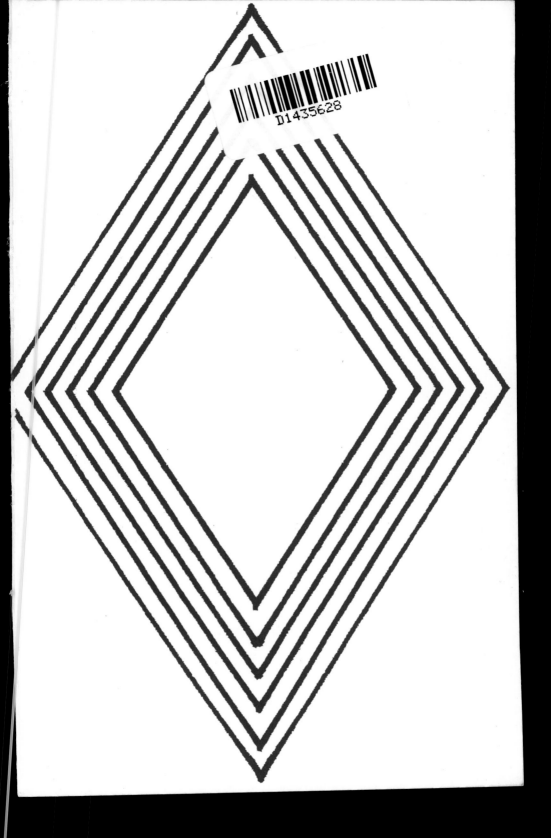

GAYLORD PHOENIX

GAYLORD PHOENIX © 2010 EDIE FAKE
PUBLISHED BY SECRET ACRES
DESIGNED BY EDIE FAKE

SECRET ACRES
200 PARK AVENUE SOUTH, 8TH FL.
NEW YORK, NY 10003

PRINTED IN HONG KONG

LIBRARY OF CONGRESS PCN: 2010928833

ISBN 13: 978 -0-9799609-8-7
ISBN 10: 0-979 9609-8-3

FOR ALL THE GAY

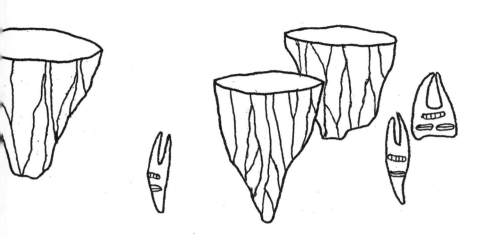

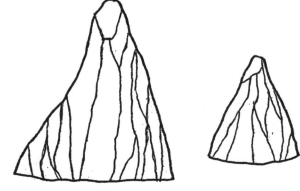

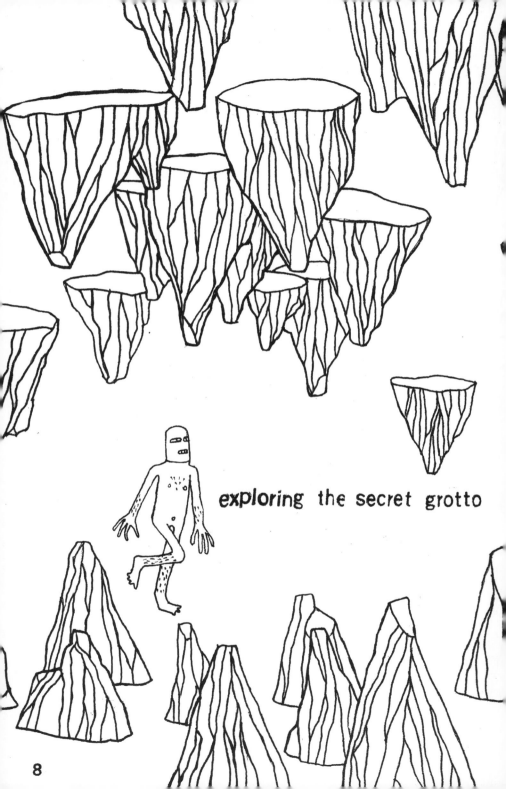

exploring the secret grotto

8

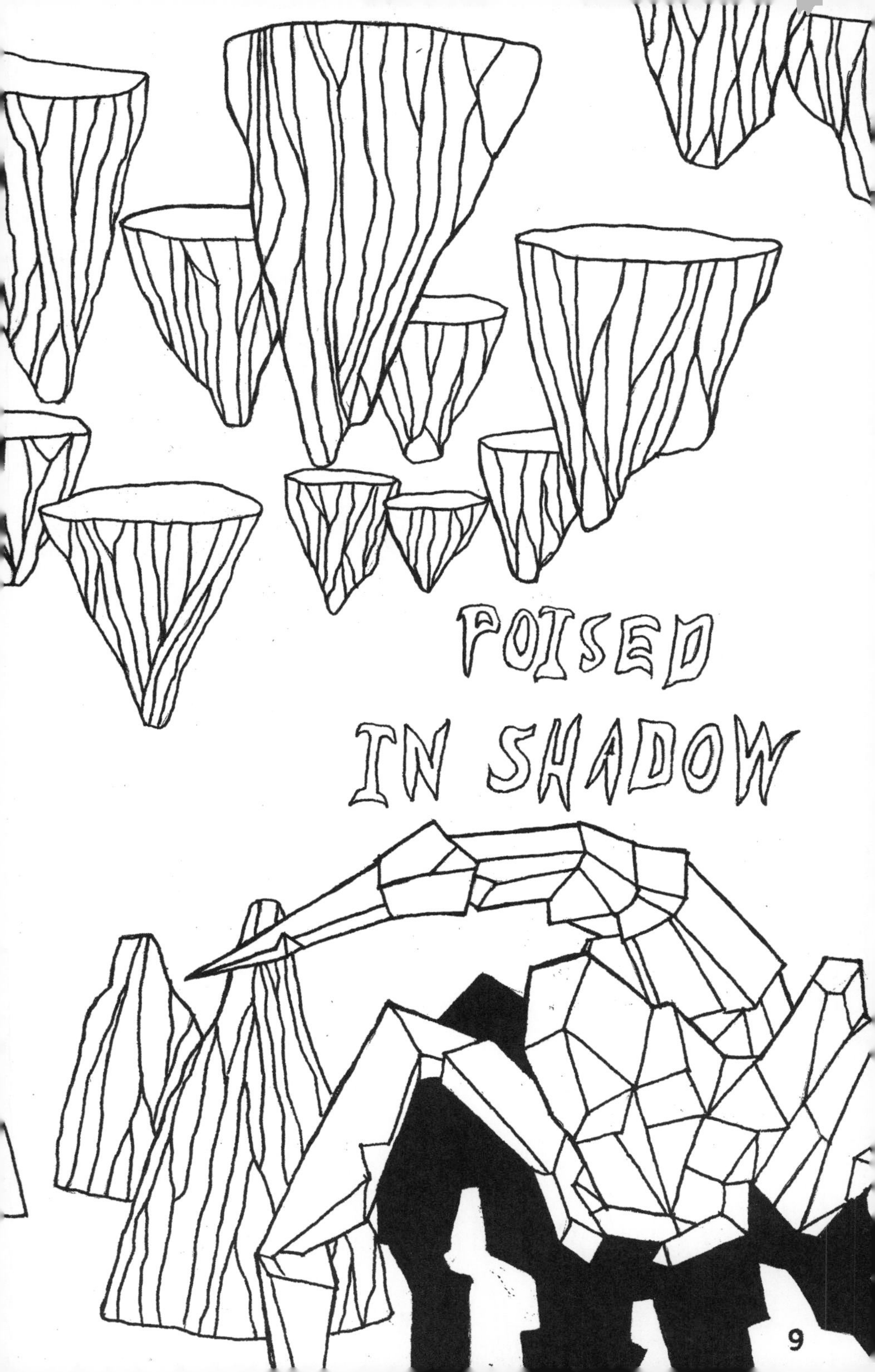
POISED
IN SHADOW

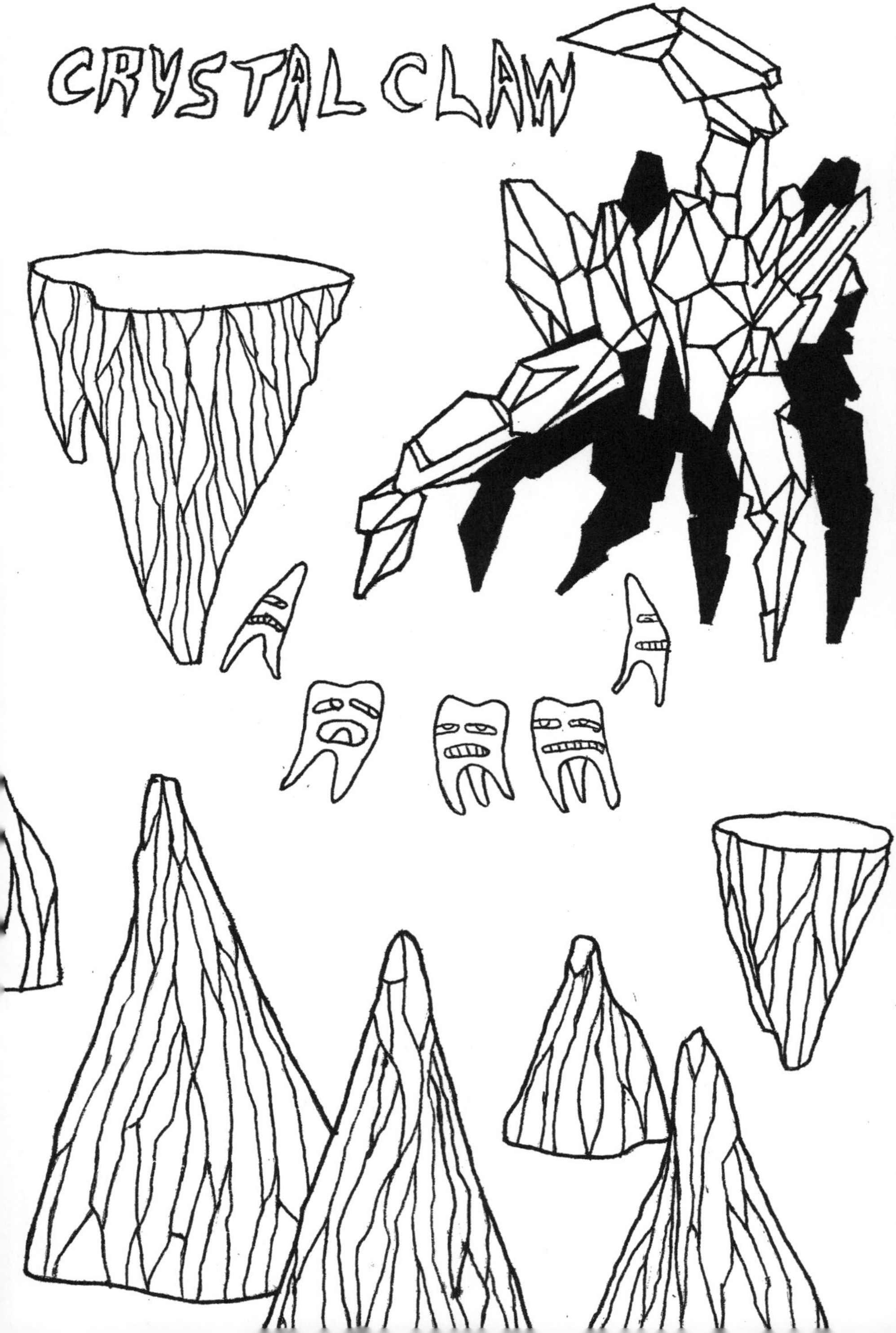
CRYSTAL CLAW

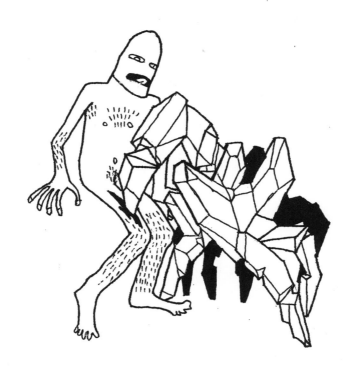

DEEP IN THE NIGHT

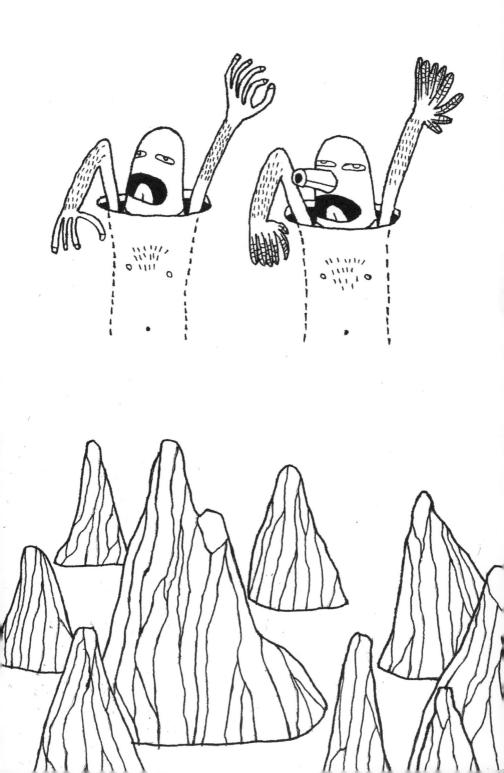

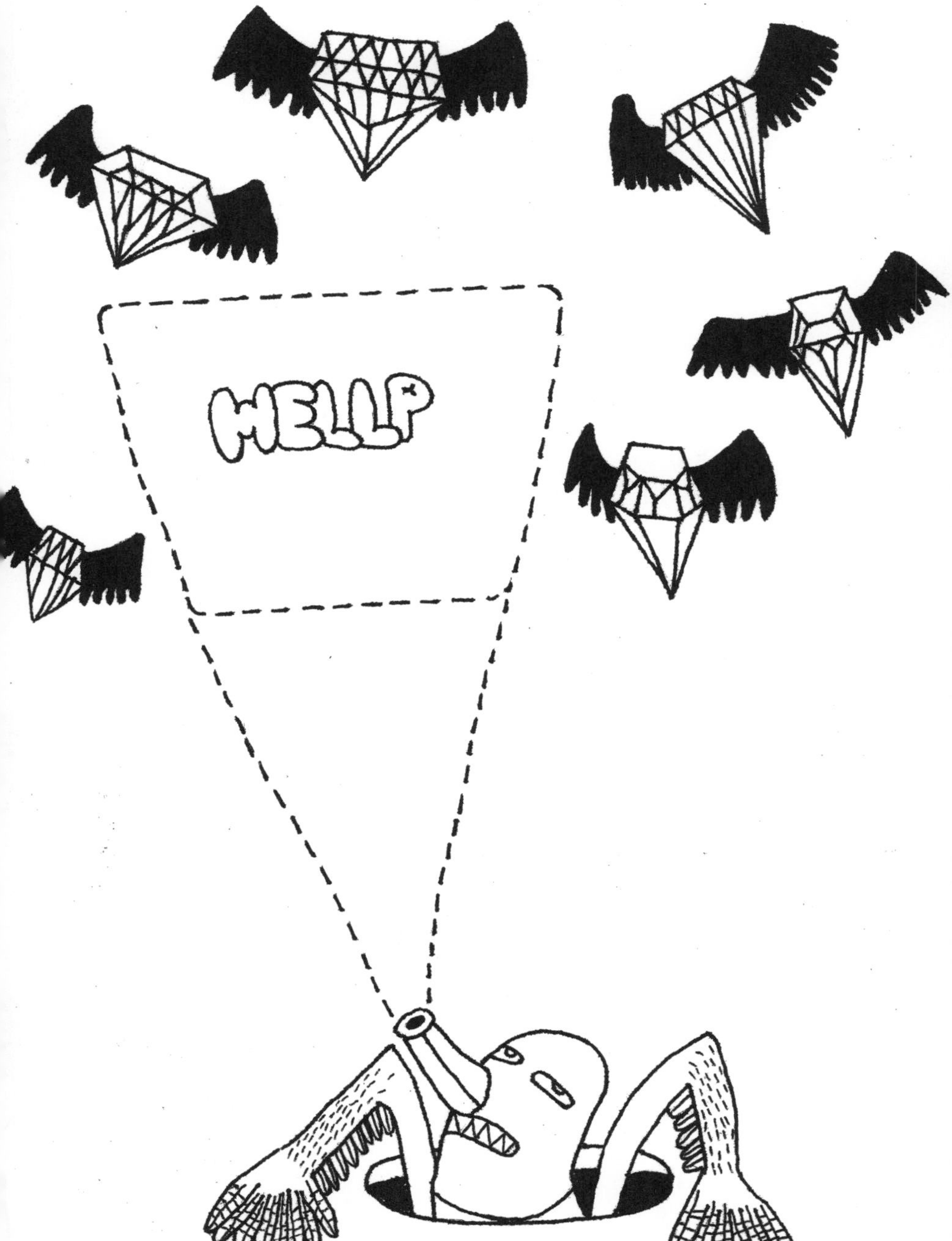
HELLP

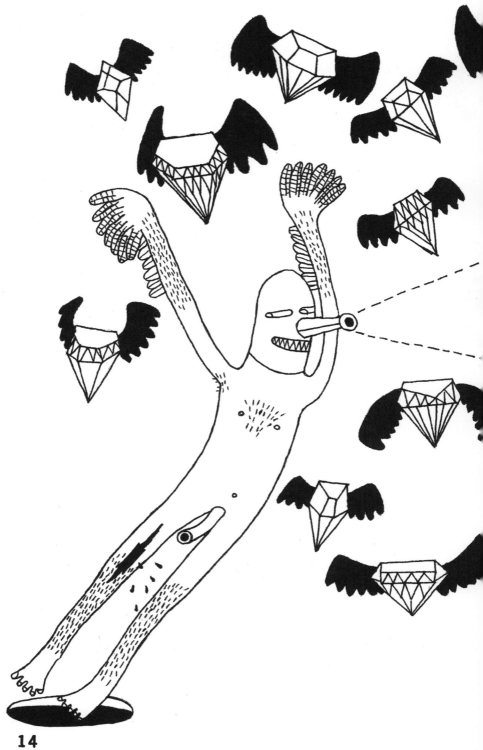

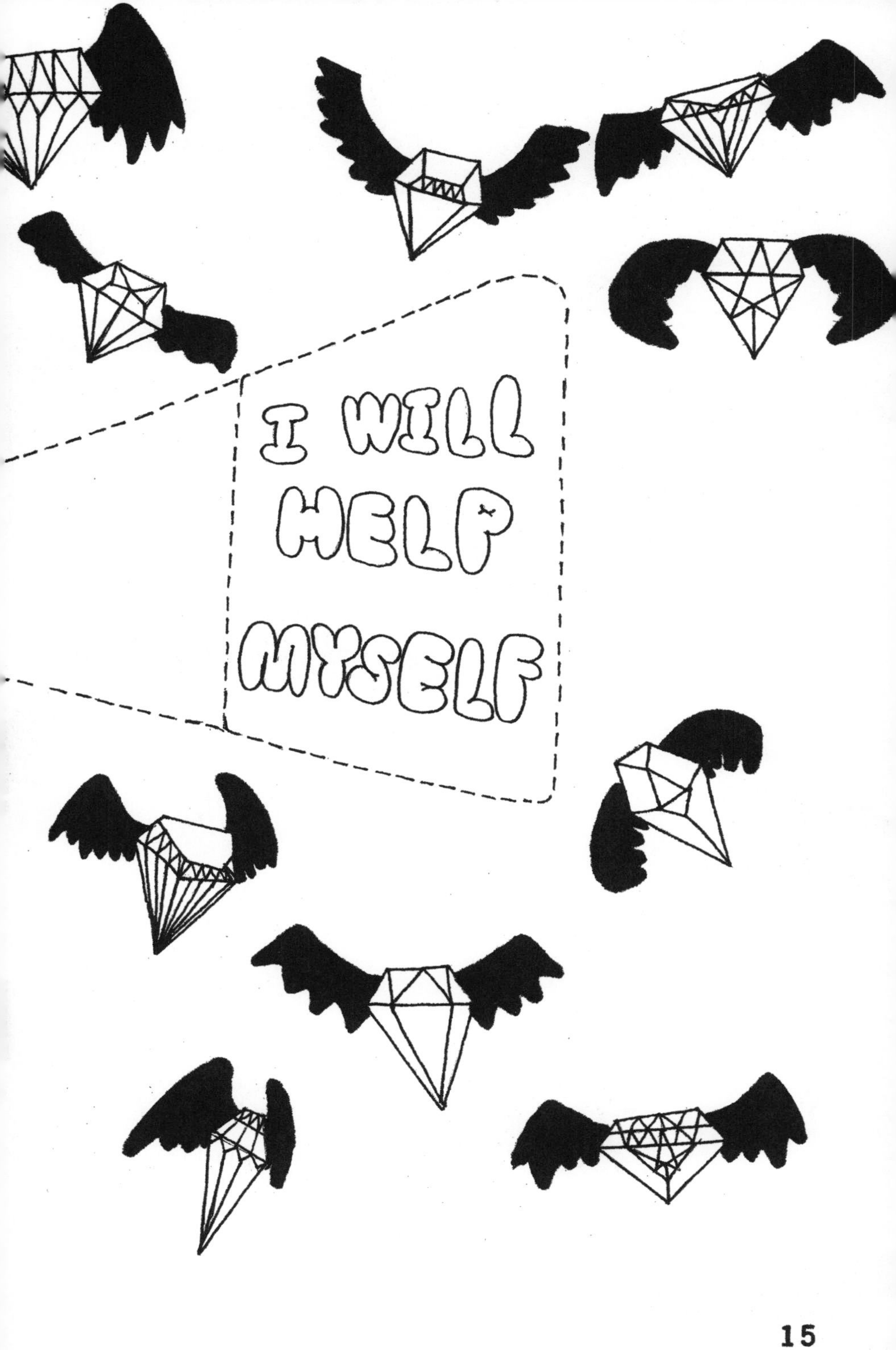
I WILL HELP MYSELF

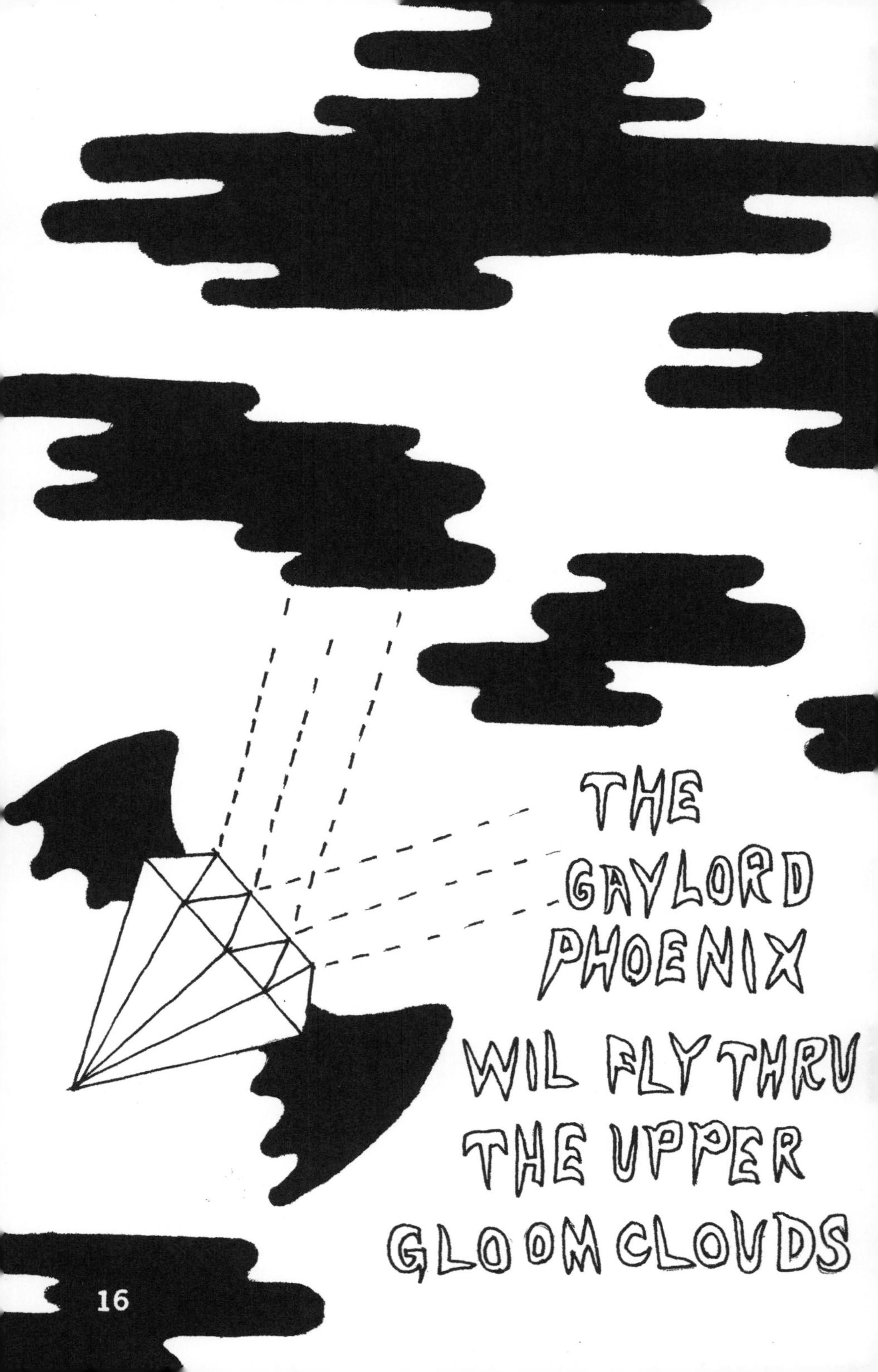
THE
GAYLORD
PHOENIX
WIL FLY THRU
THE UPPER
GLOOM CLOUDS

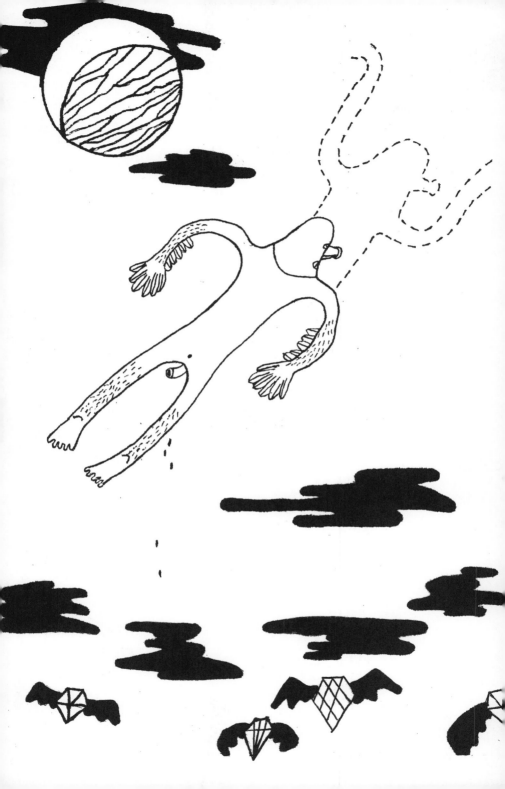

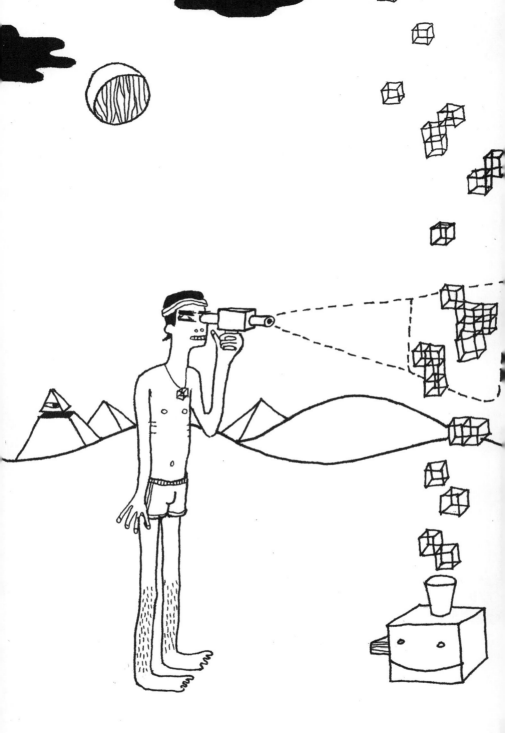

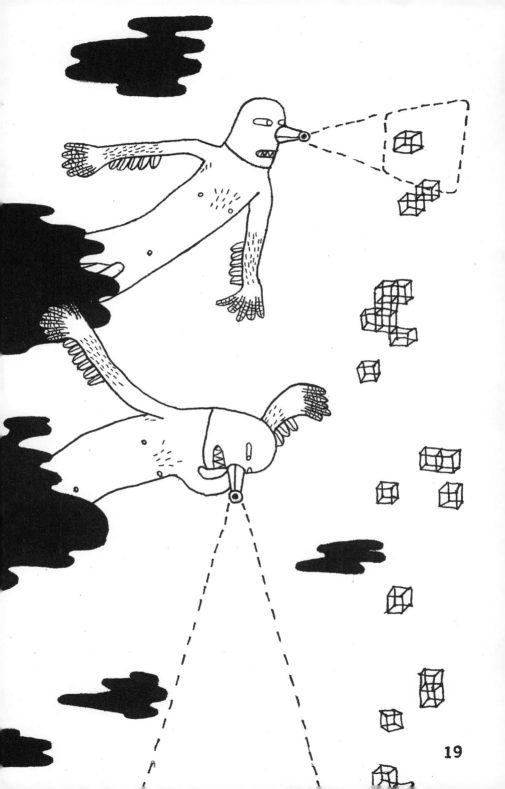

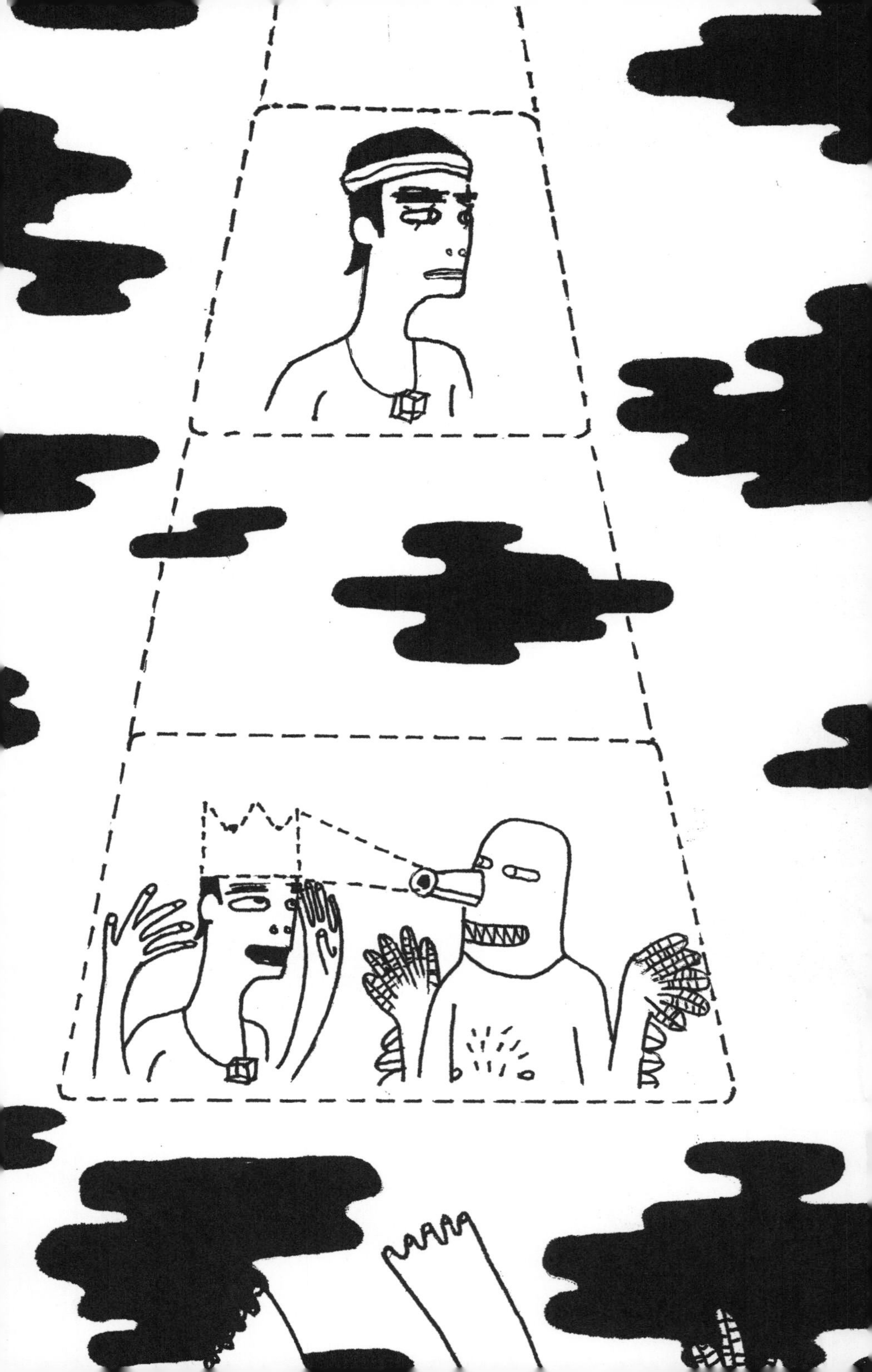

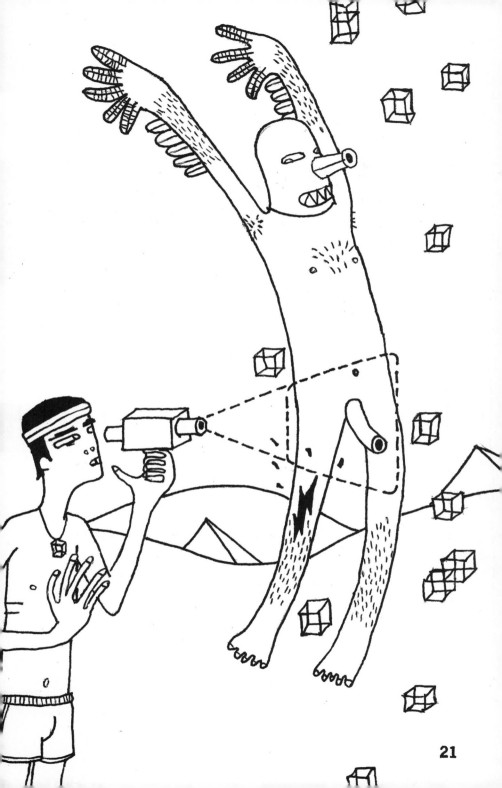

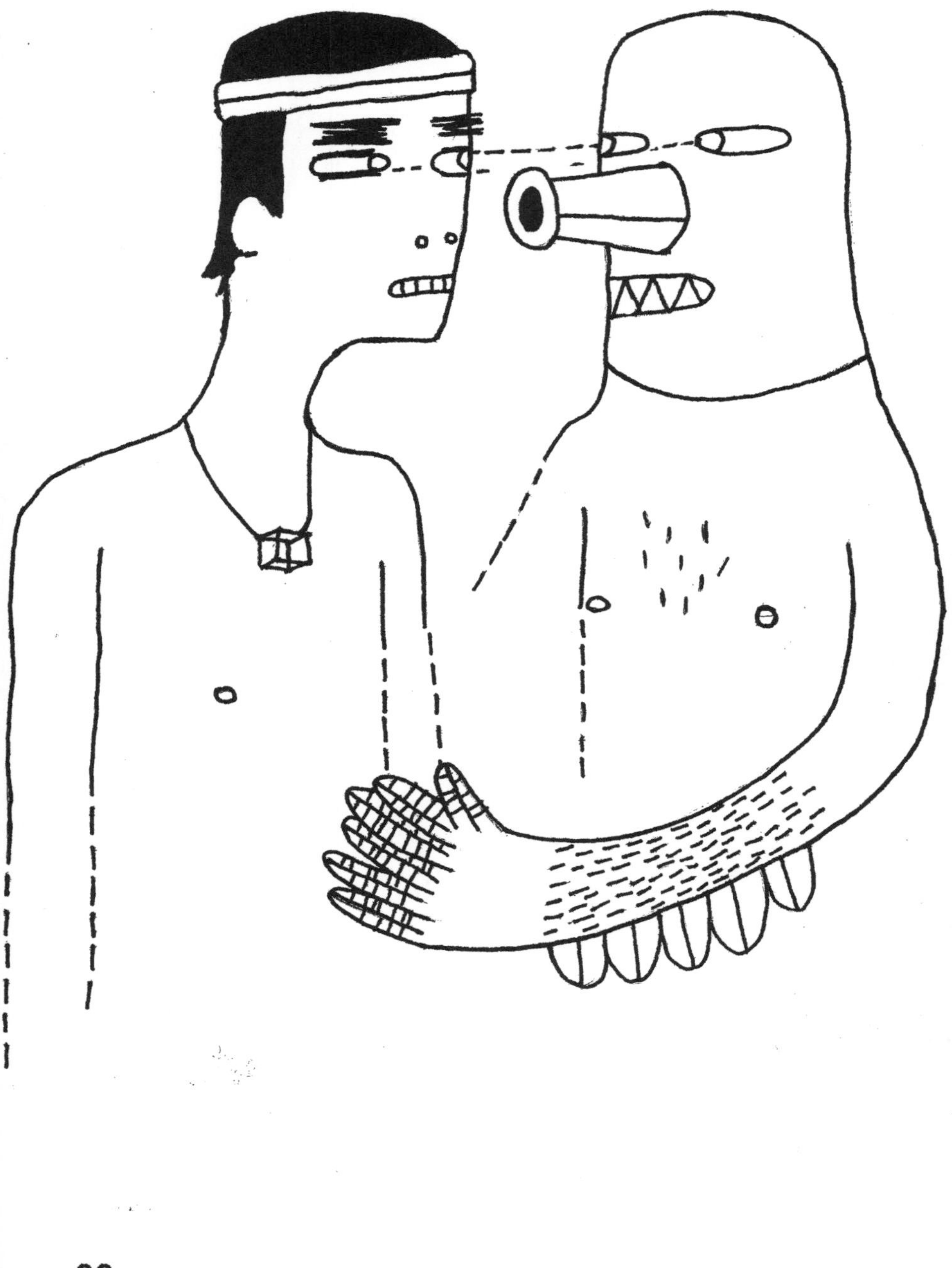

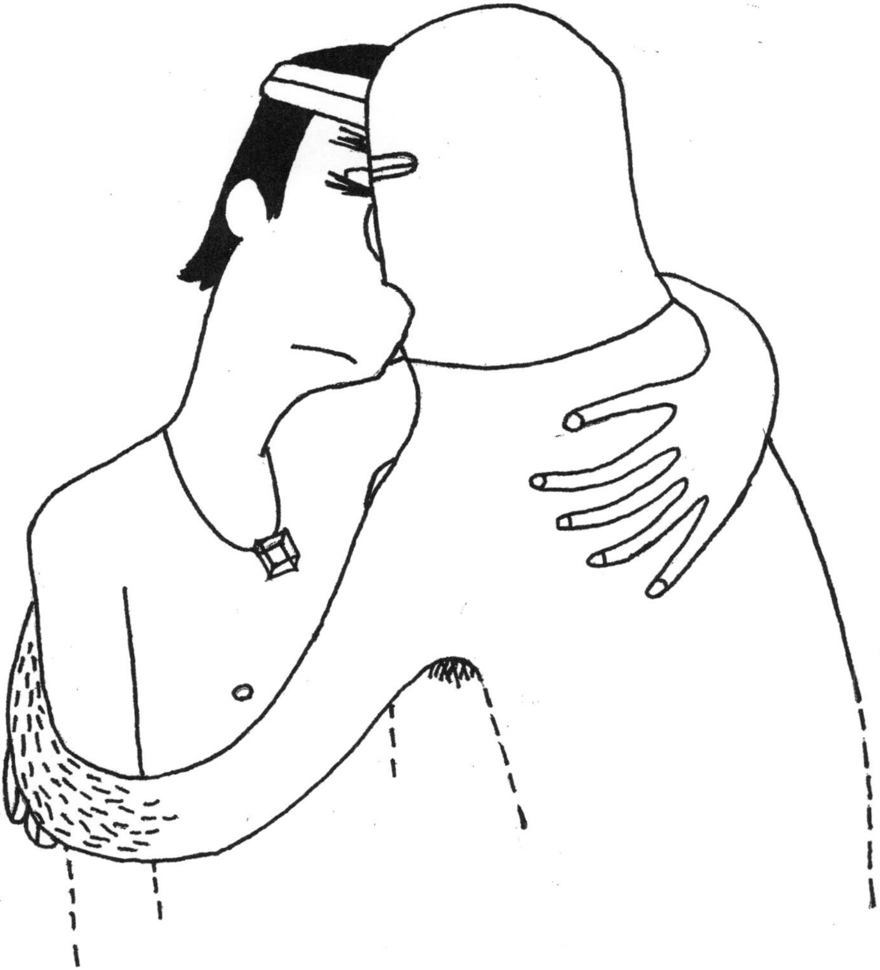

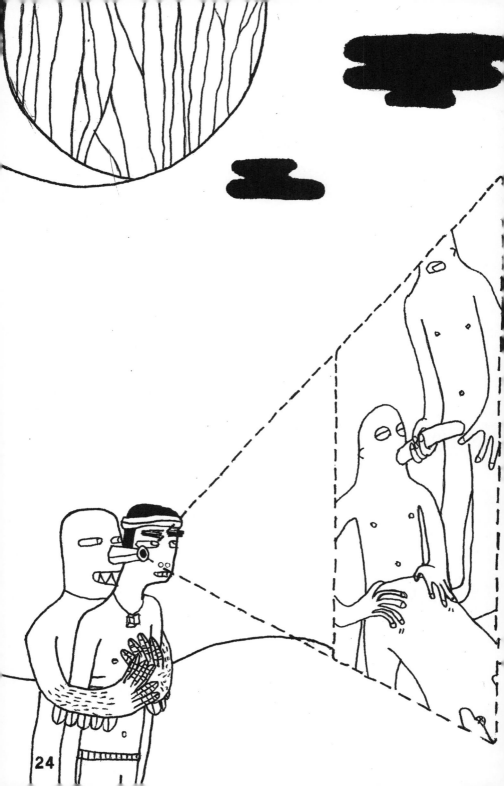

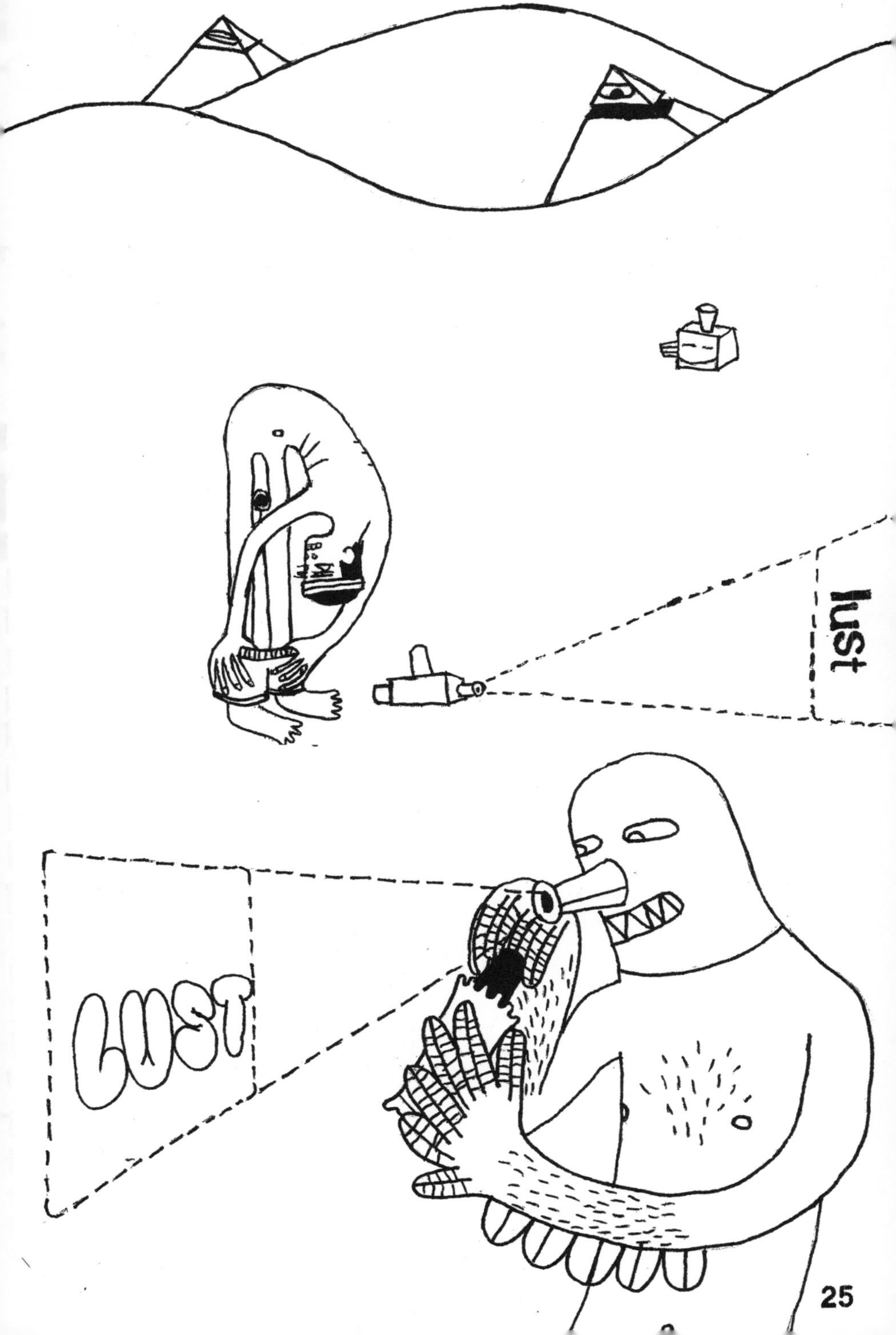
lust
LUST

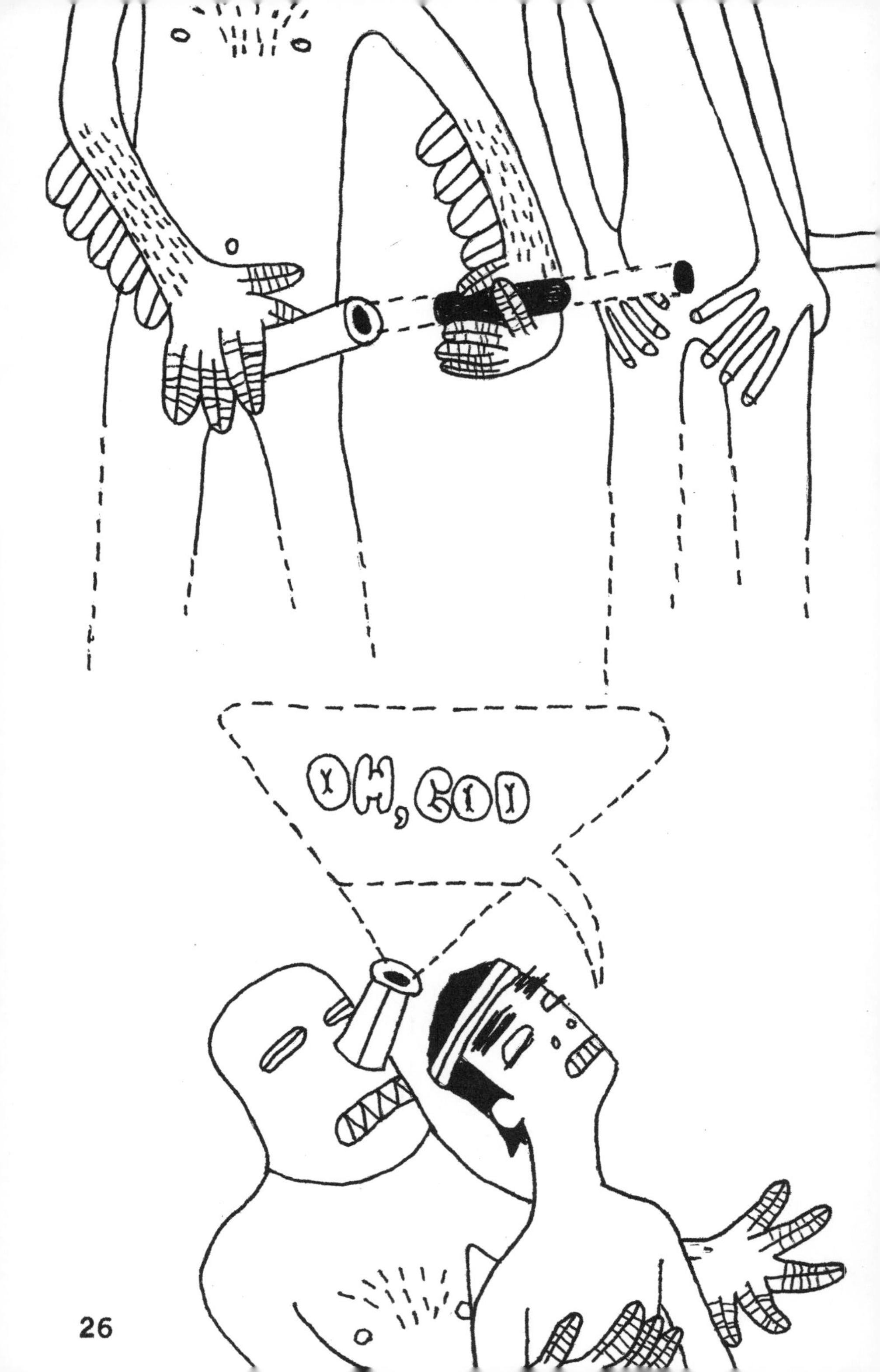
OH, GOD

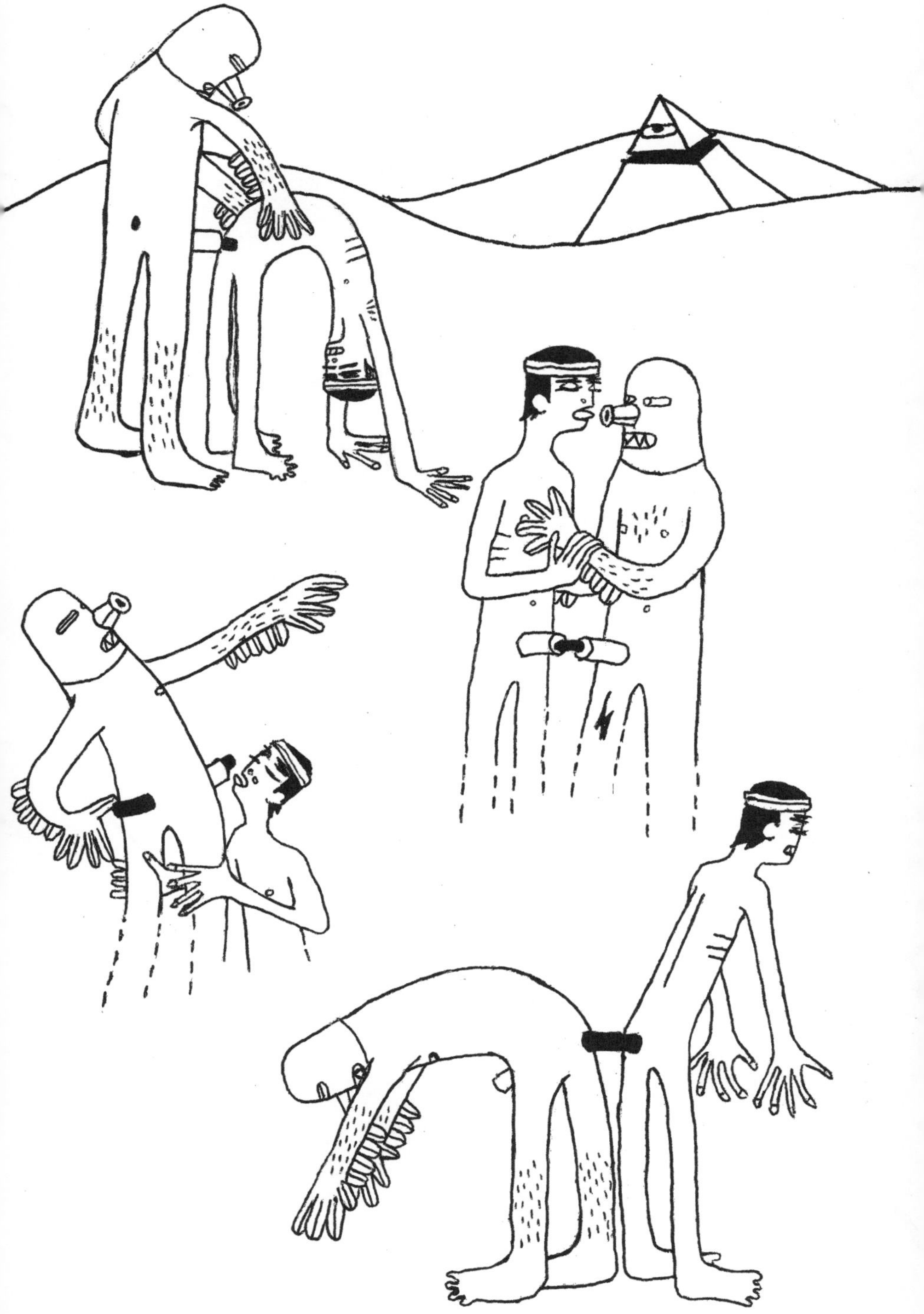

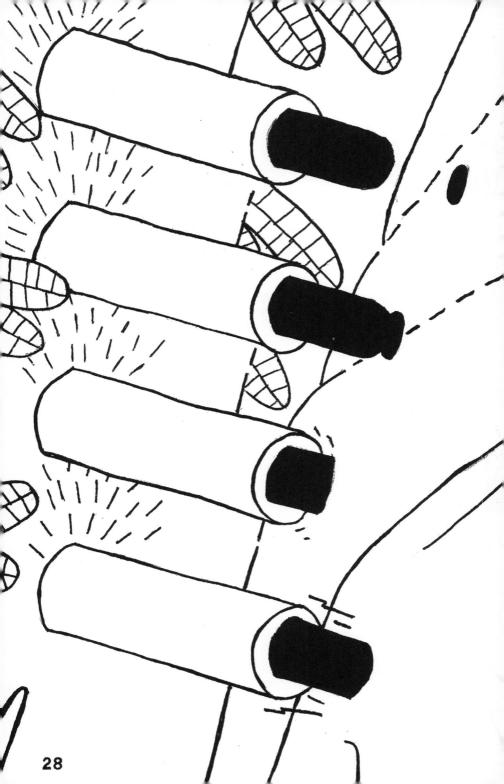

28

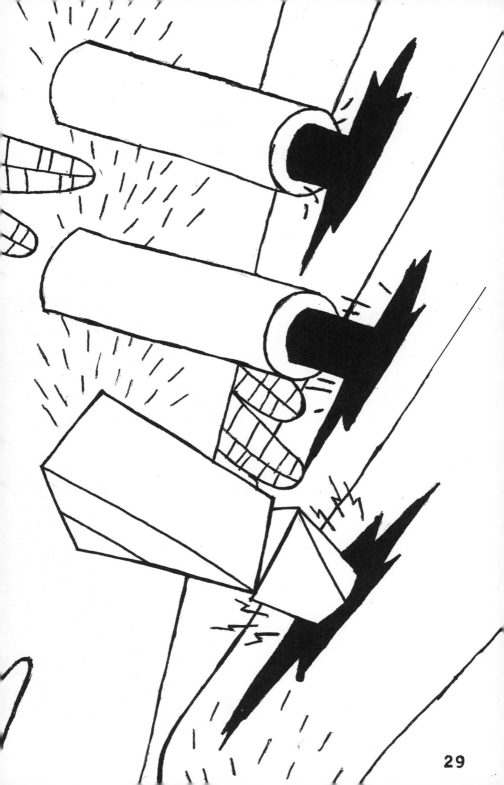

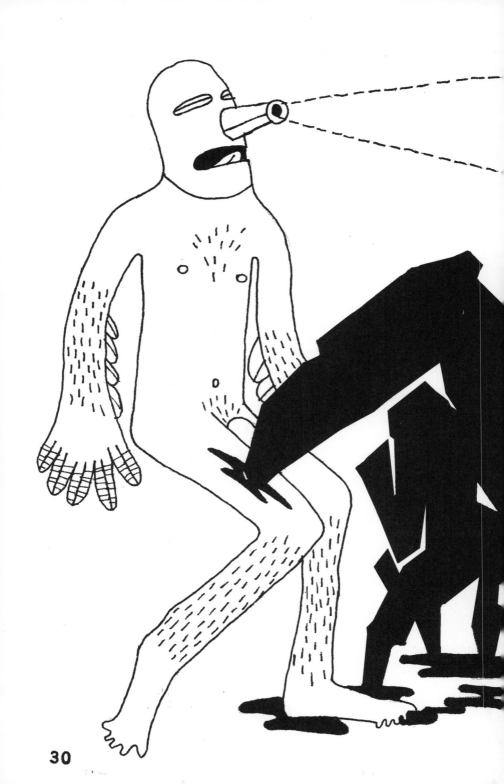

I HAVE CRYSTAL BLOODLUST

AN AWFUL TRANSFORM

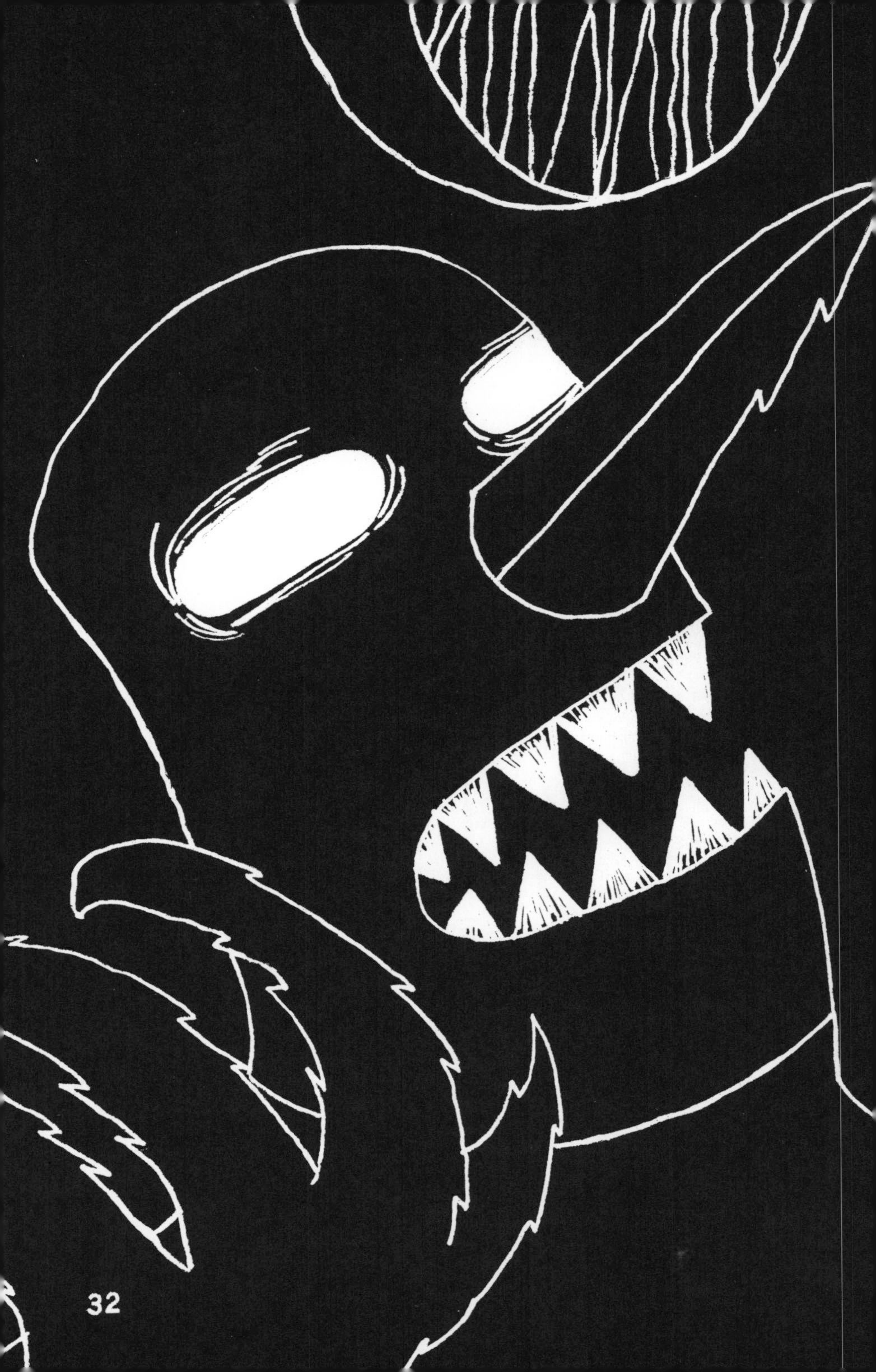

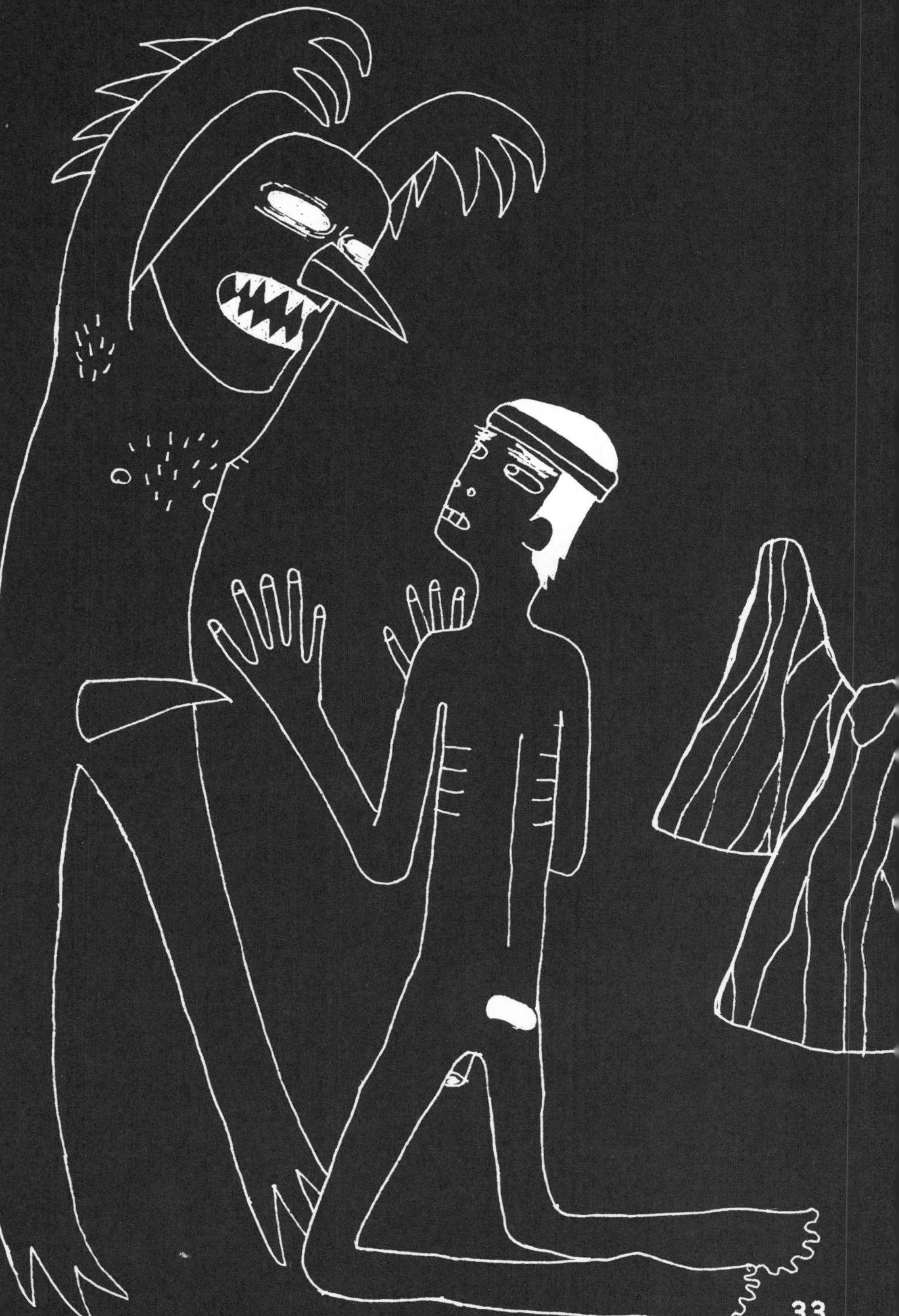

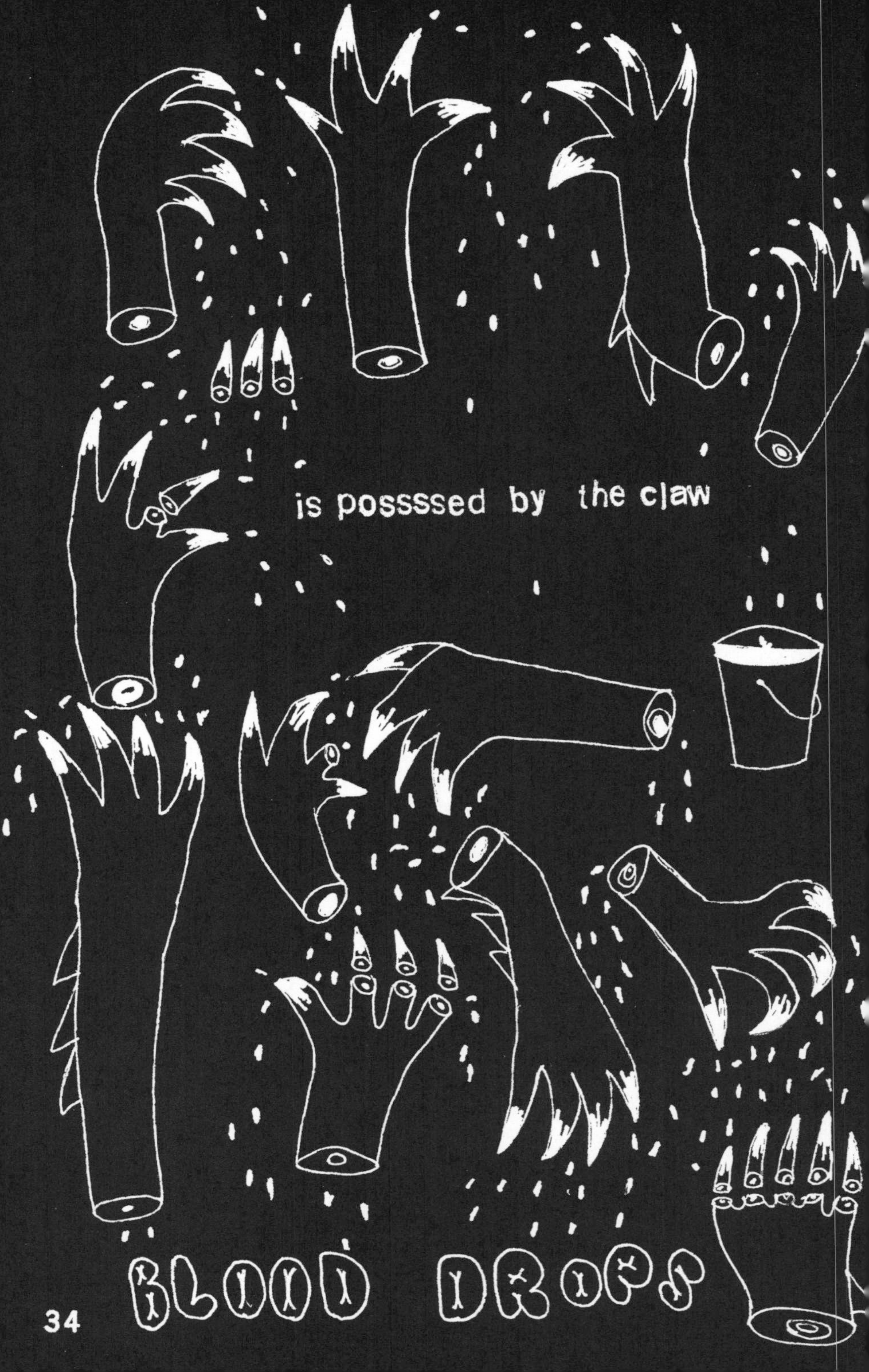
is posssed by the claw
BLOOD DROPS

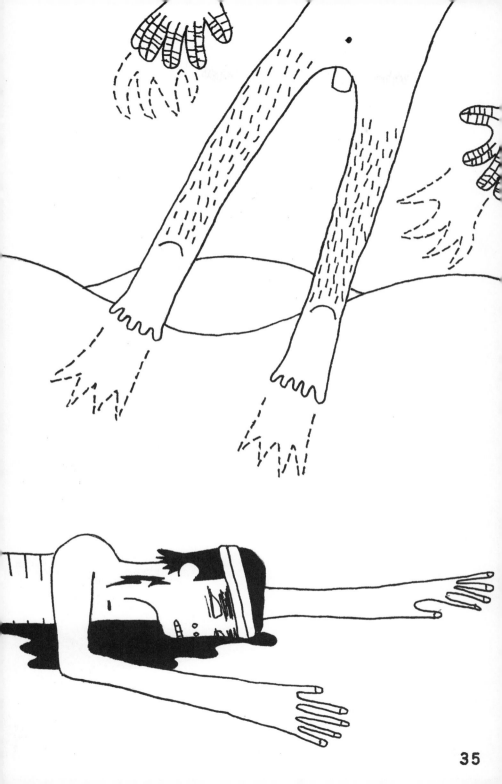

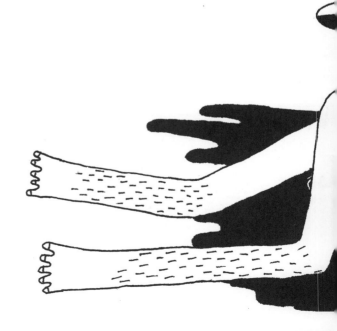

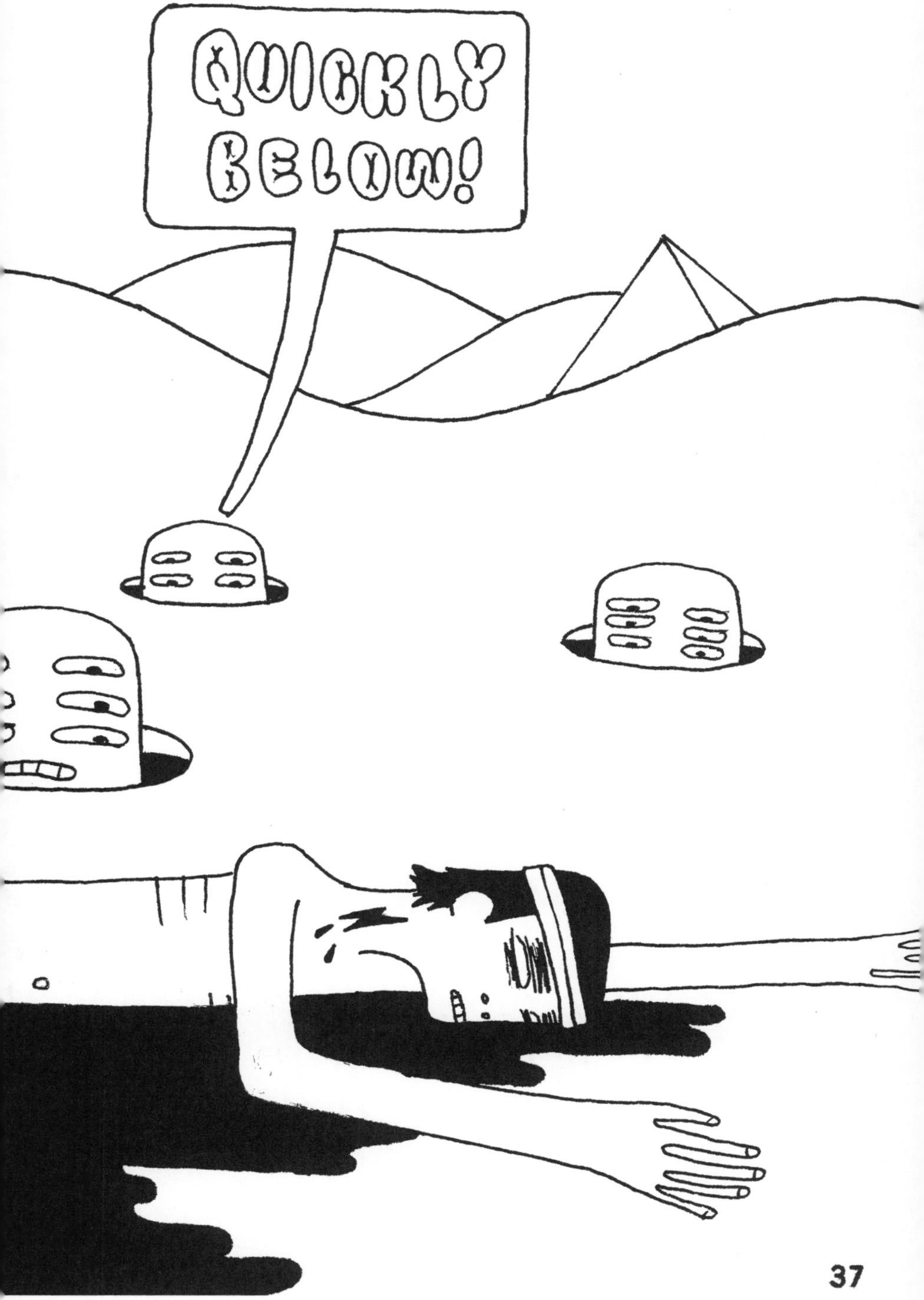
QUICKLY BELOW!

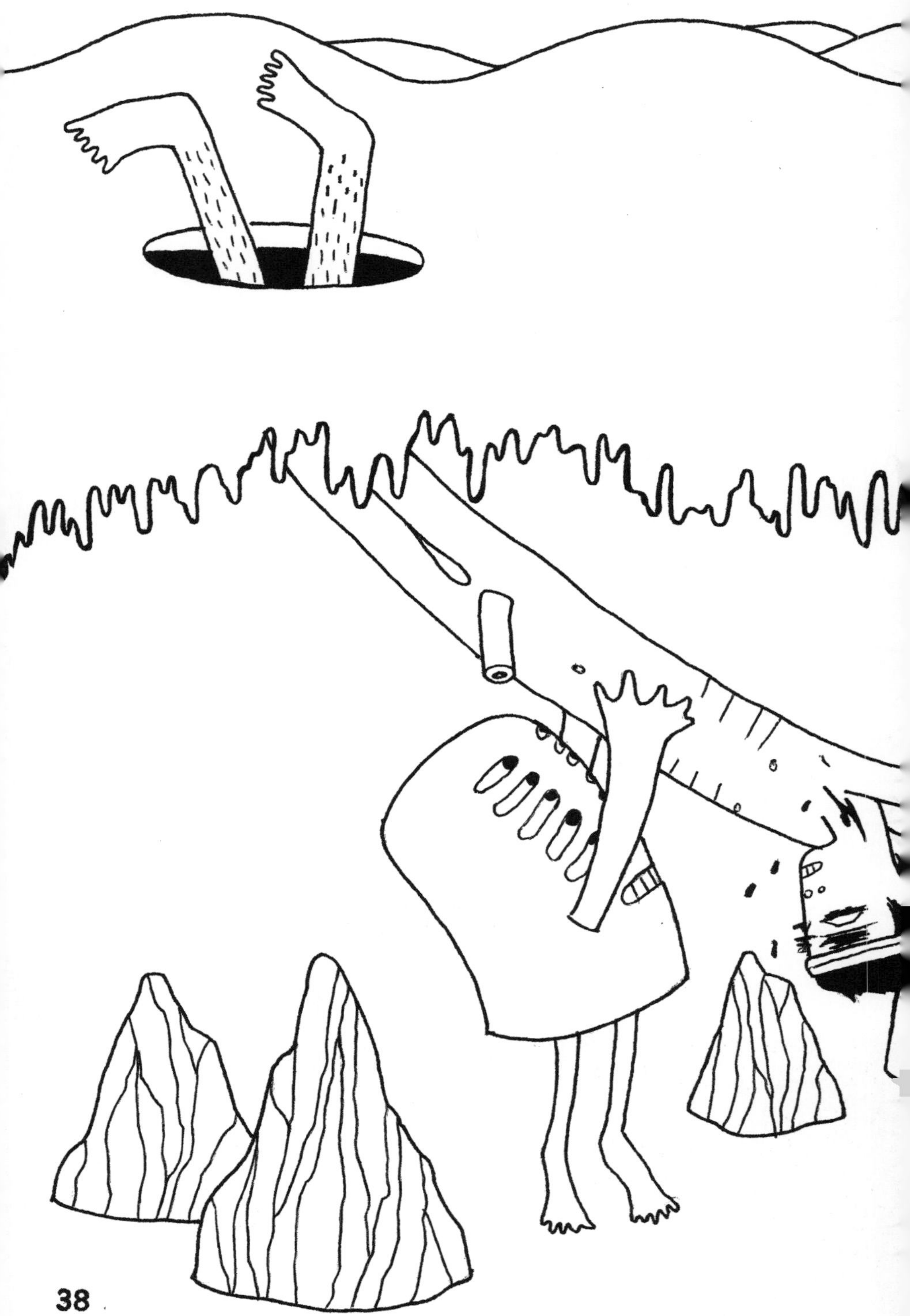

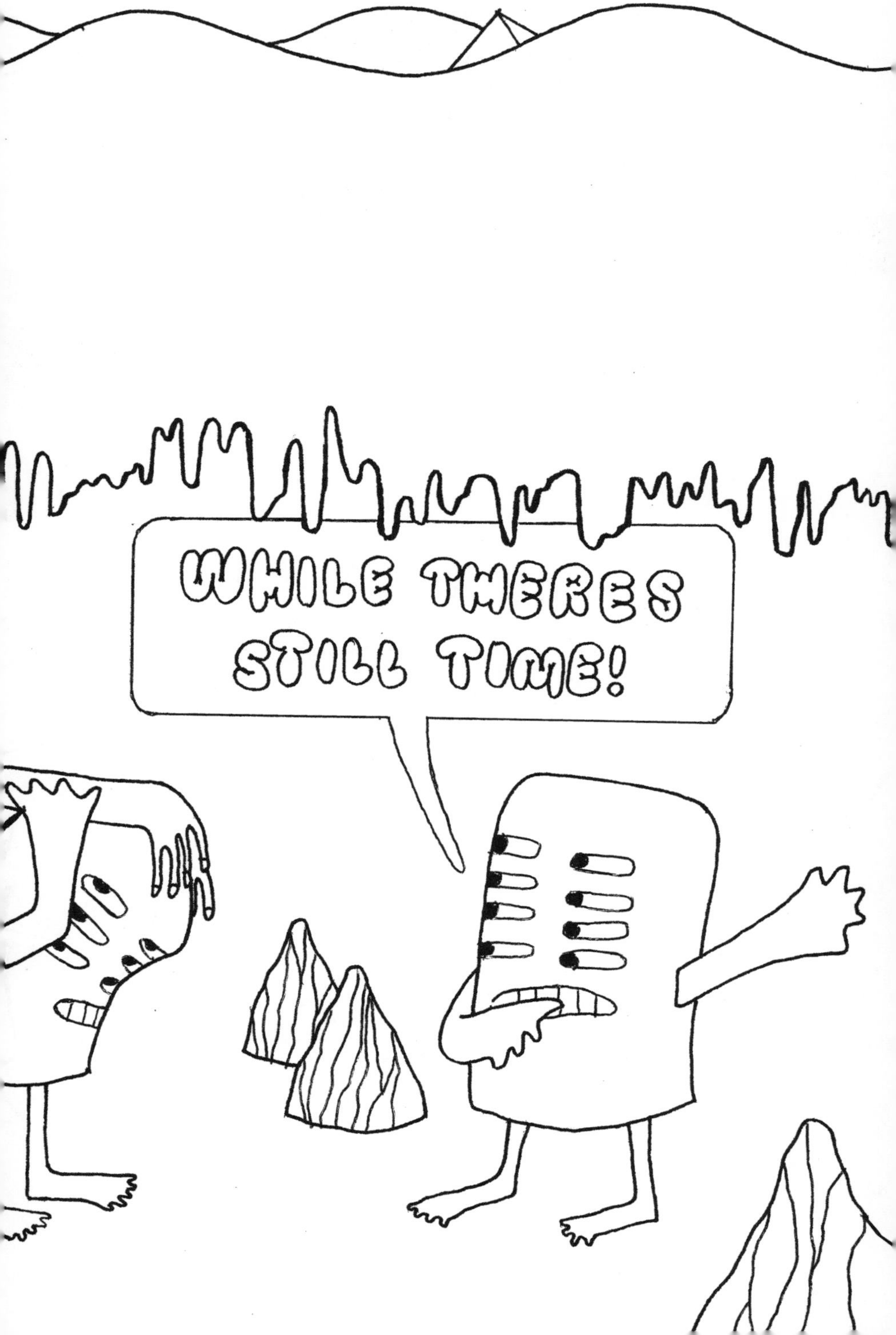
WHILE THERES STILL TIME!

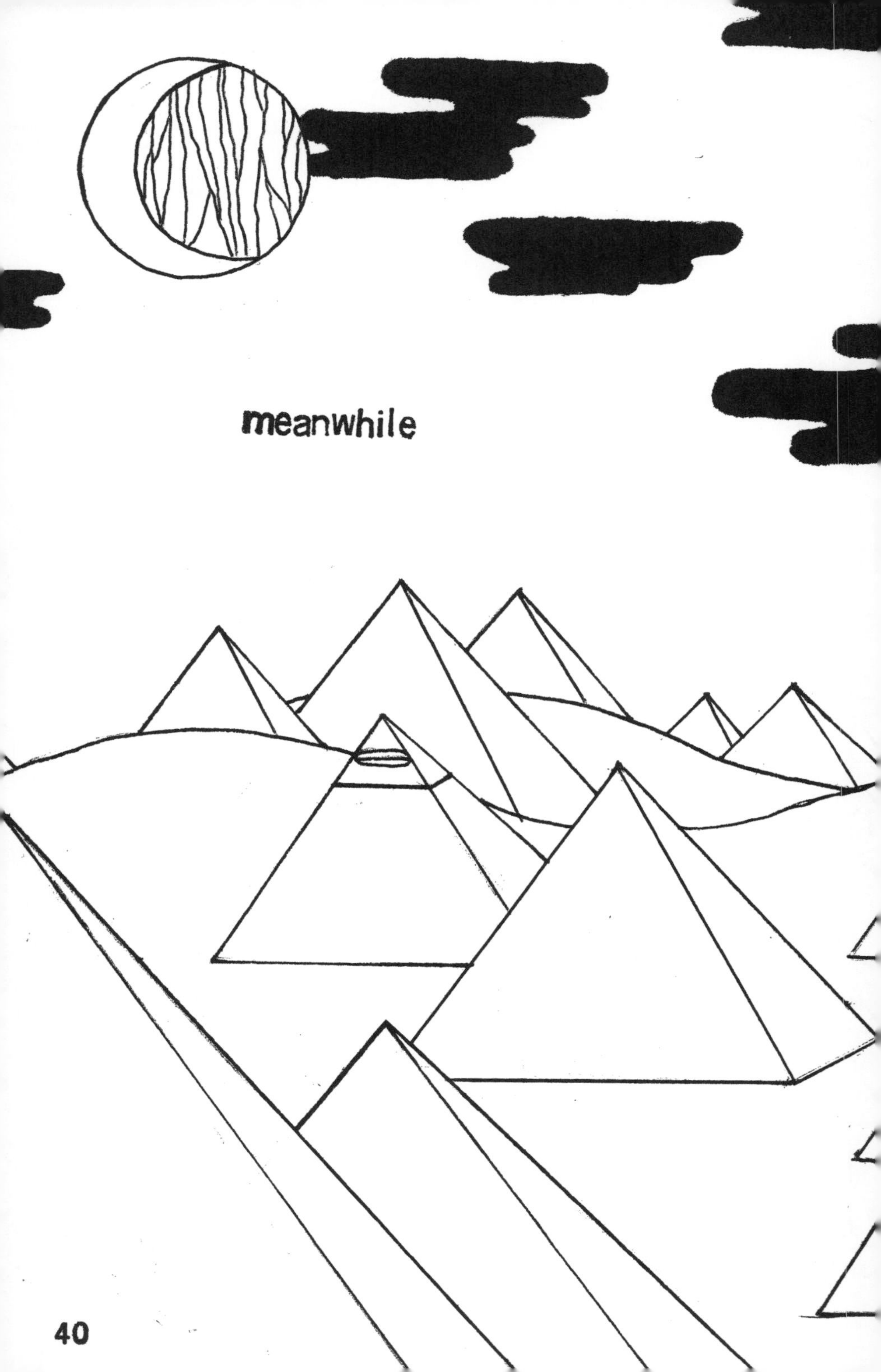
meanwhile

over the pyramidal city

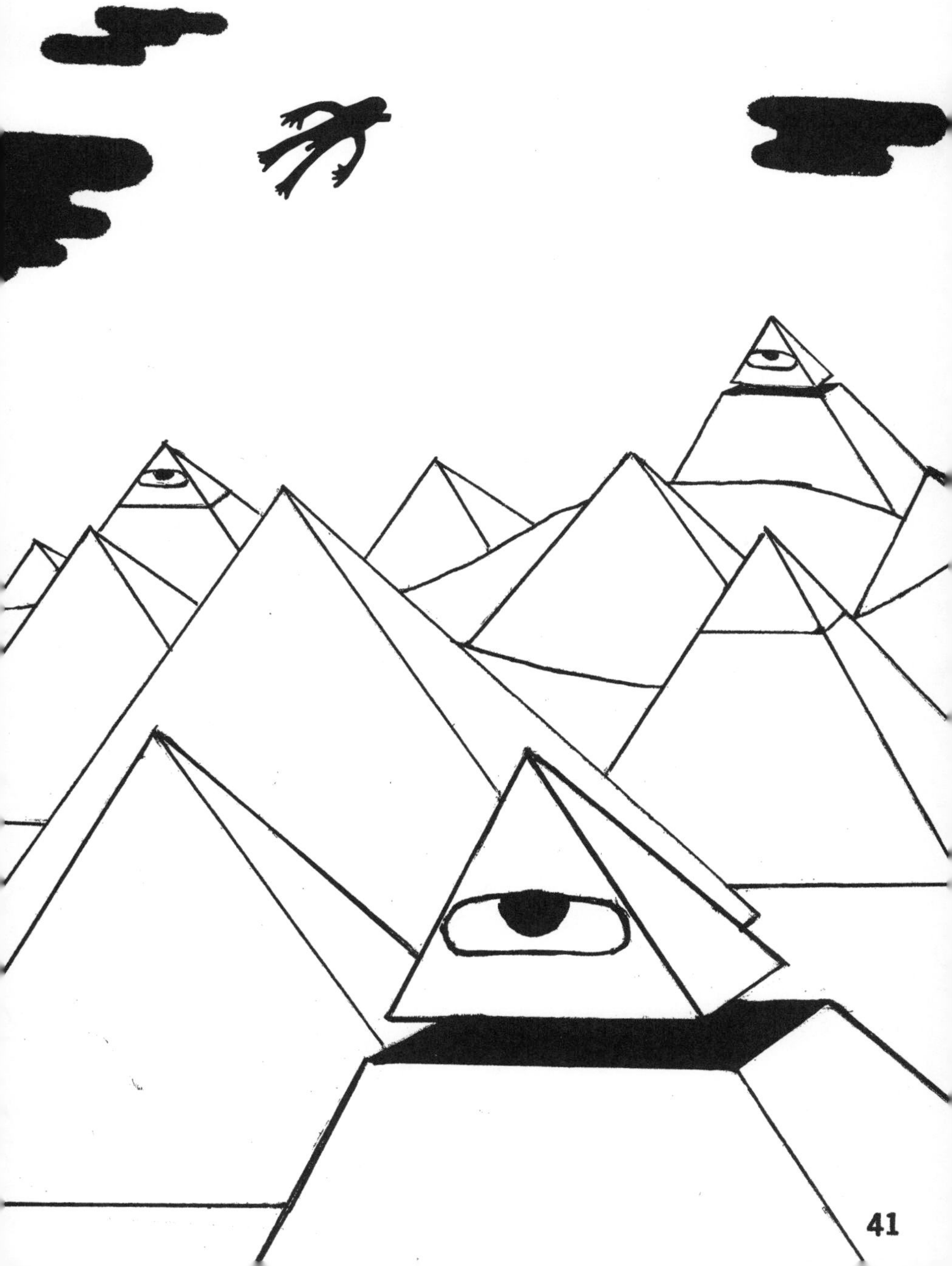

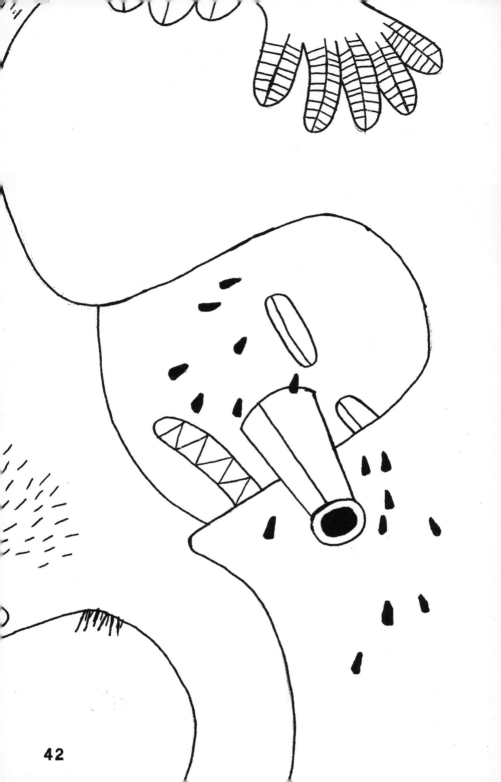

above

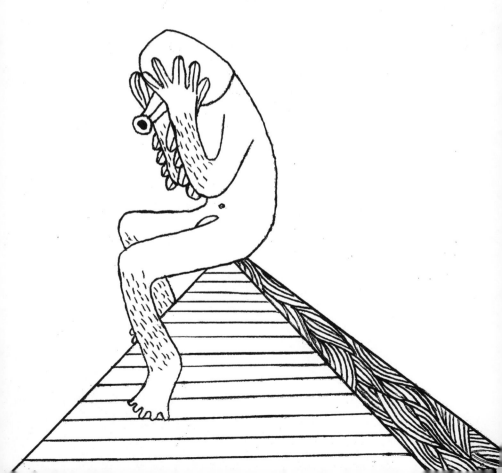

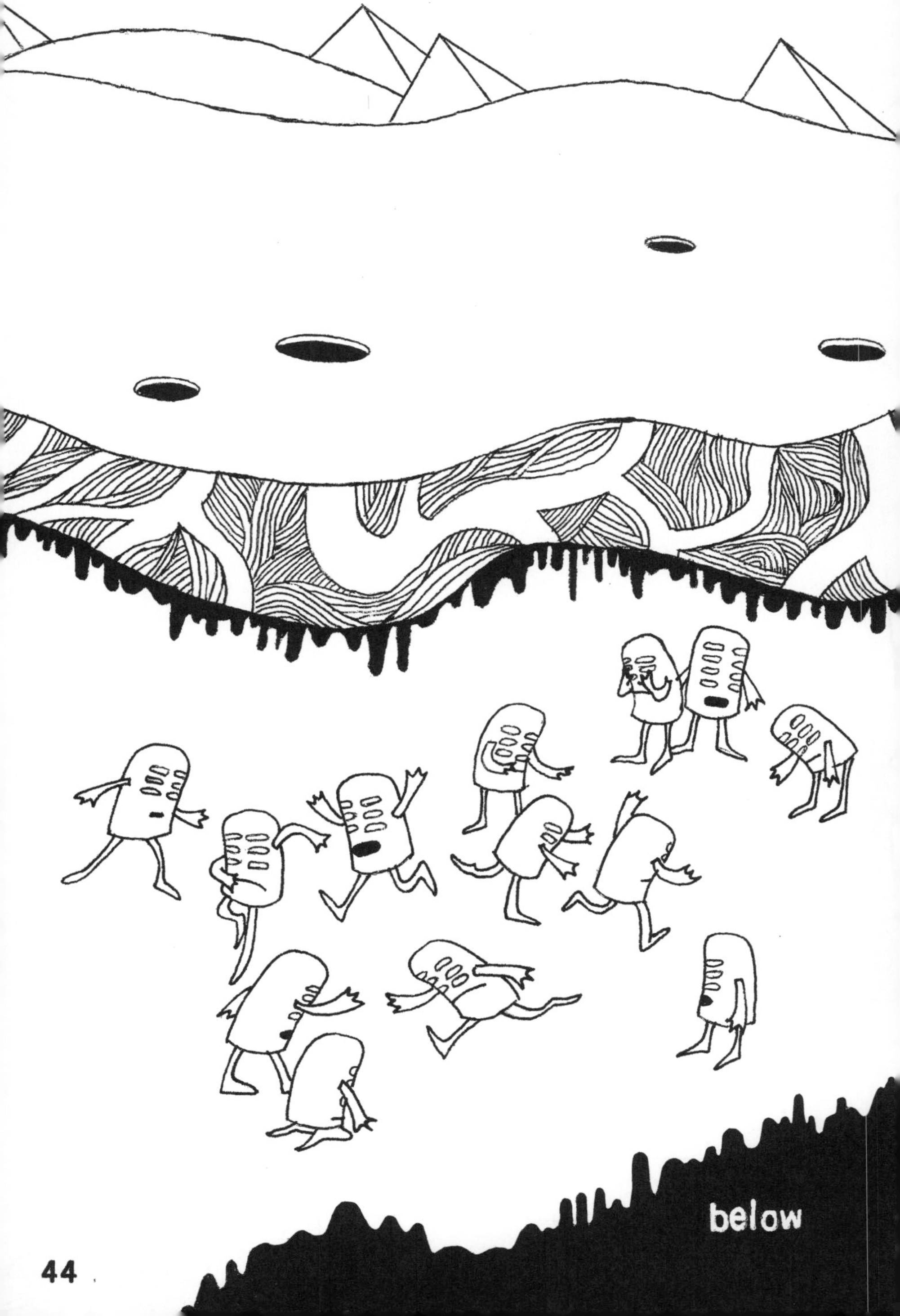
below

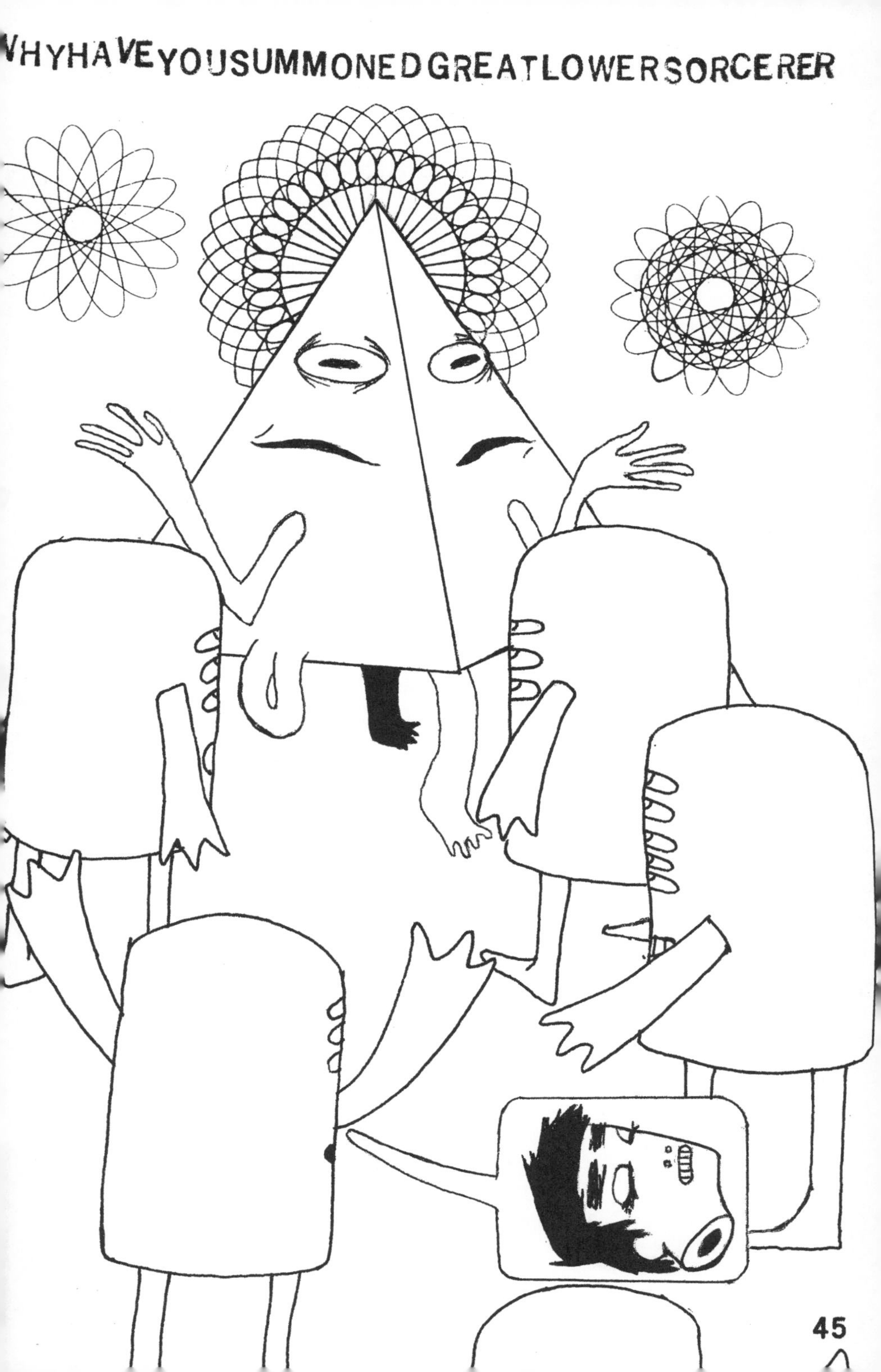
VHYHAVEYOUSUMMONEDGREATLOWERSORCERER

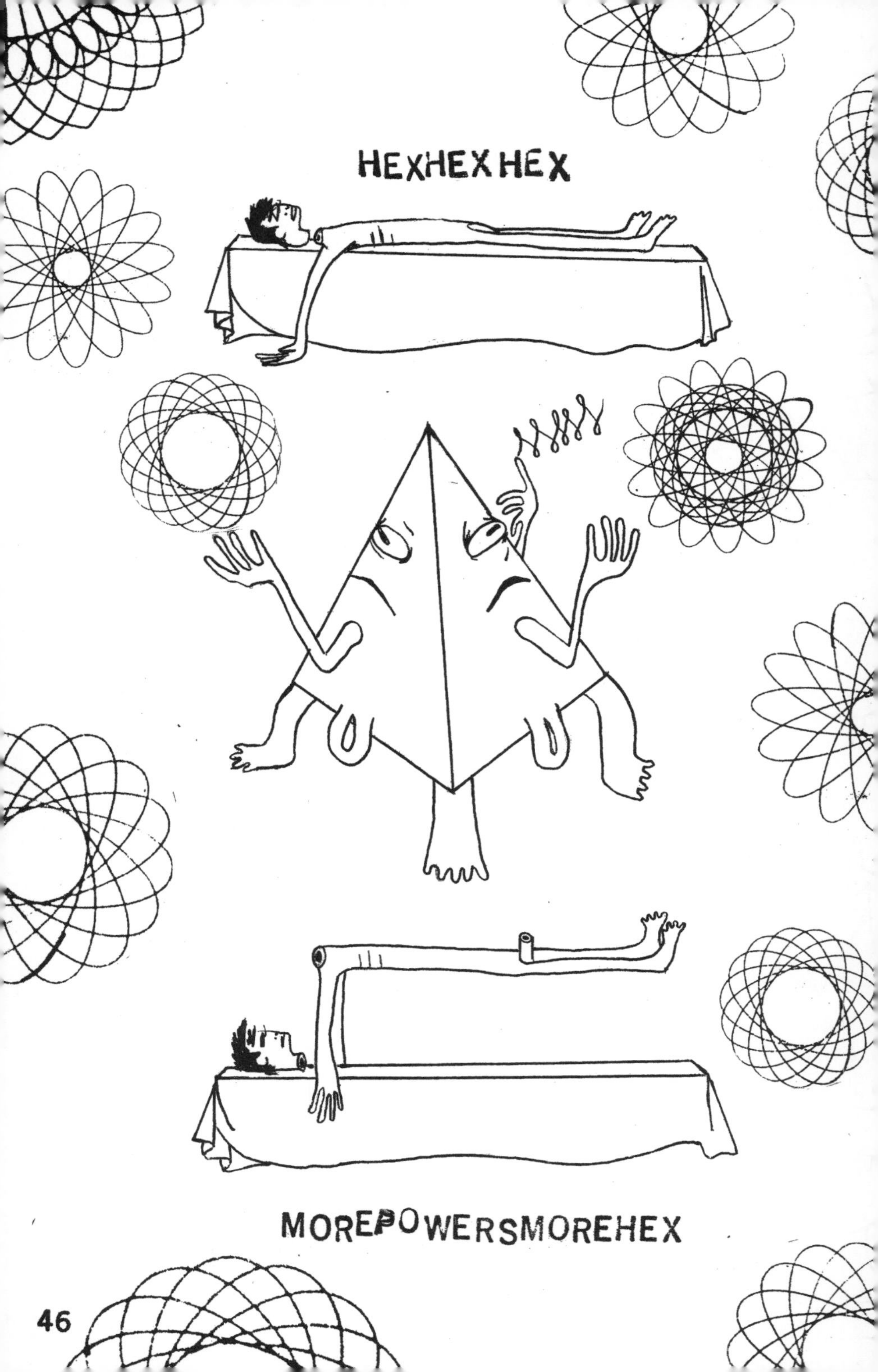
HEXHEXHEX
MOREPOWERSMOREHEX

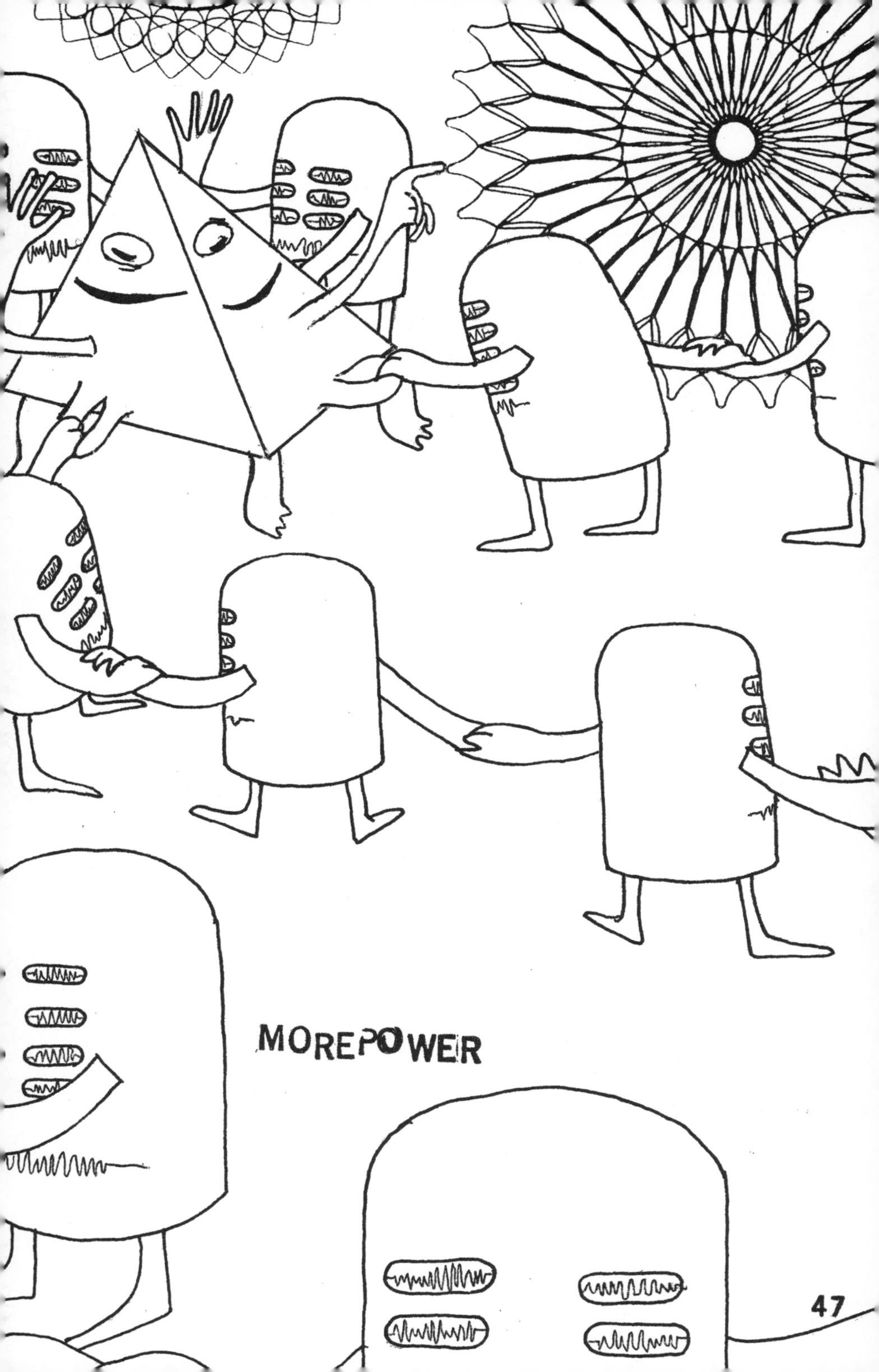
MOREPOWER

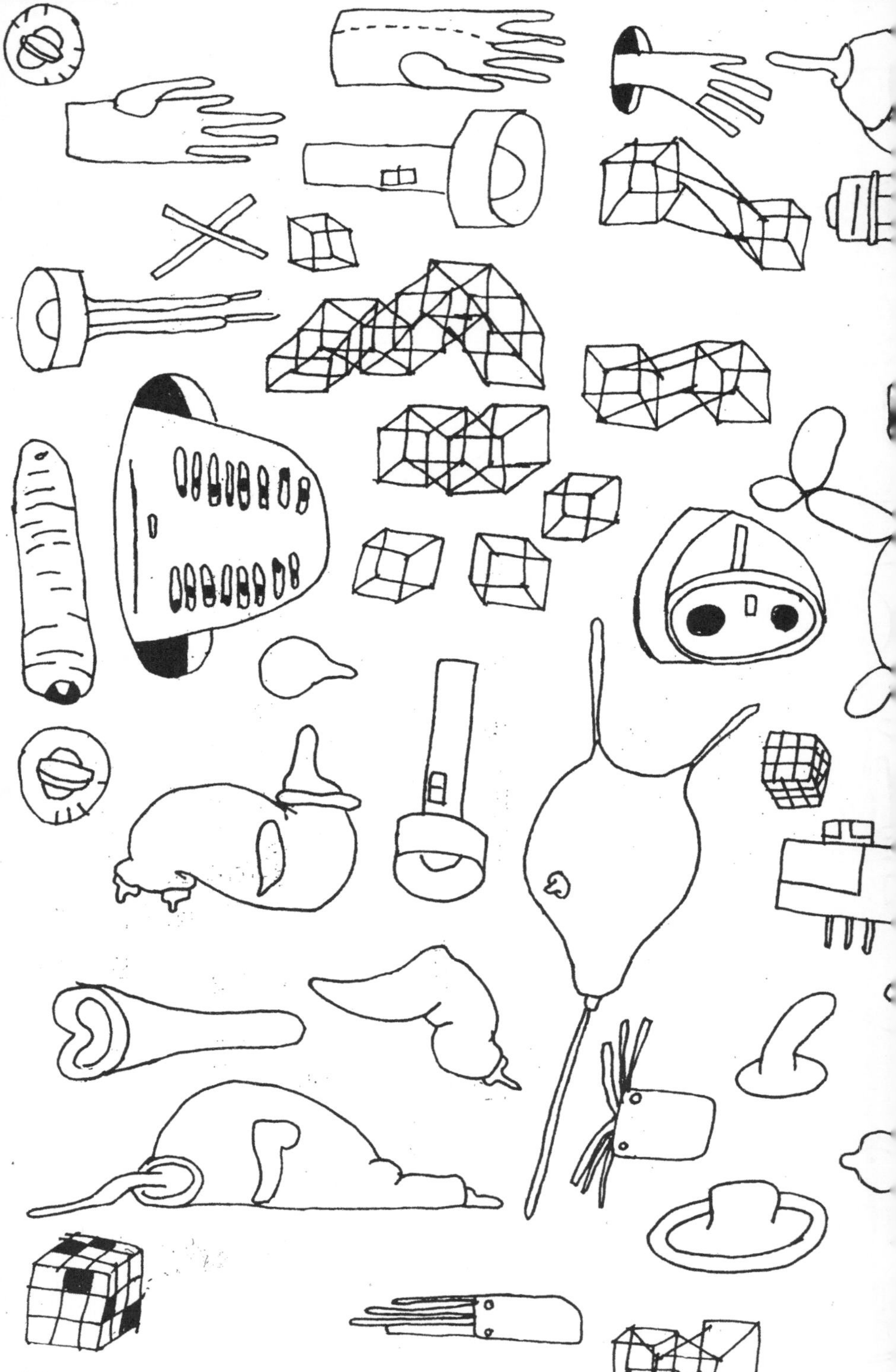

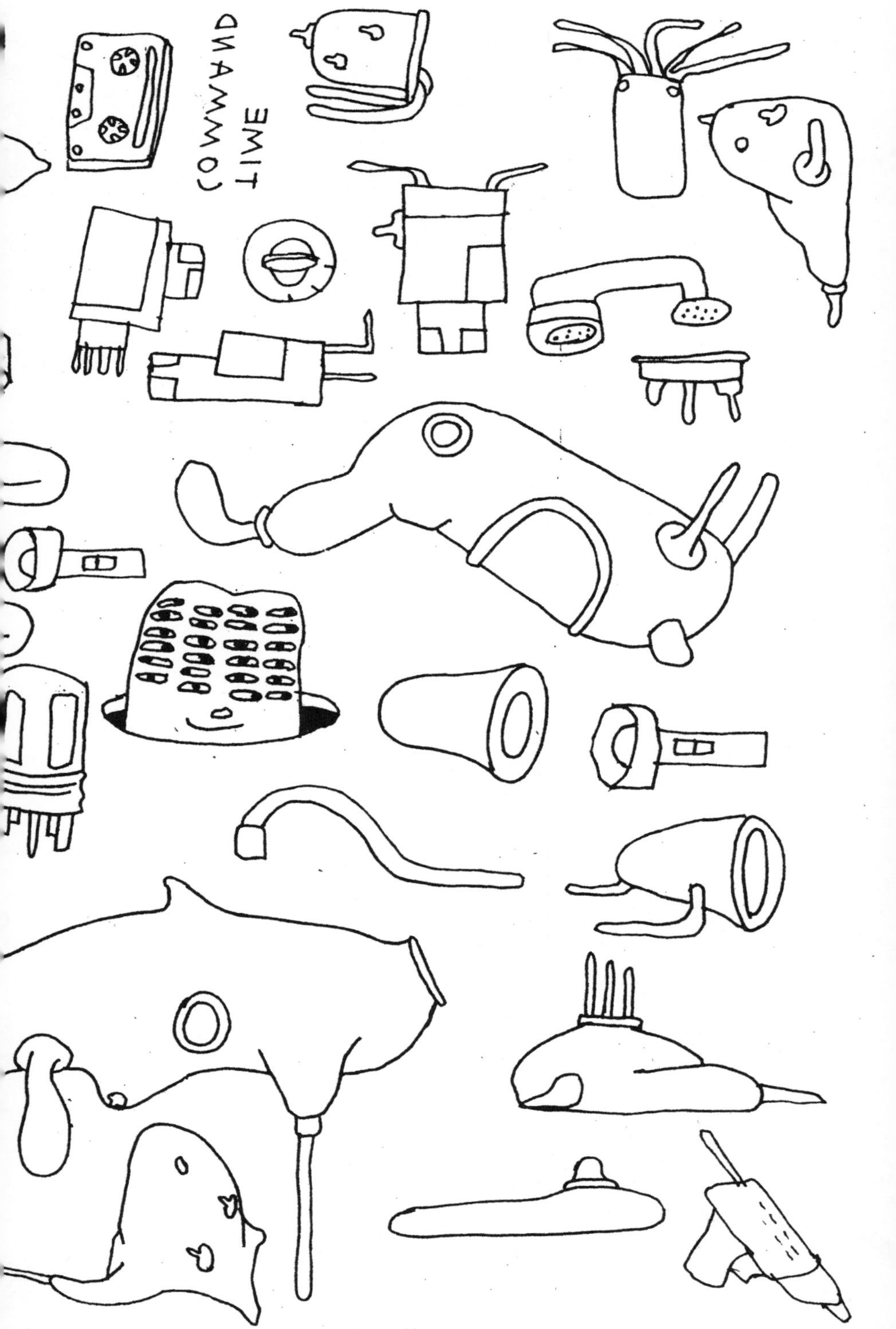
COMMAND
TIME

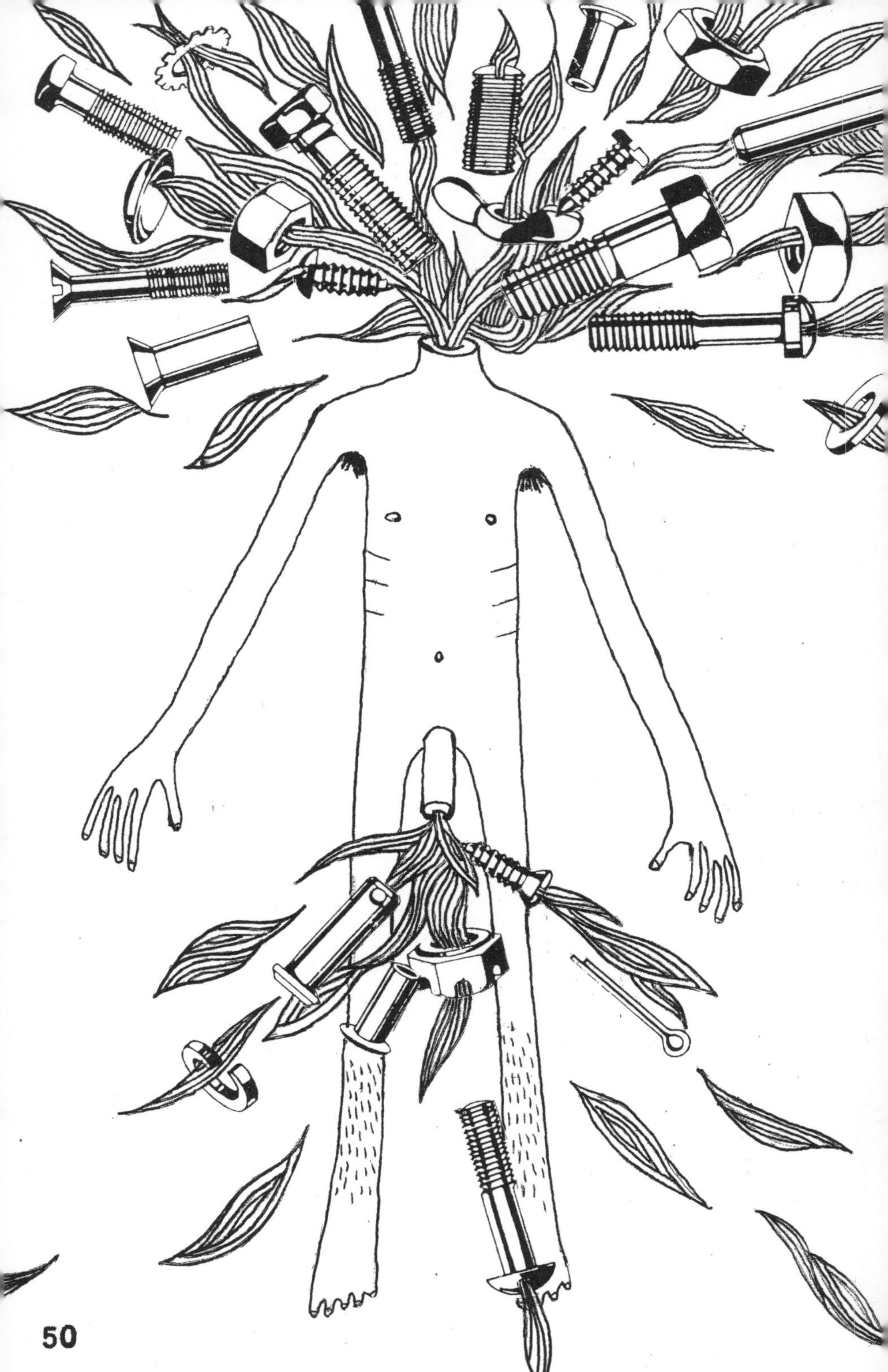

then

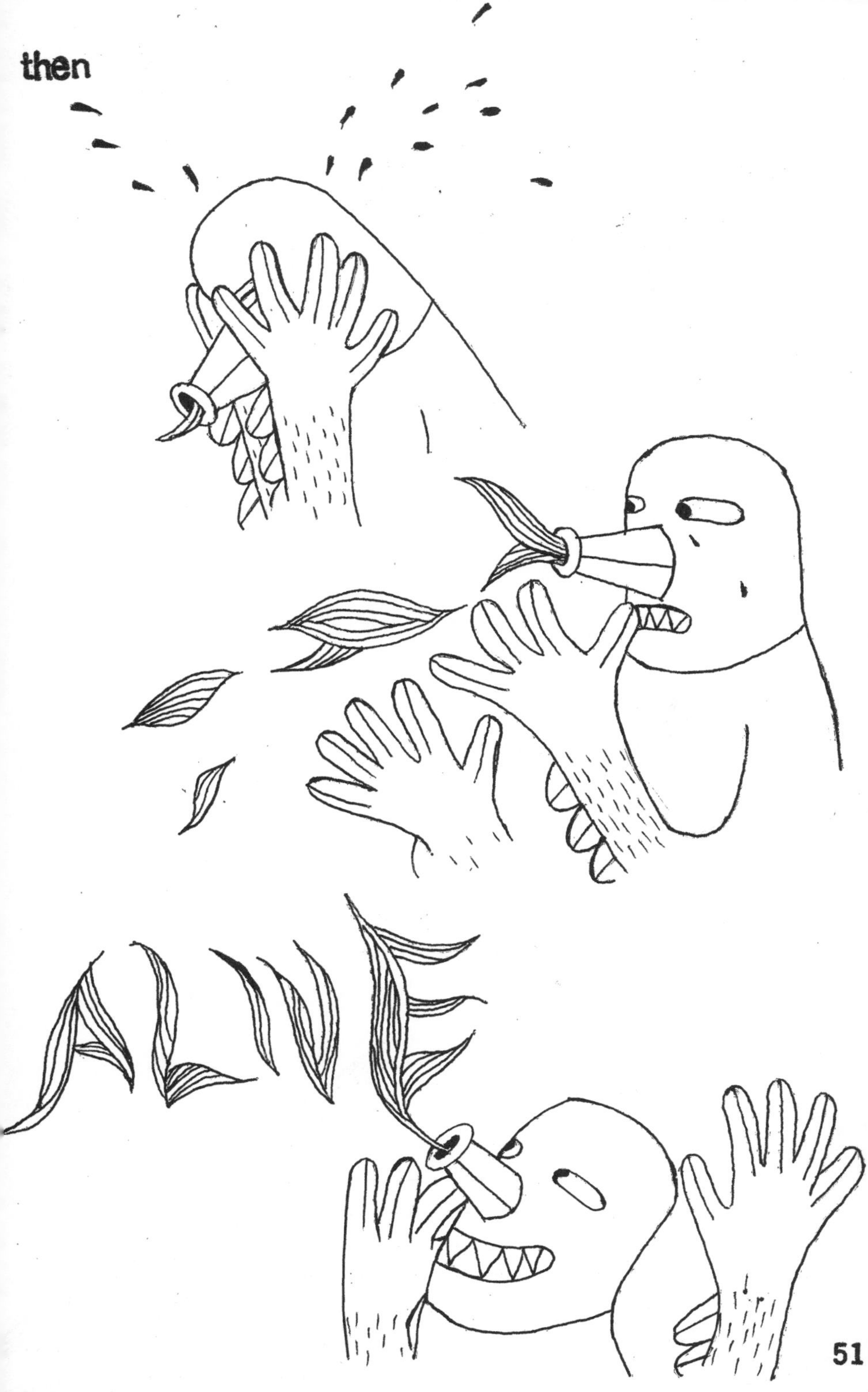
ALIVE

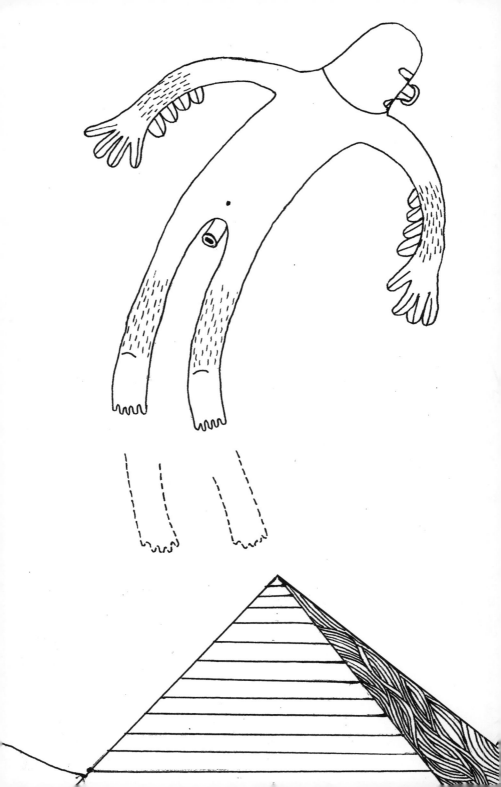

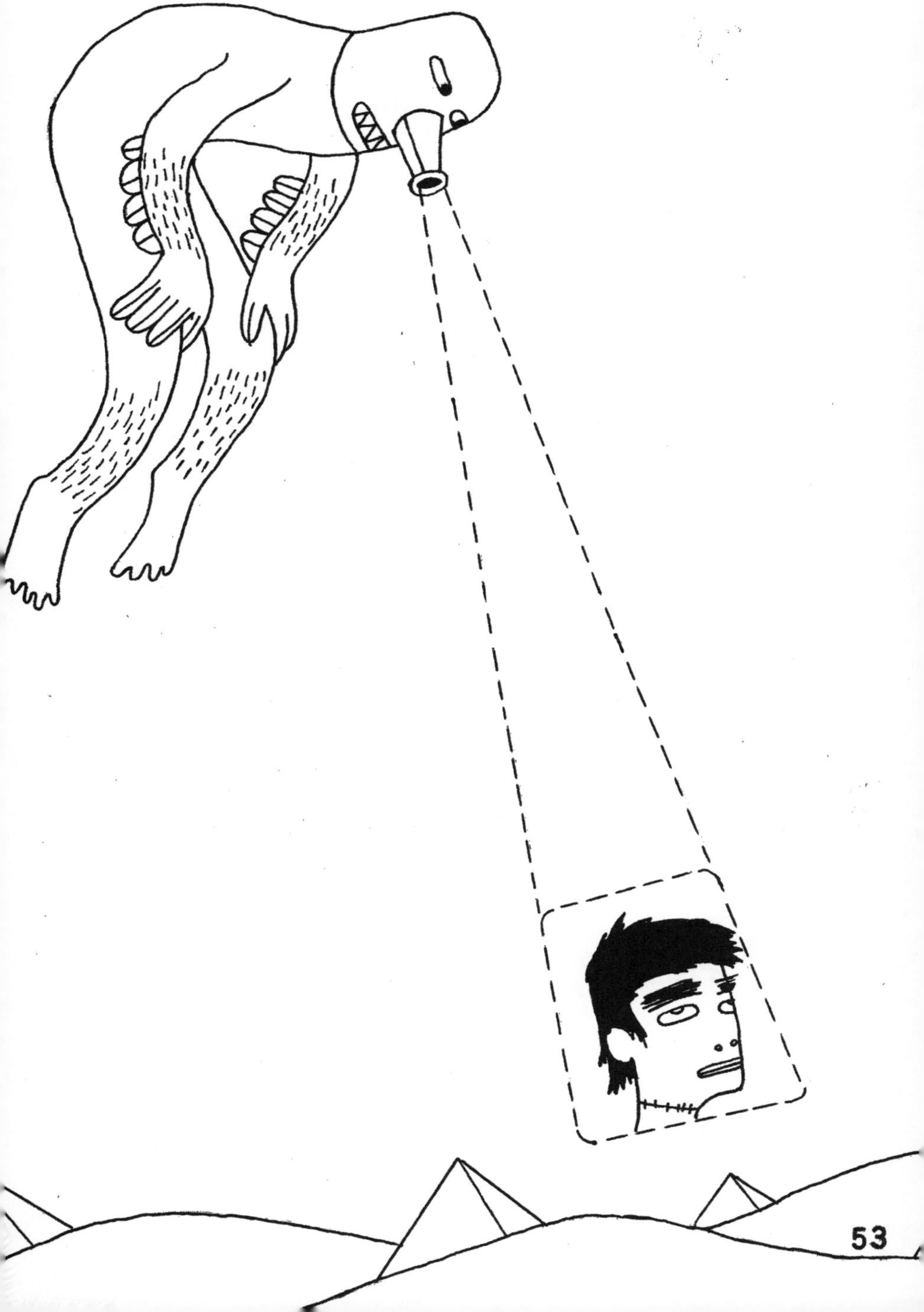

I MUST GO

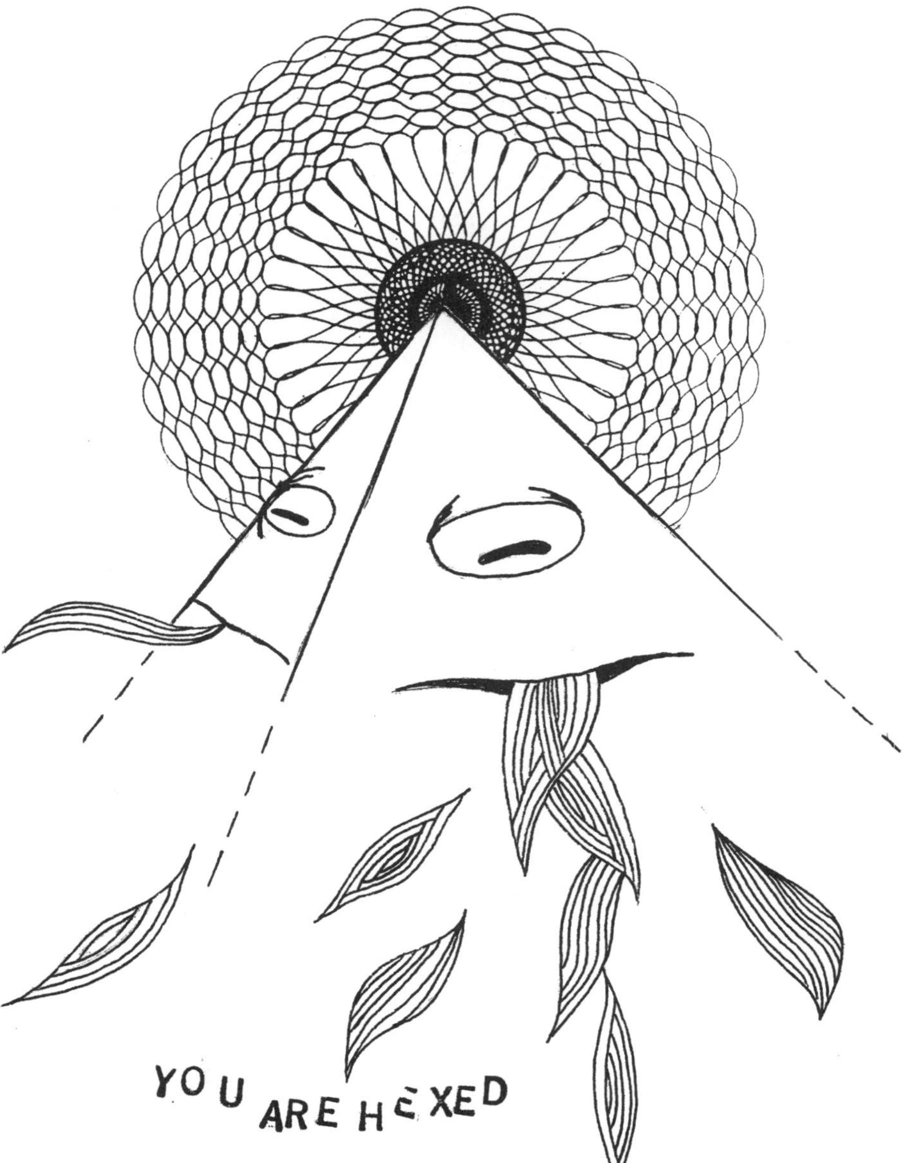

YOU ARE HEXED

YOU MUST ASCEND TO

5 TH TEMPLE

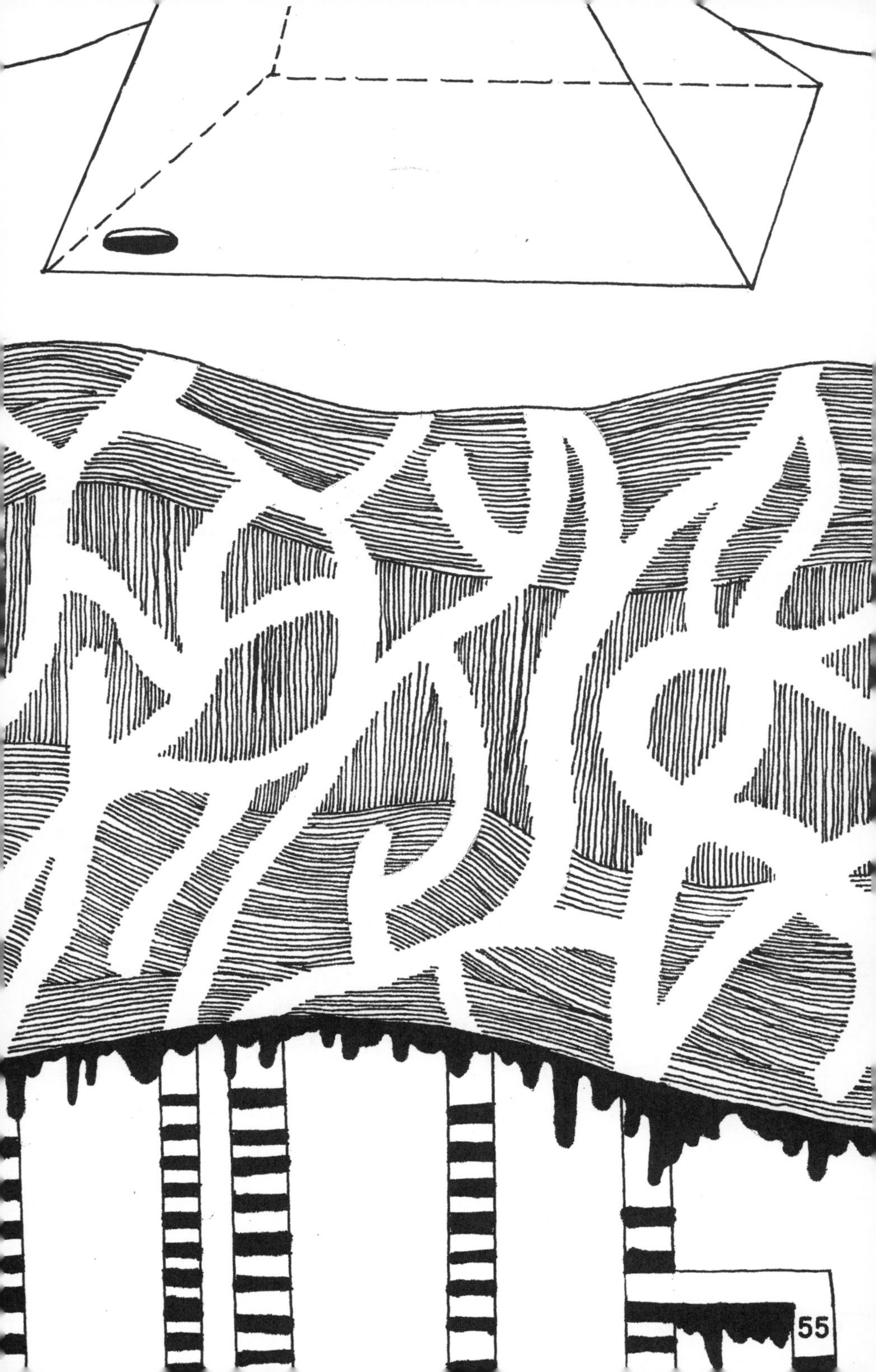

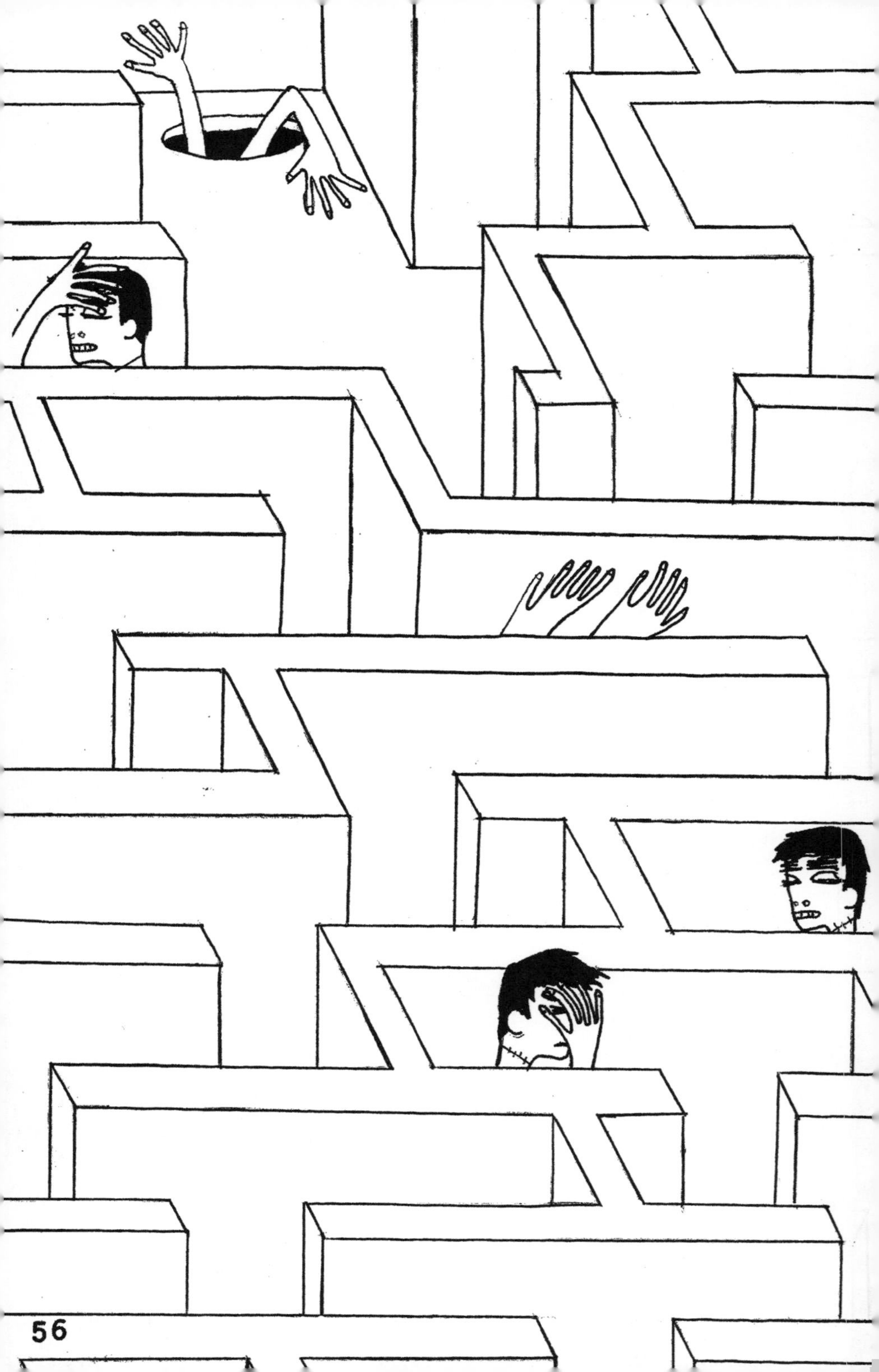

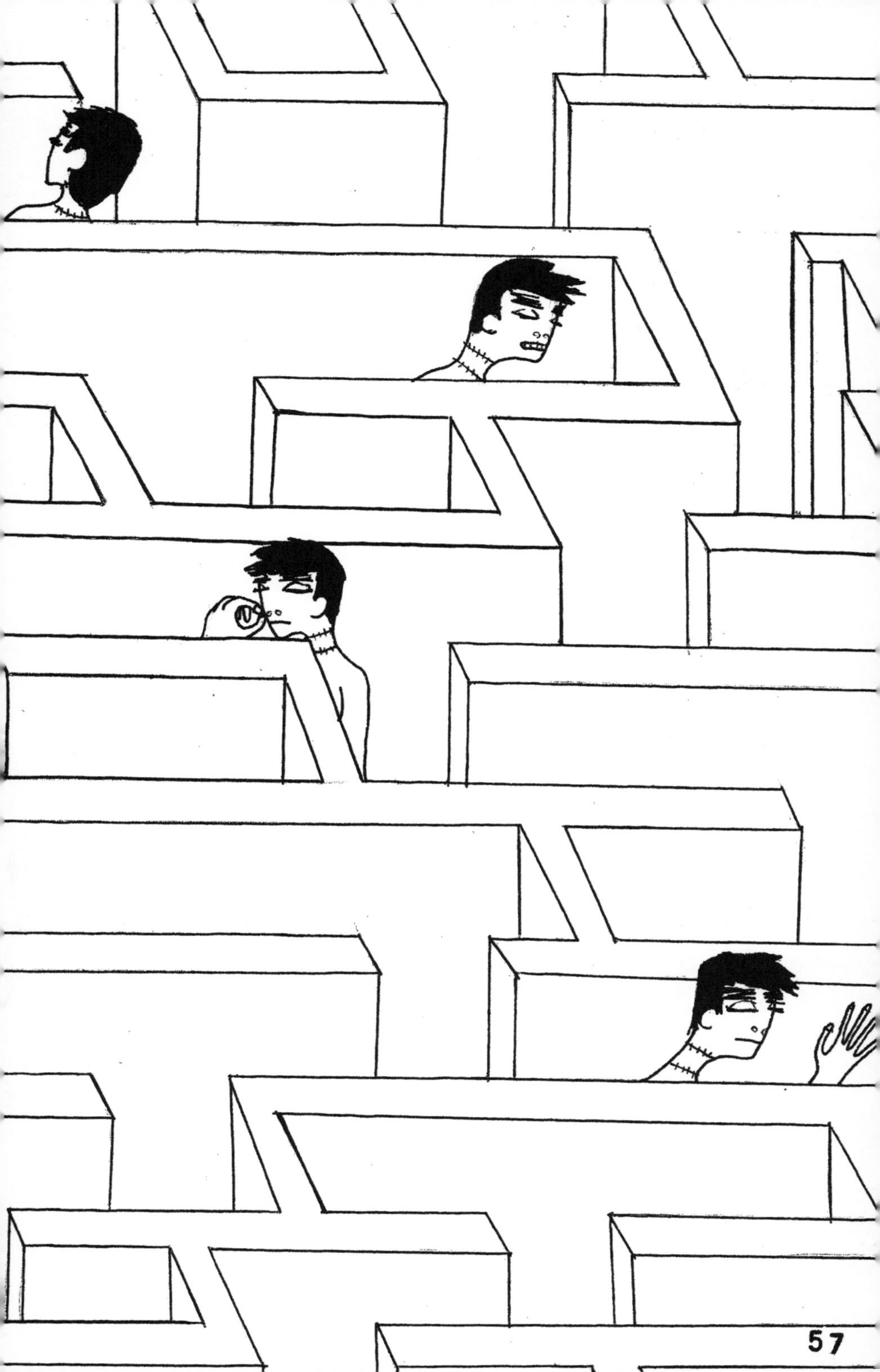

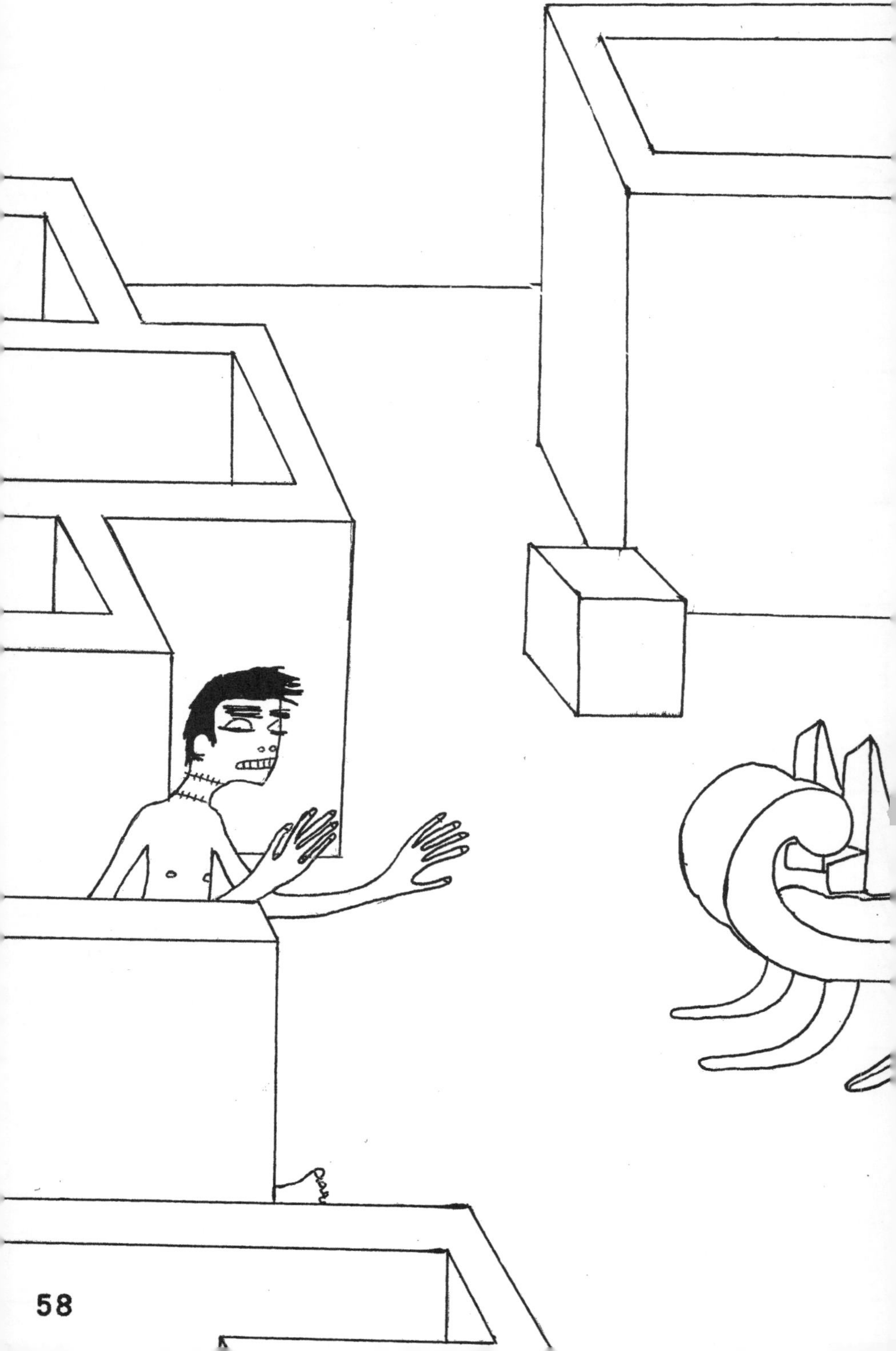

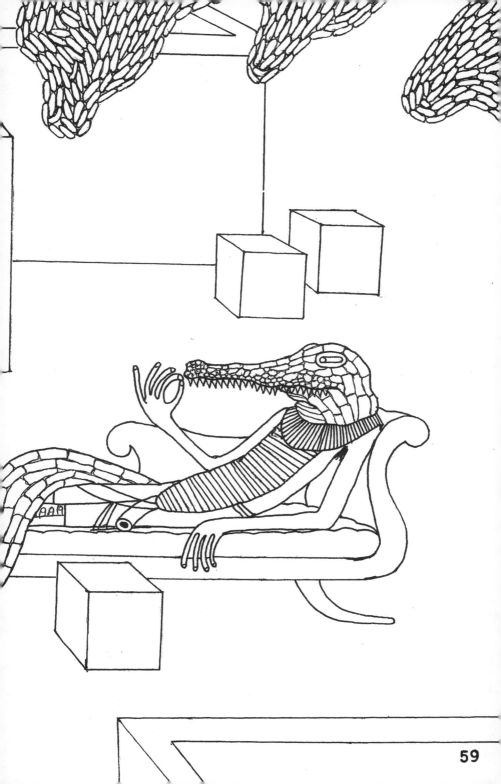

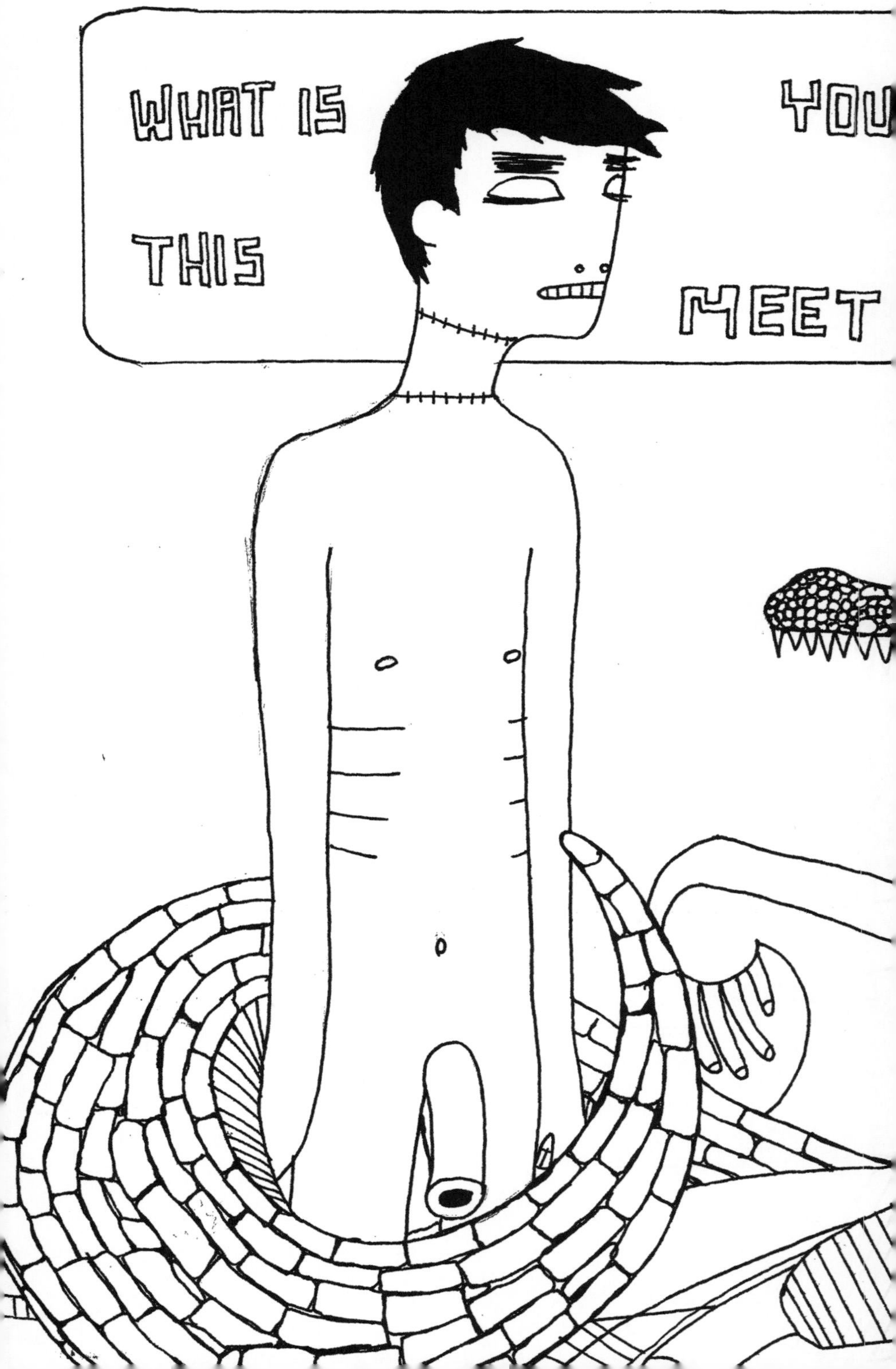
WHAT IS
THIS
YOU
MEET

HAVE THE LOWER MAGIC

YR EMPERER

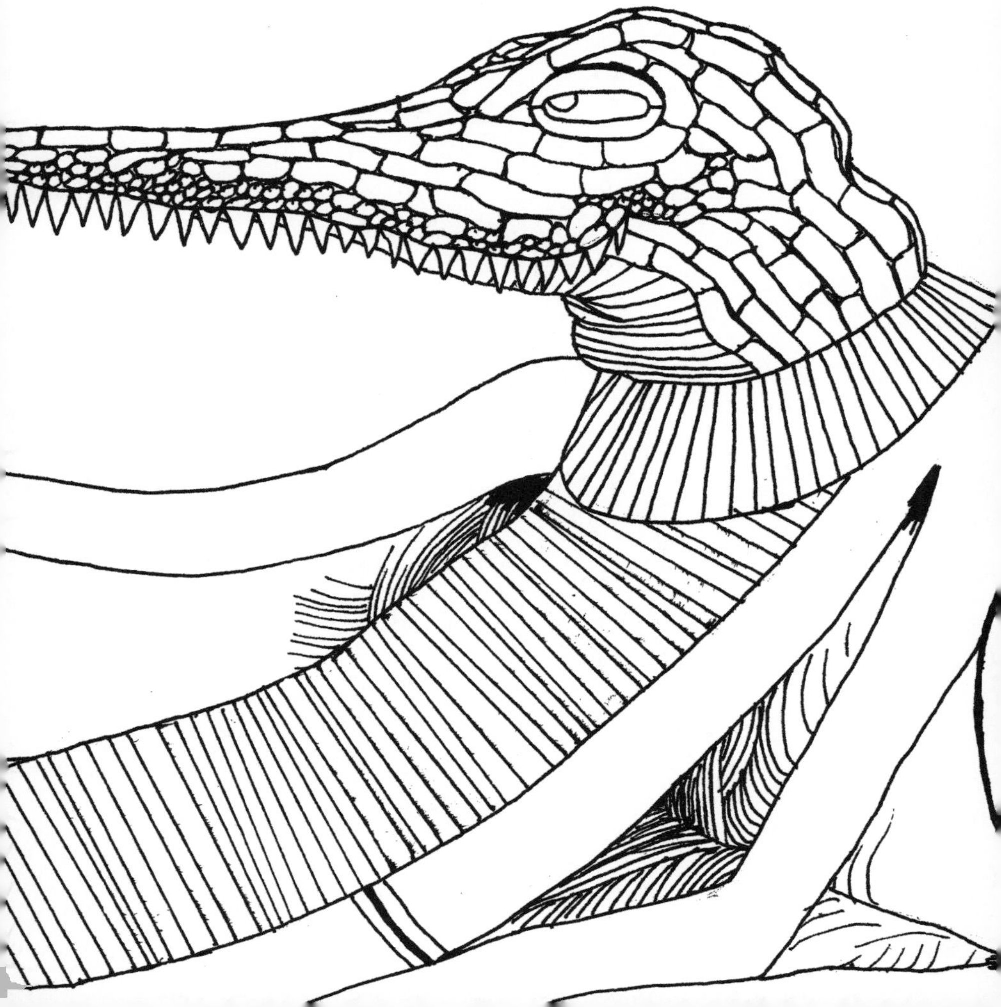

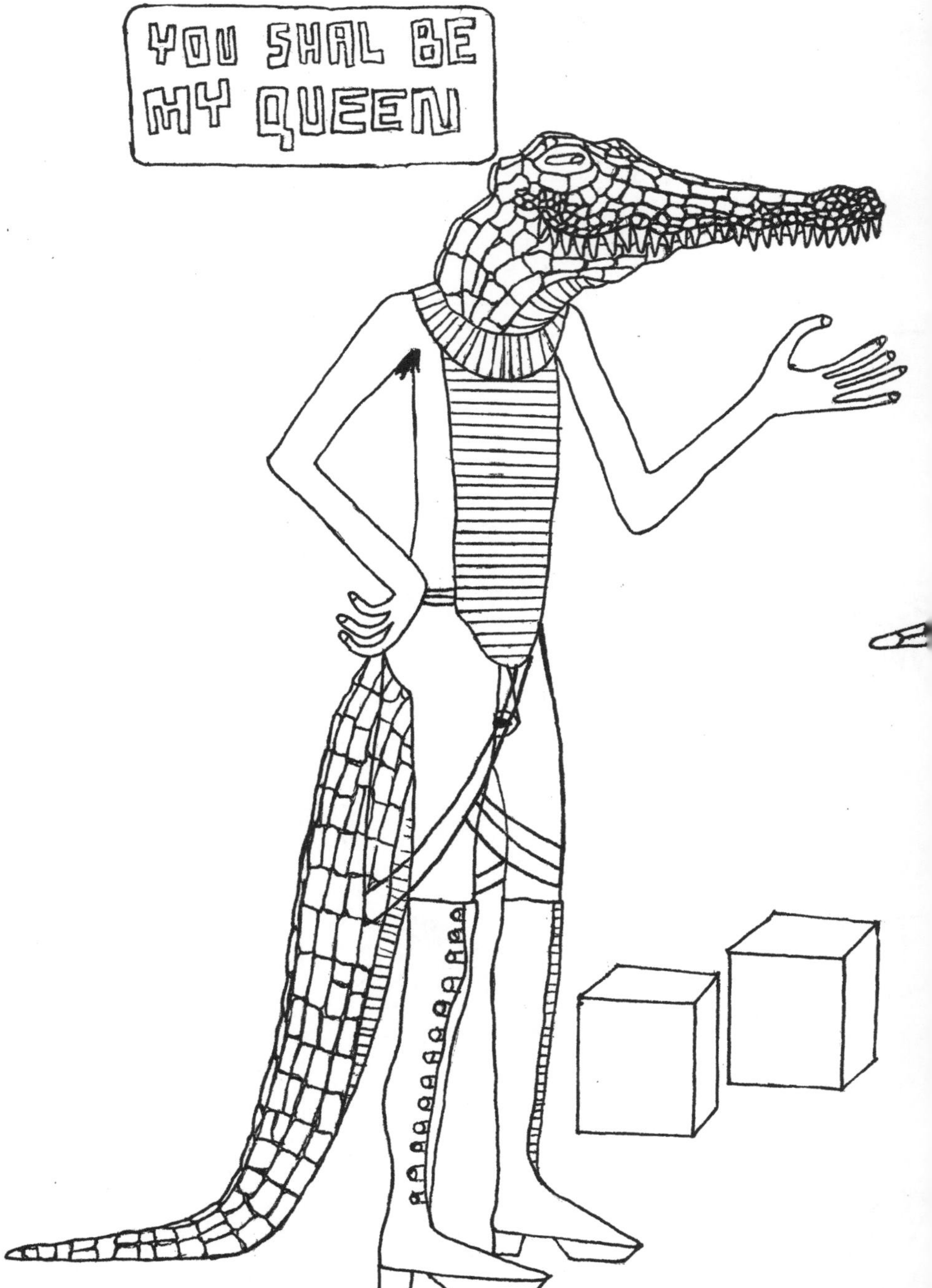
YOU SHAL BE MY QUEEN

deep seduction

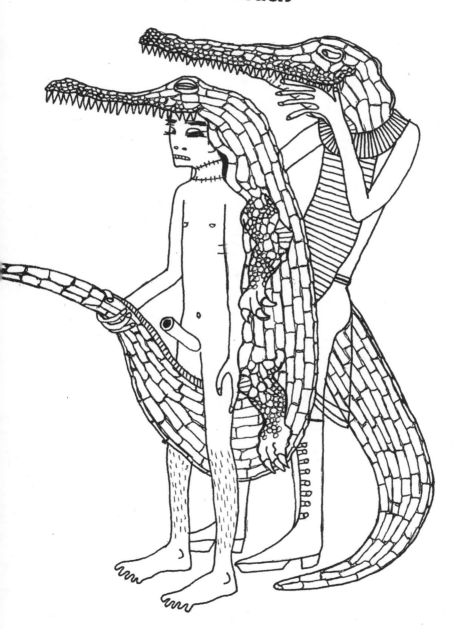

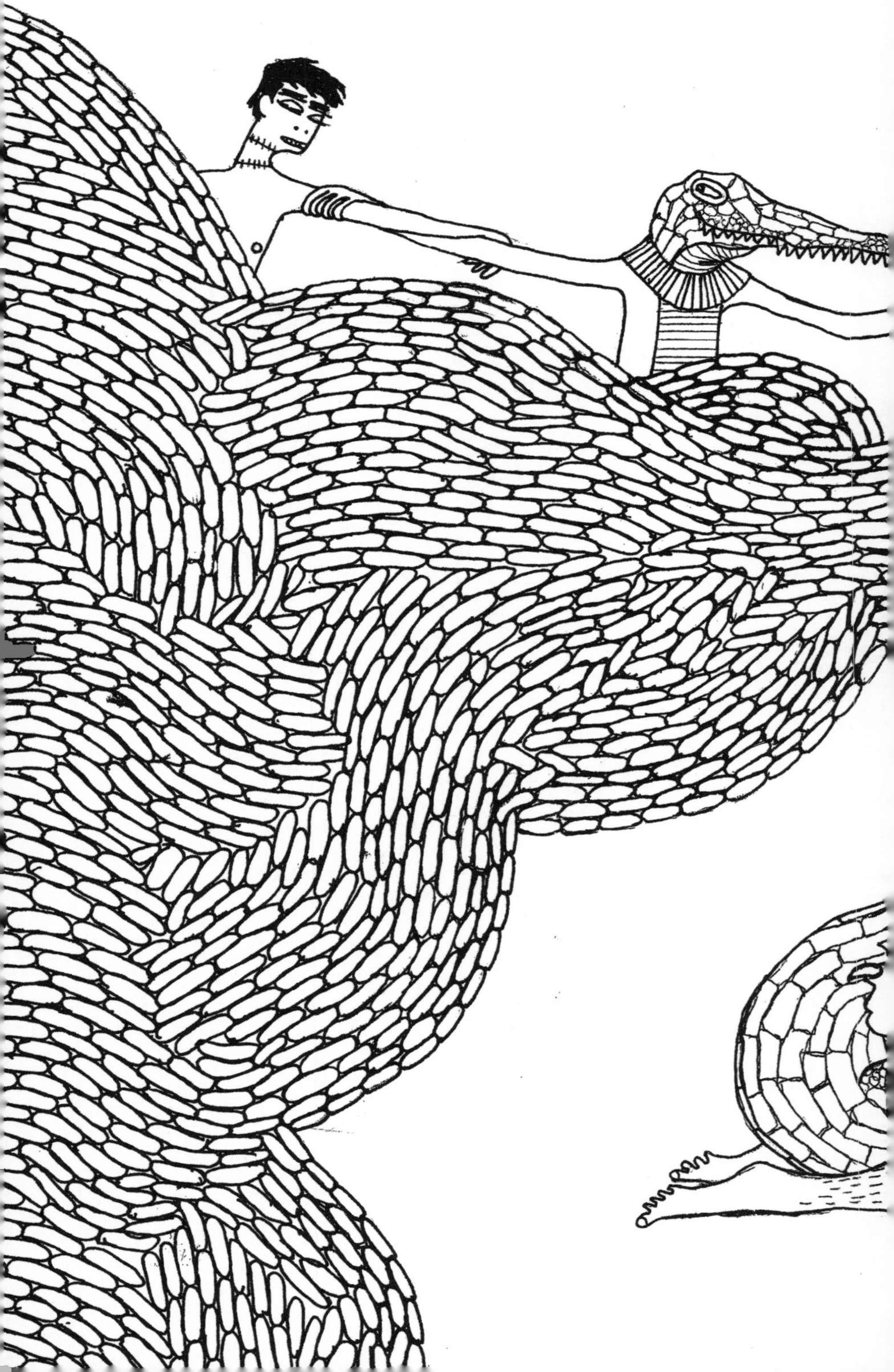

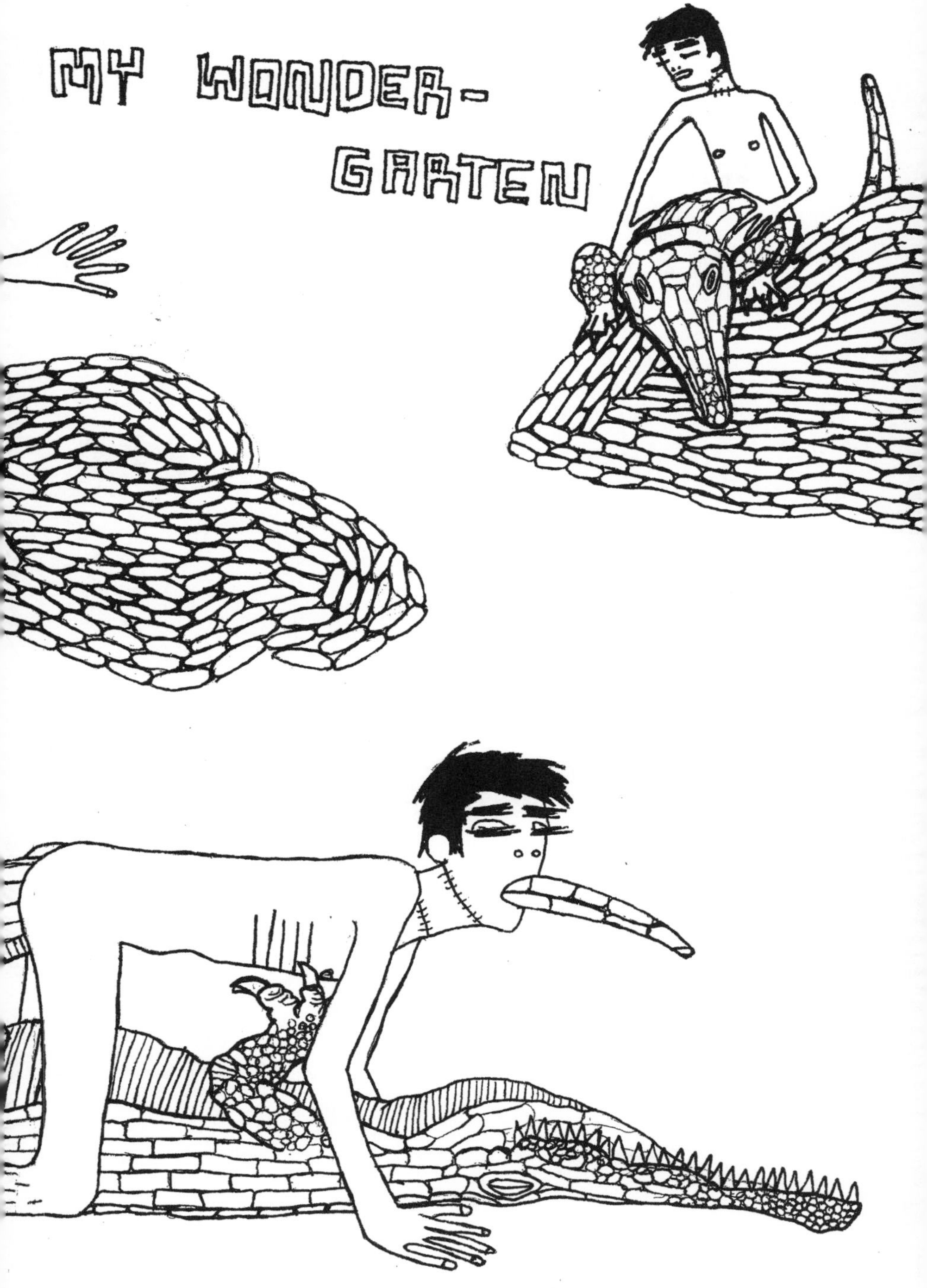
MY WONDER-
GARTEN

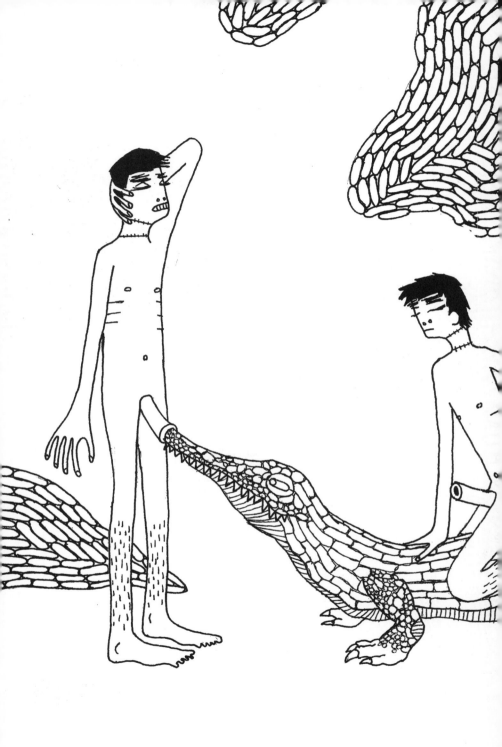

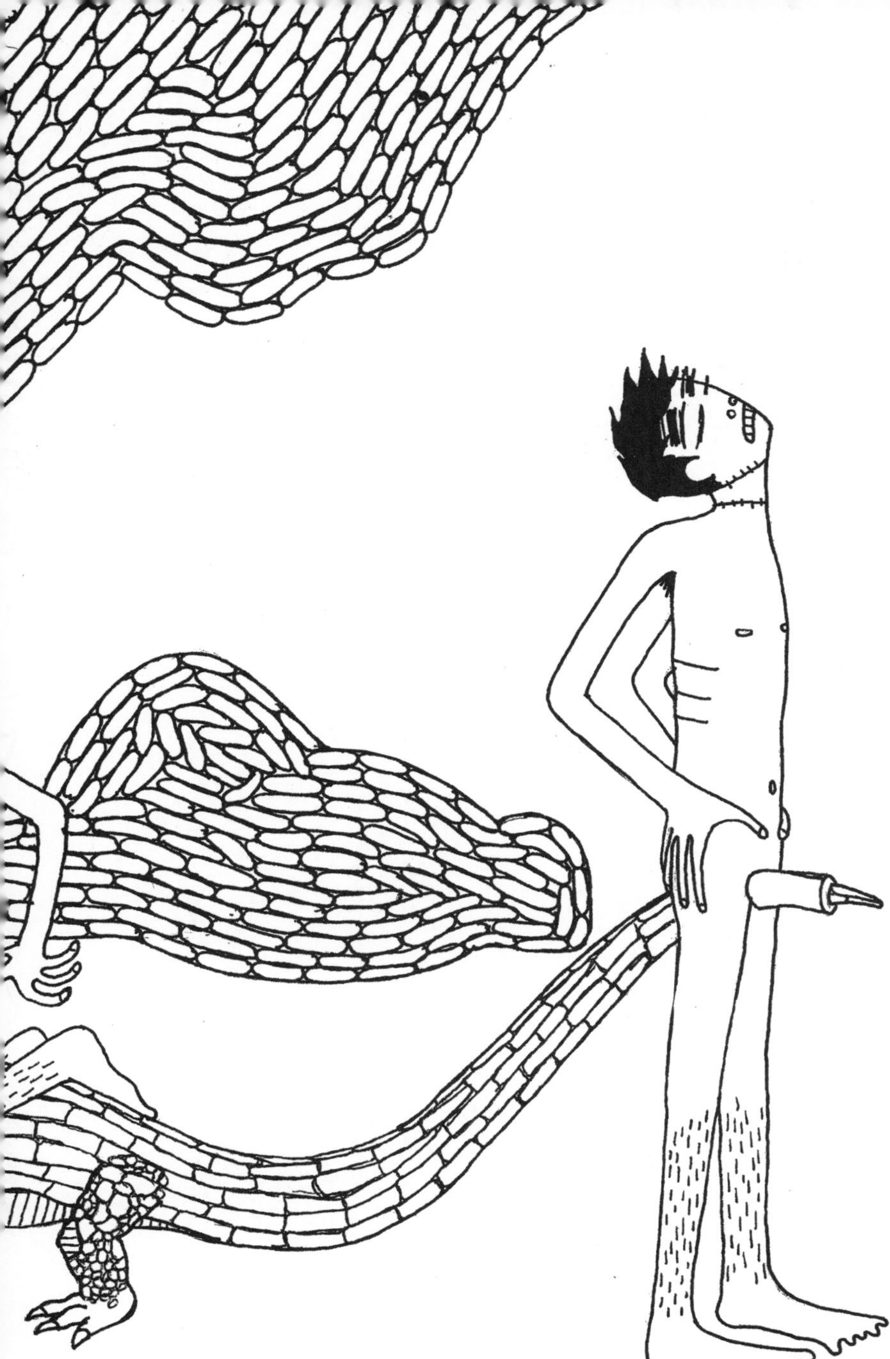

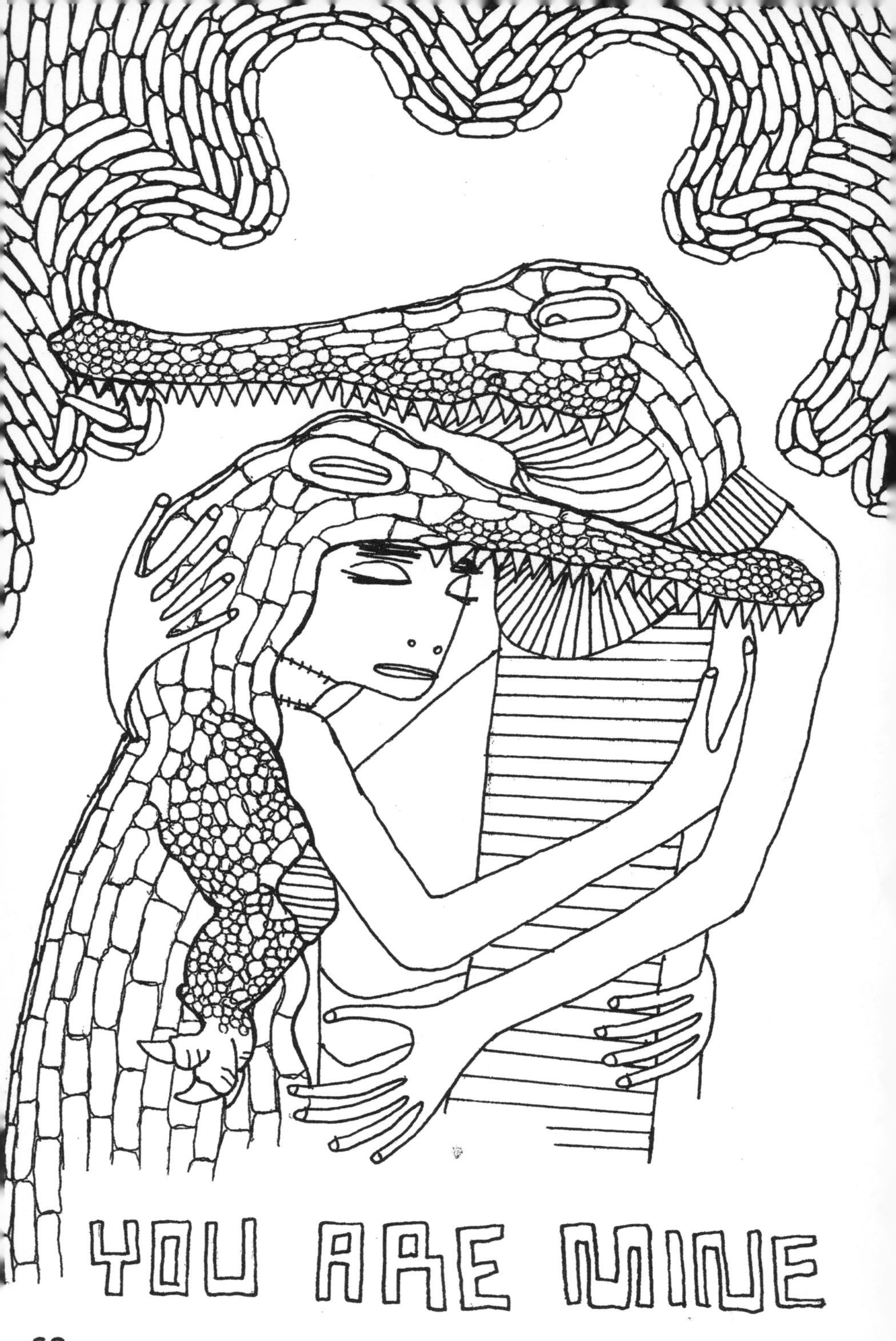
YOU ARE MINE

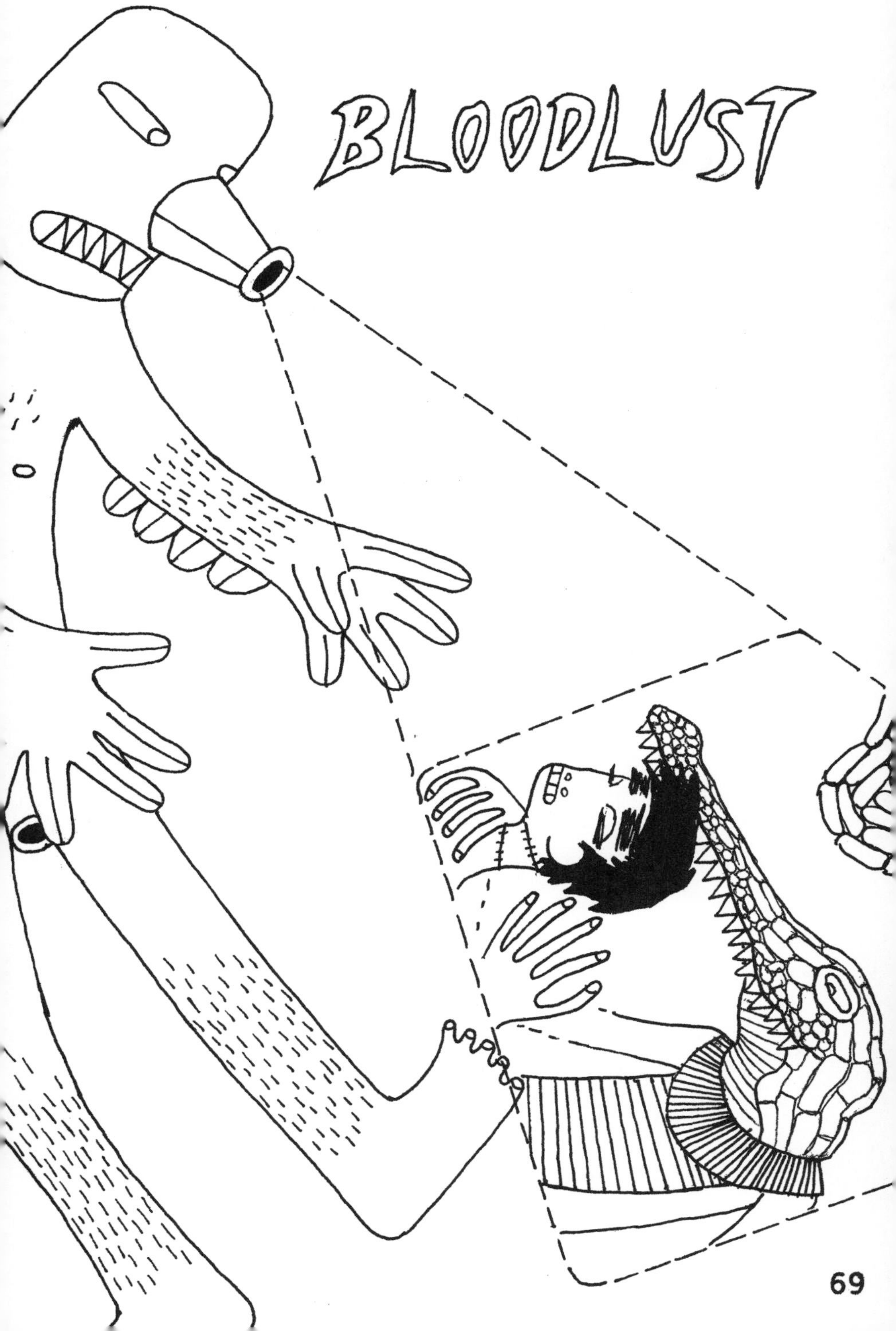
BLOODLUST

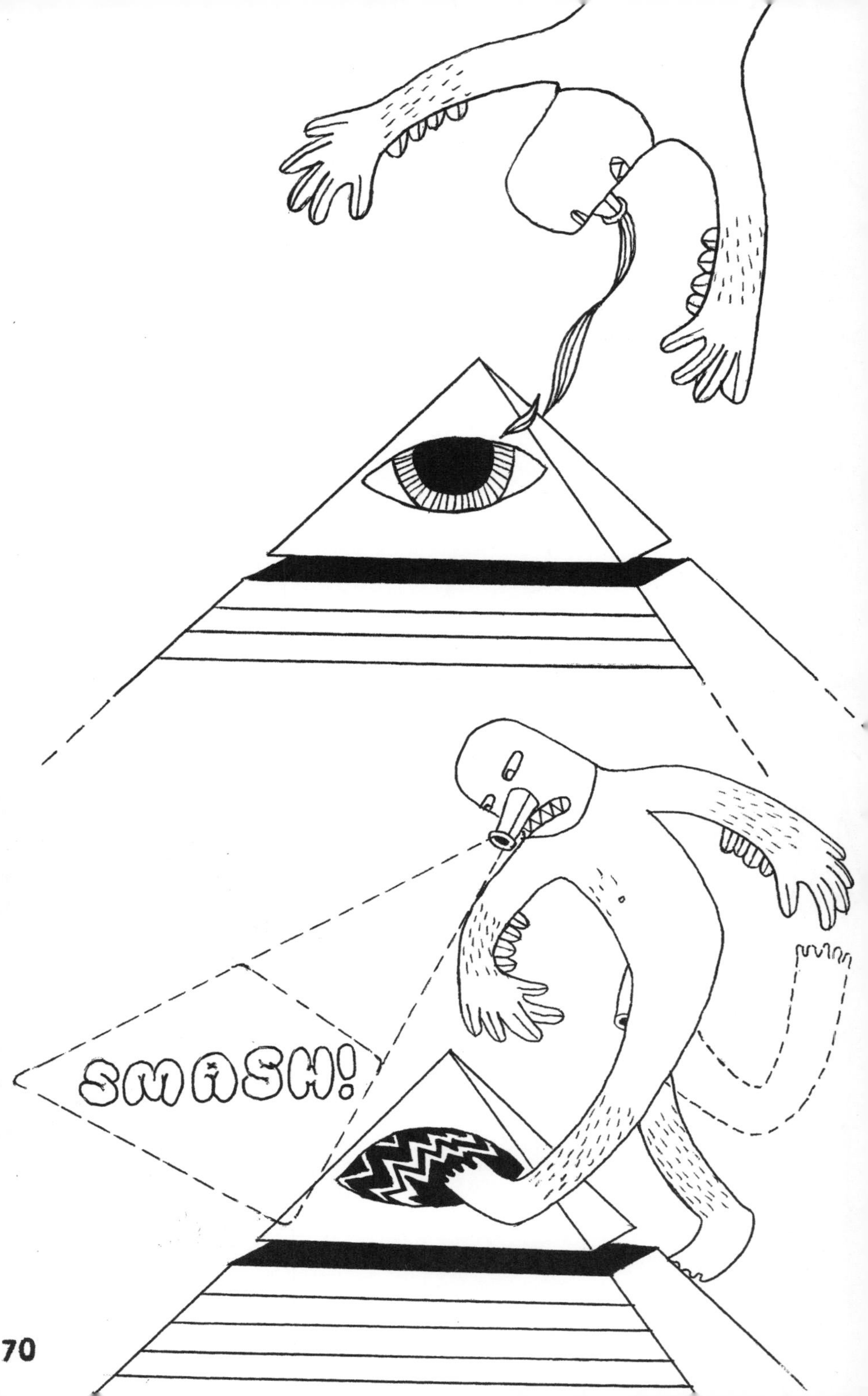
SMASH!

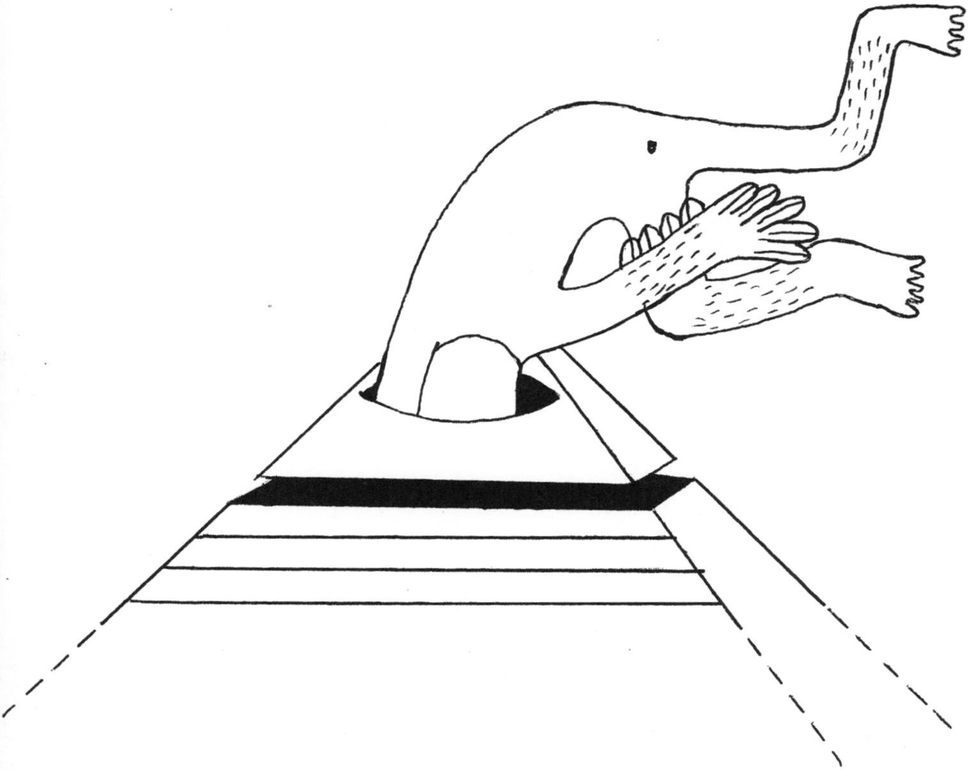

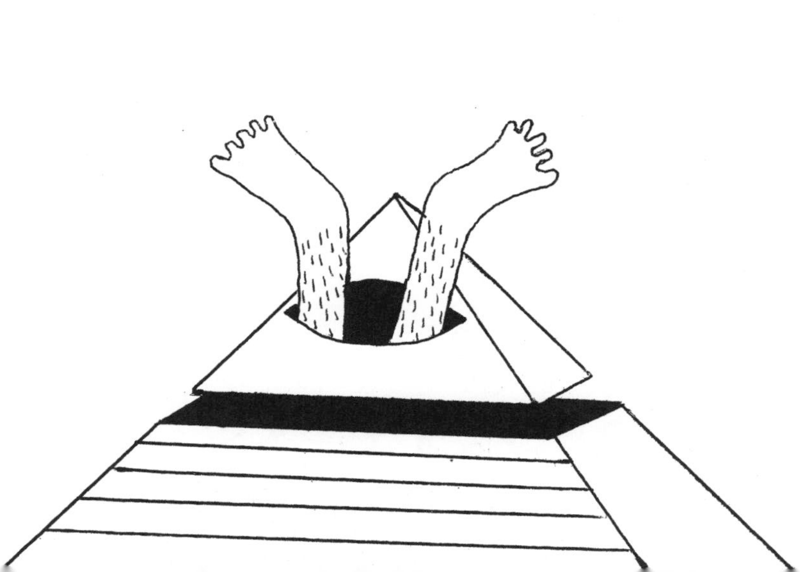

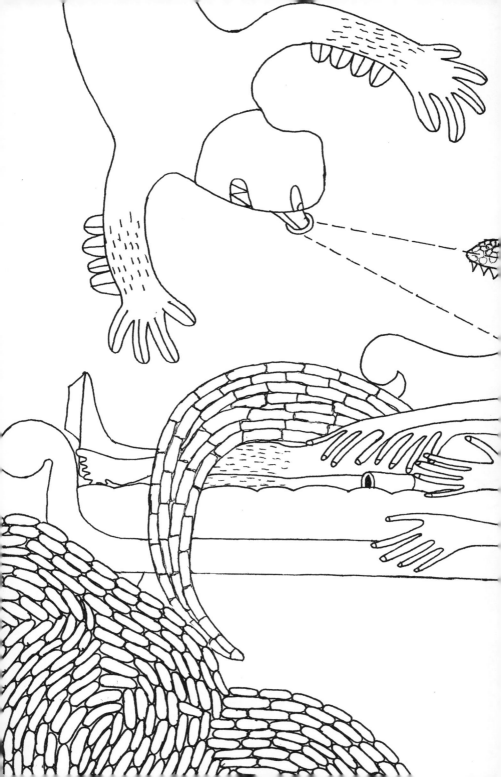

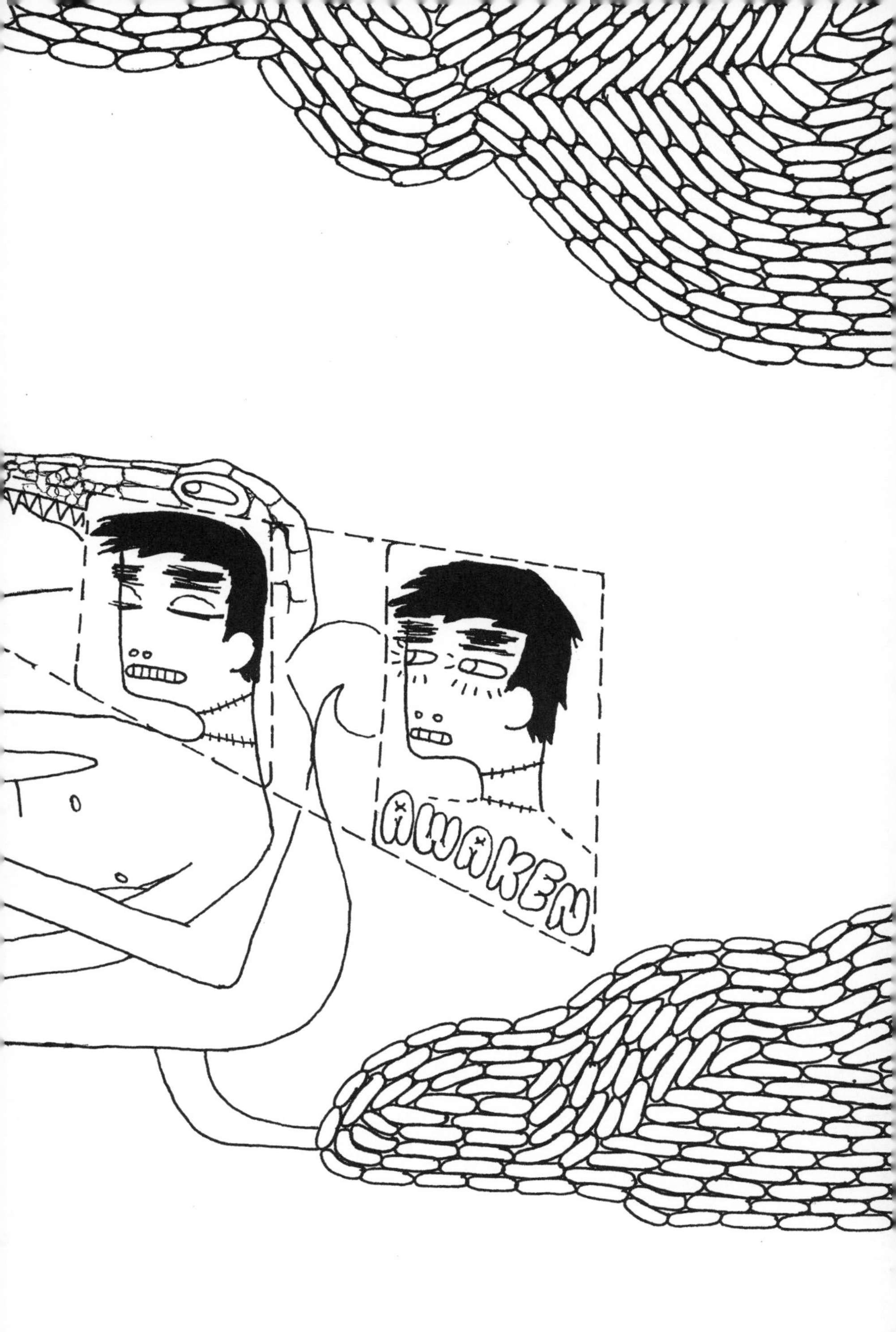
AWAKEN

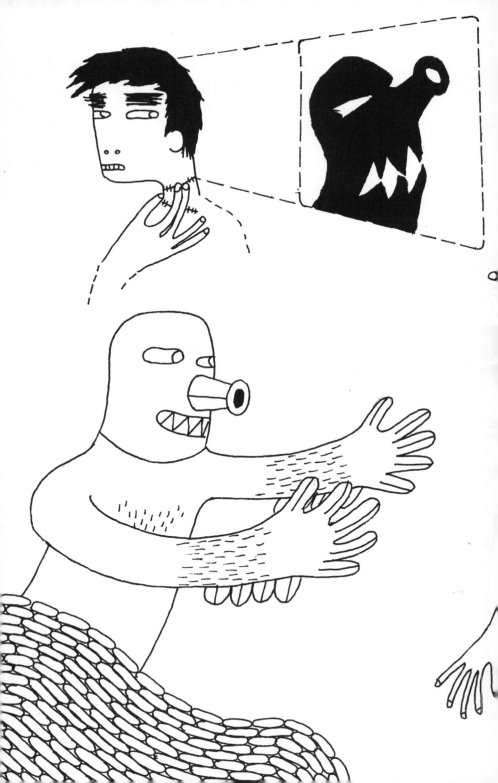

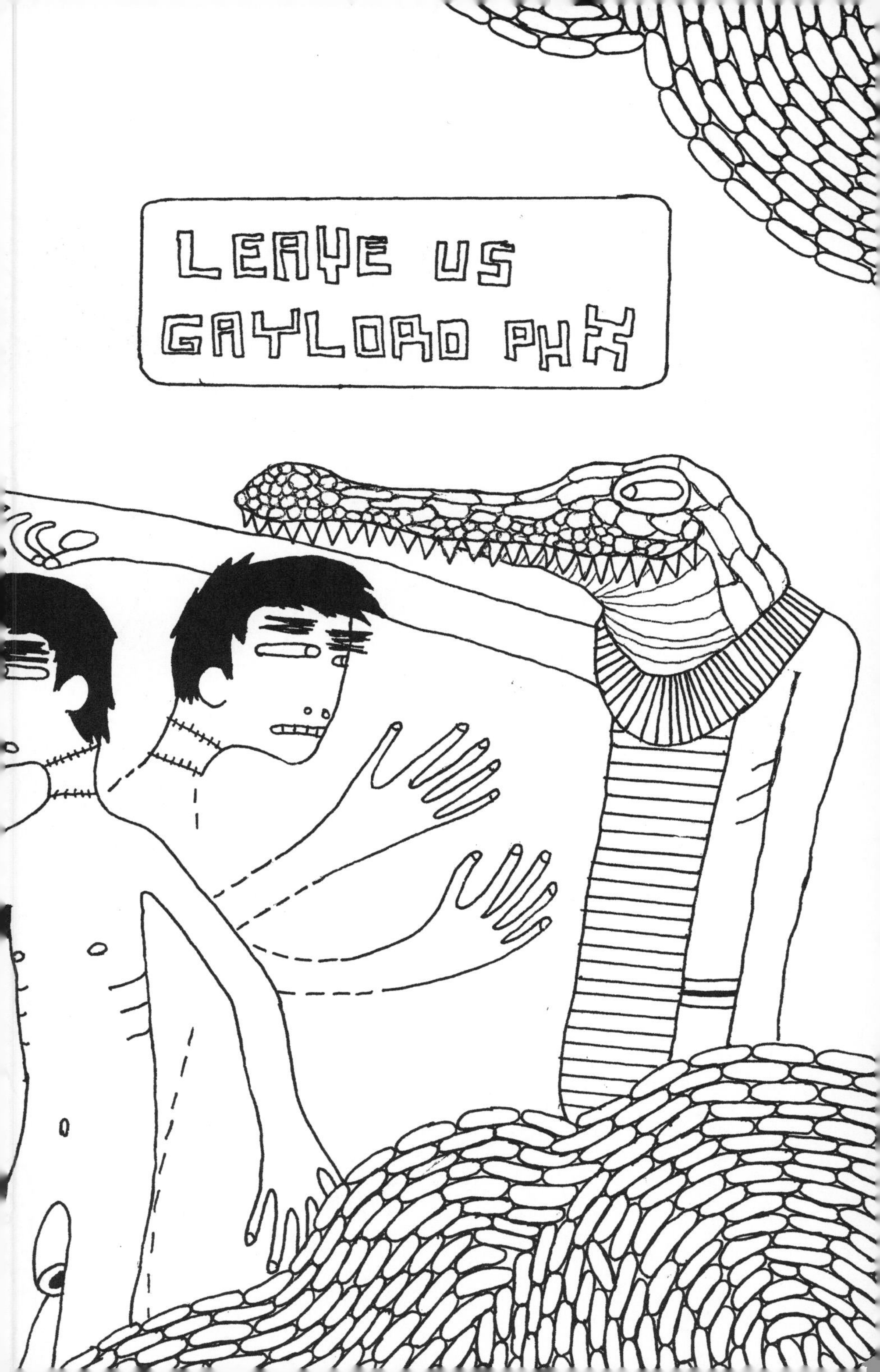
LEAVE US
GAYLORD PHX

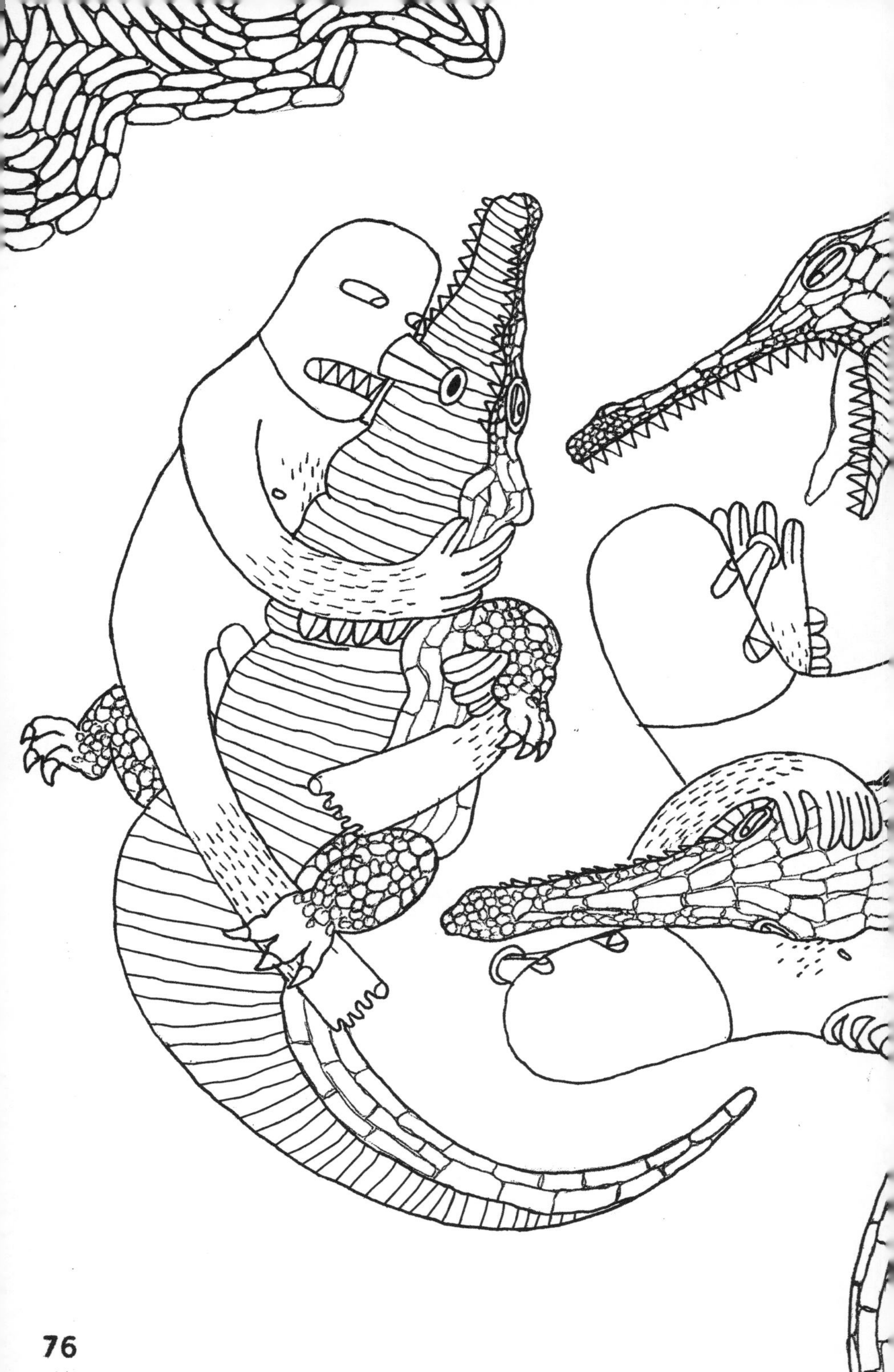

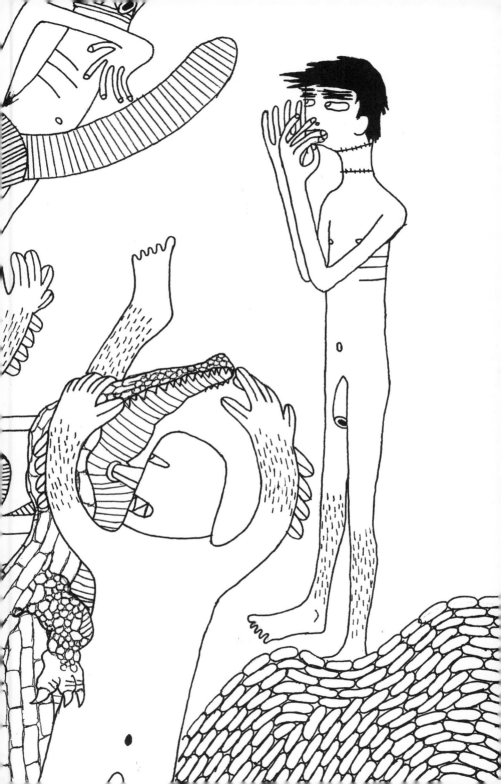

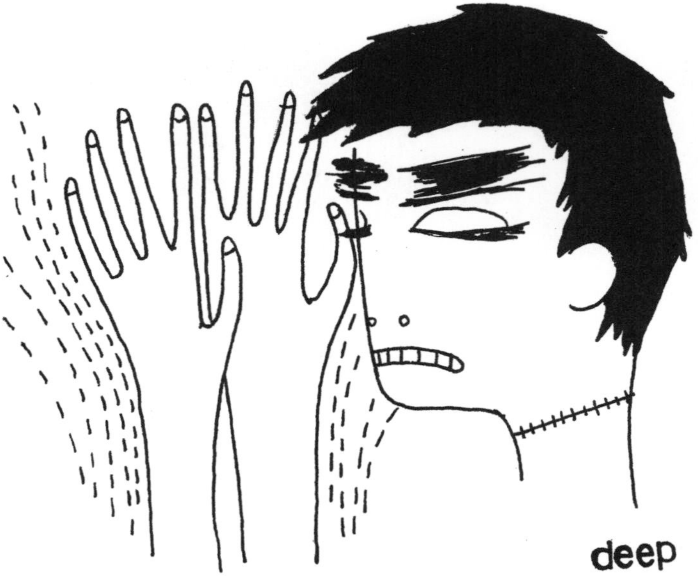

deep

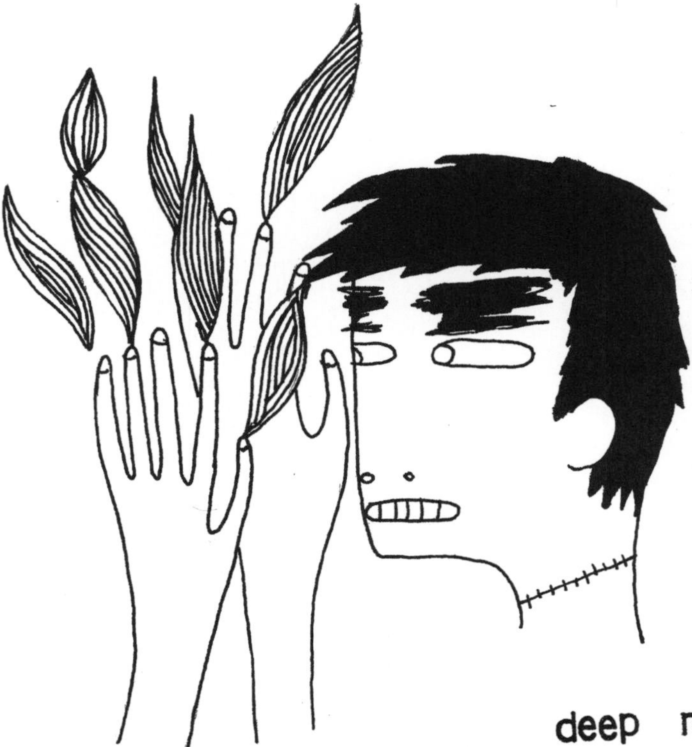

deep magic

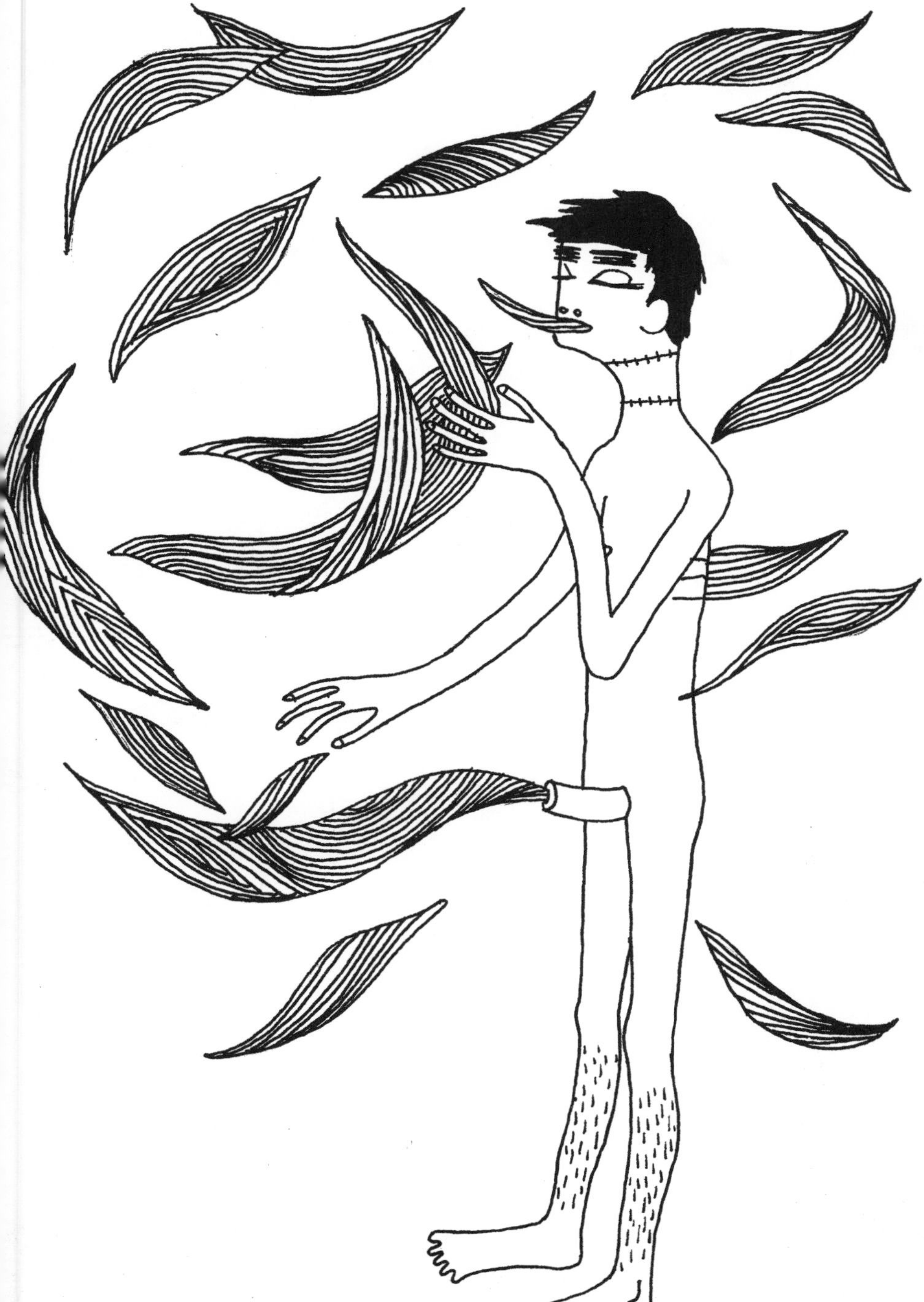

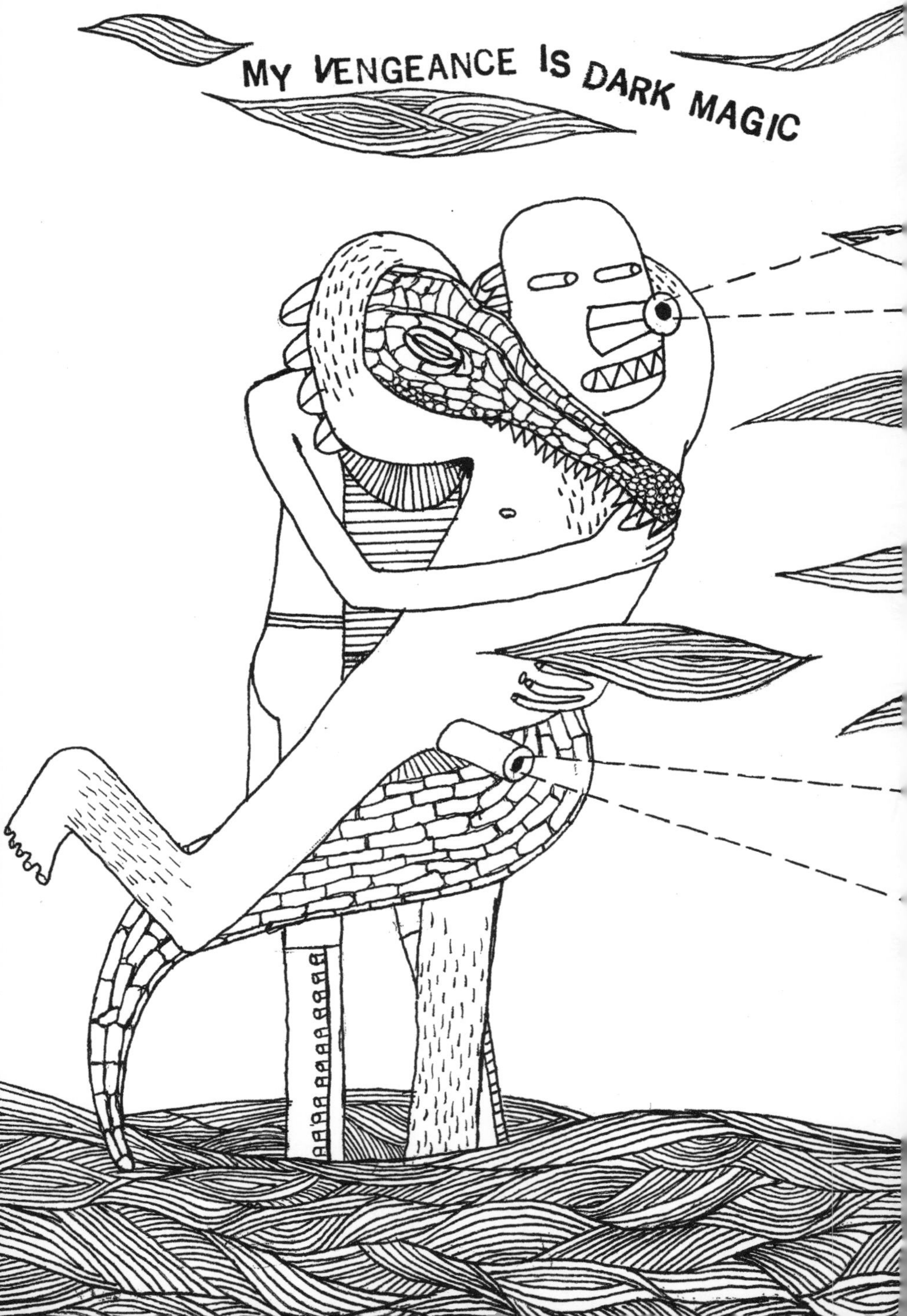
MY VENGEANCE IS DARK MAGIC

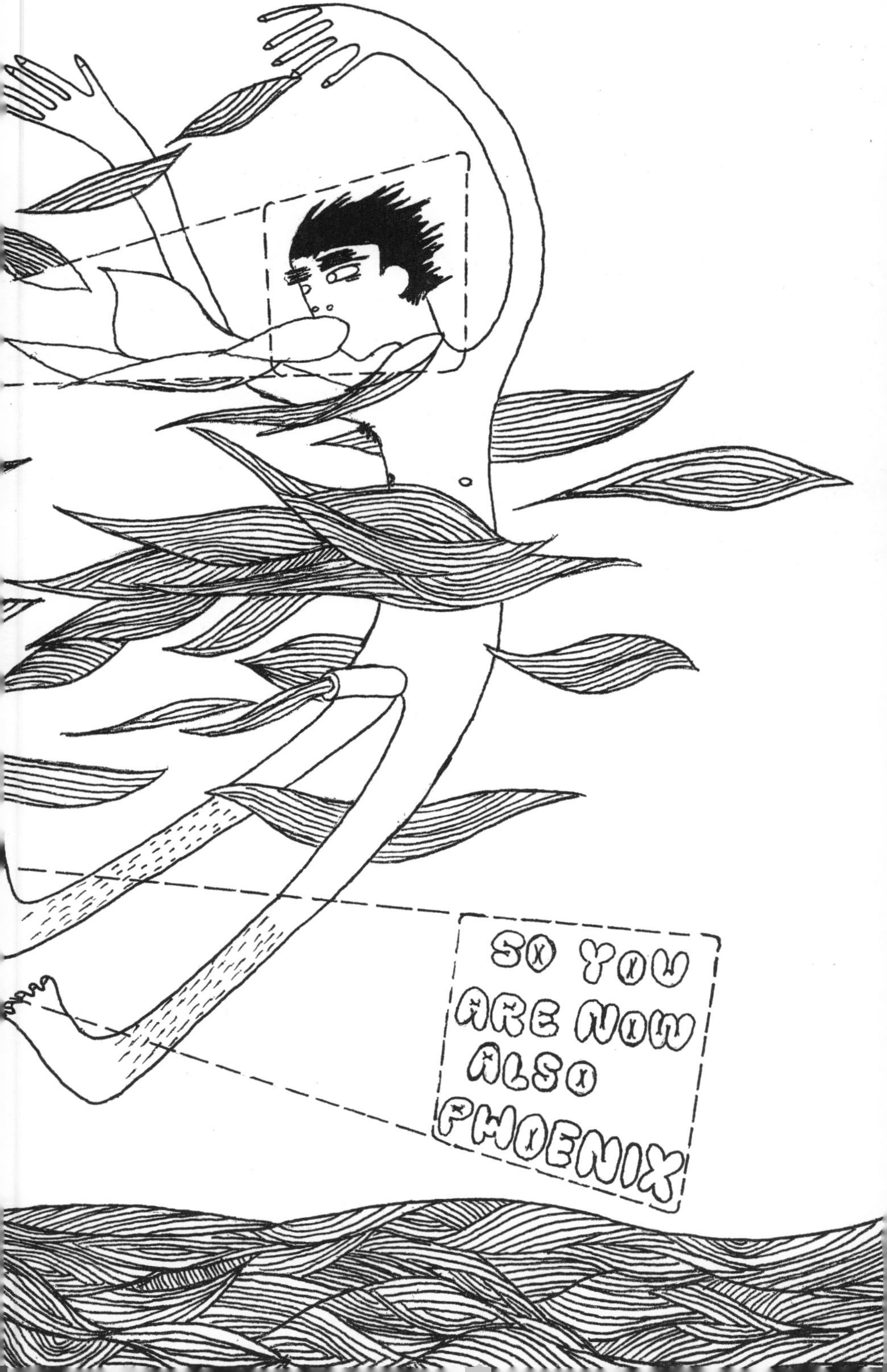
SO YOU
ARE NOW
ALSO
PHOENIX

MY VENGEANCE IS

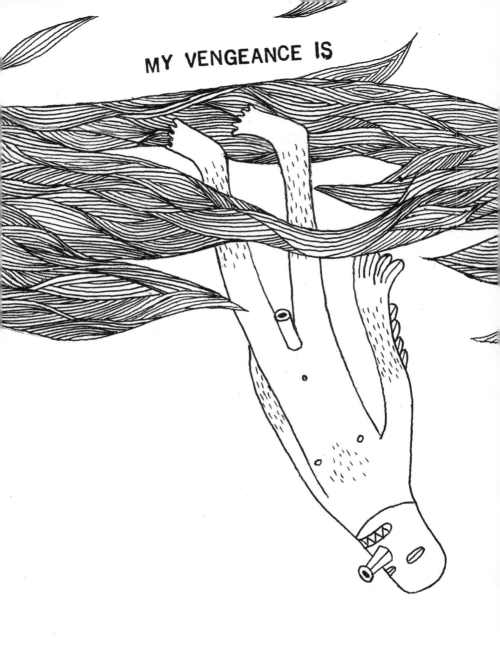

A NEW OCEAN

of tears

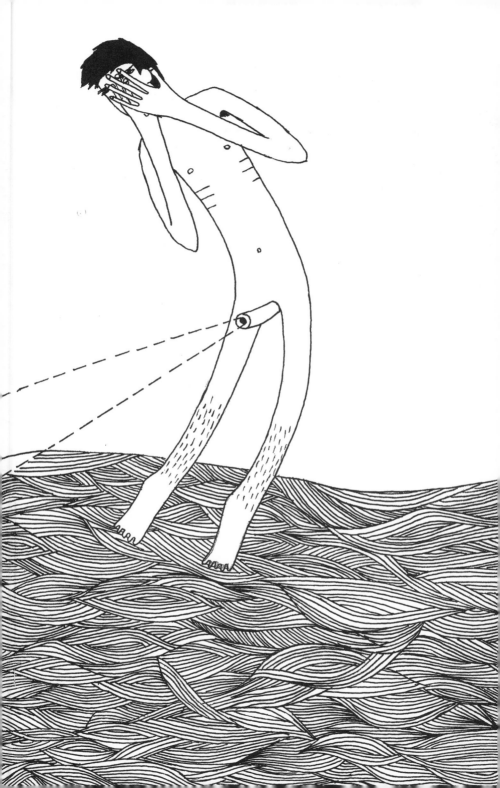

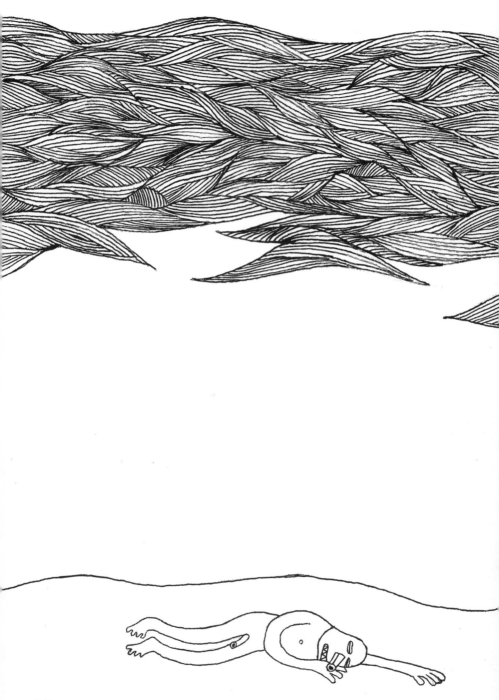

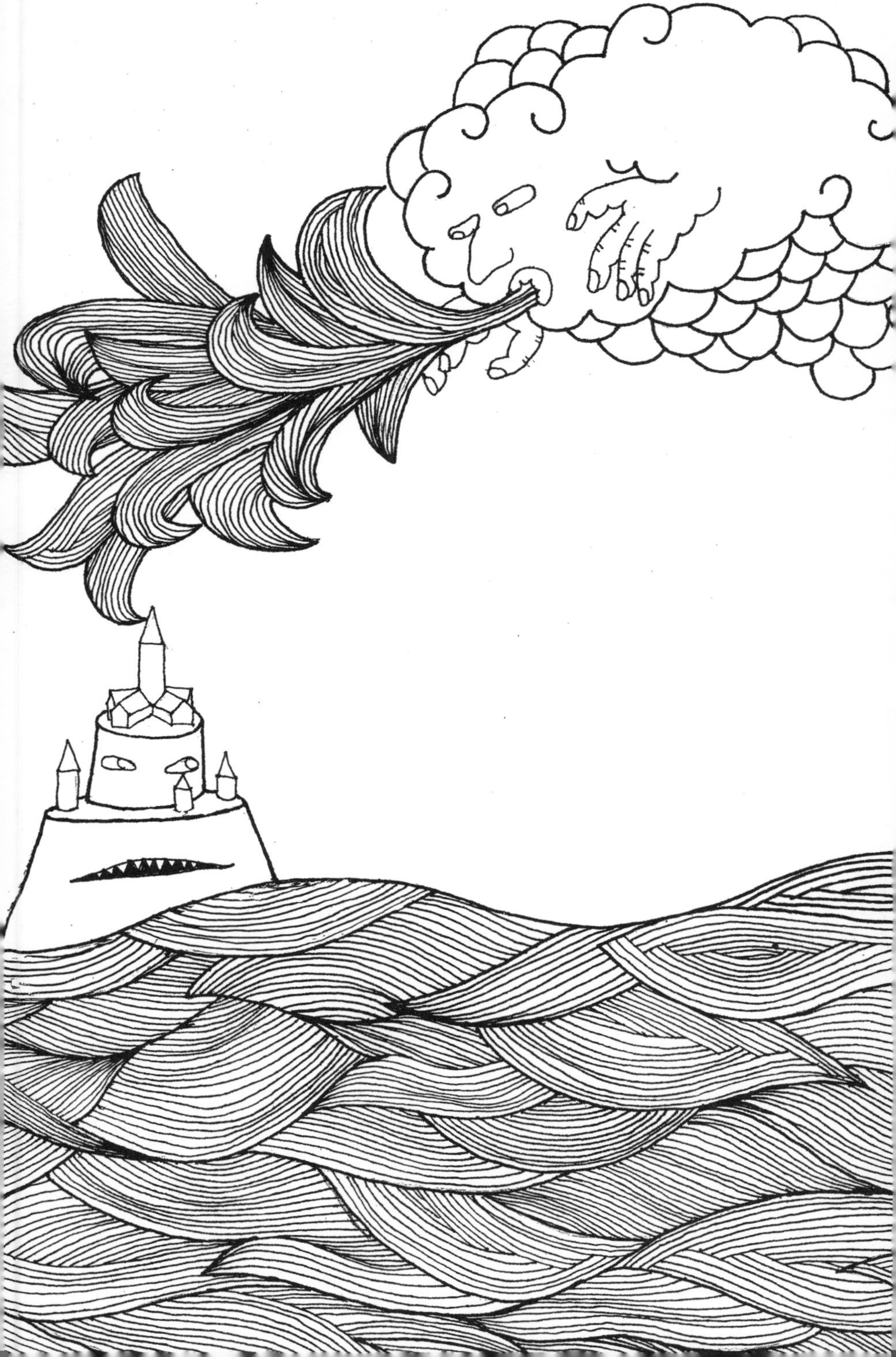

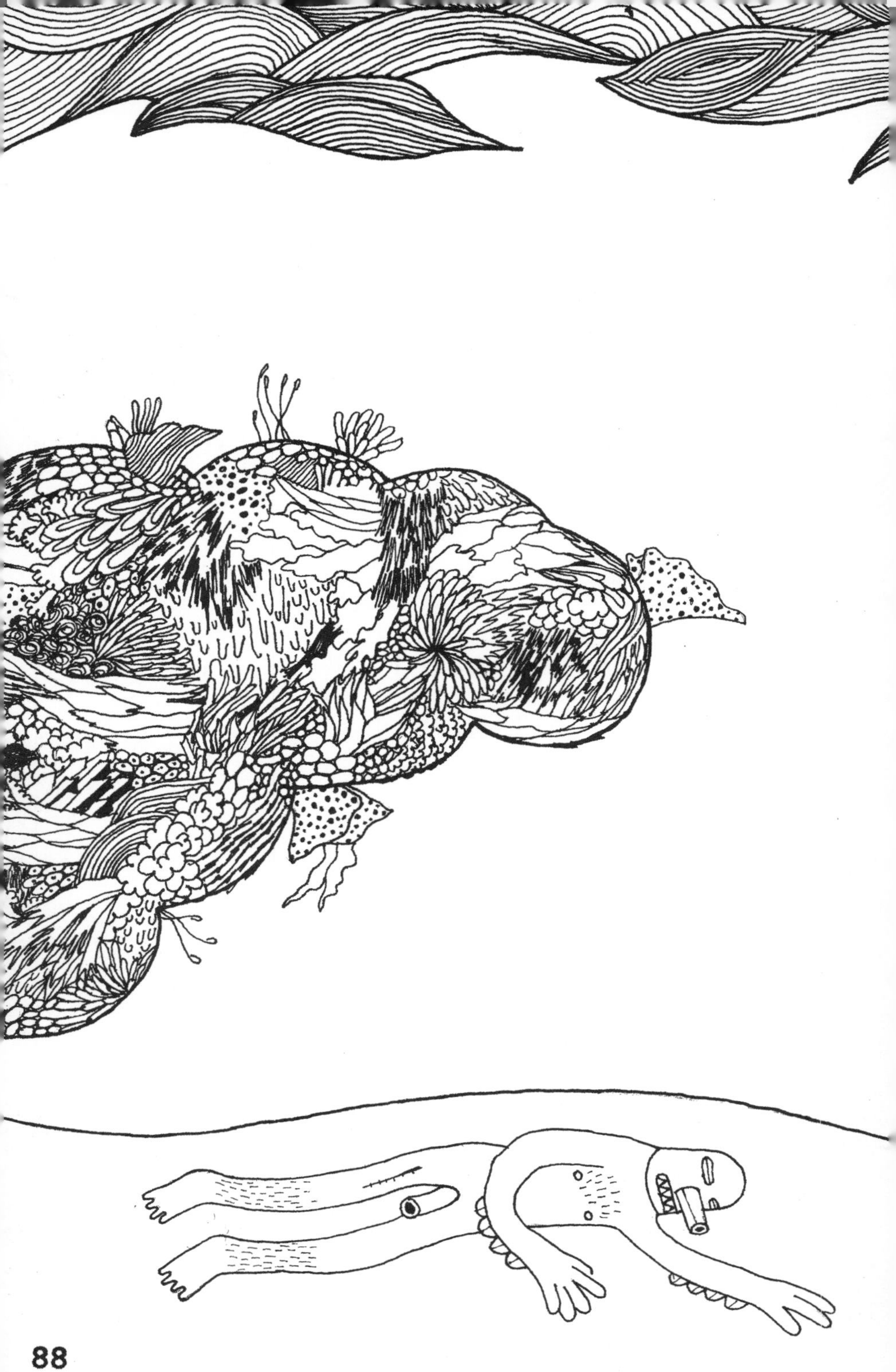

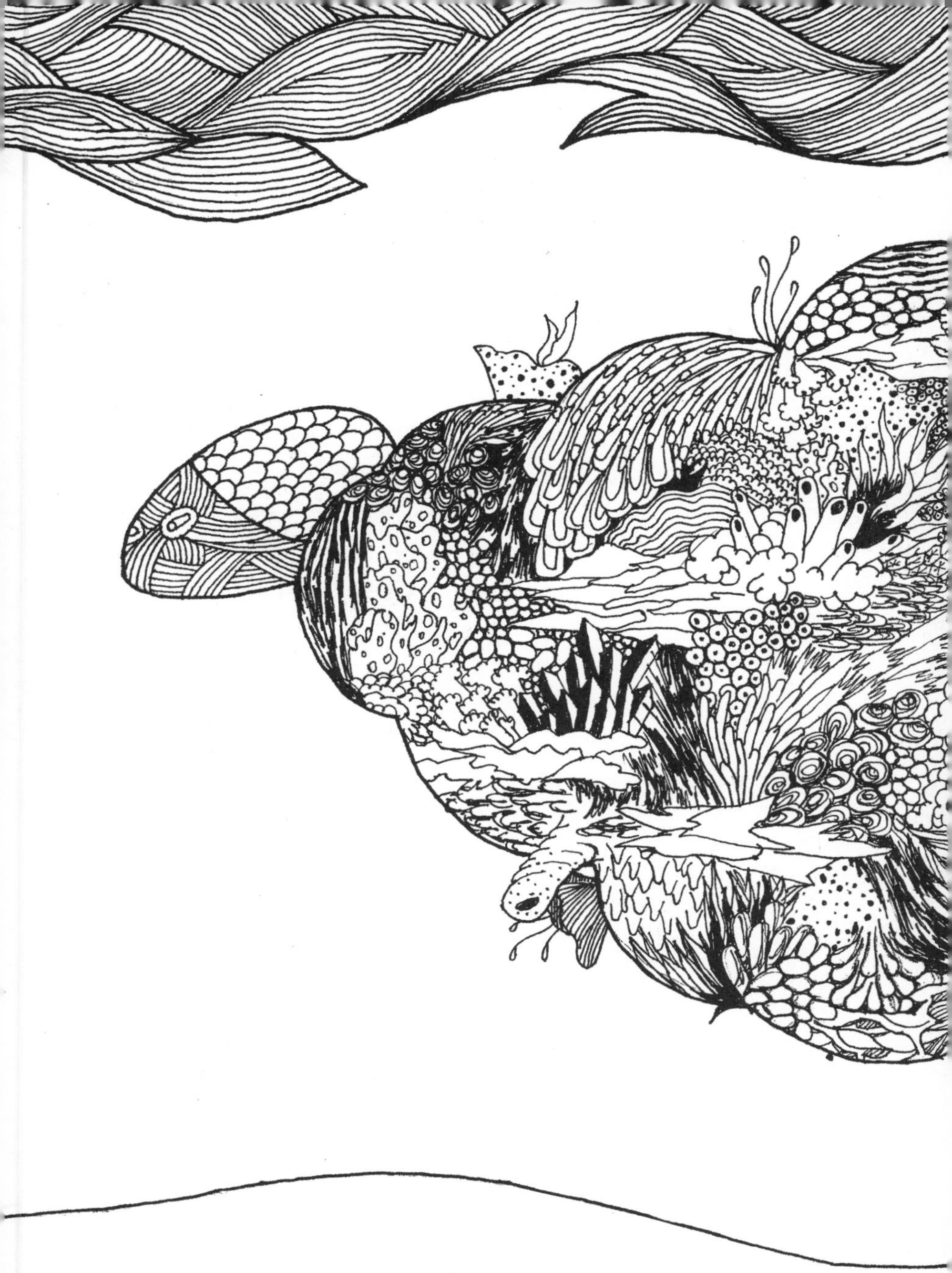

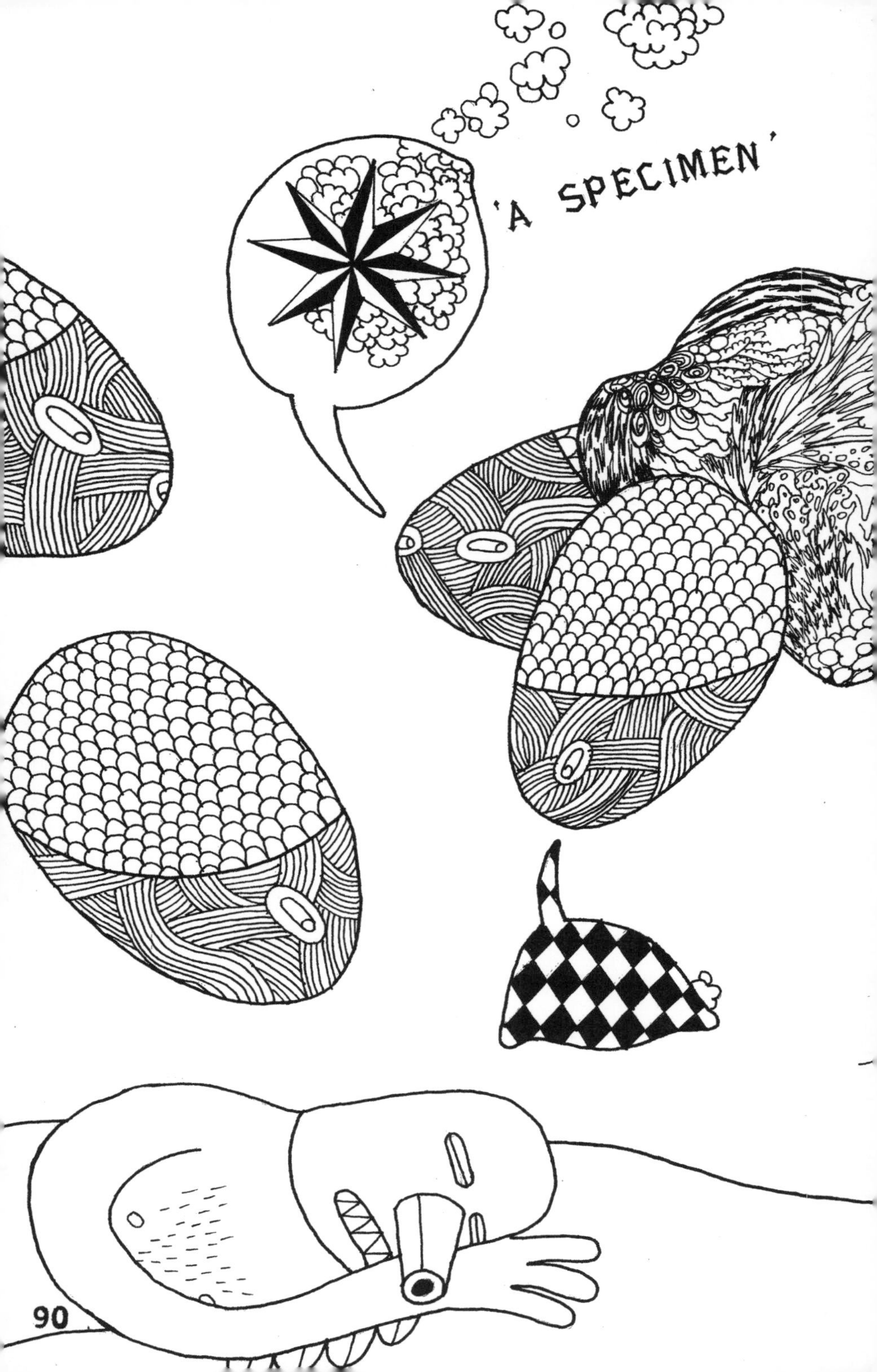
'A SPECIMEN'

'NOT A SEA CREATURE'

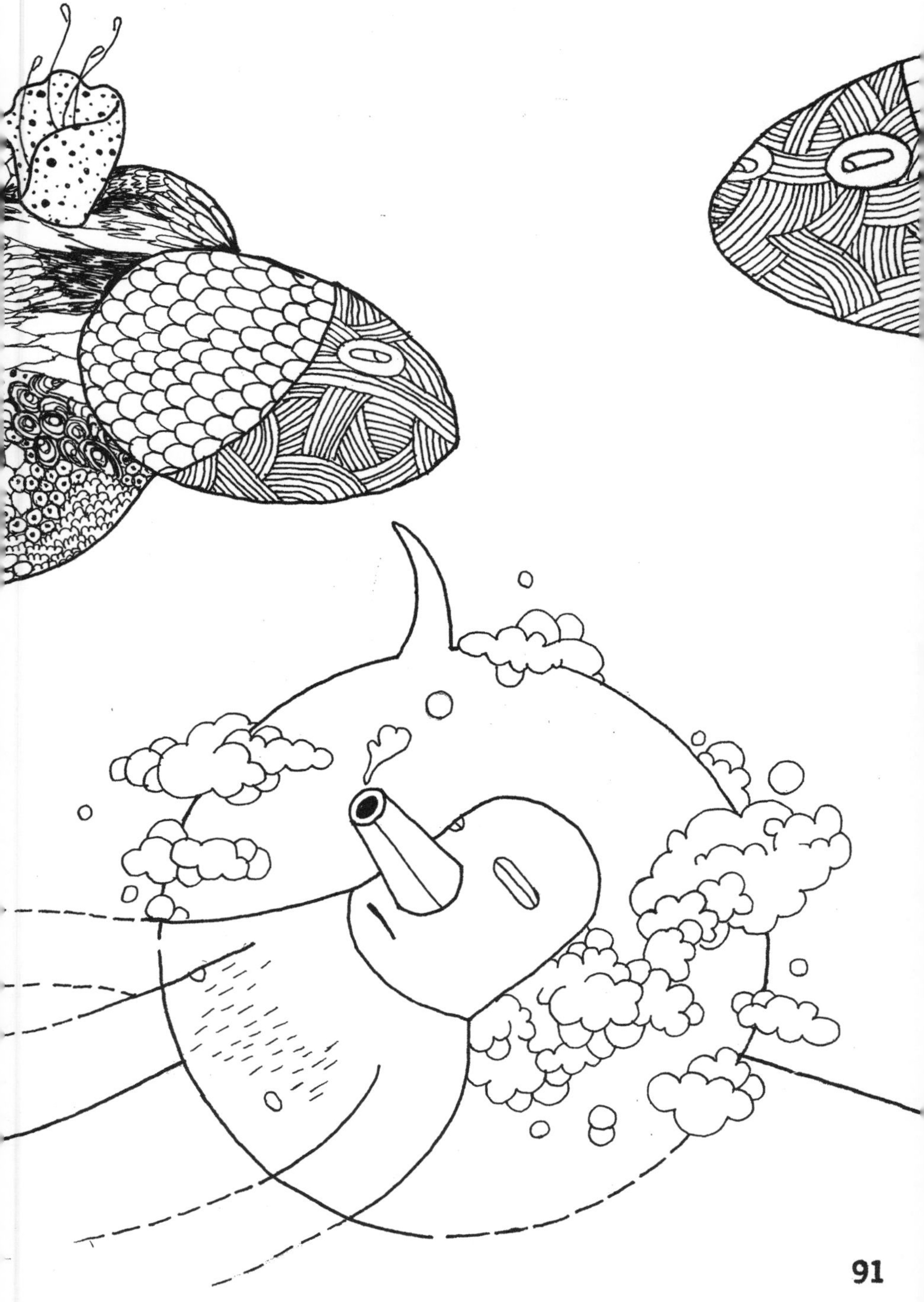

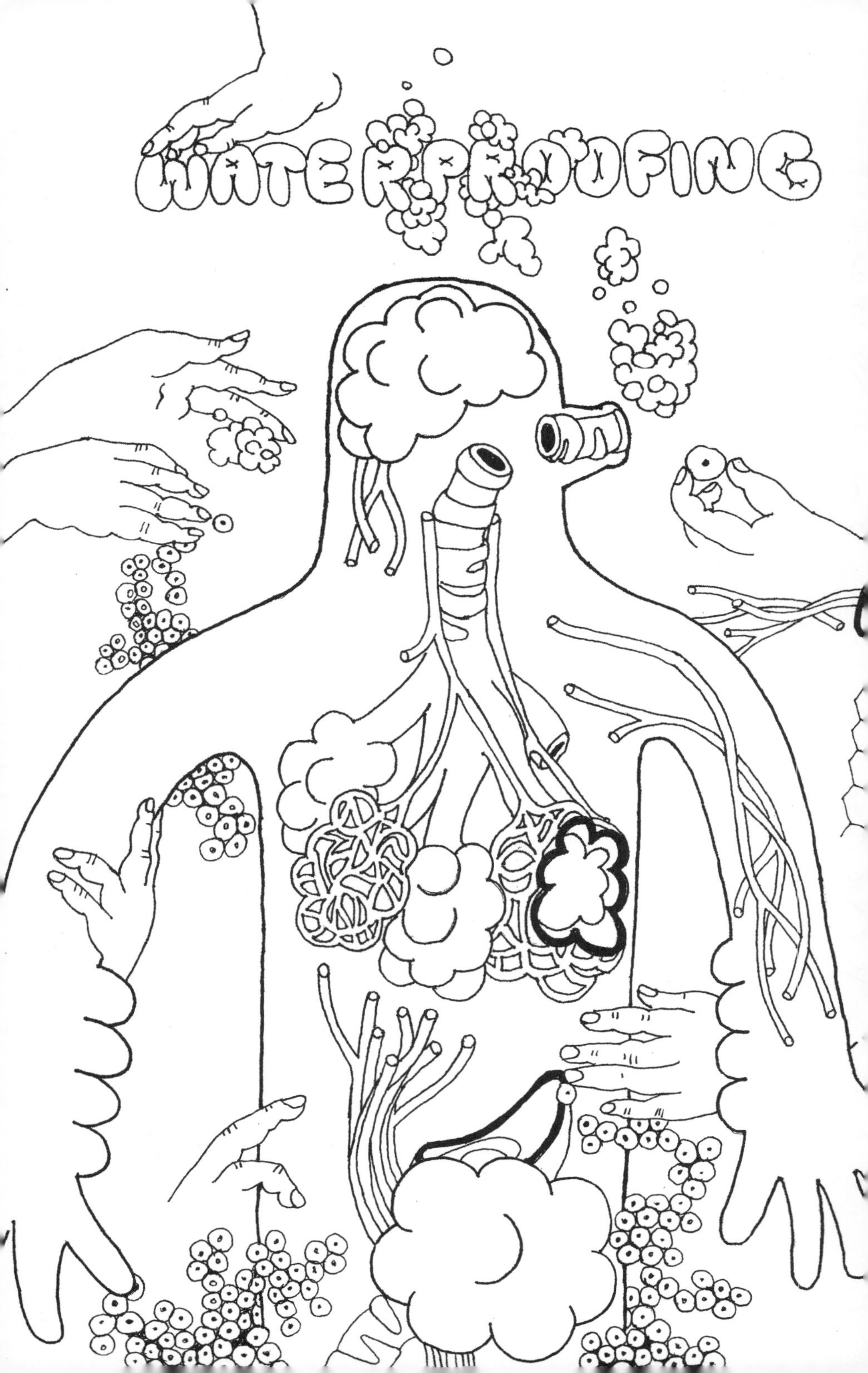
WATERPROOFING

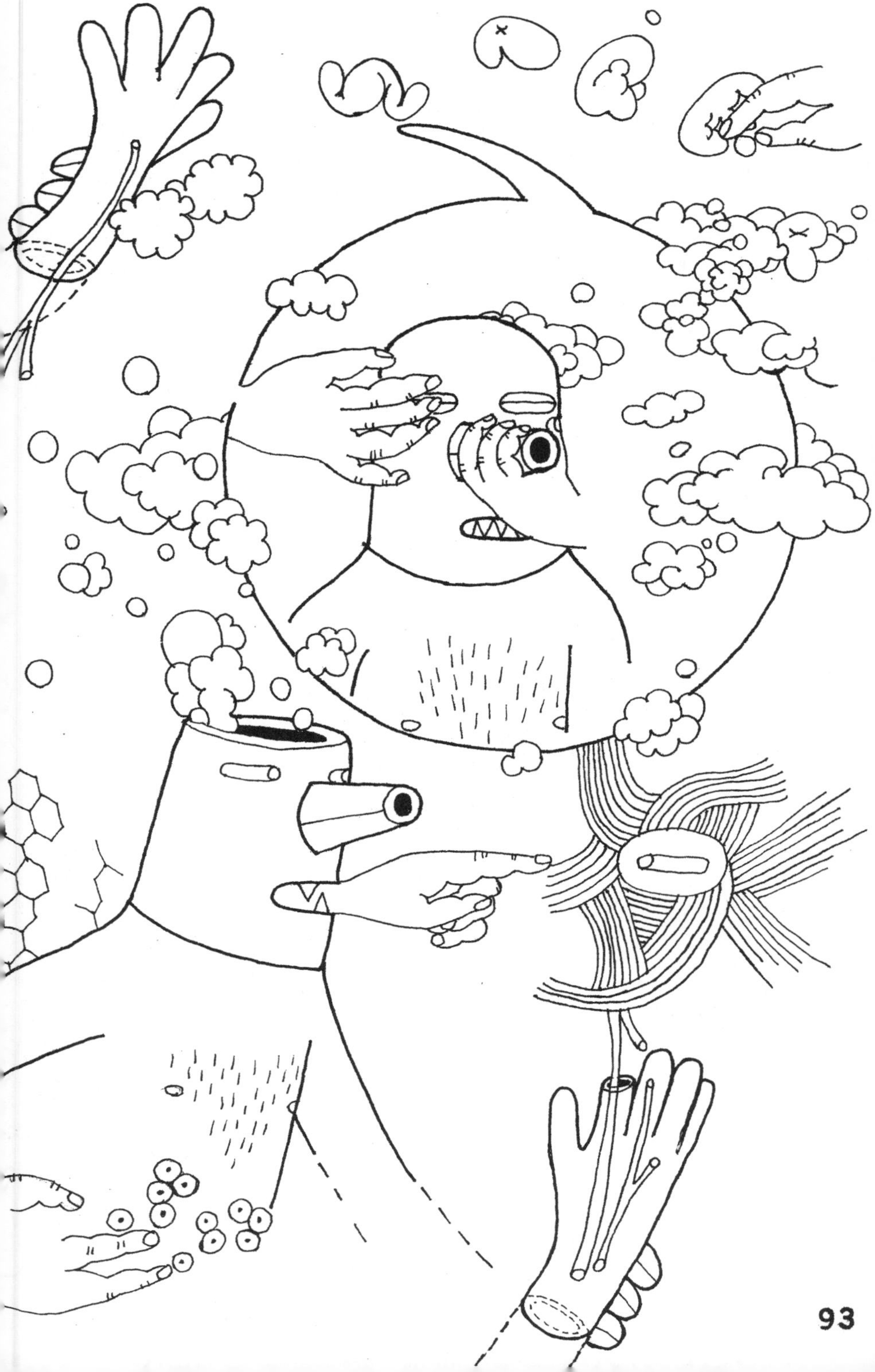

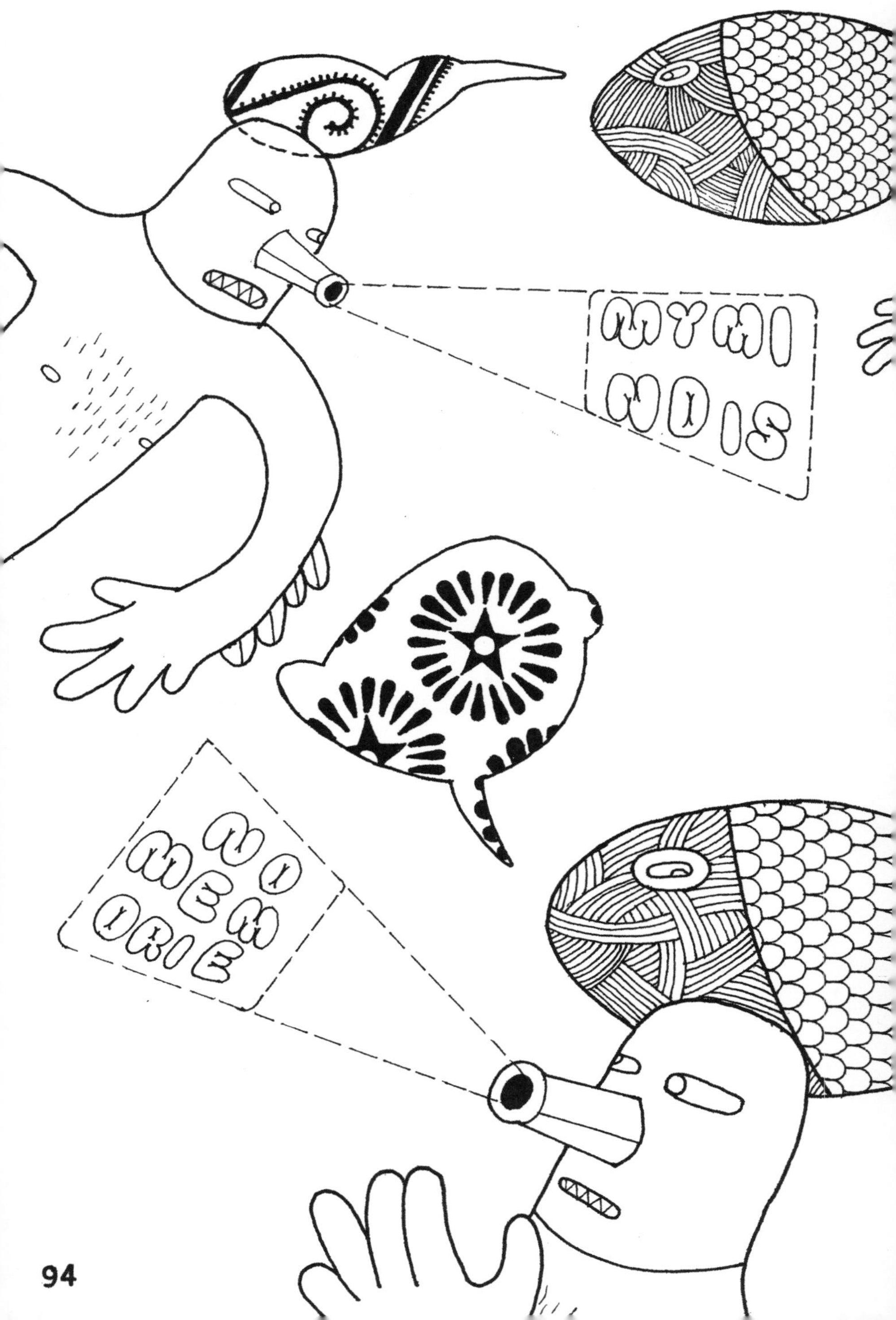
MYMI
NDIS
NI
MEM
ORIE

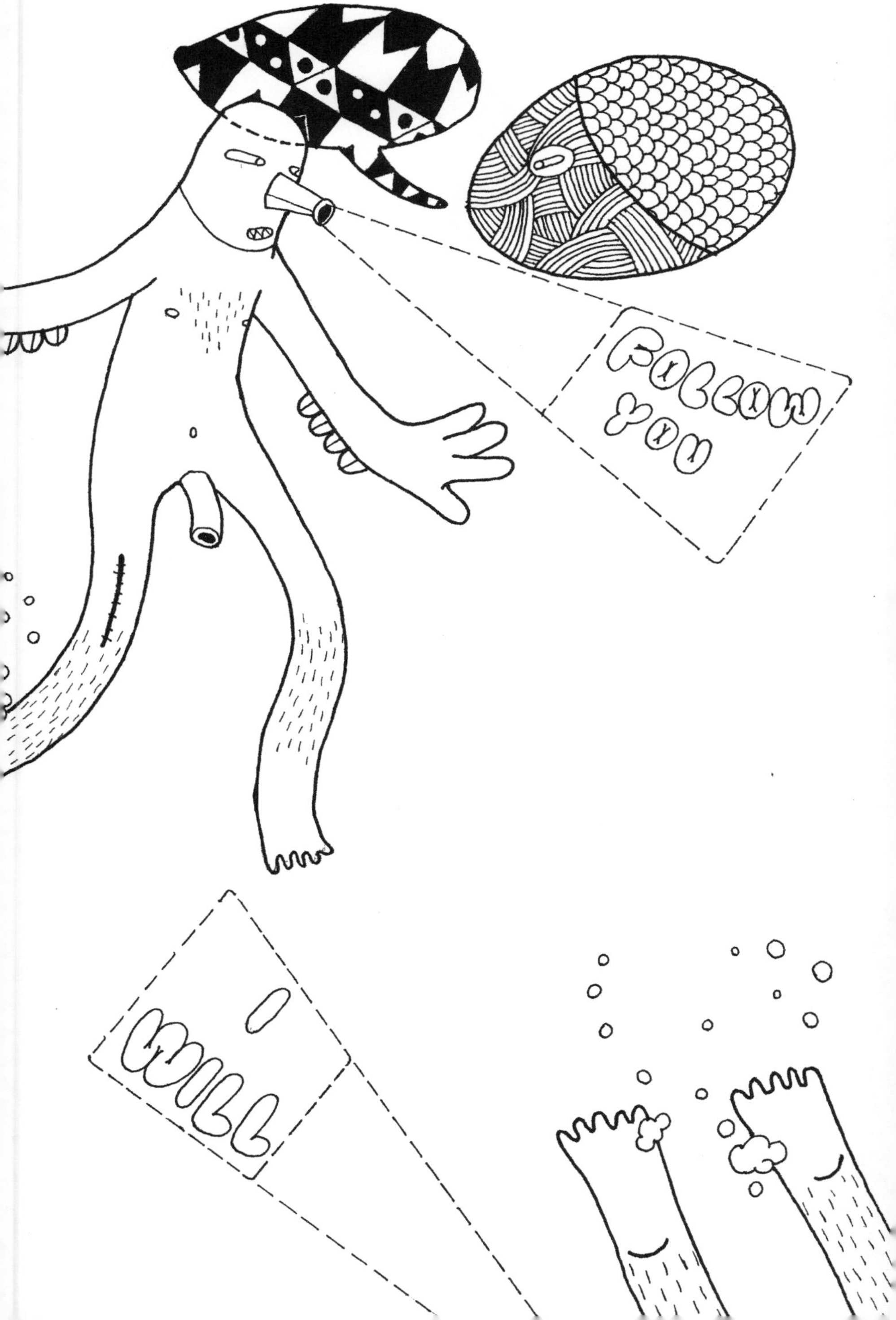
FOLLOW YOU
I WILL

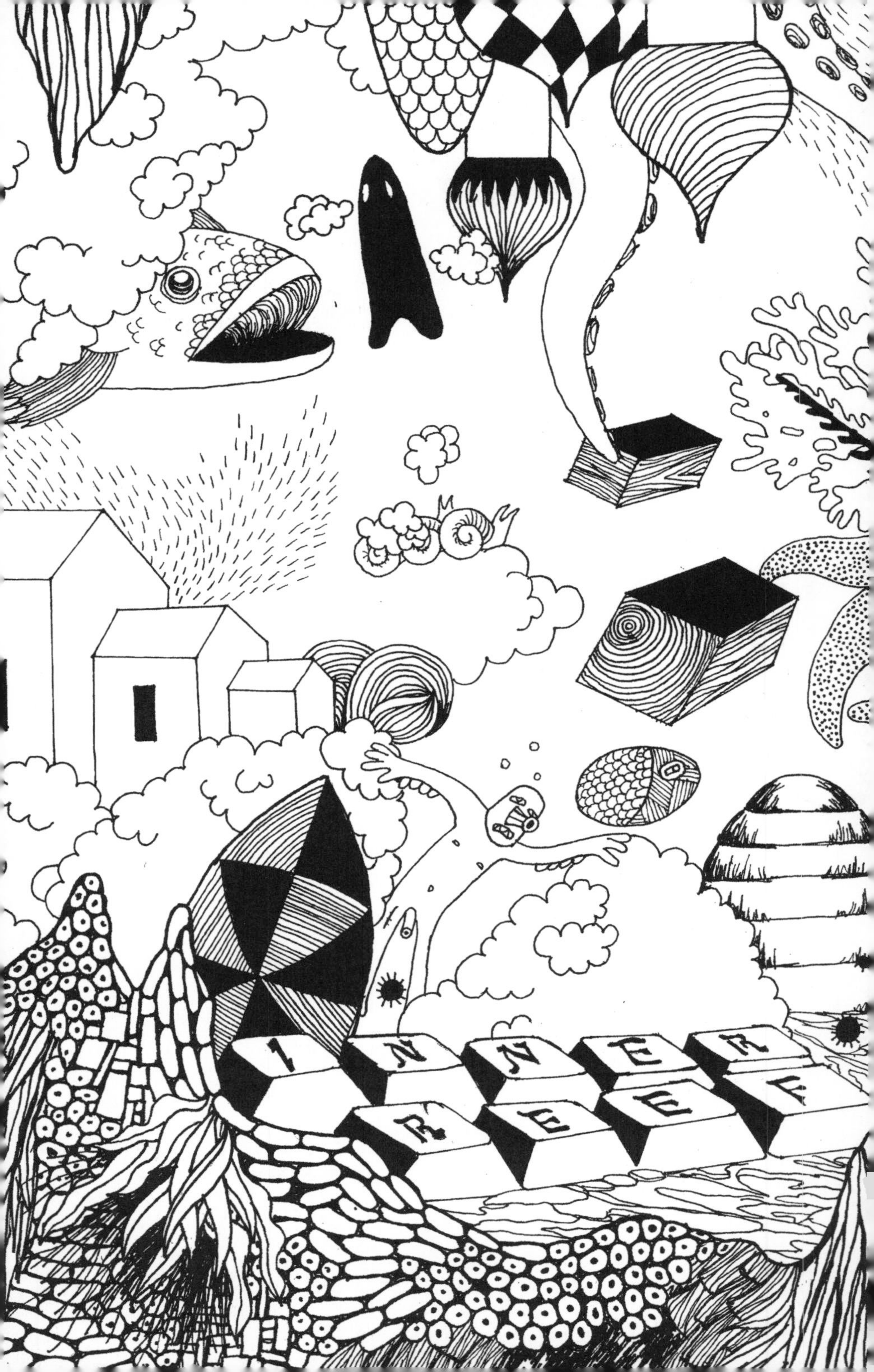
INNER
REEF

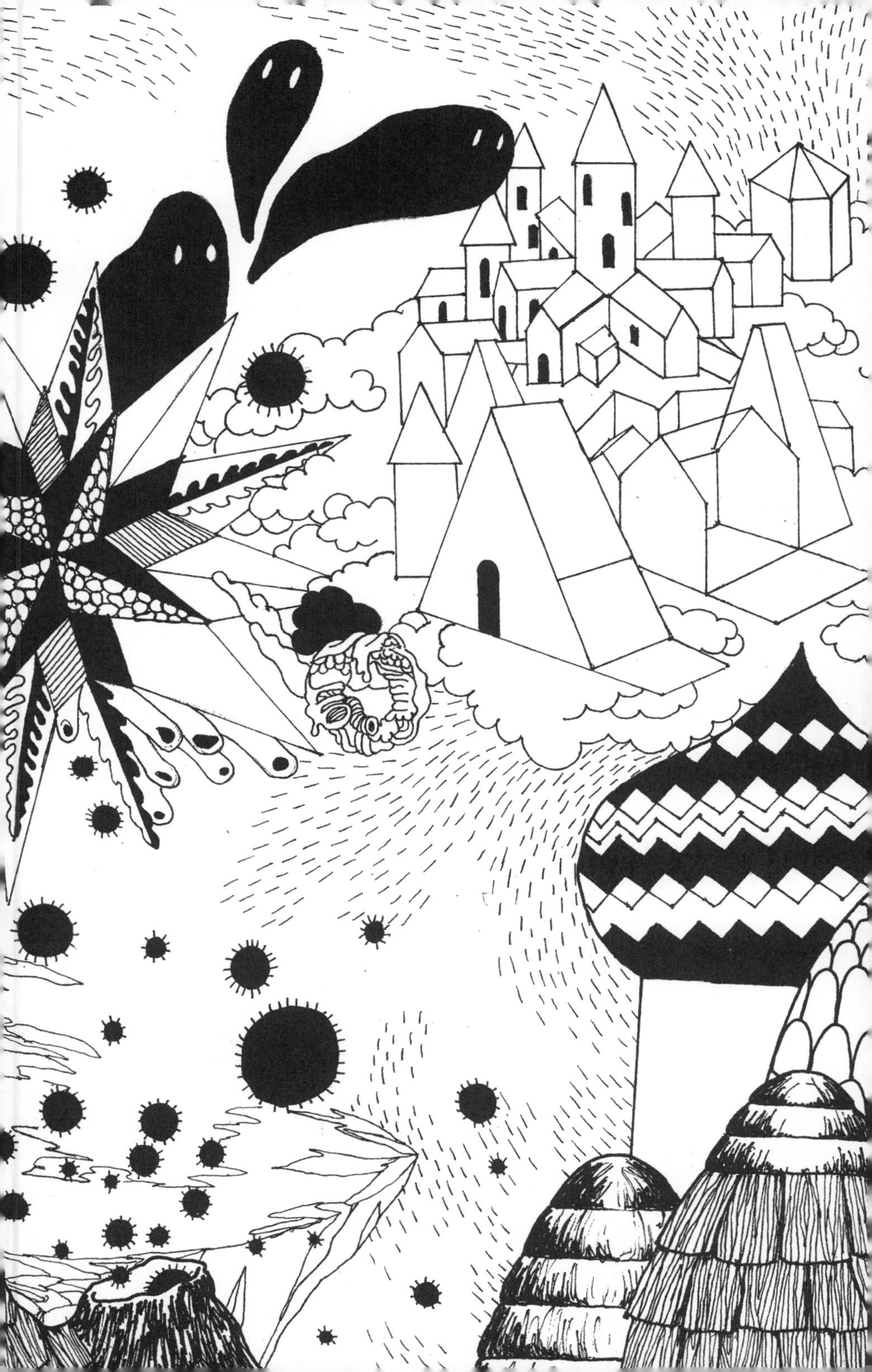

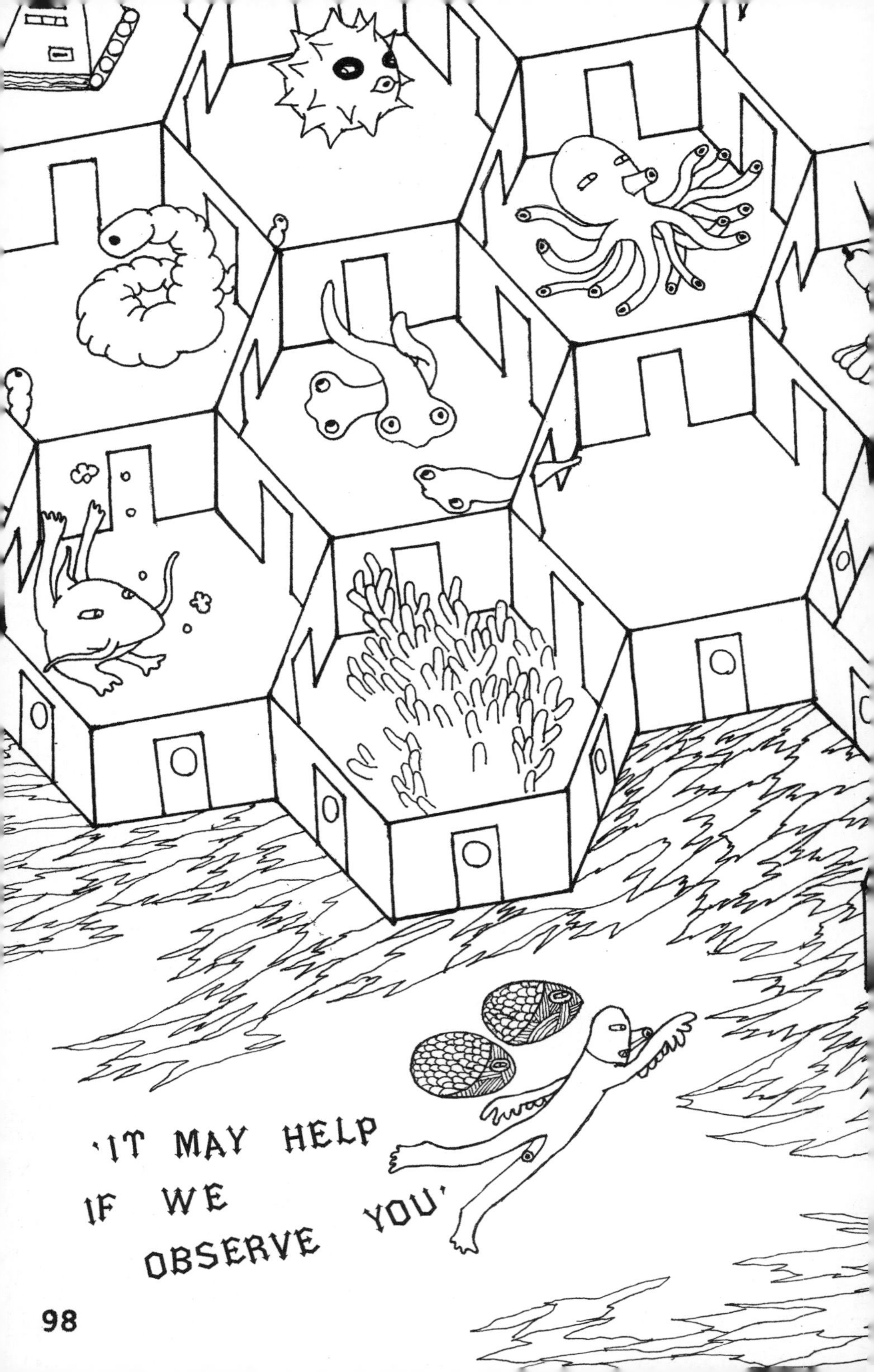
'IT MAY HELP
IF WE
OBSERVE YOU'

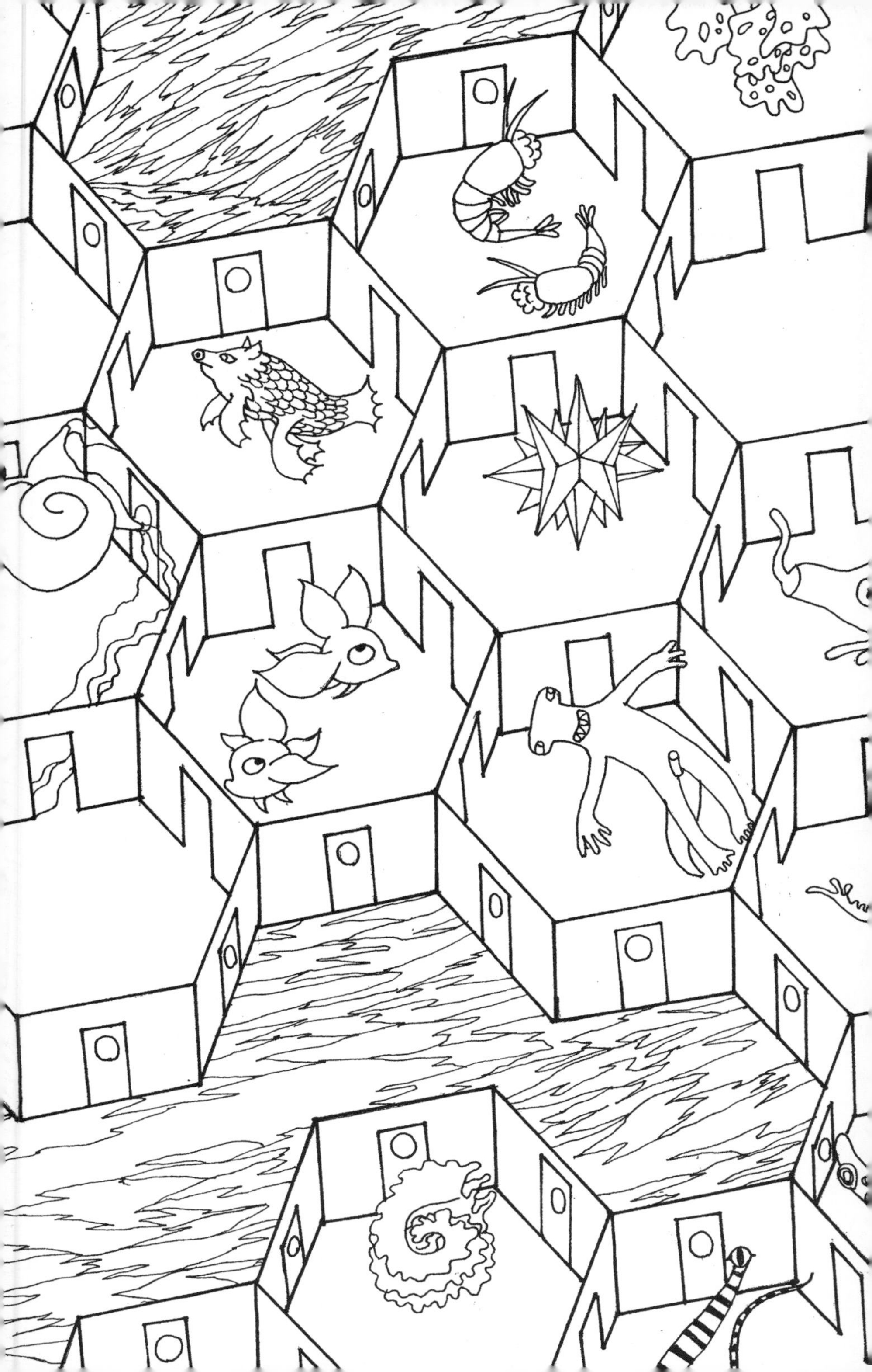

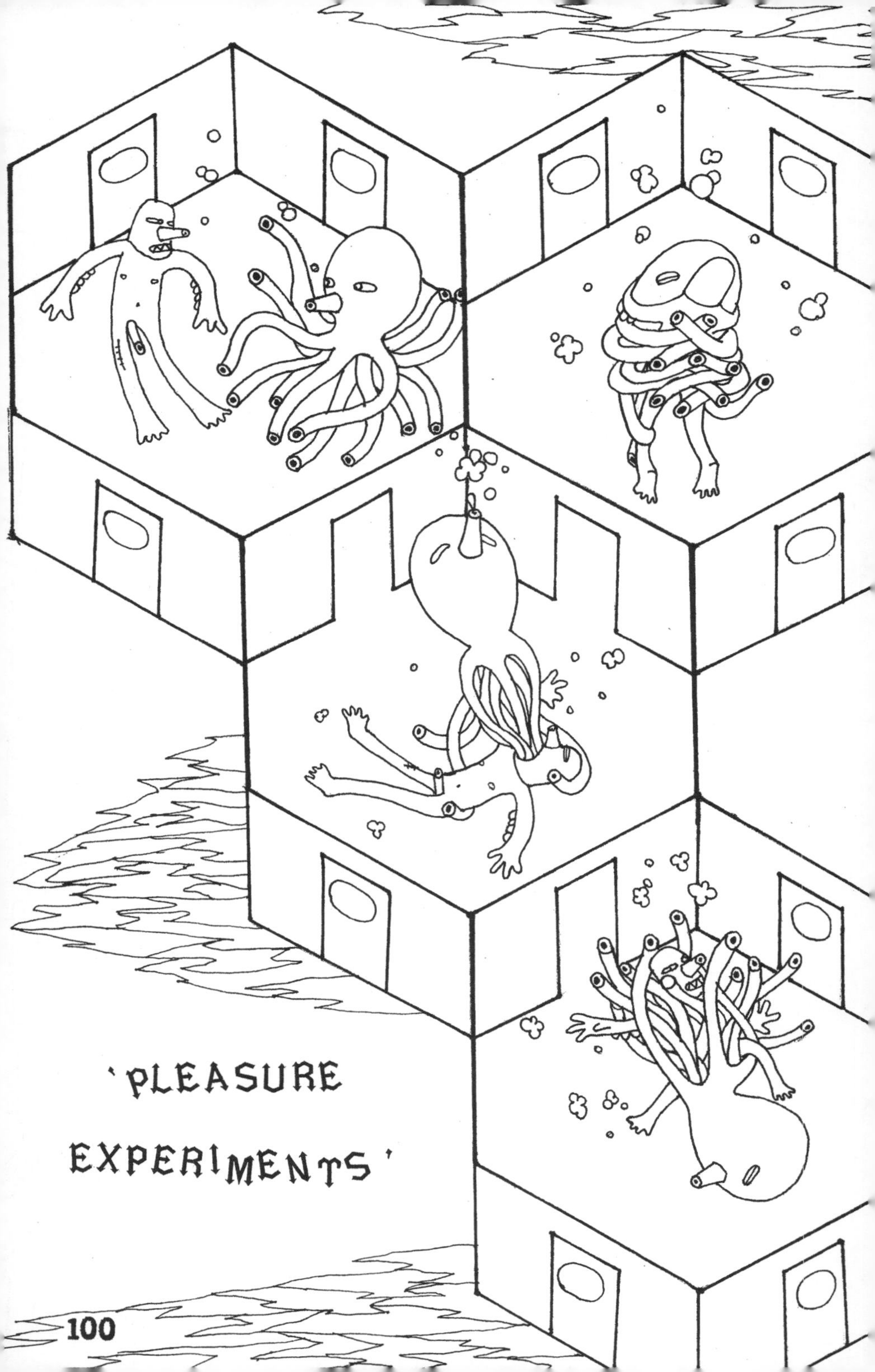
'PLEASURE
EXPERIMENTS'

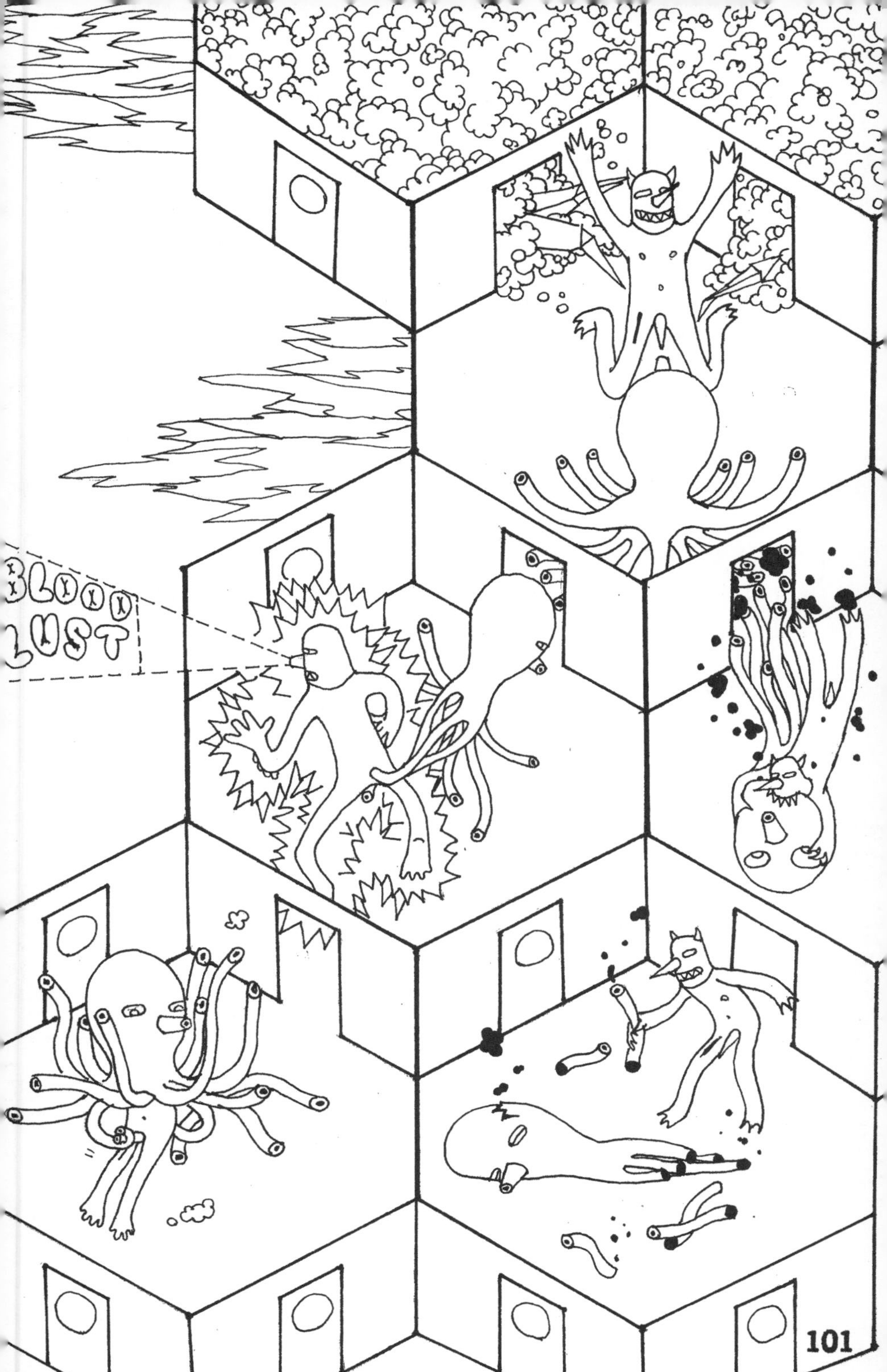
BLOOD
LUST

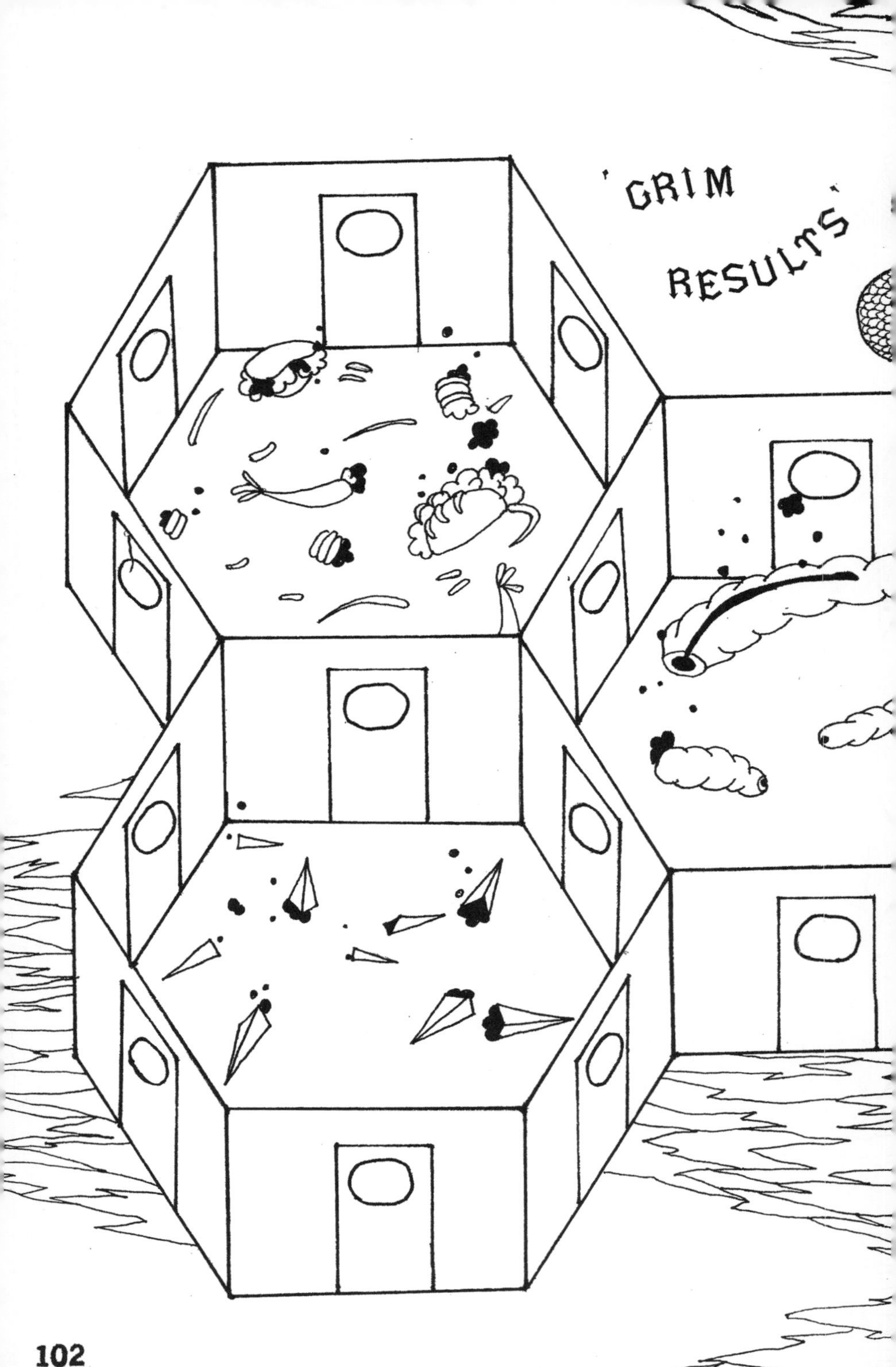
GRIM RESULTS

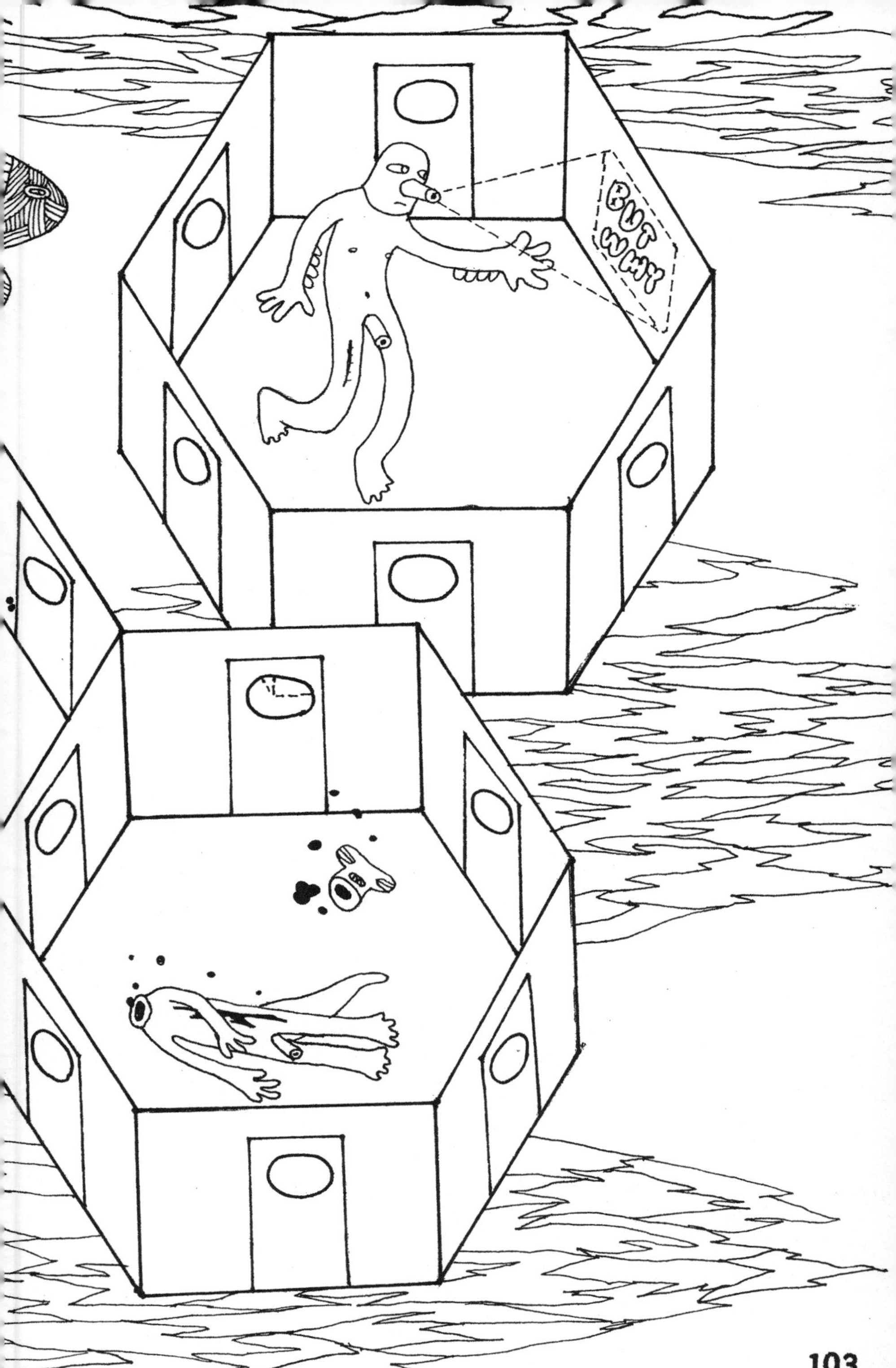
BUT WHY

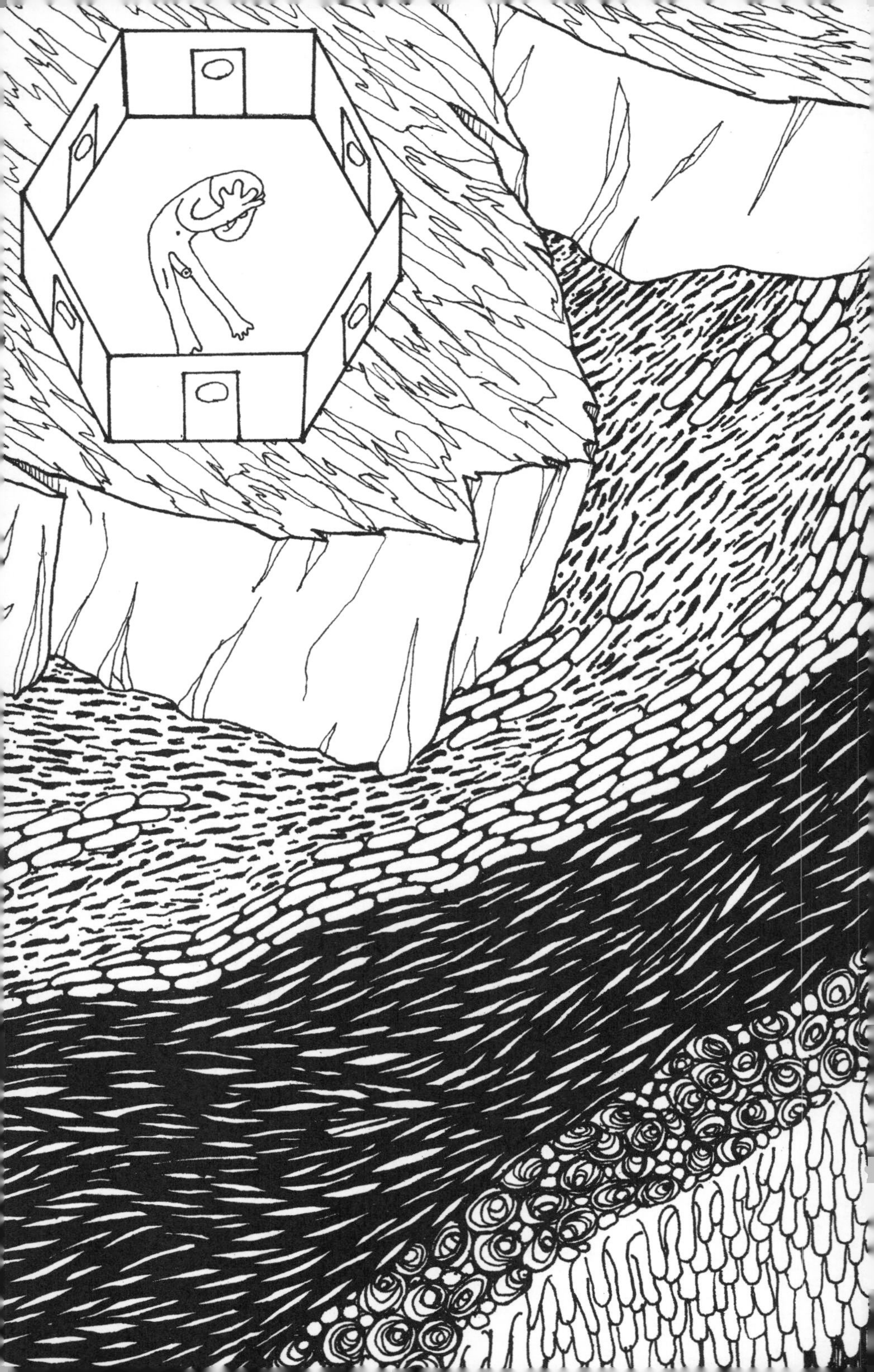

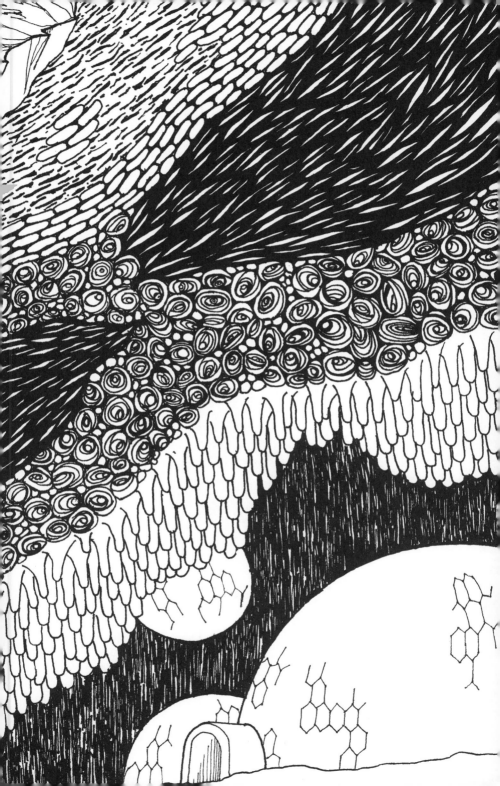

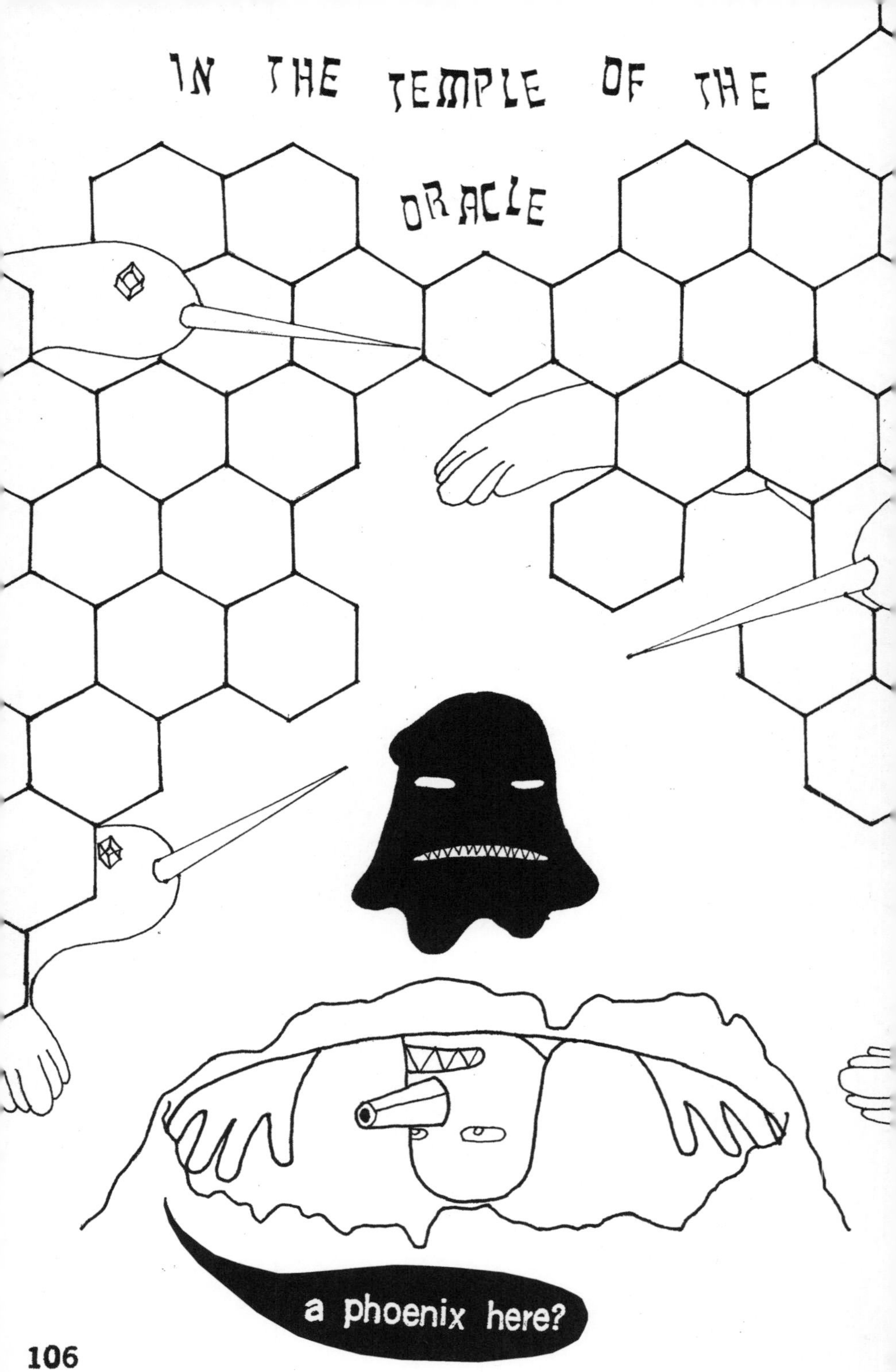
IN THE TEMPLE OF THE
ORACLE
a phoenix here?

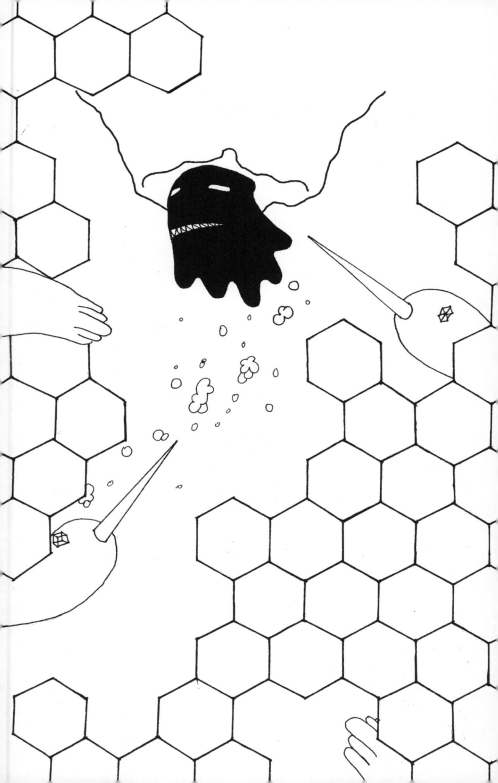

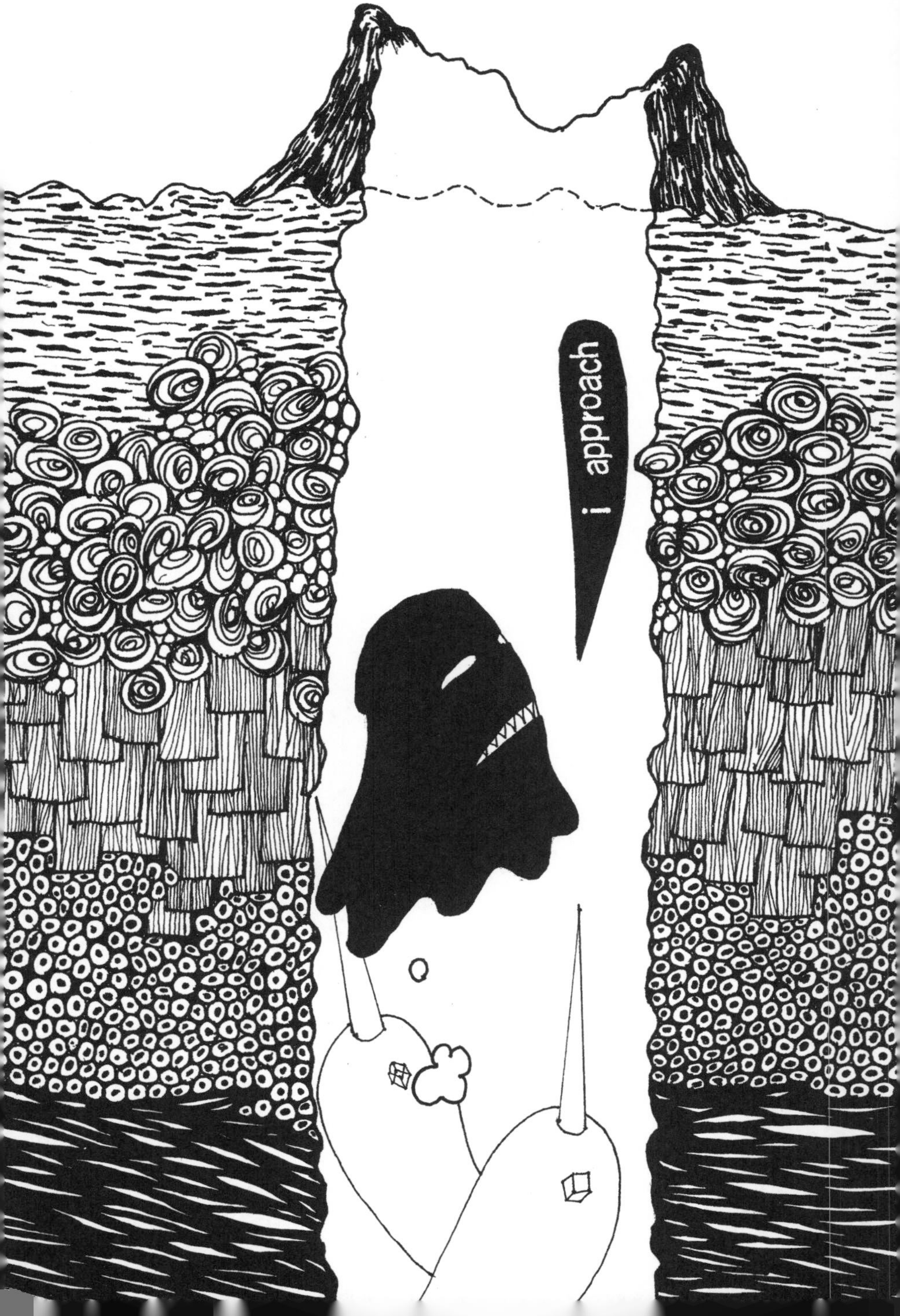
i approach

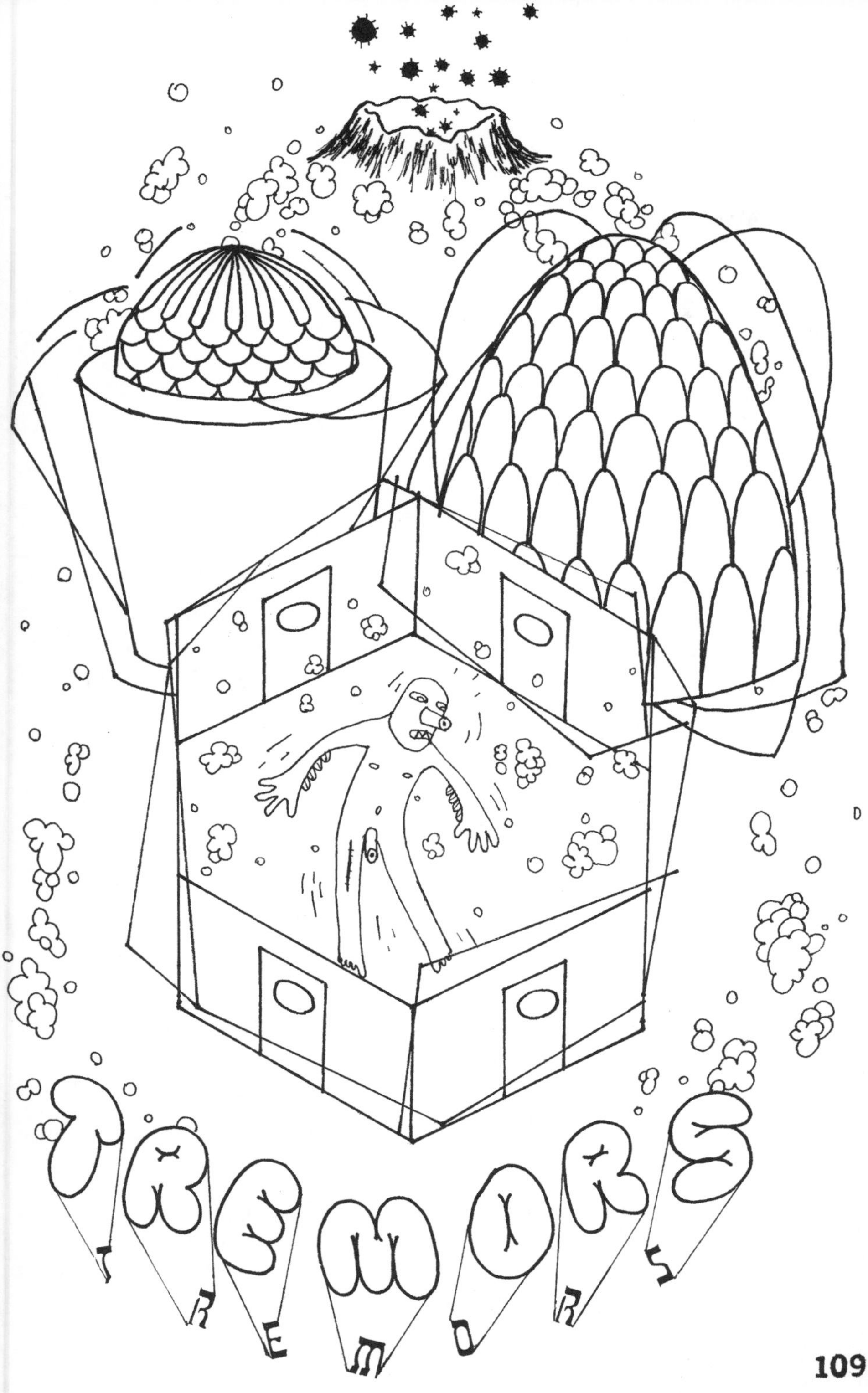
TREMORS

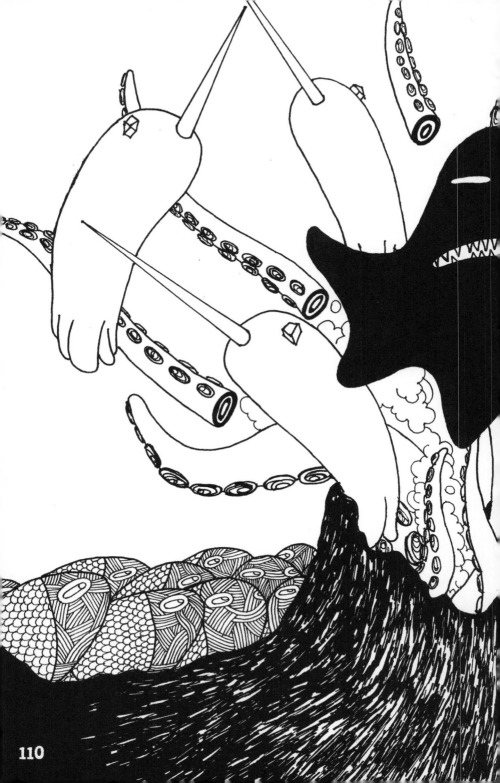

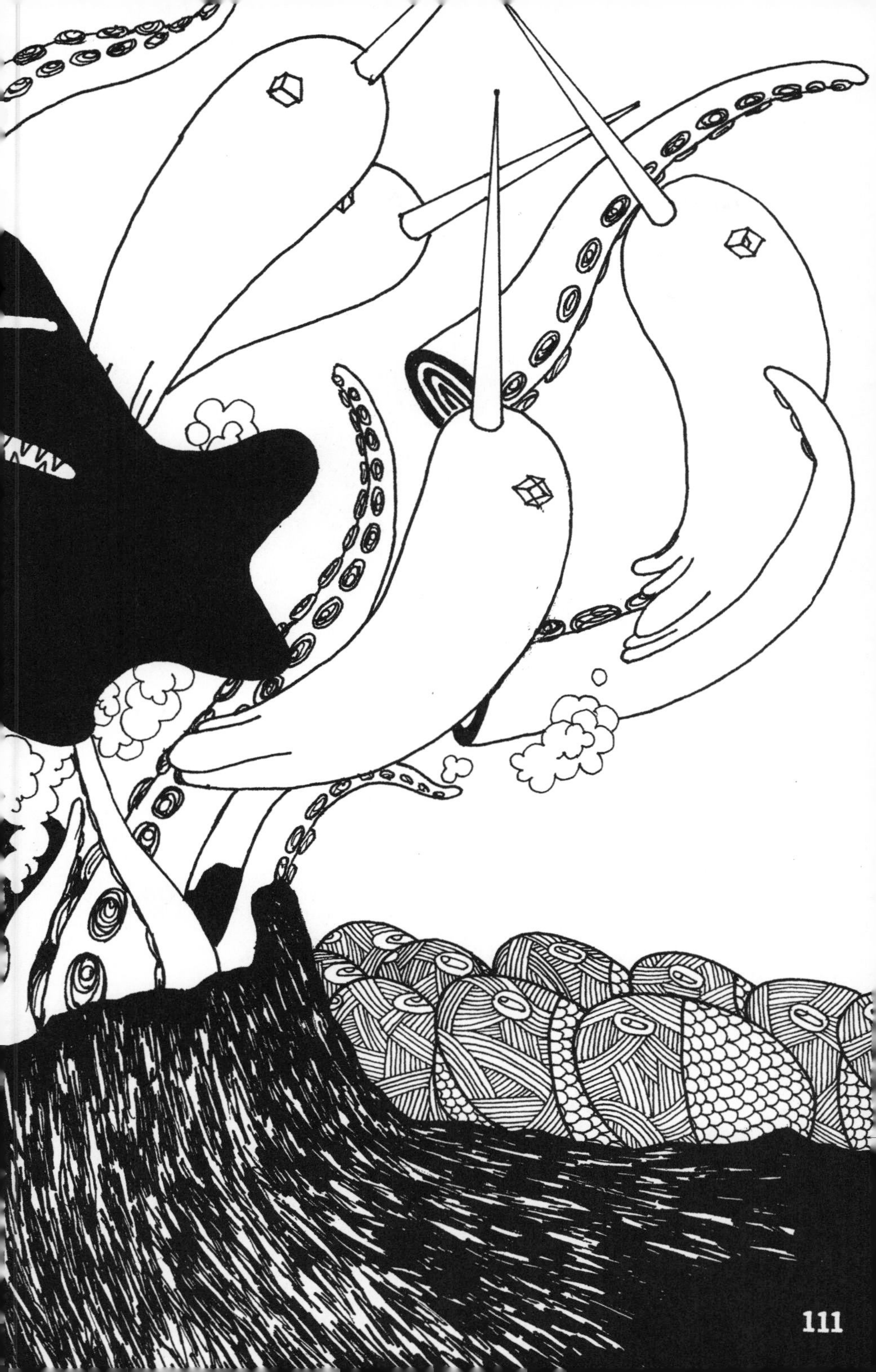

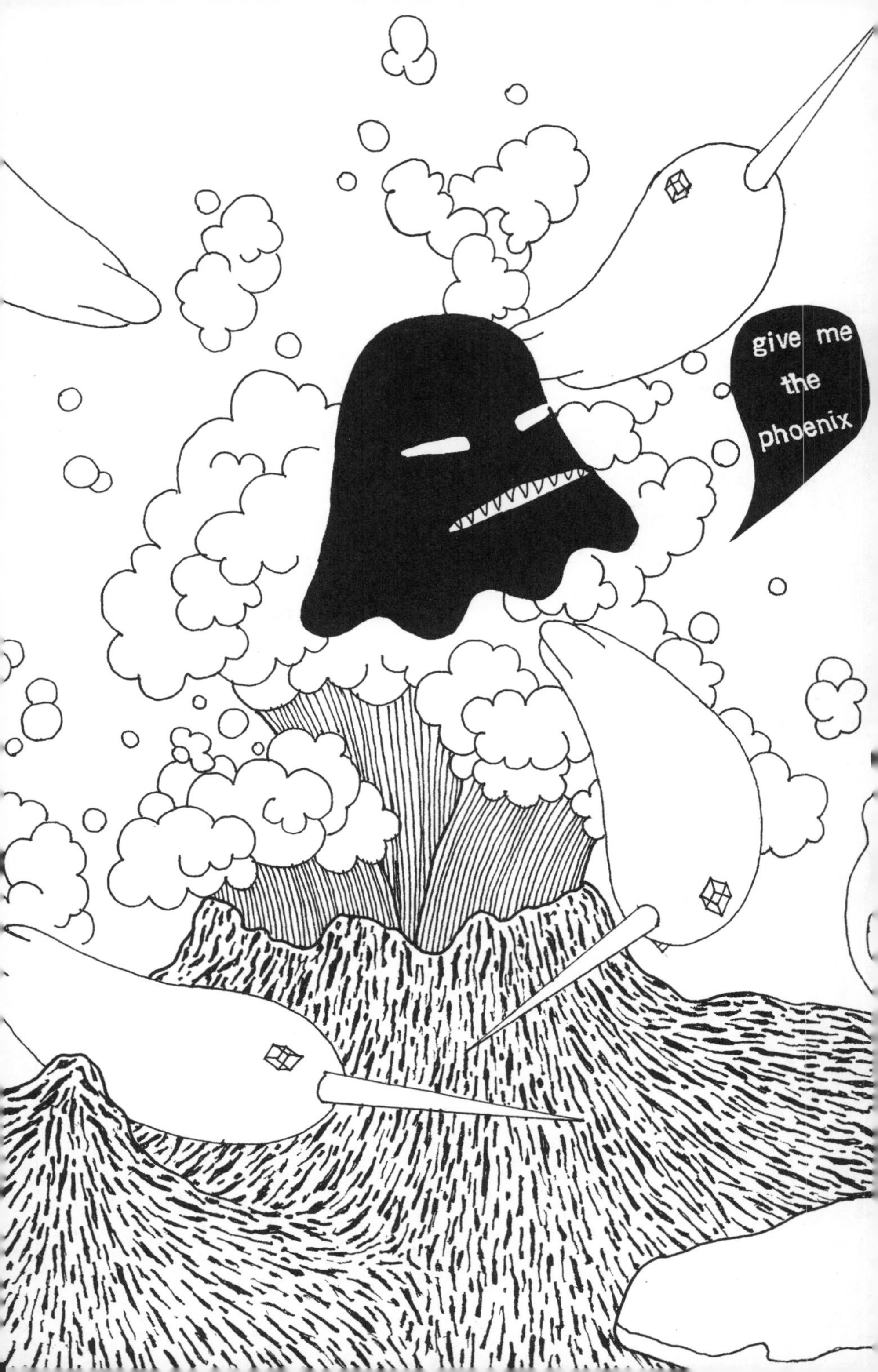
give me the phoenix

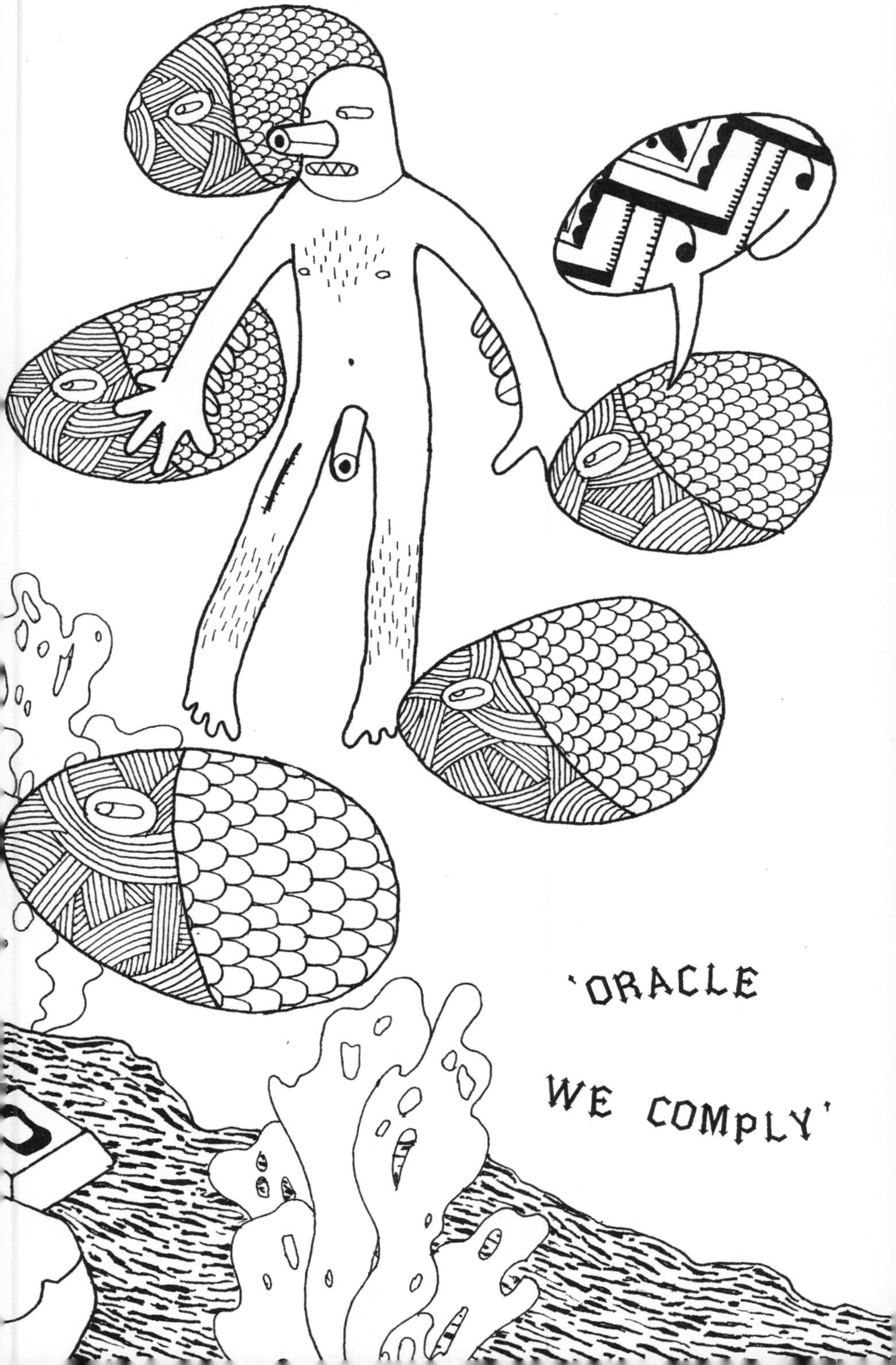
'ORACLE
WE COMPLY'

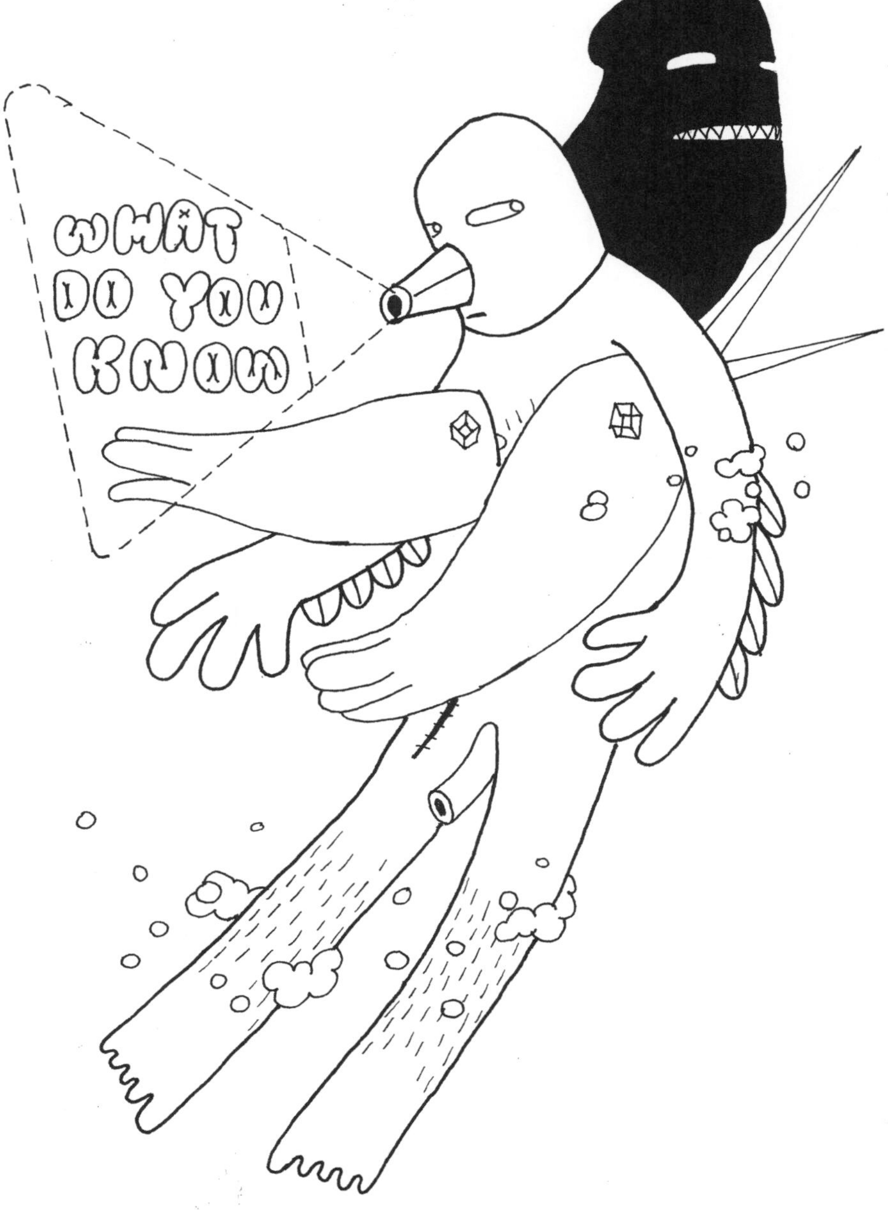
WHAT
DO YOU
KNOW

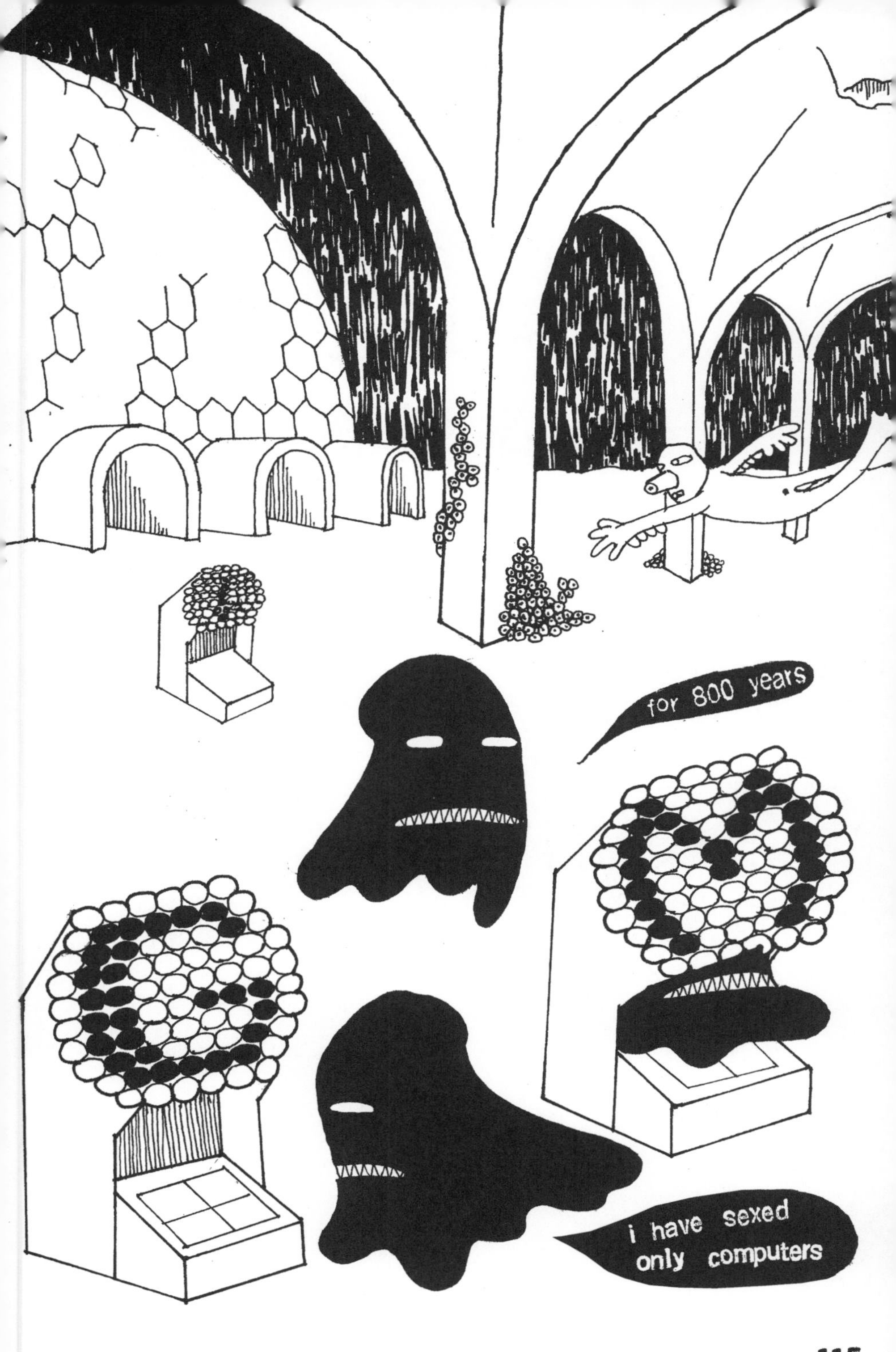
for 800 years
i have sexed only computers

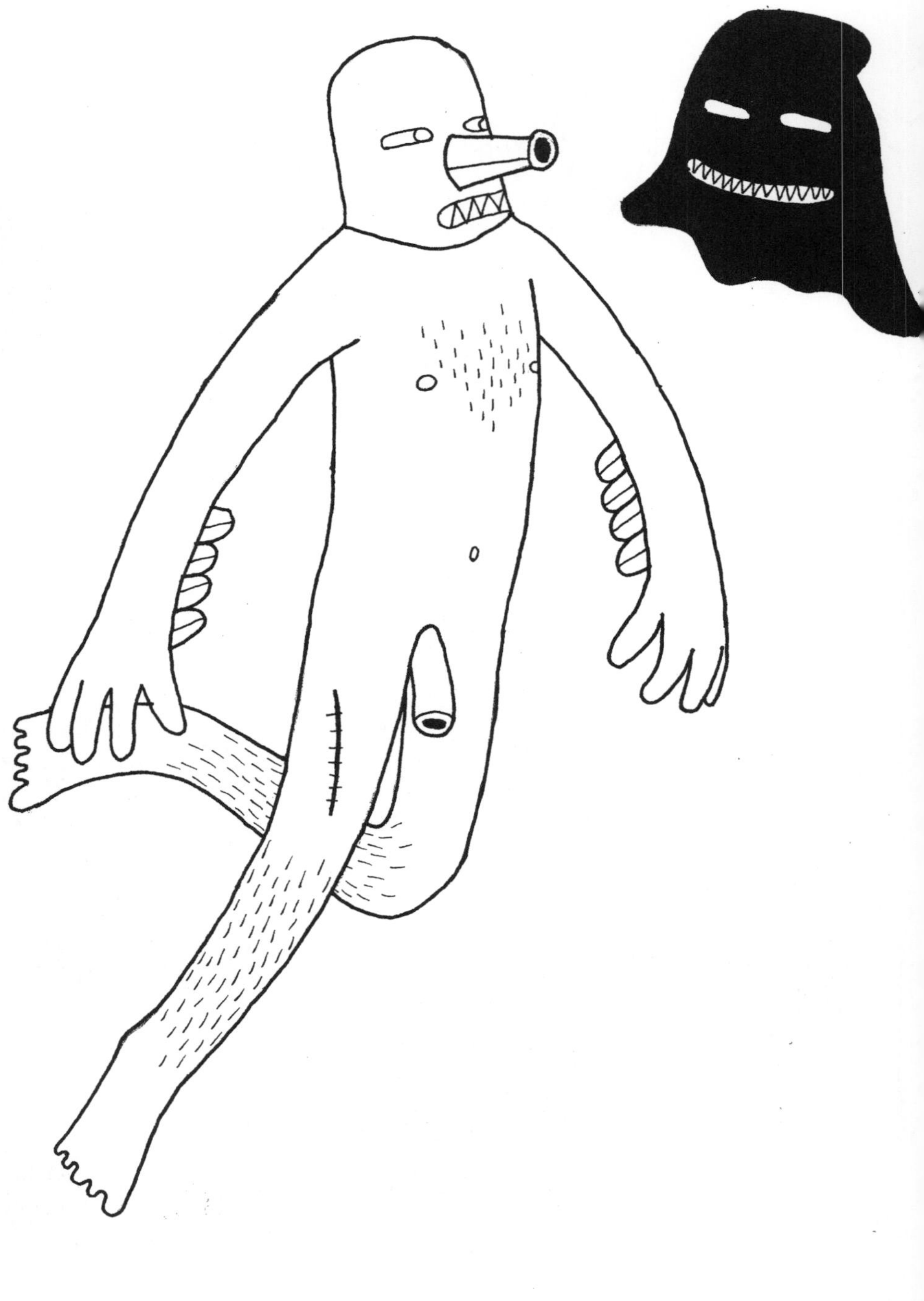

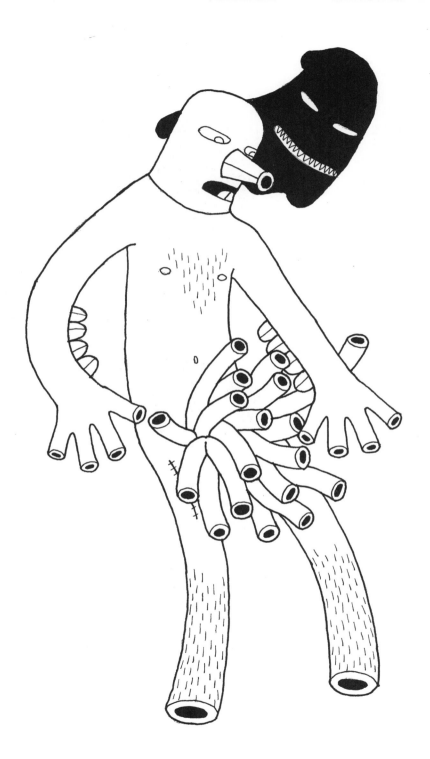

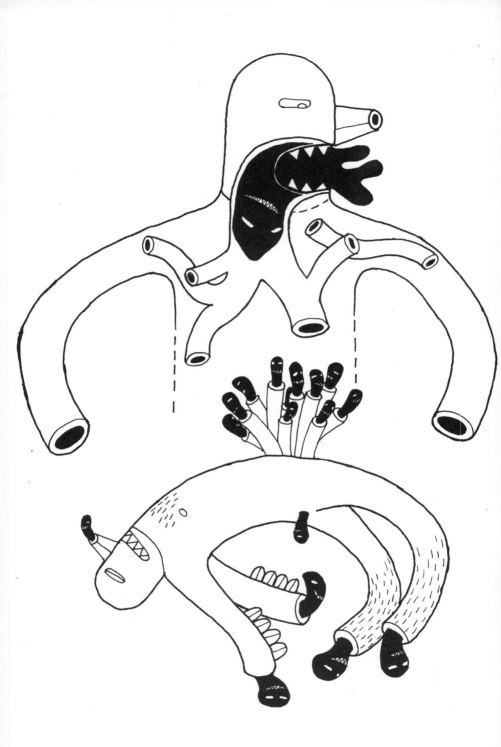

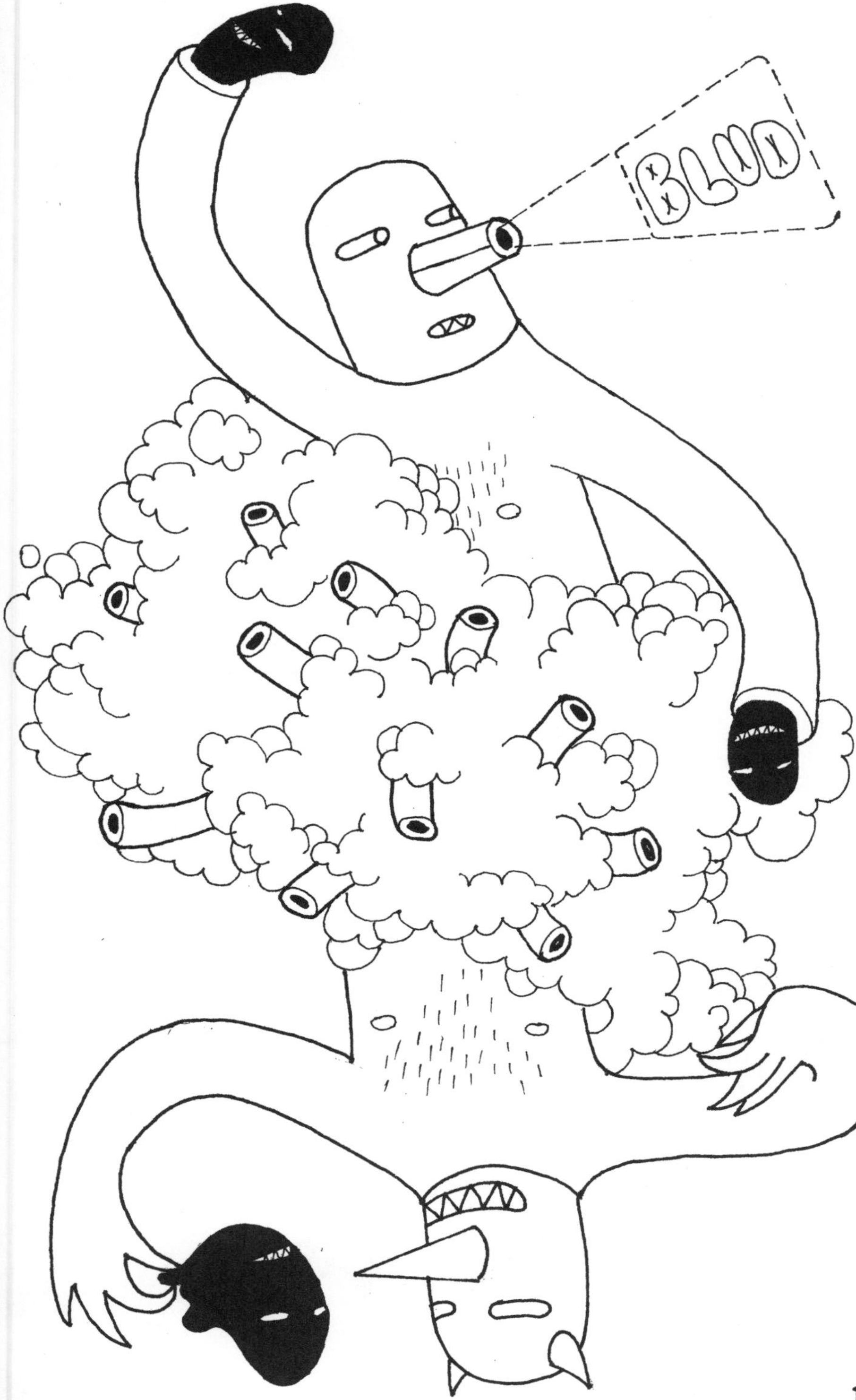
BLUD

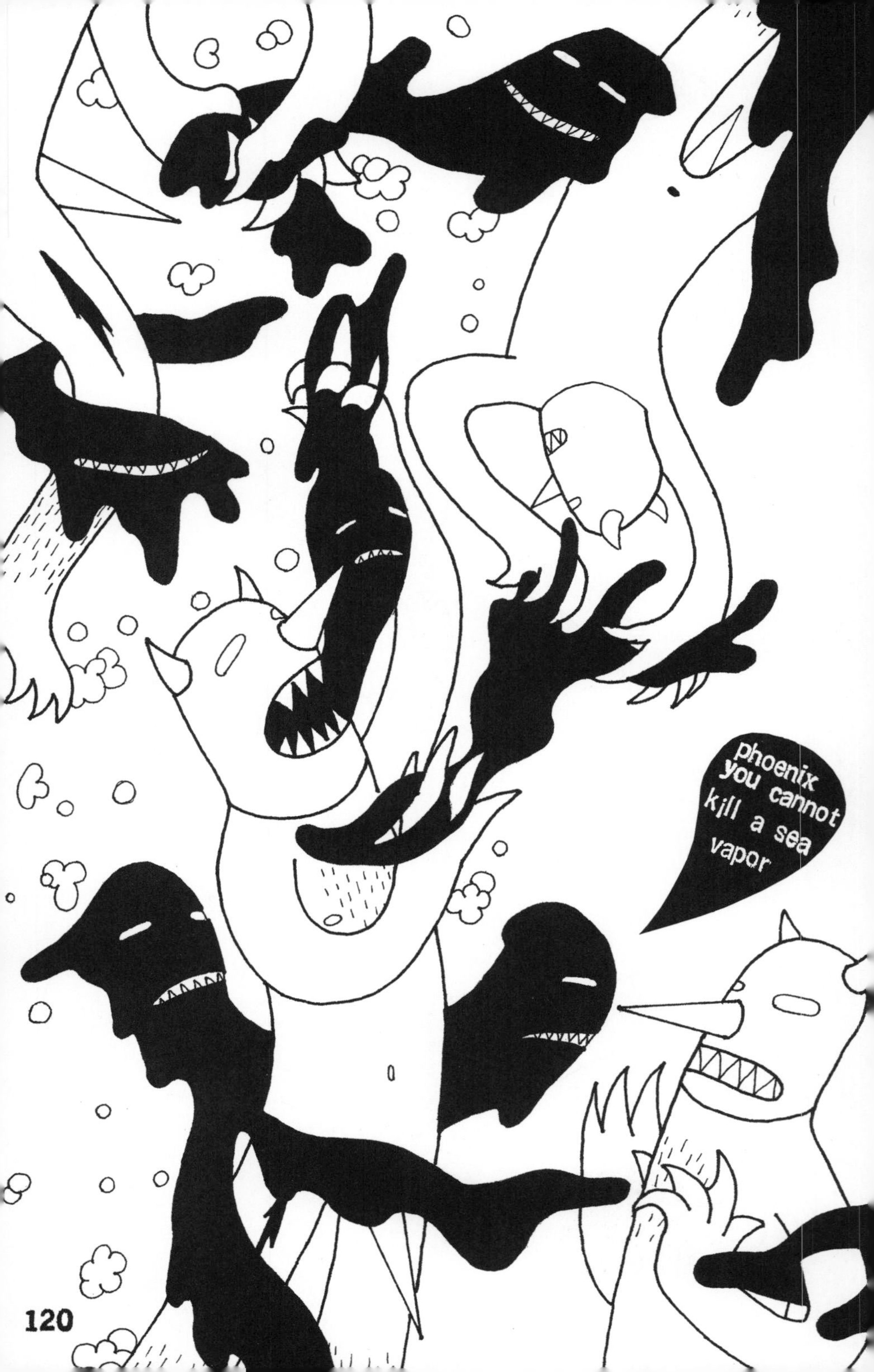
phoenix you cannot kill a sea vapor

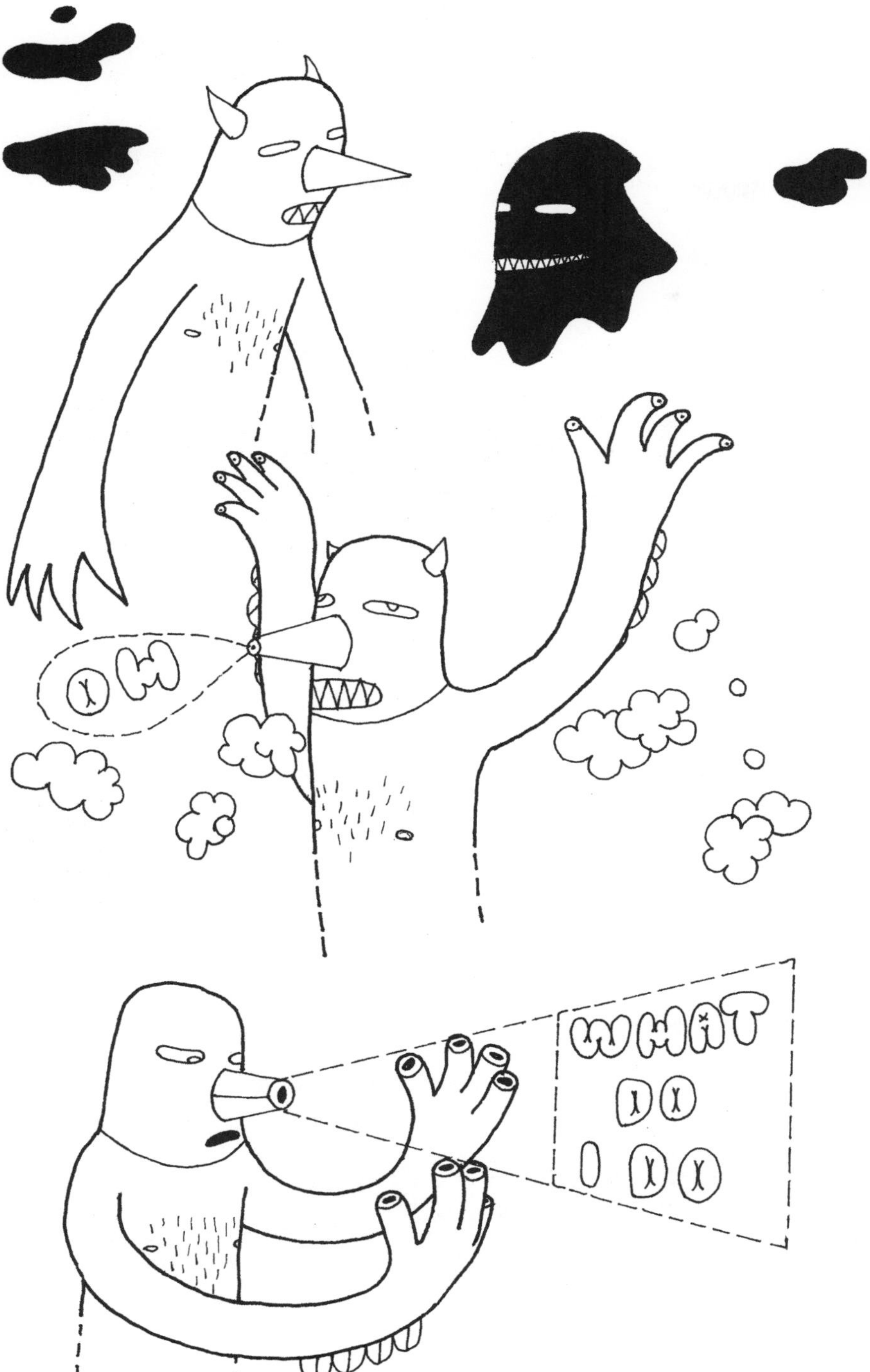
OH
WHAT DO I DO

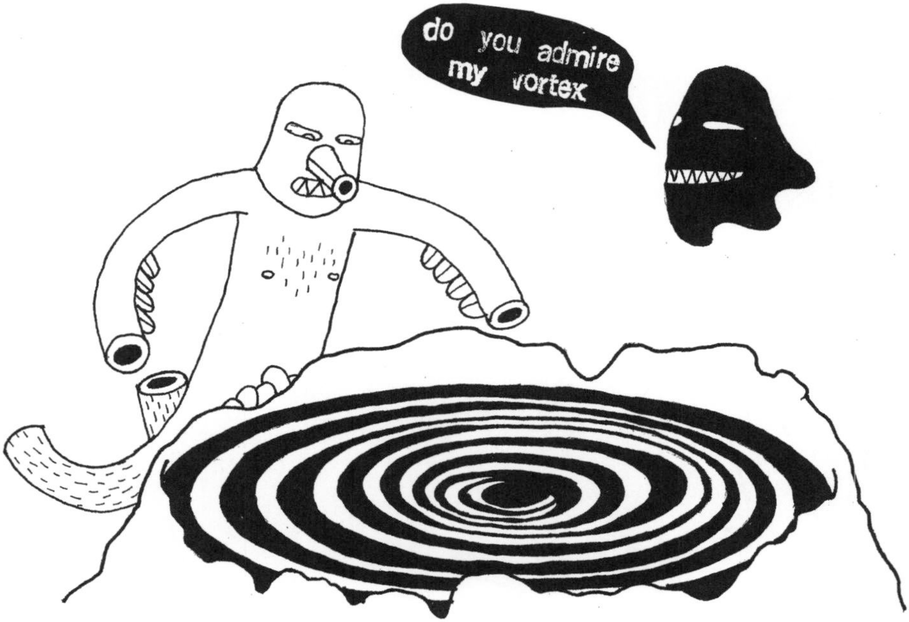
do you admire my vortex

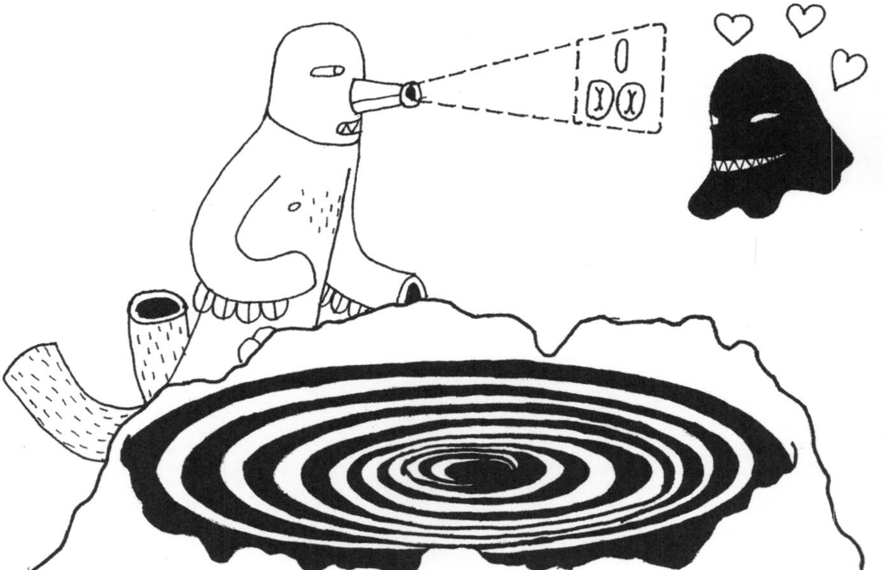

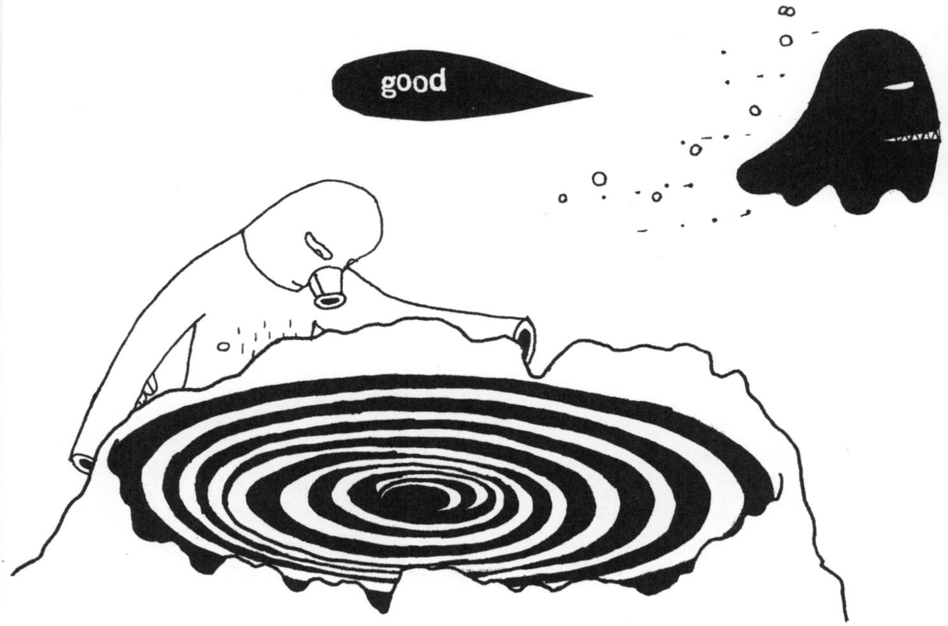
good

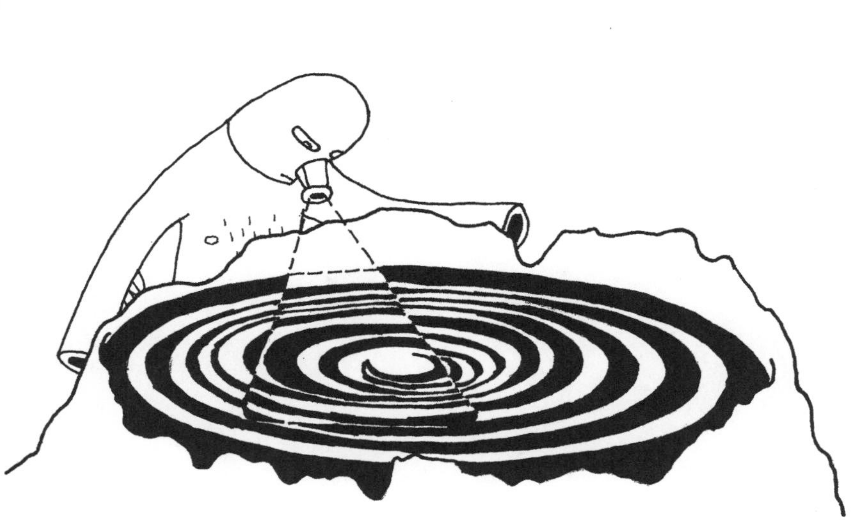

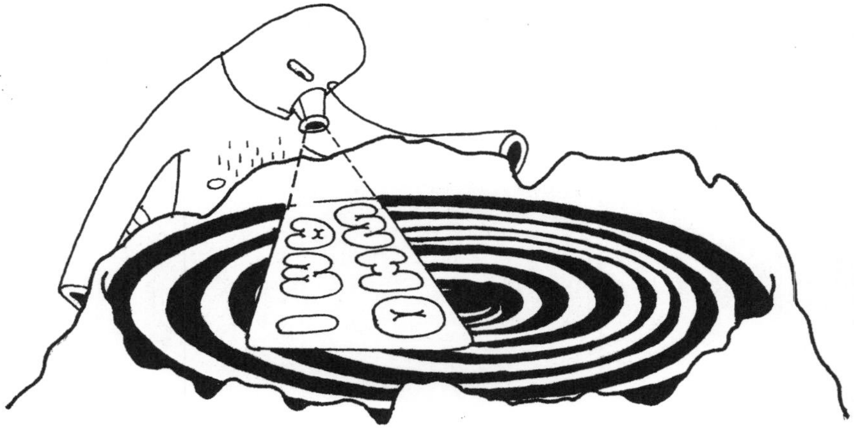

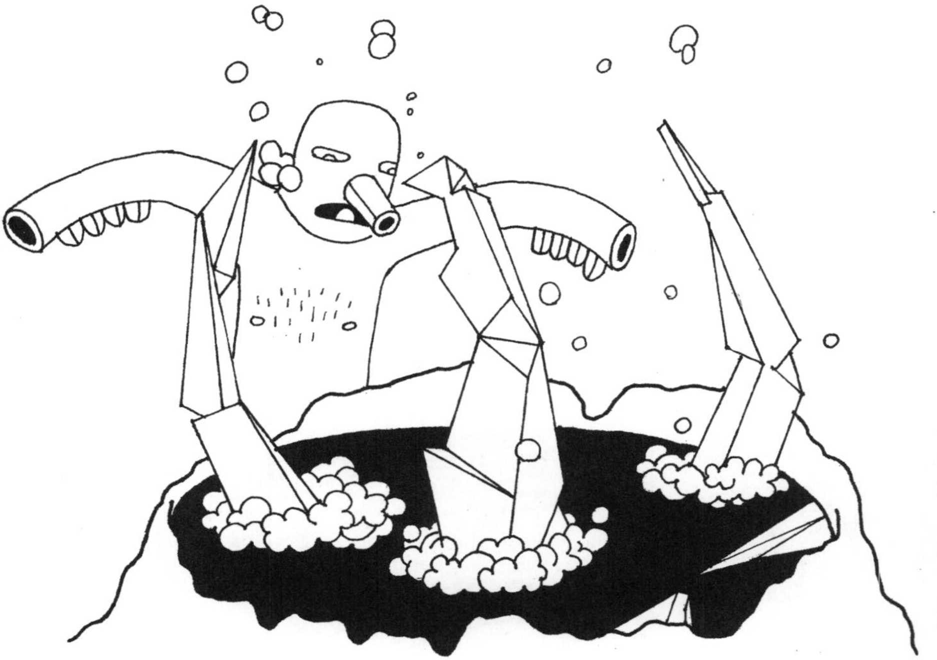

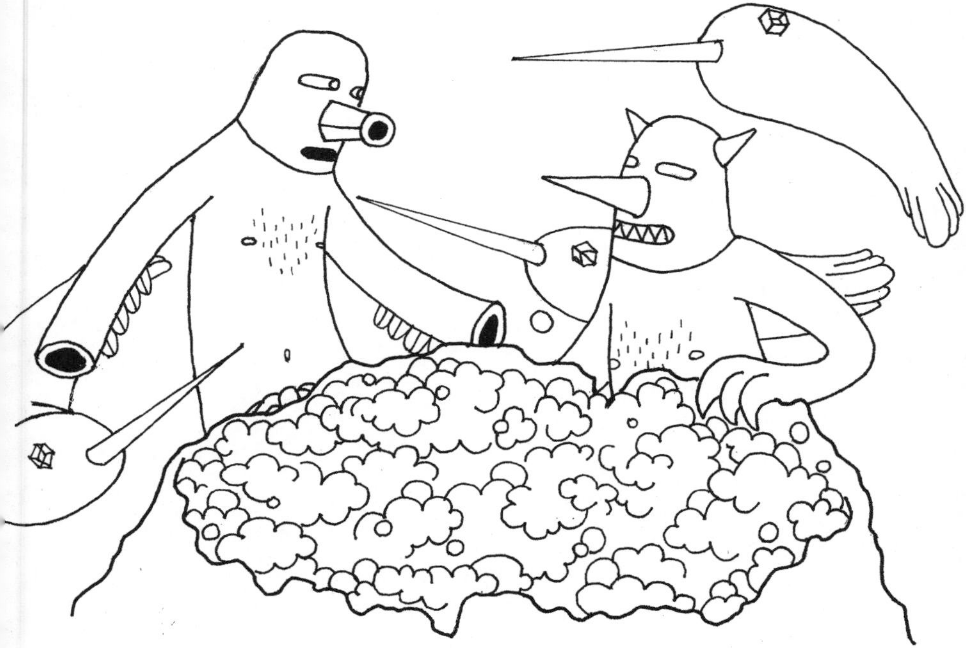

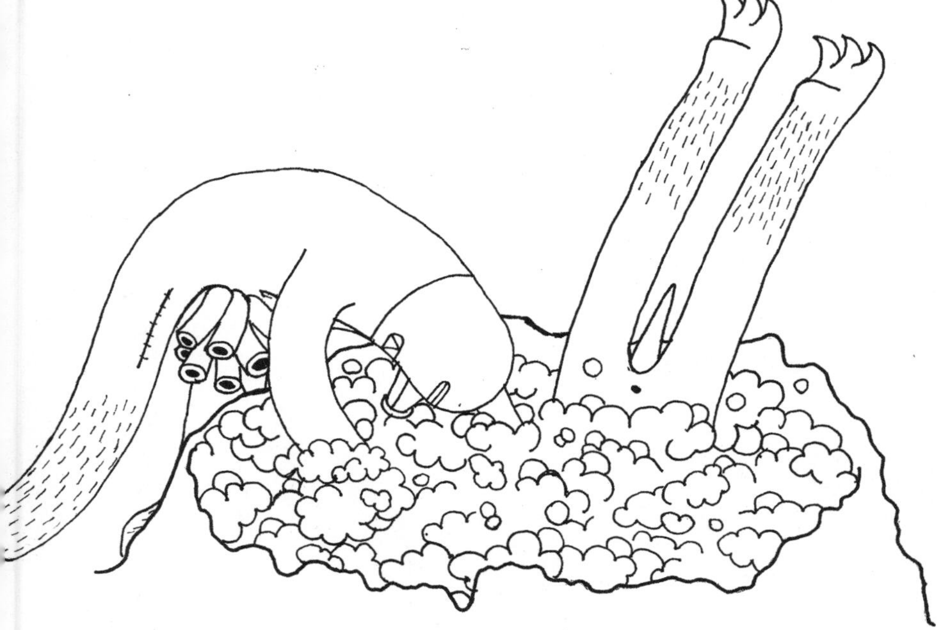

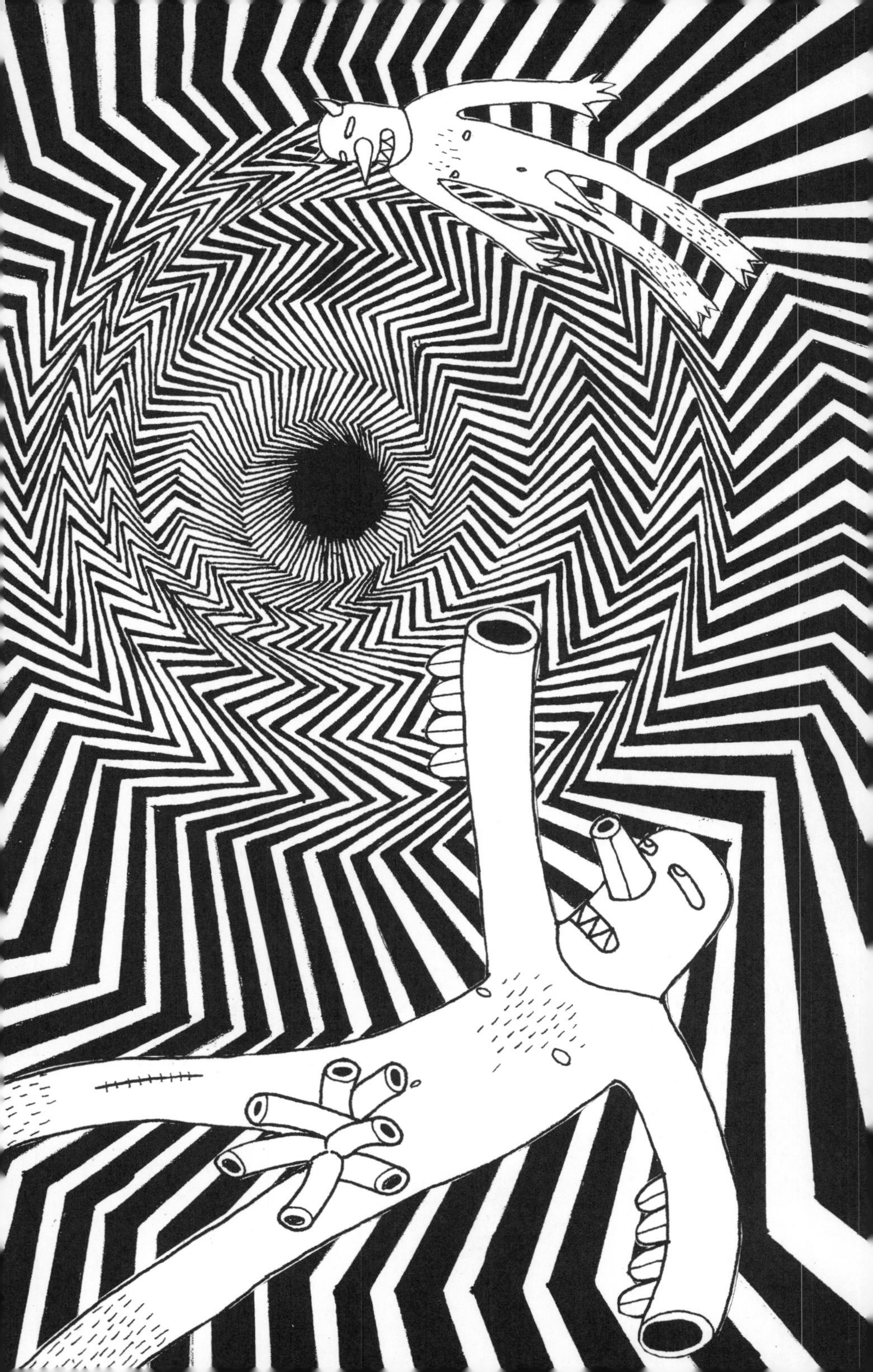

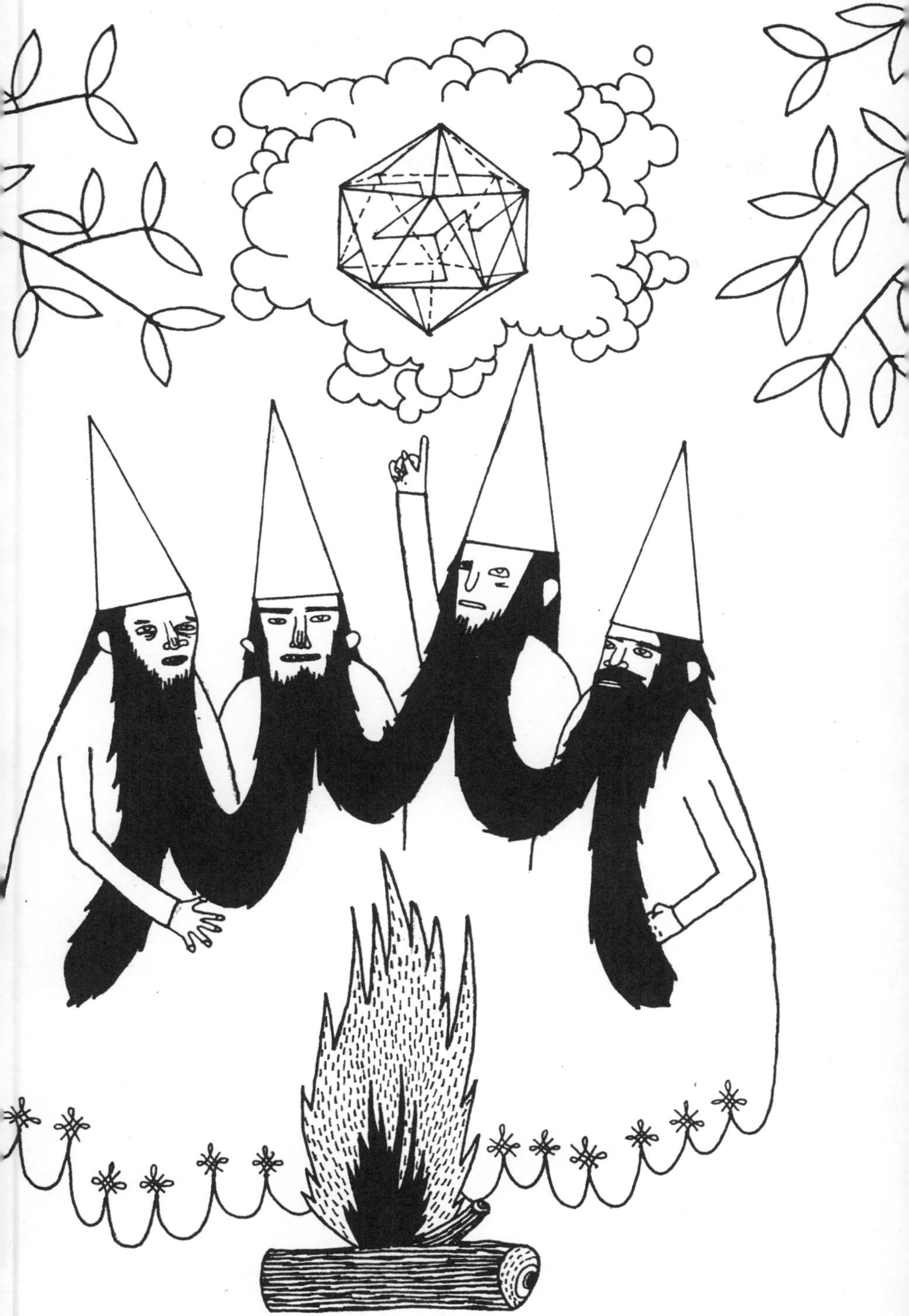

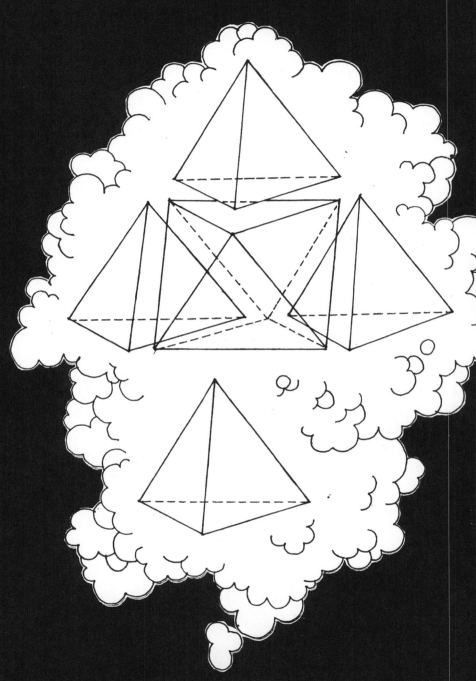

THE GEOMETRIC RITES

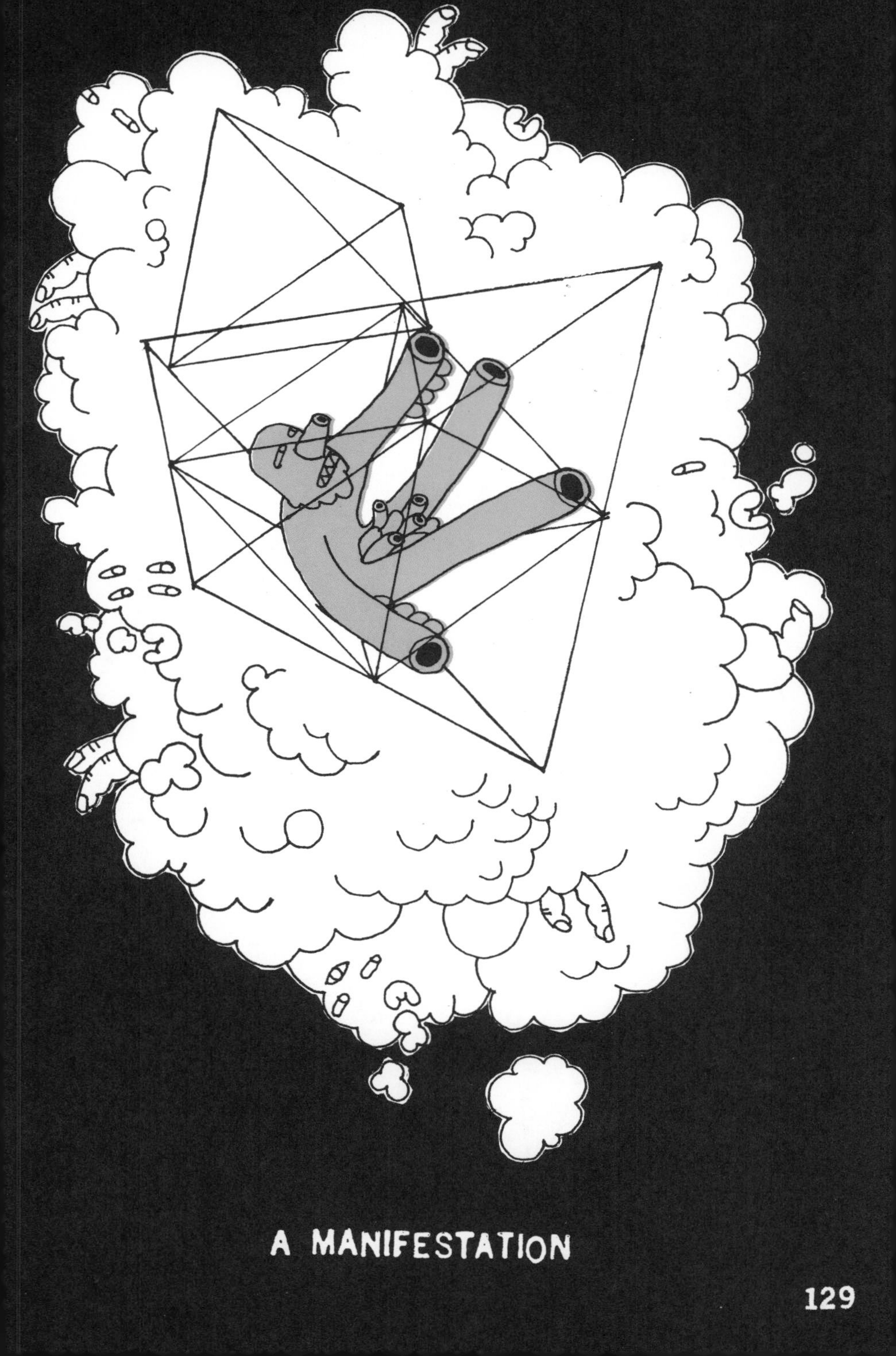

A MANIFESTATION

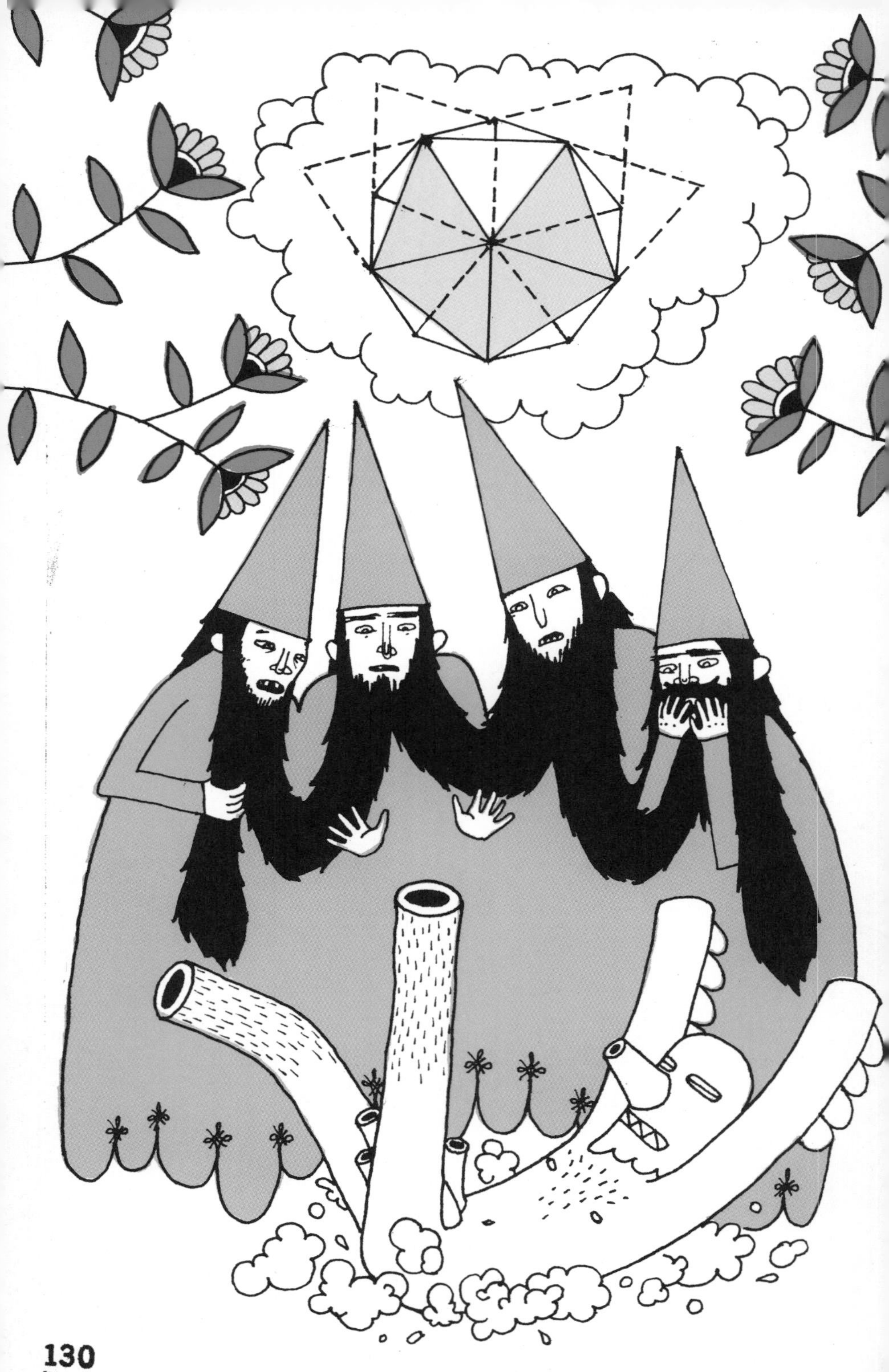

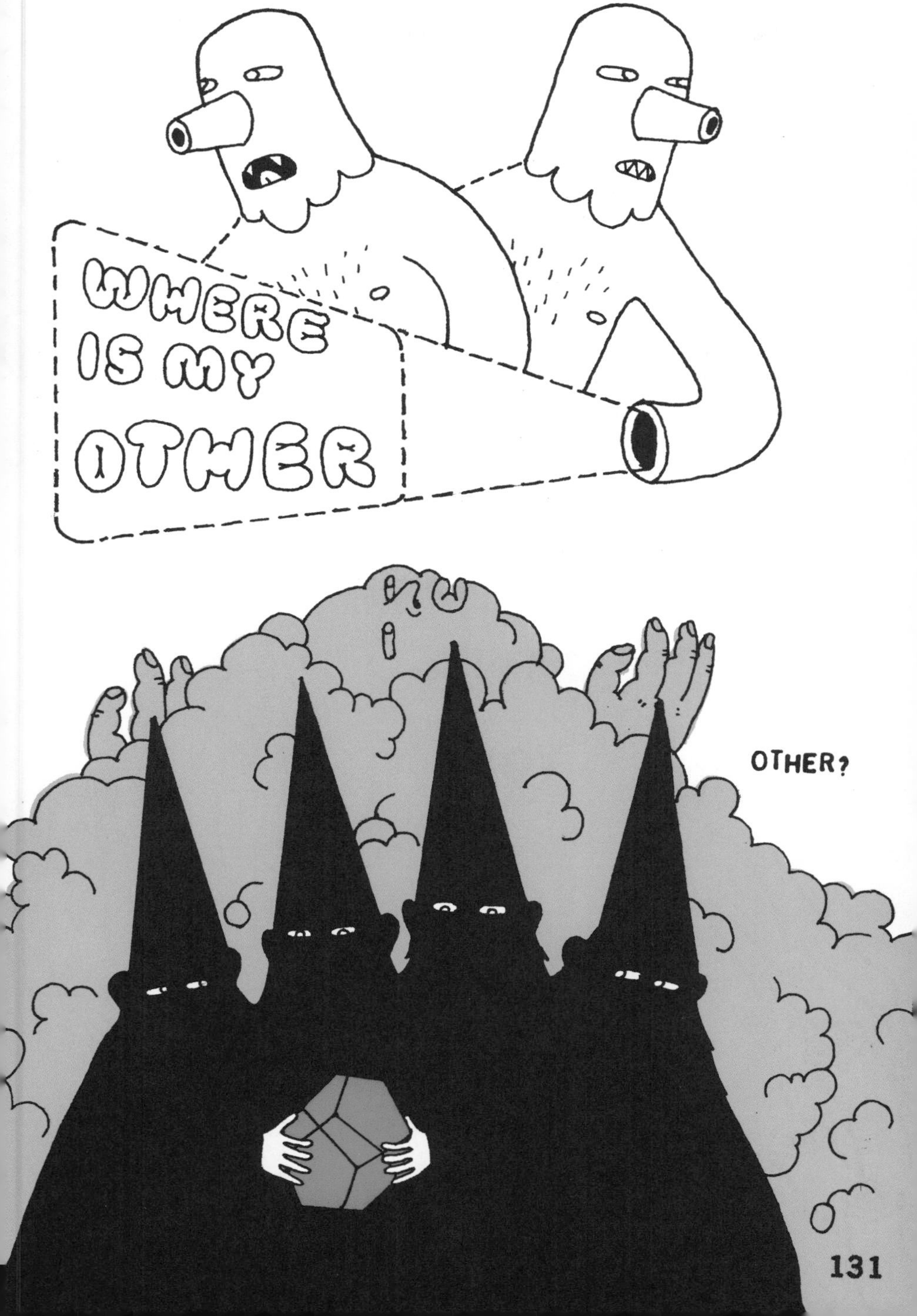
WHERE IS MY OTHER
OTHER?

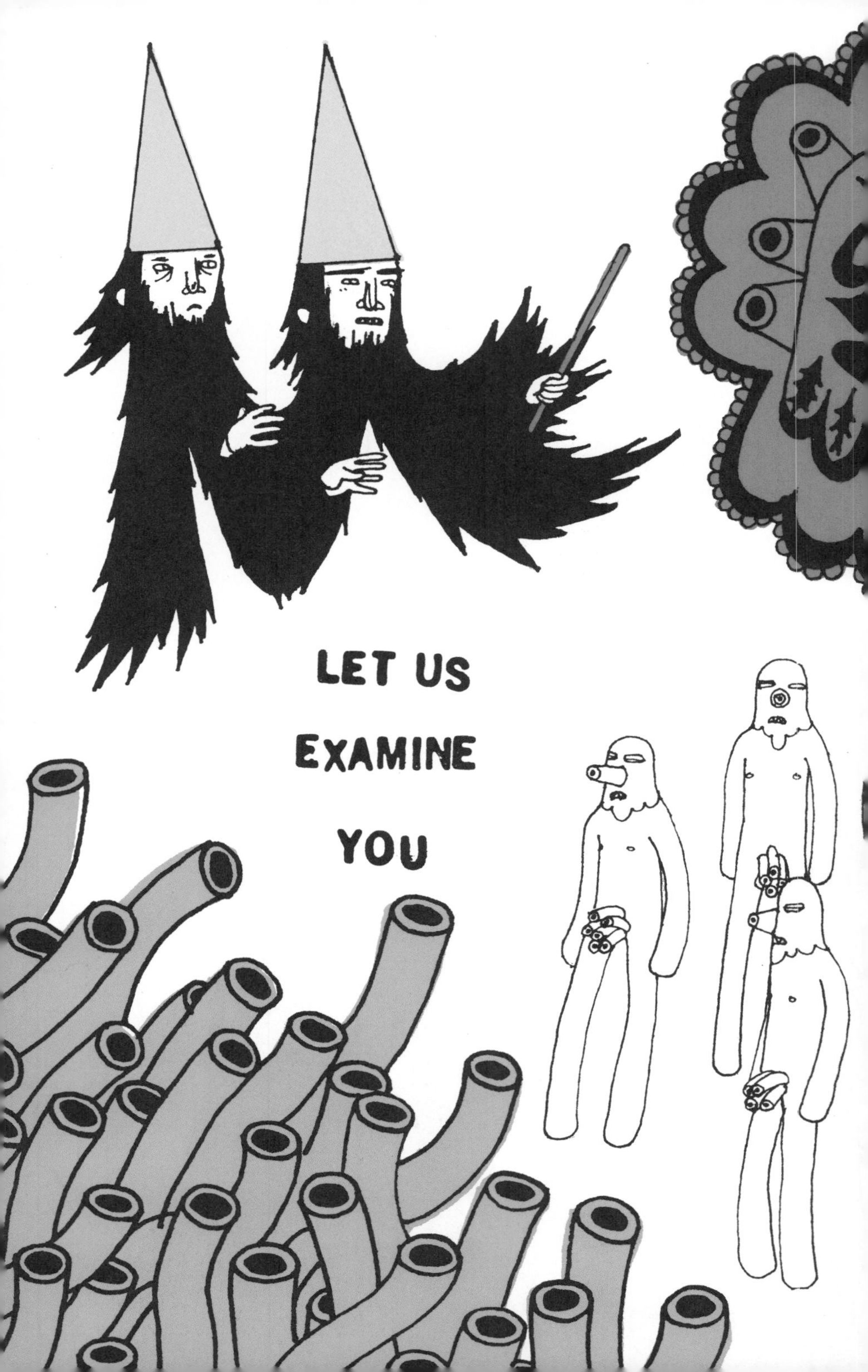
LET US
EXAMINE
YOU

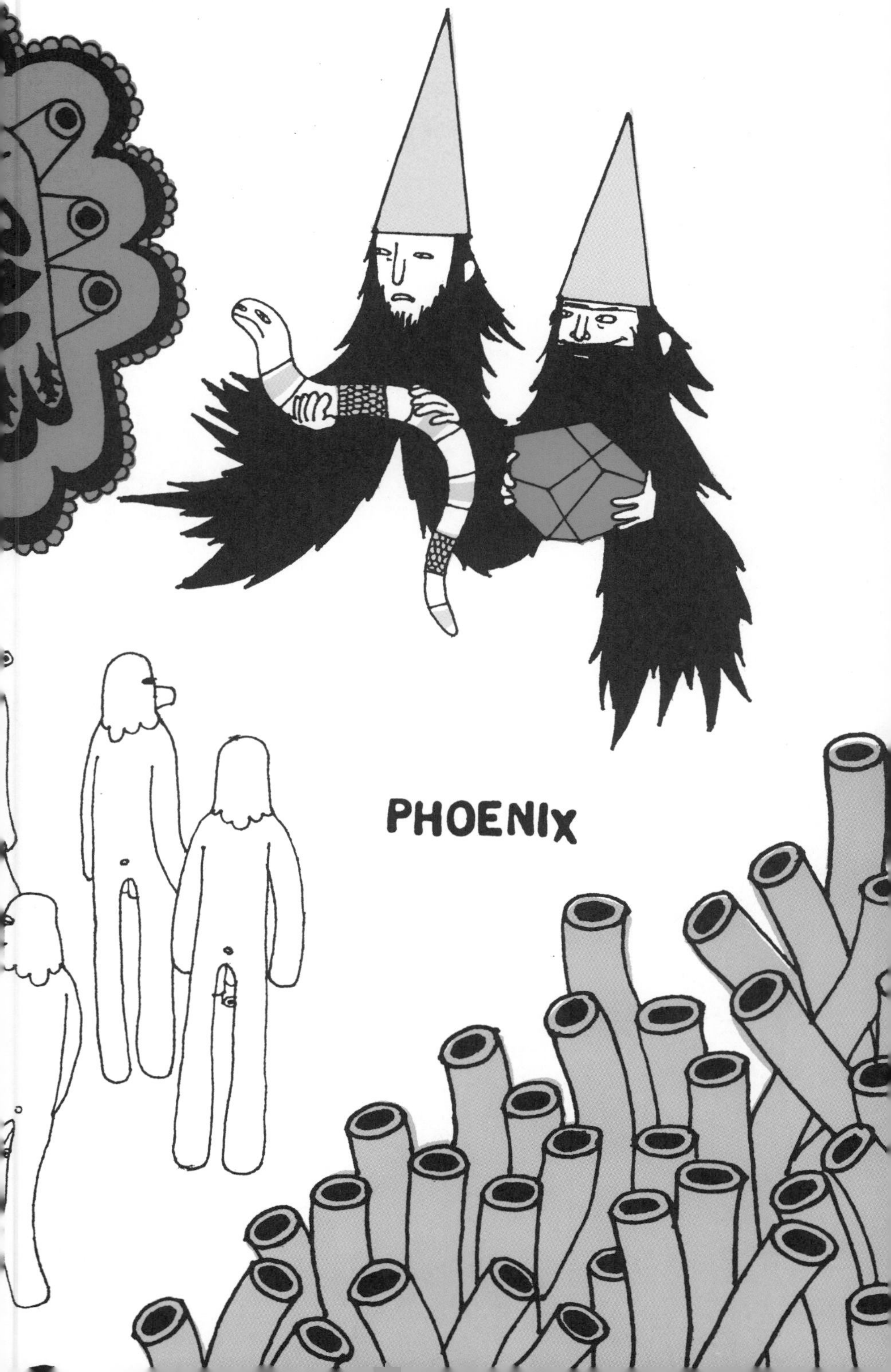
PHOENIX

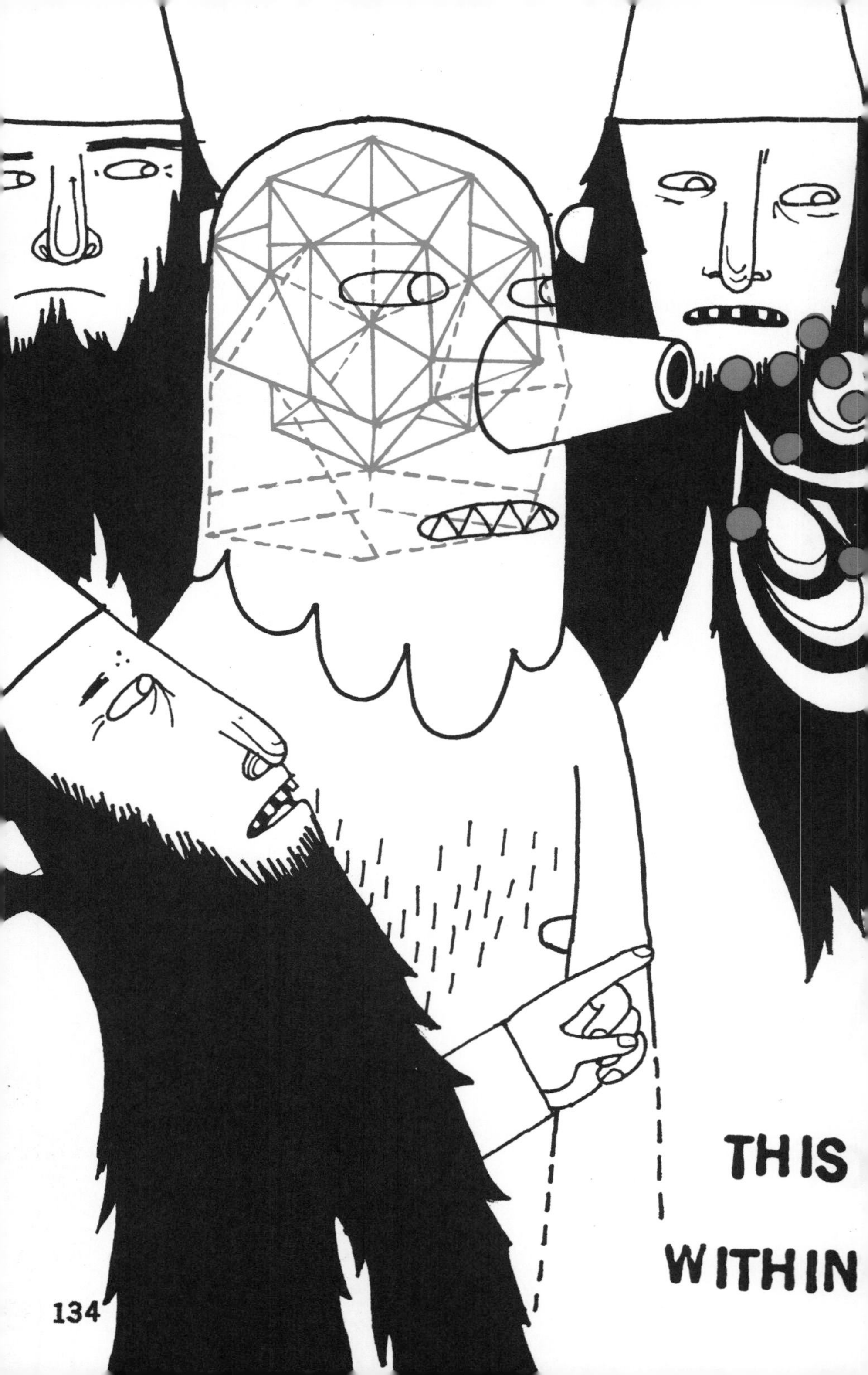
THIS
WITHIN

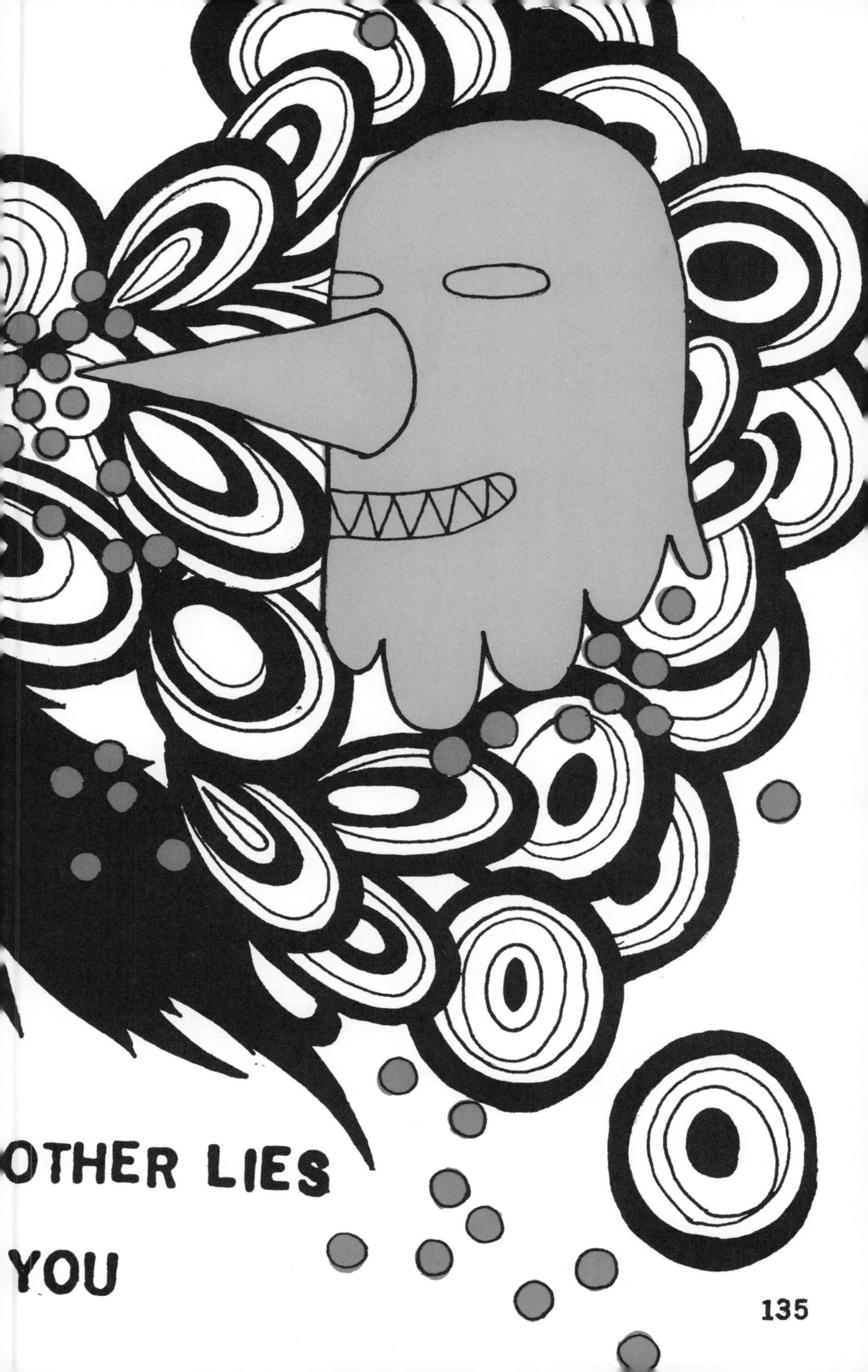
OTHER LIES
YOU

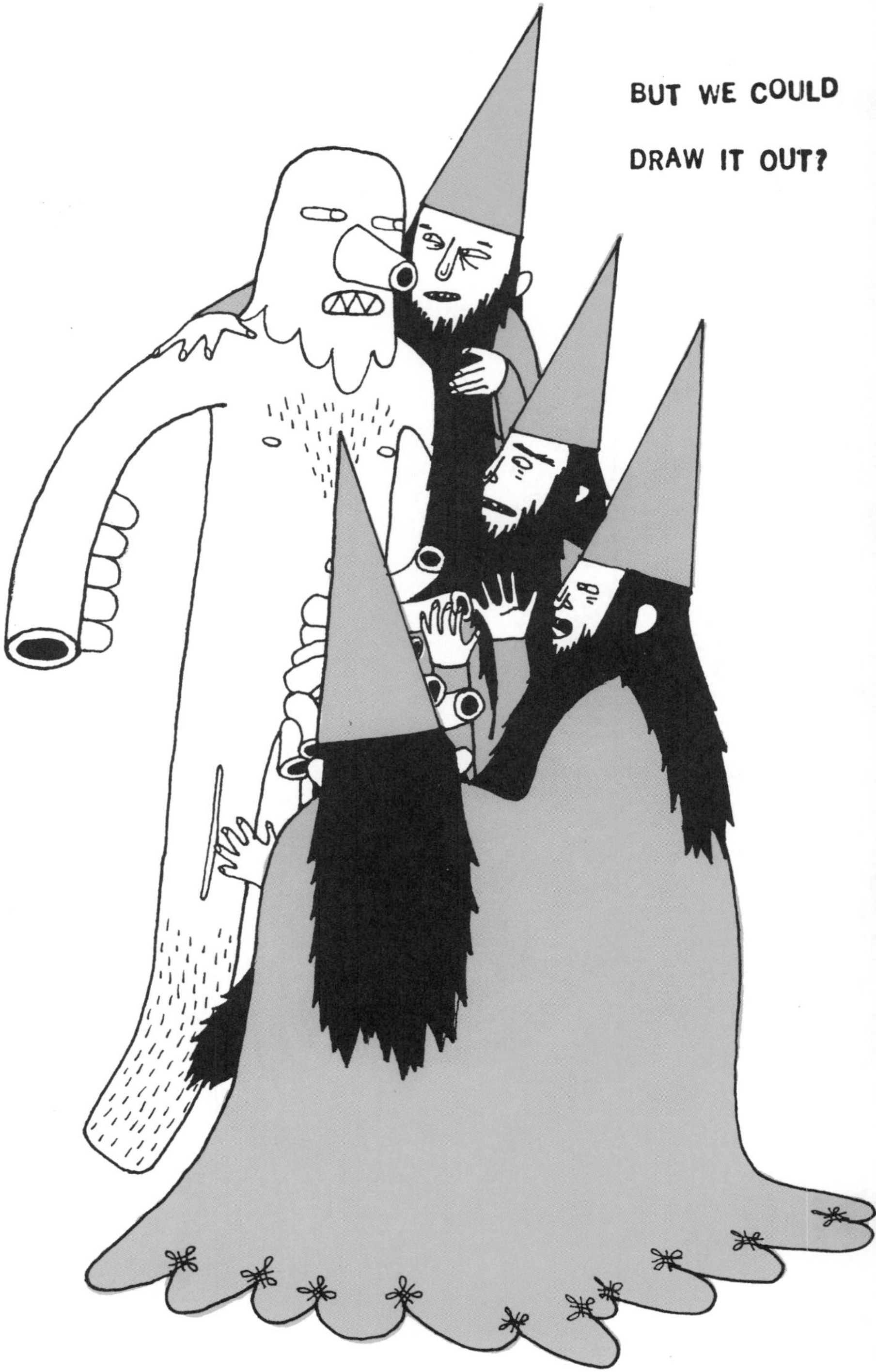
BUT WE COULD
DRAW IT OUT?

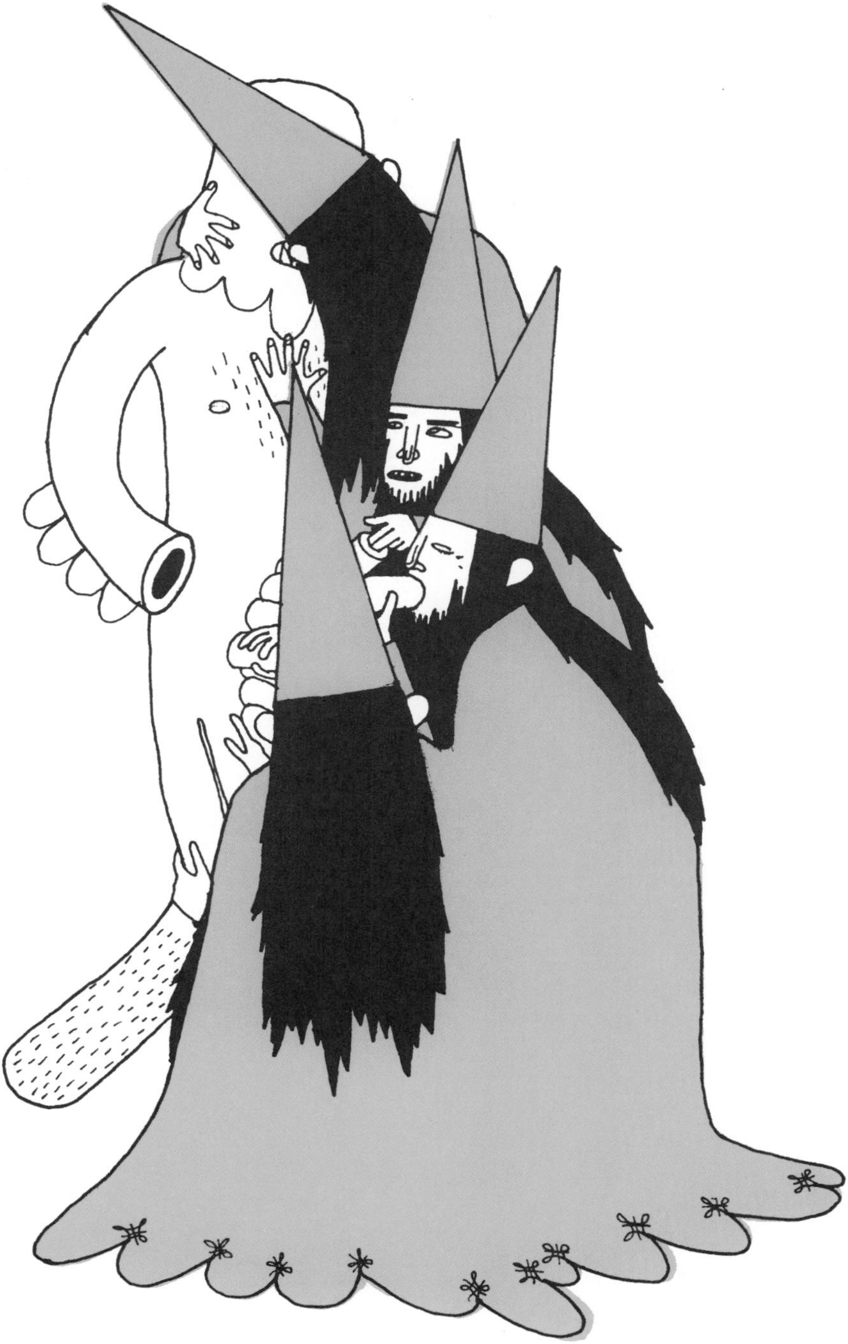

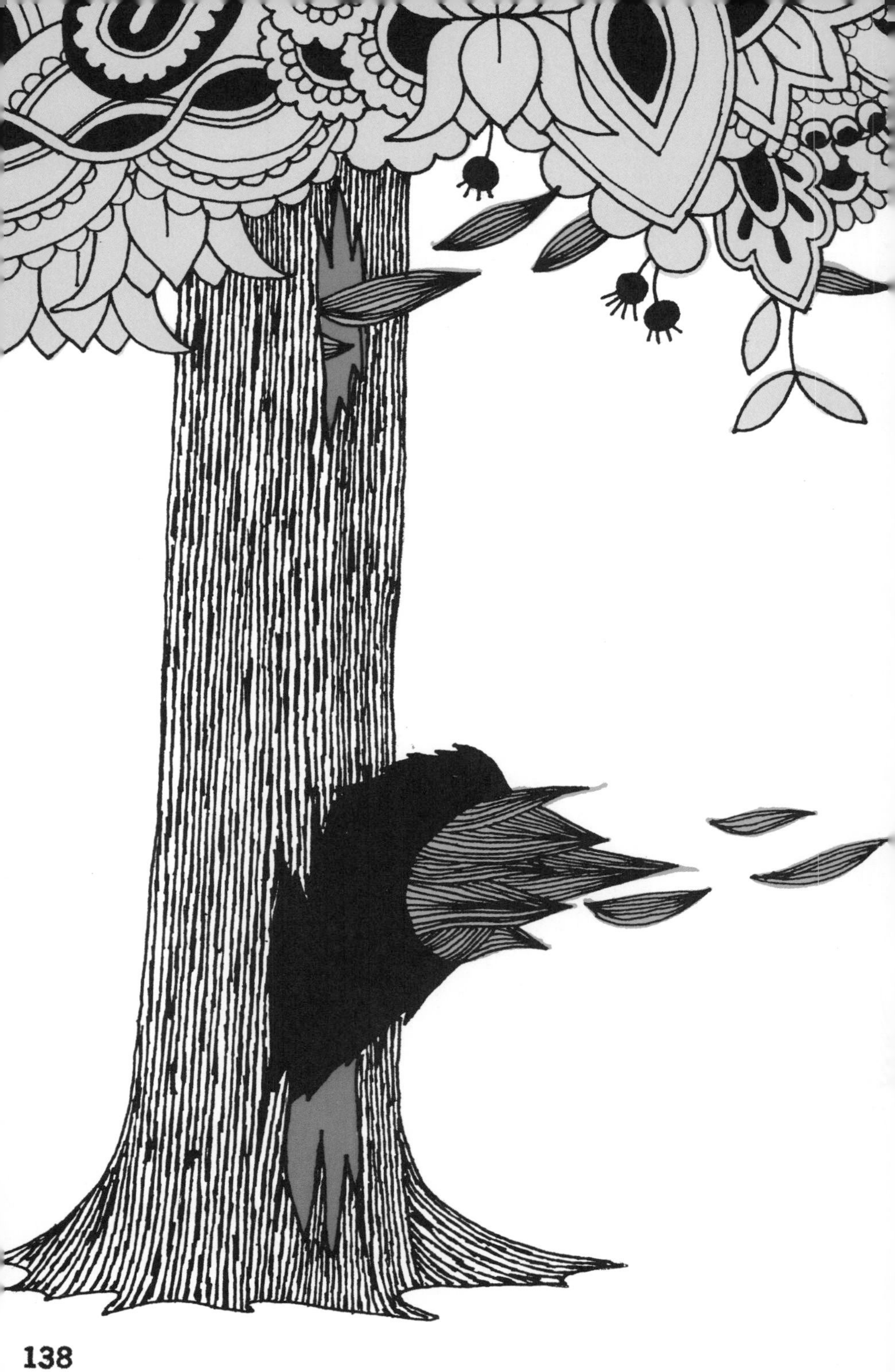

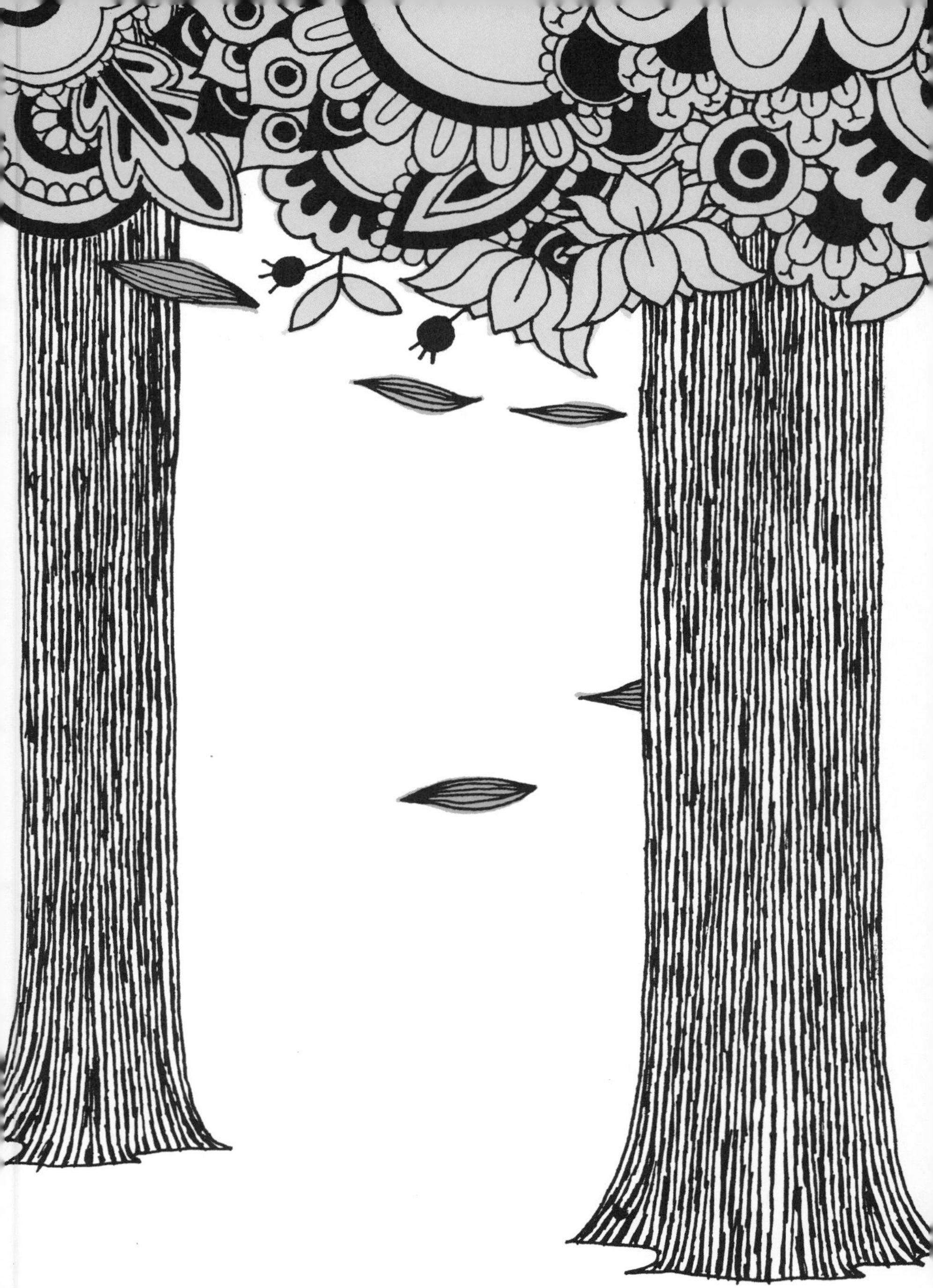

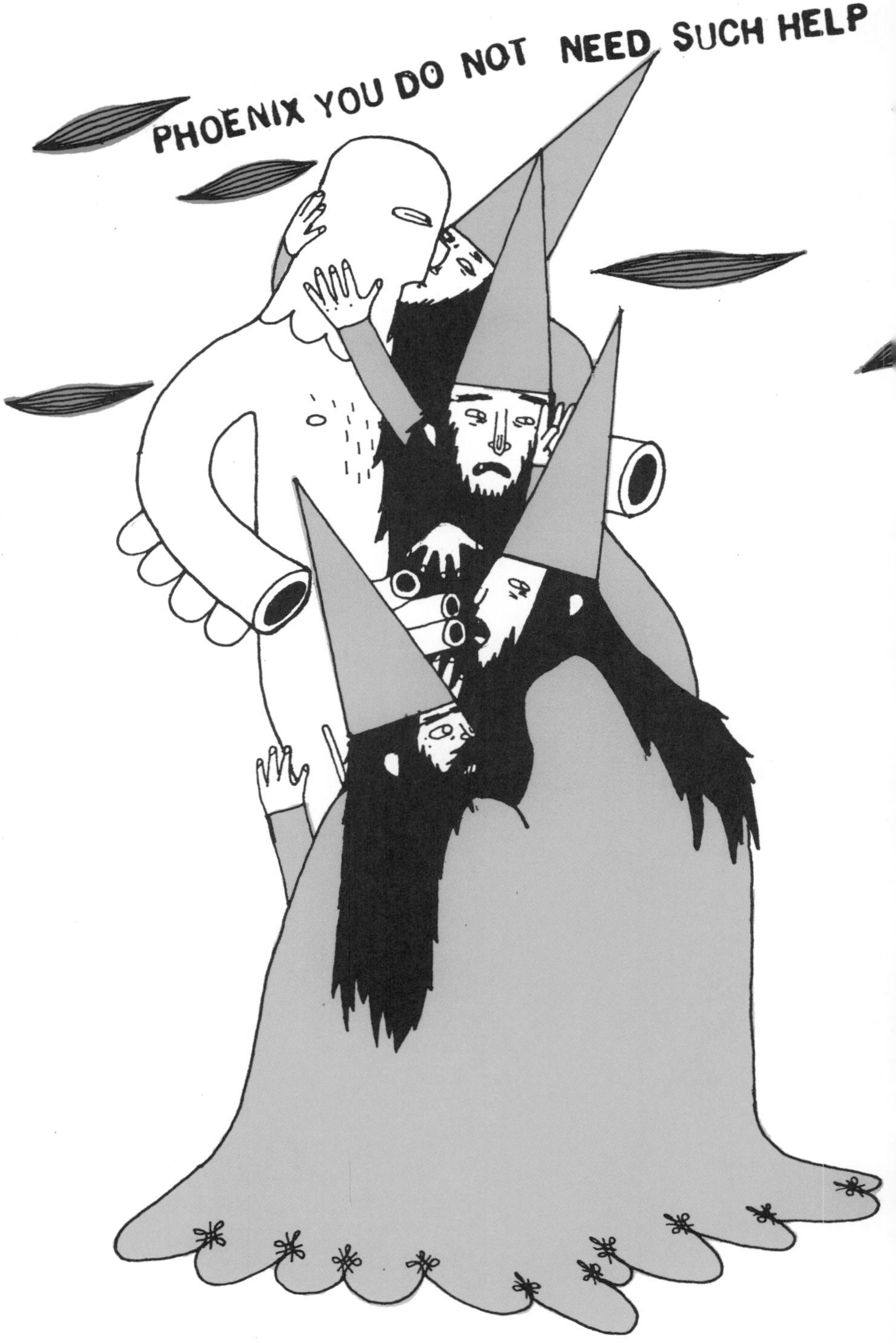
PHOENIX YOU DO NOT NEED SUCH HELP

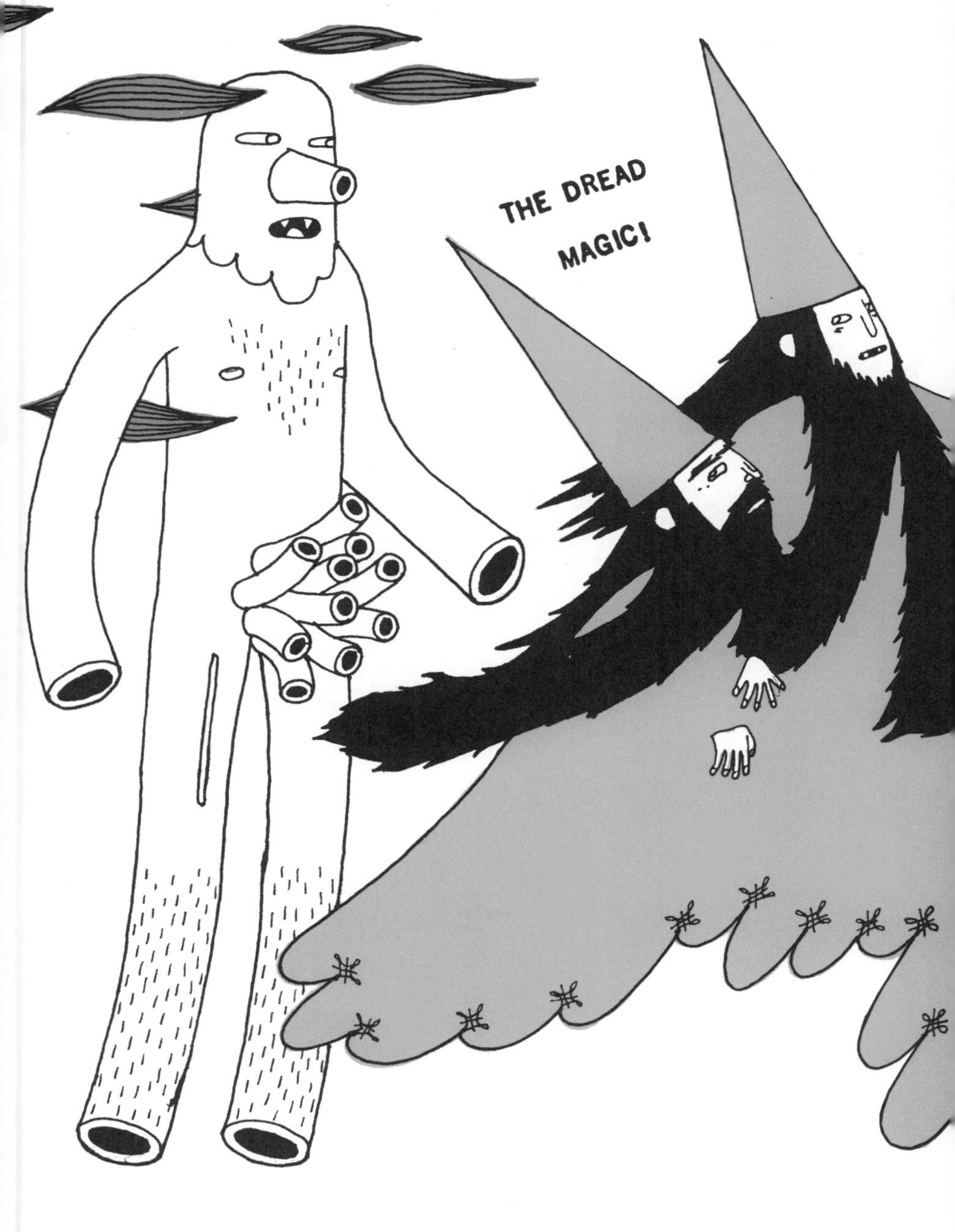
THE DREAD MAGIC!

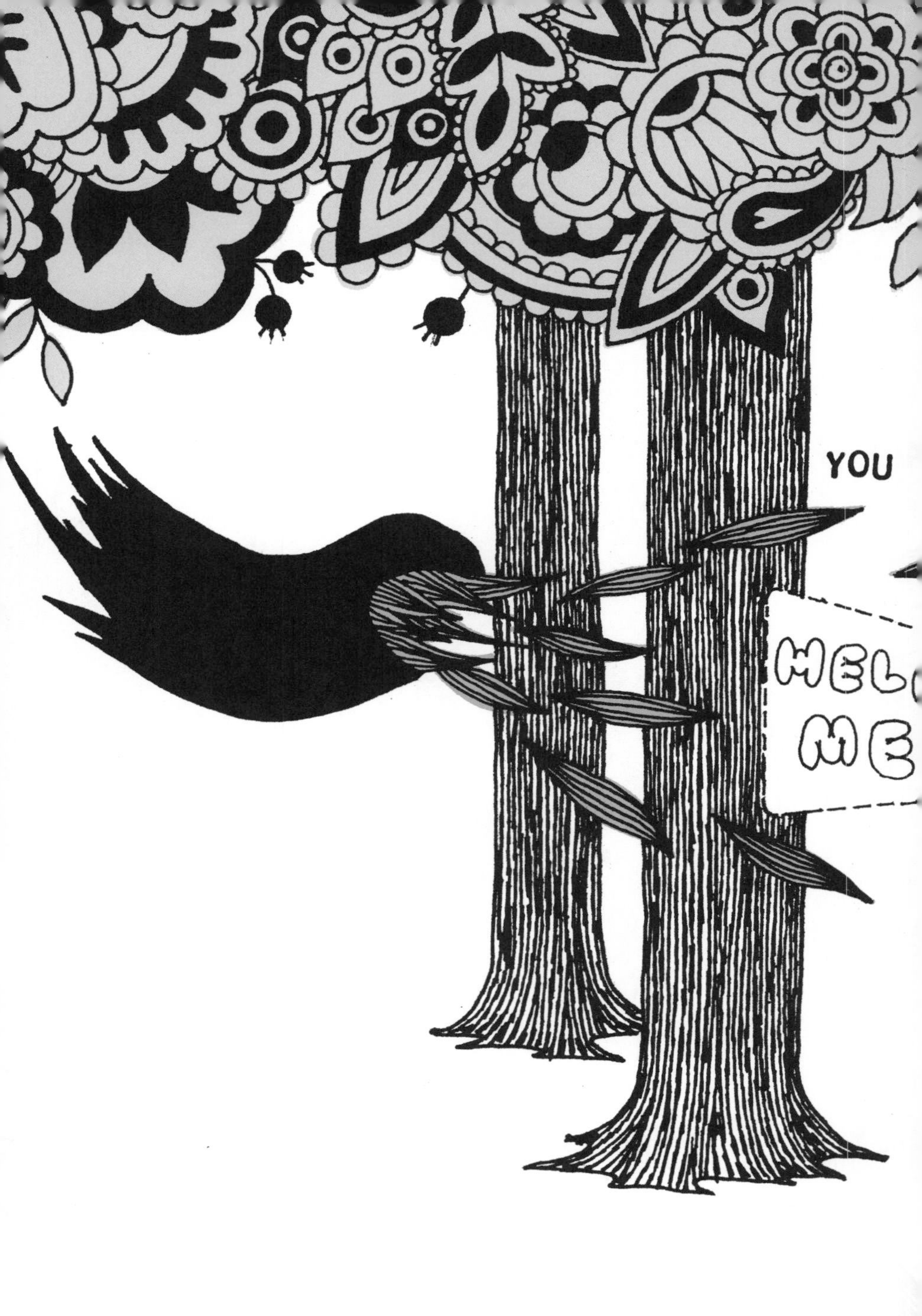
YOU
HEL
ME

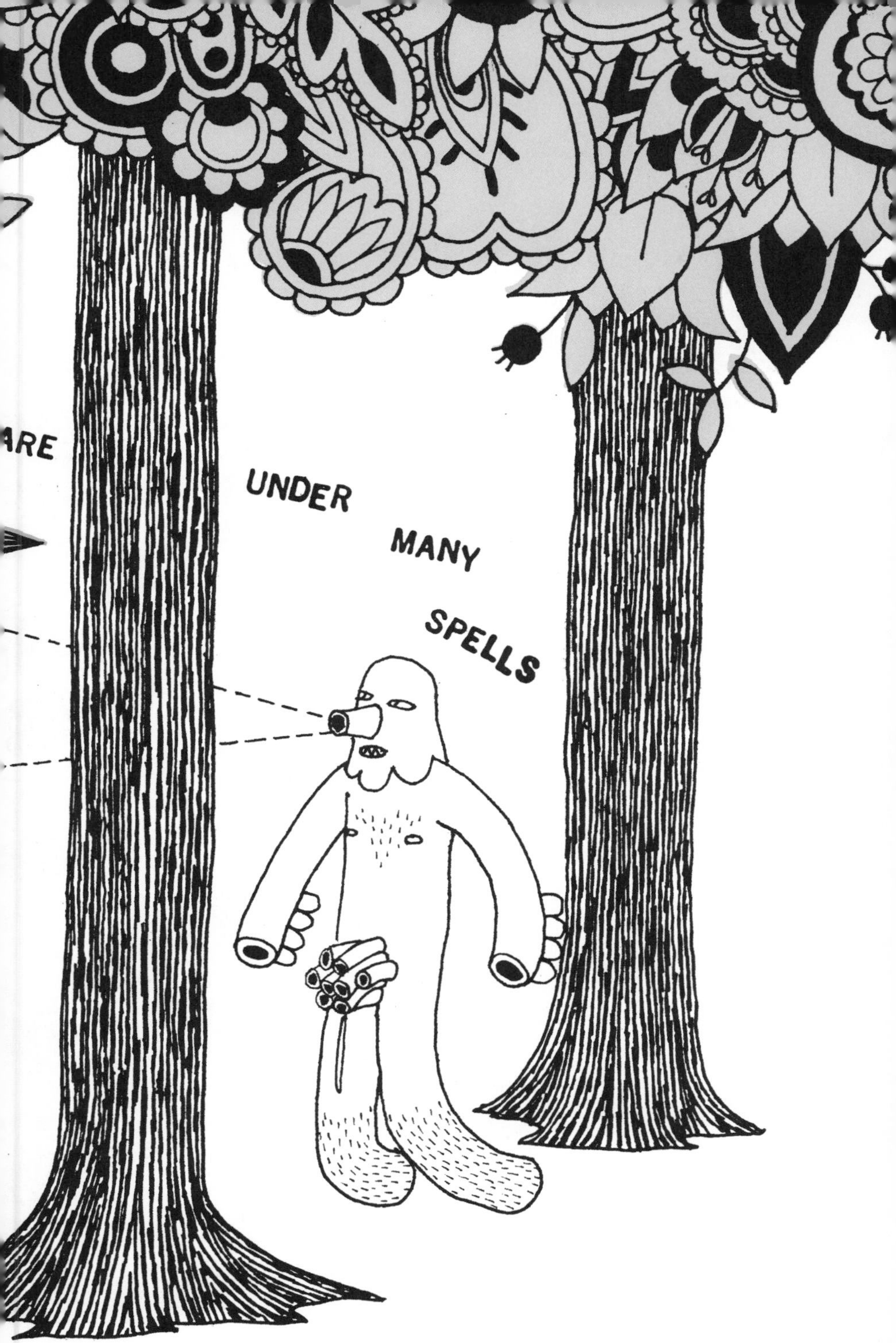
ARE
UNDER
MANY
SPELLS

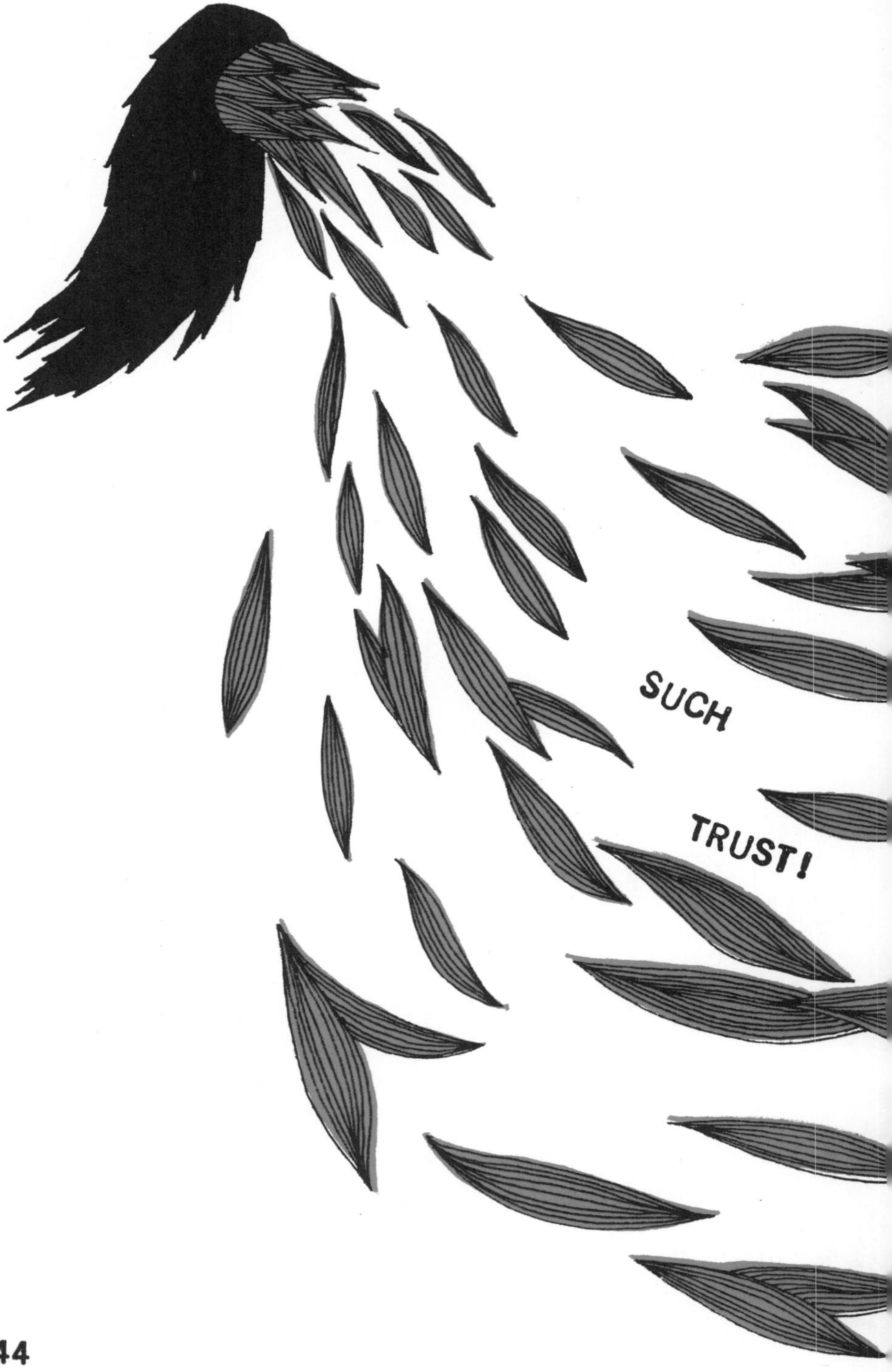
SUCH
TRUST!

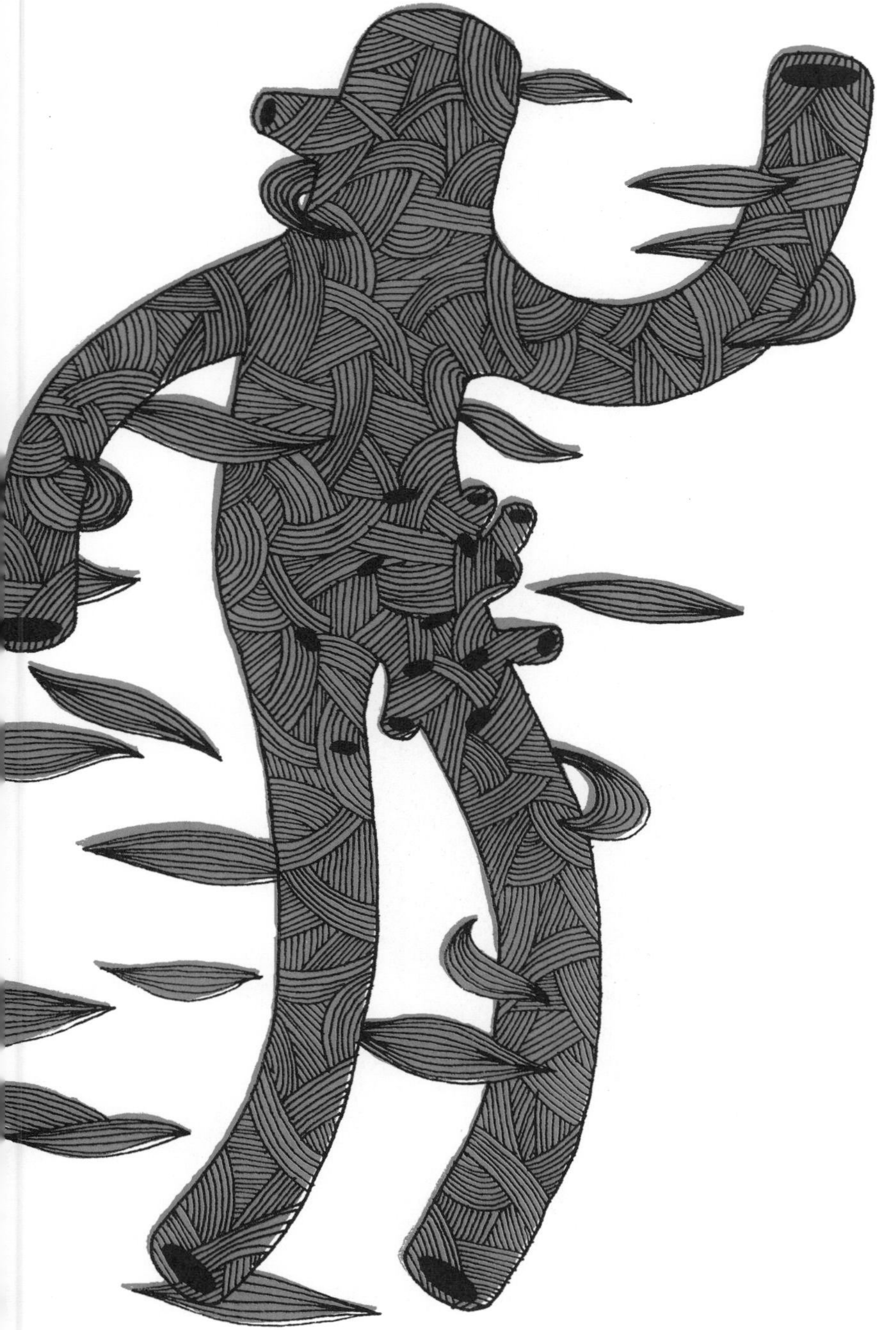

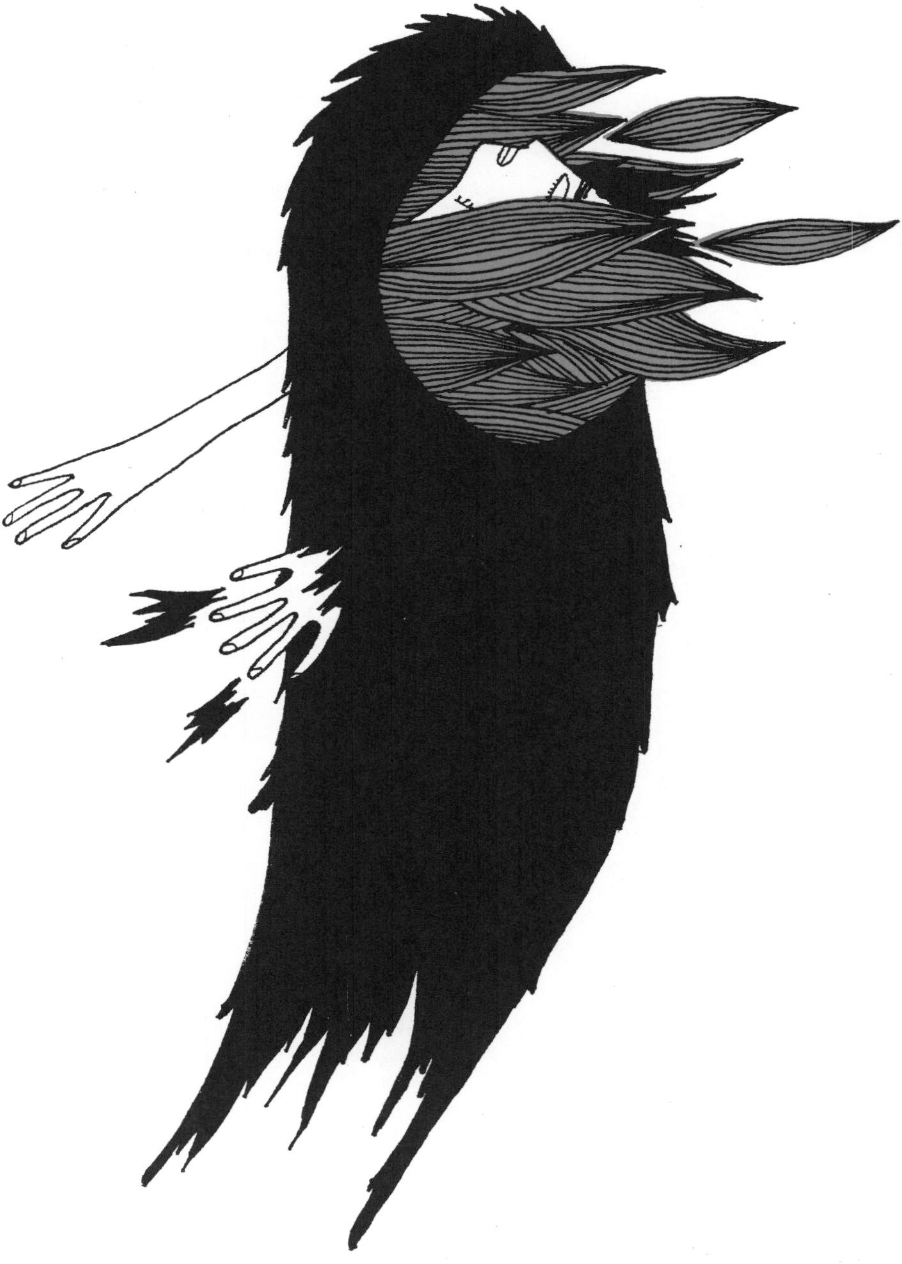

BEHOLD THE LOWER PHOENIX!

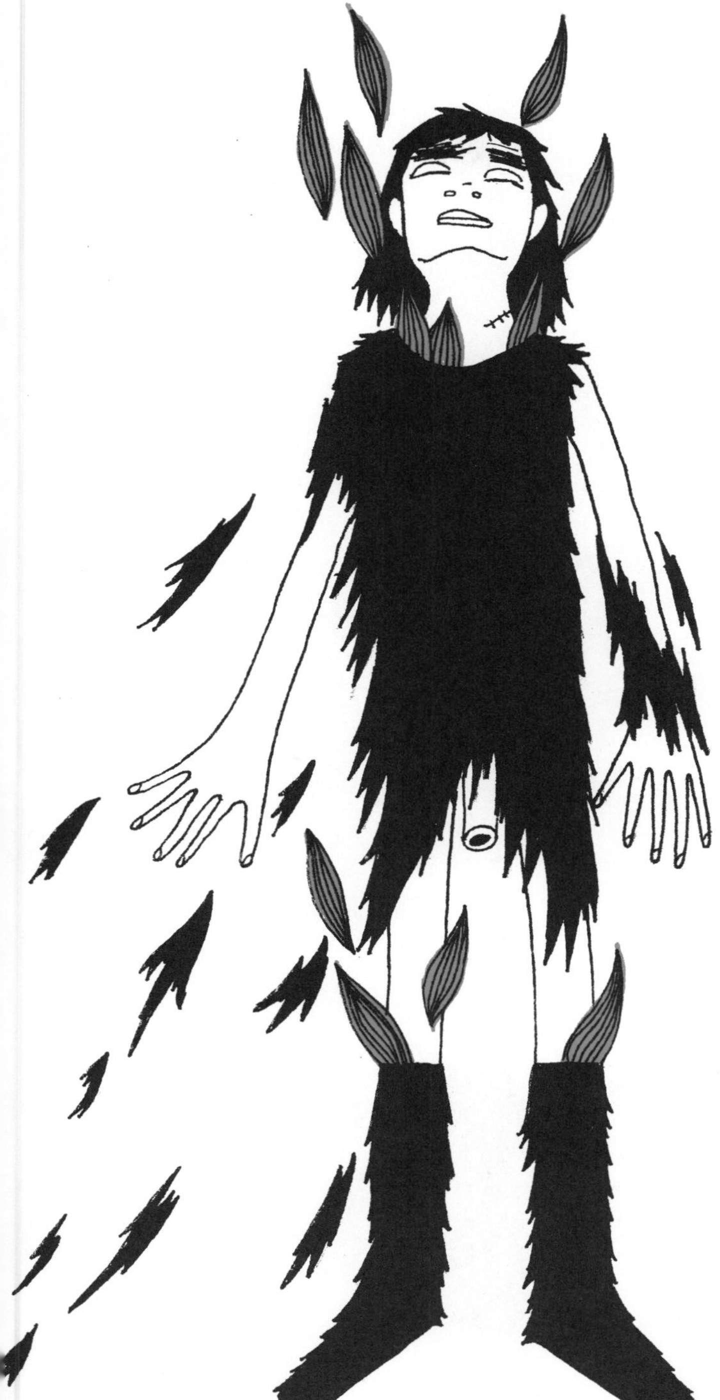

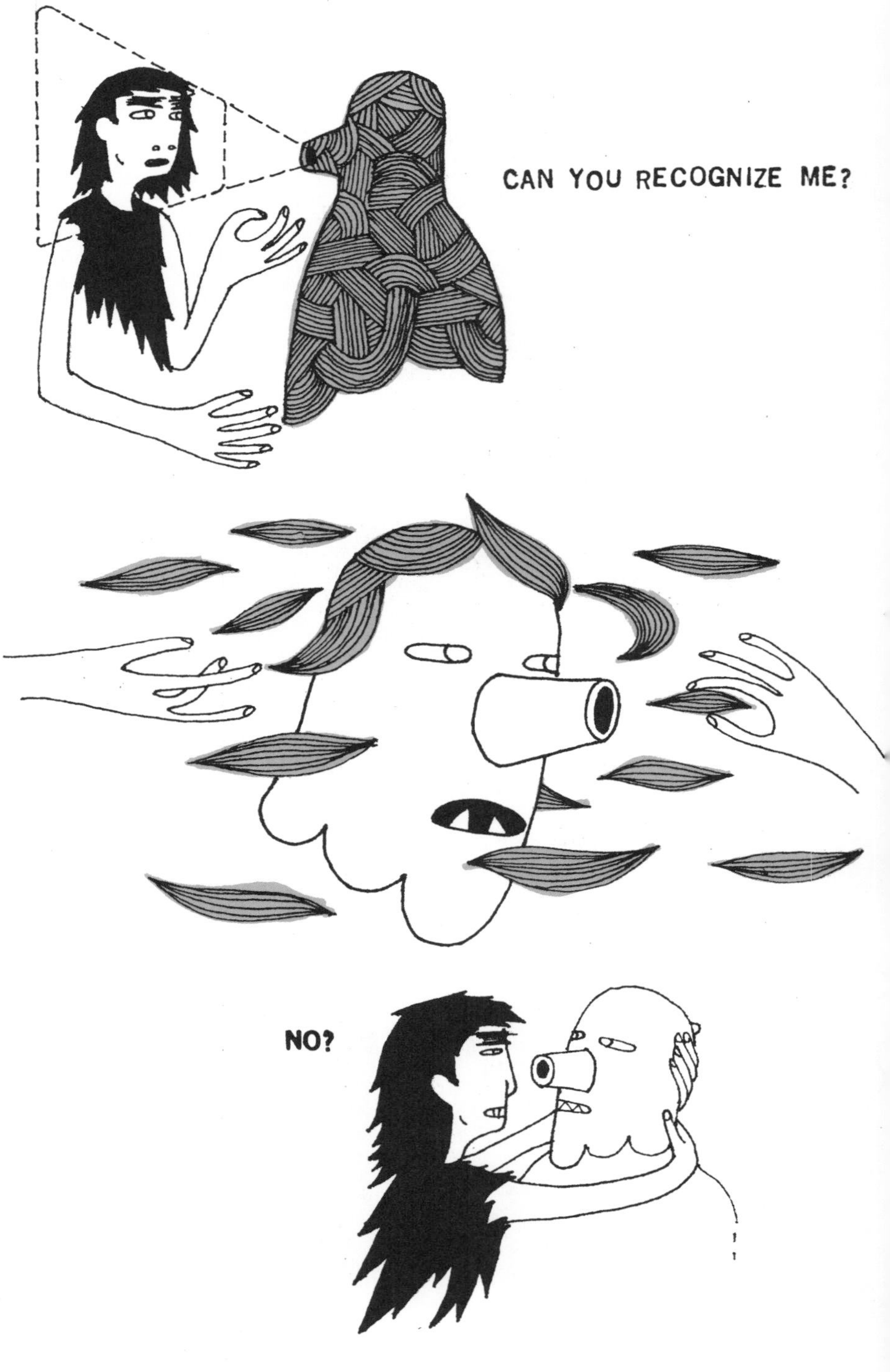
CAN YOU RECOGNIZE ME?
NO?

I CAN HELP YOU

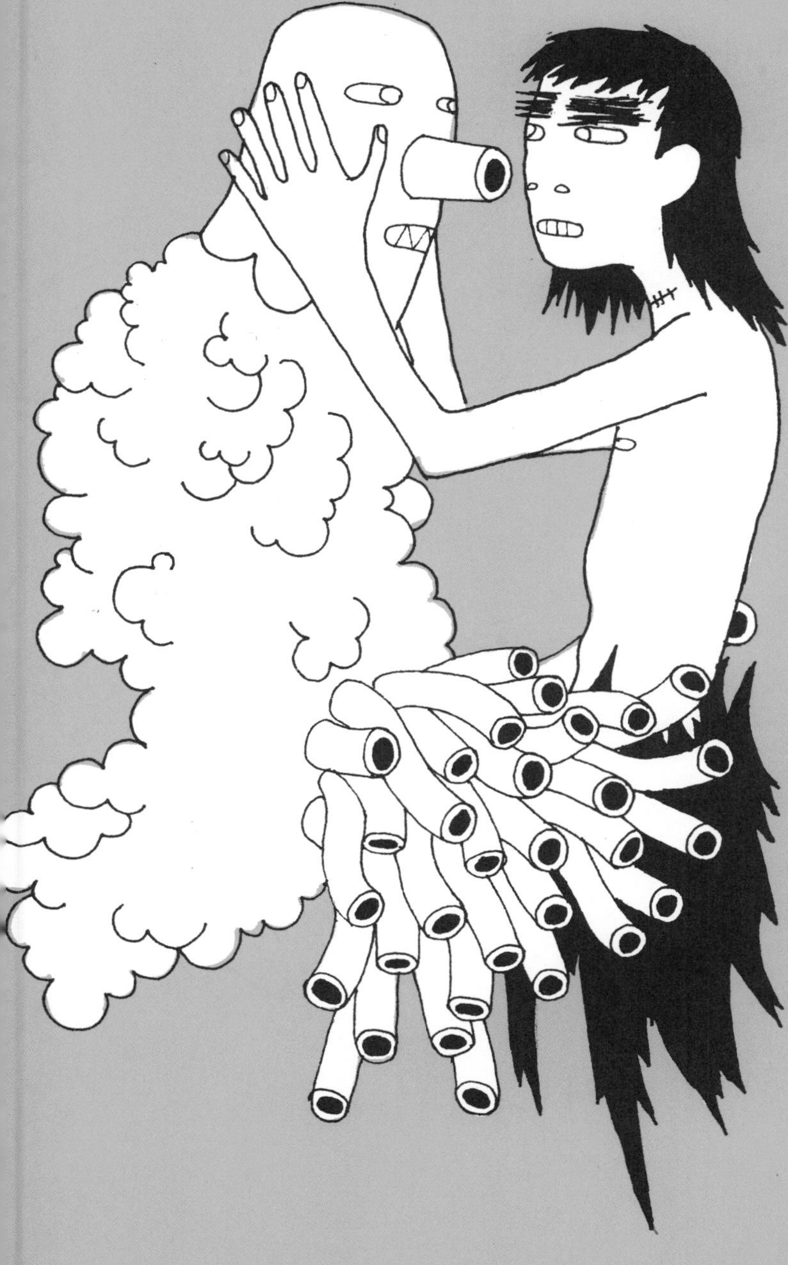

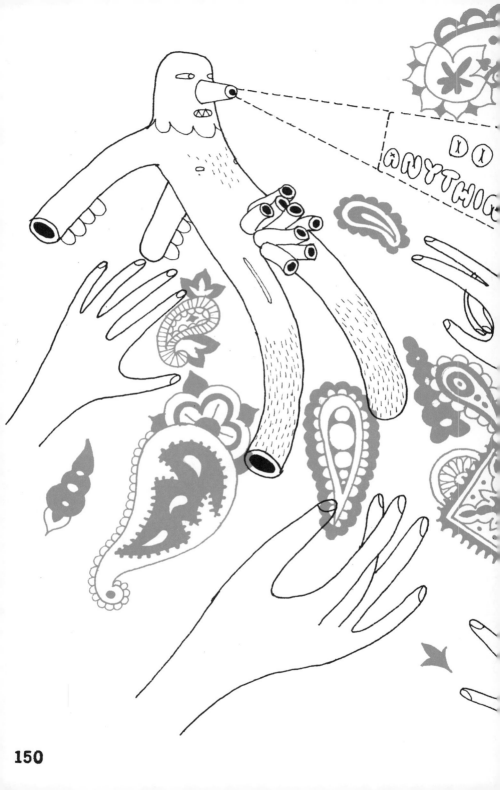

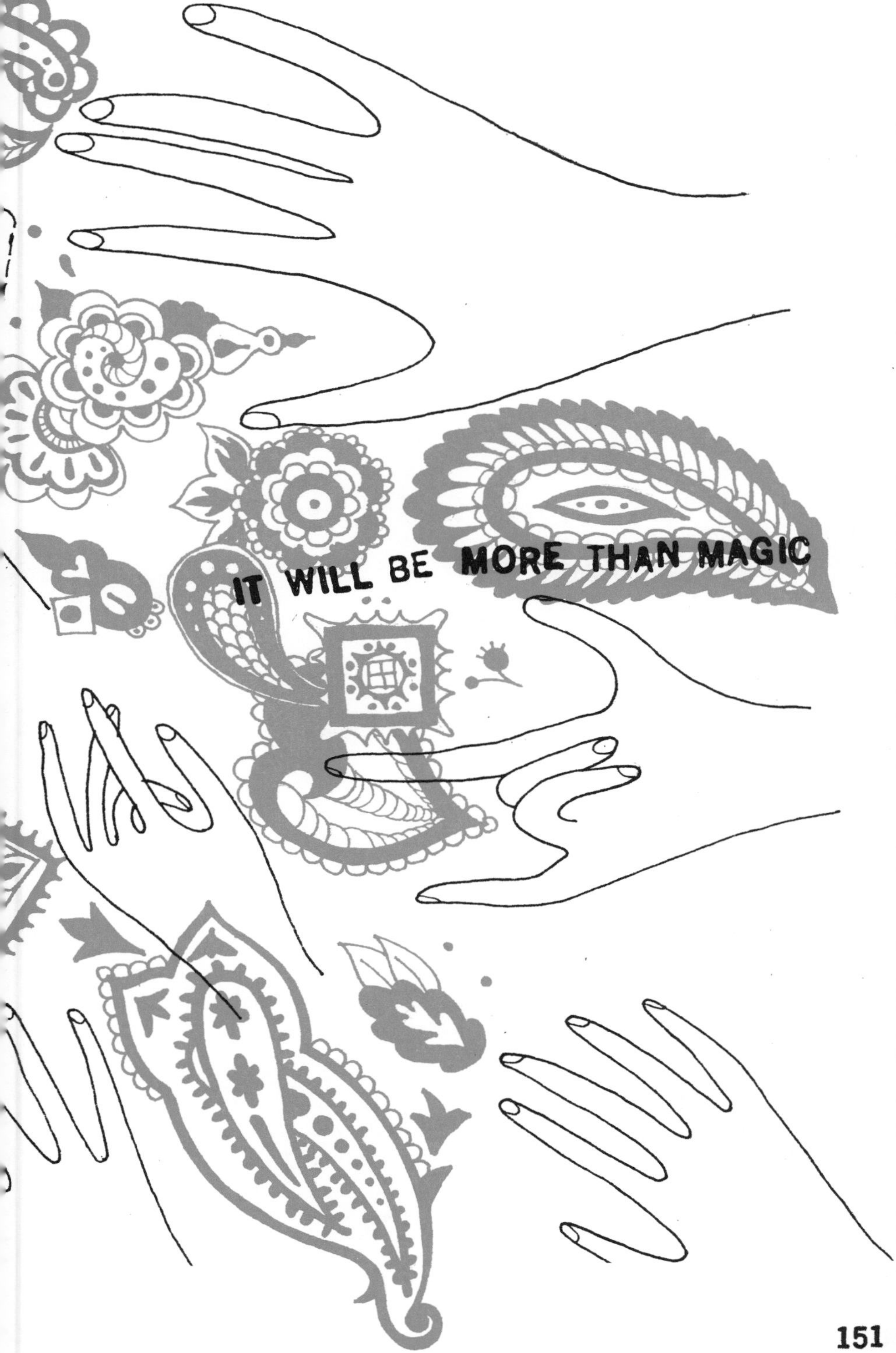
IT WILL BE MORE THAN MAGIC

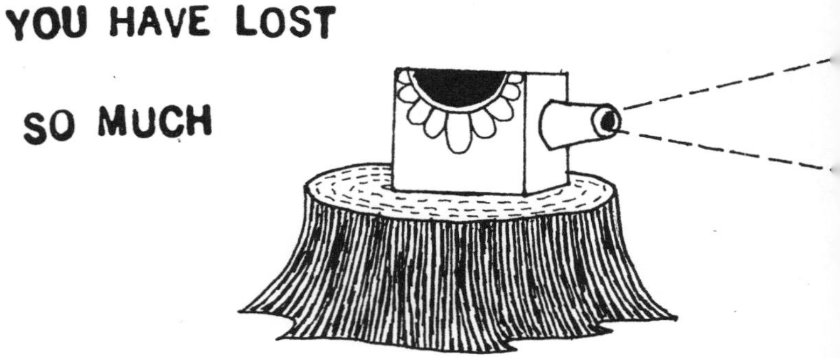
YOU HAVE LOST
SO MUCH

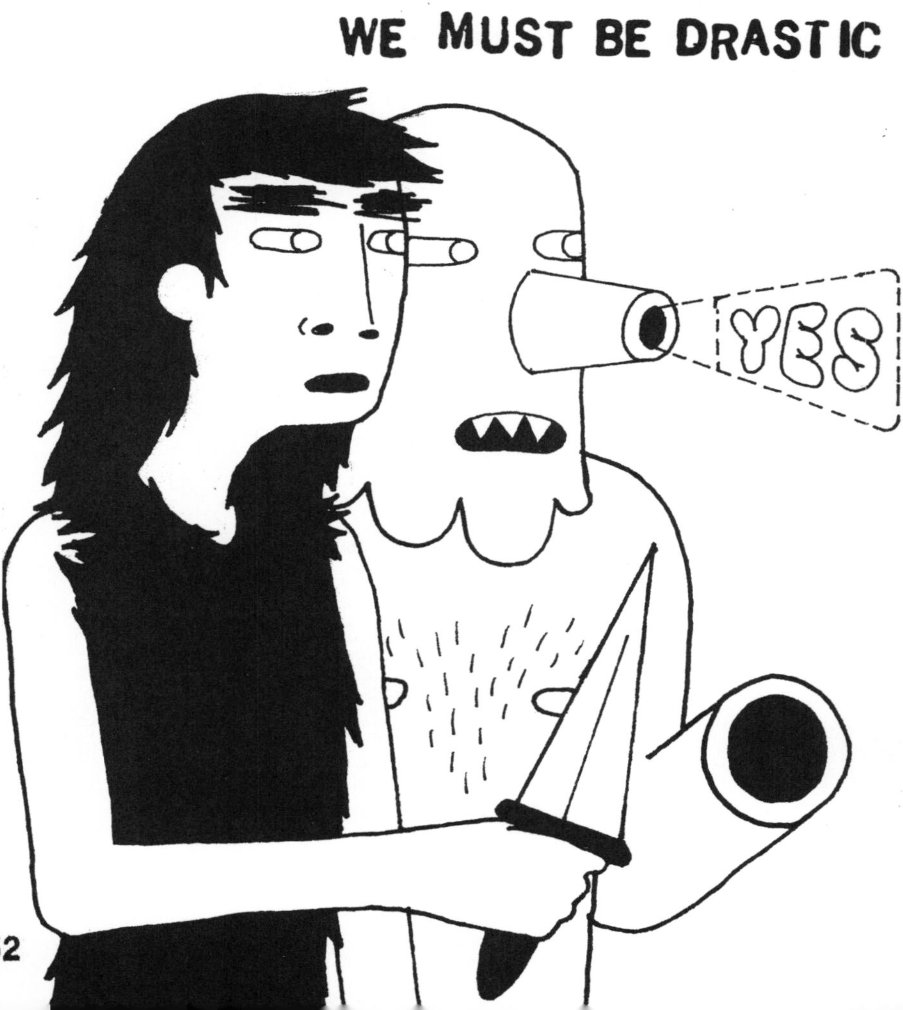
WE MUST BE DRASTIC
YES

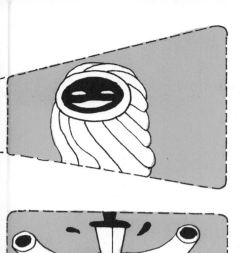
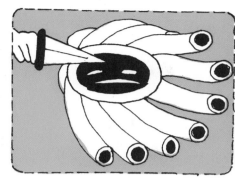
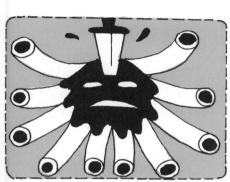
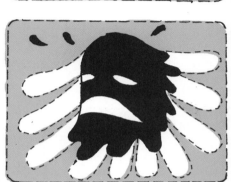

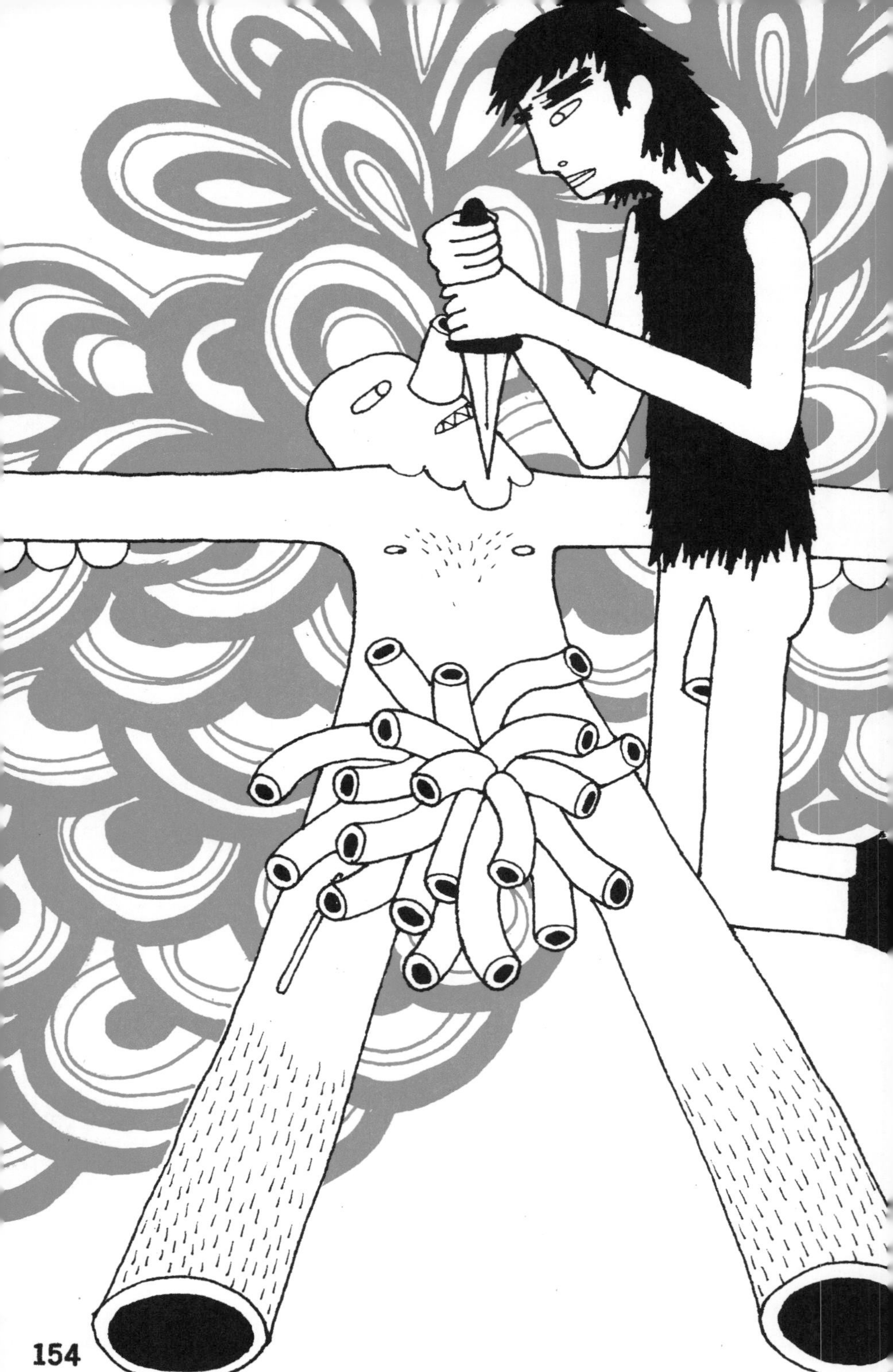

EXORCHASM

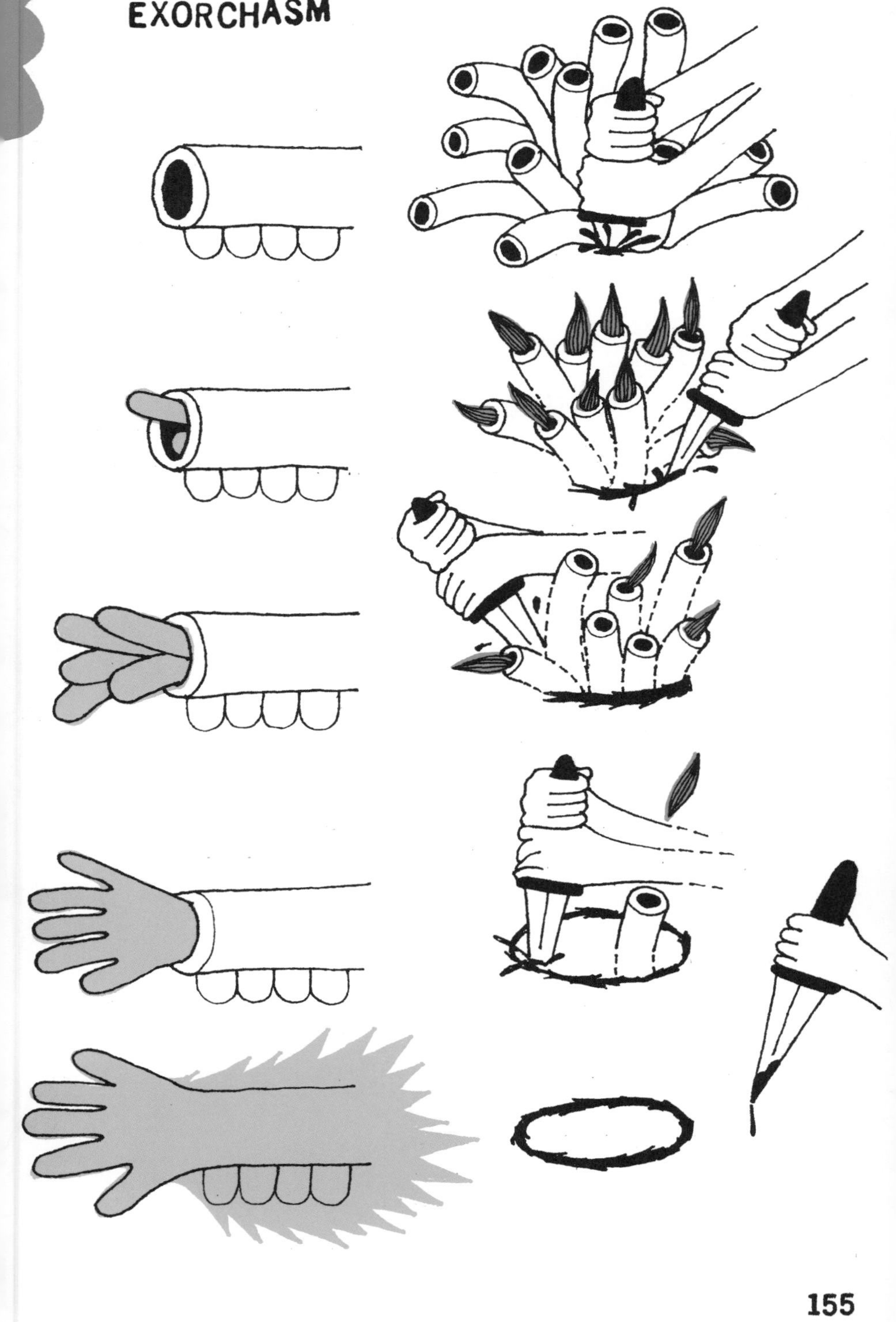

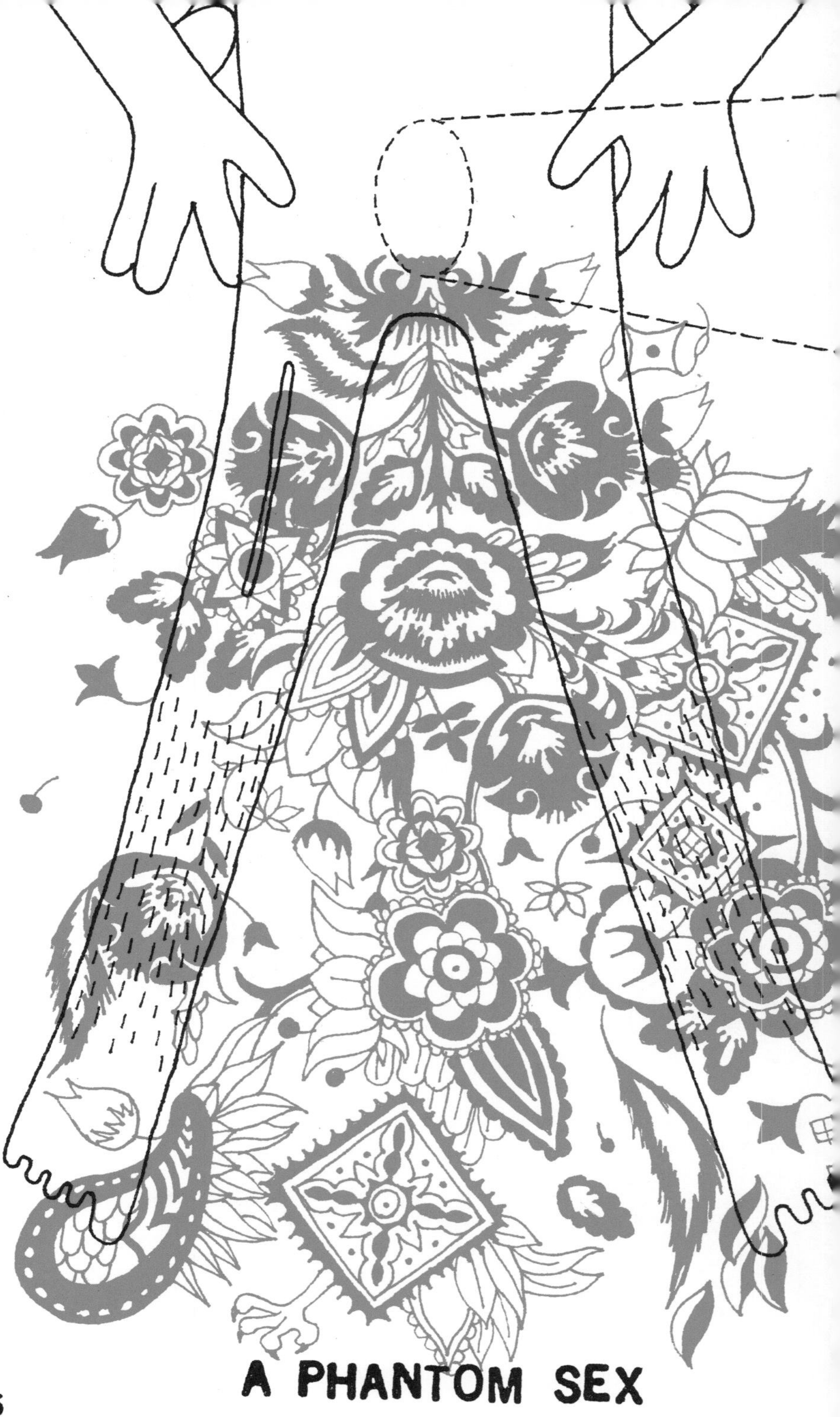

A PHANTOM SEX

IT IS WHAT I HAVE WANTED

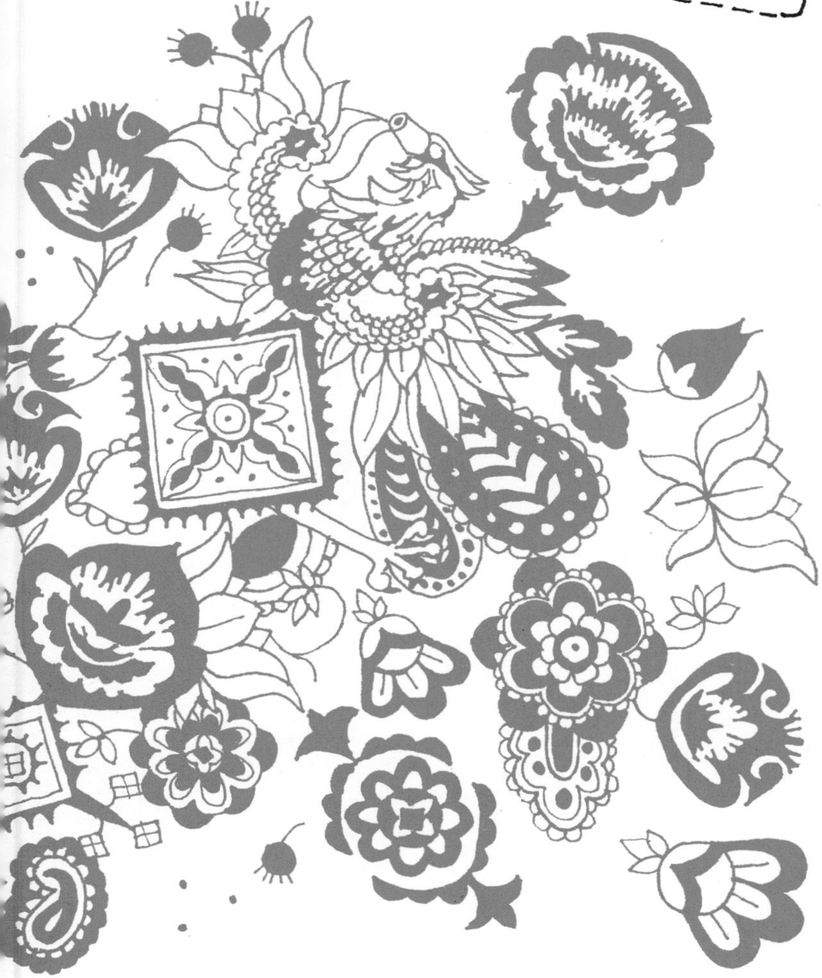

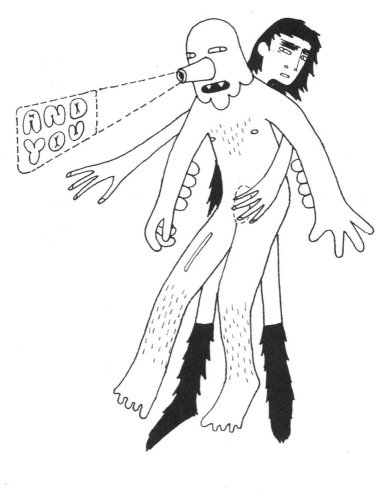

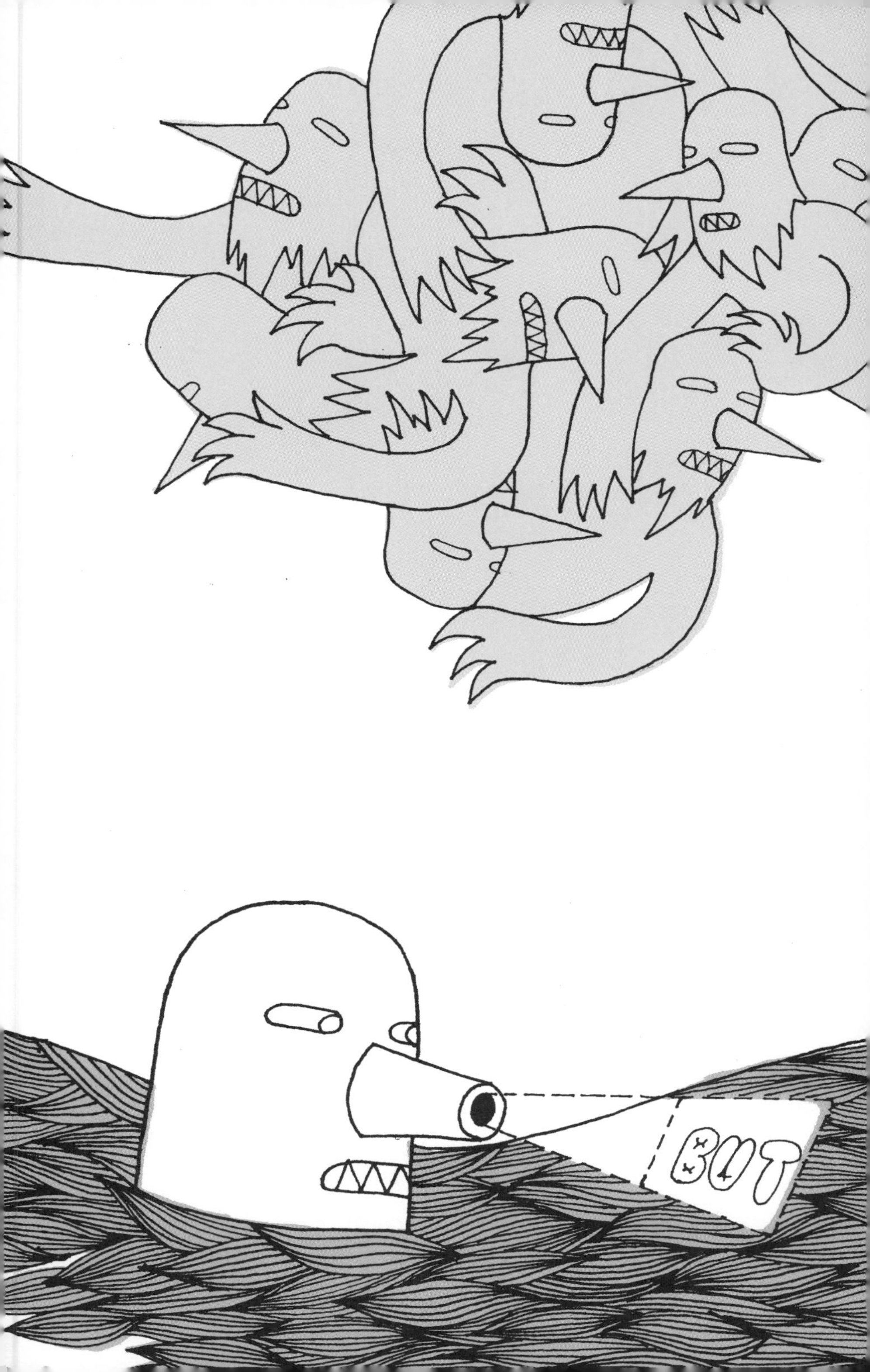
BUT

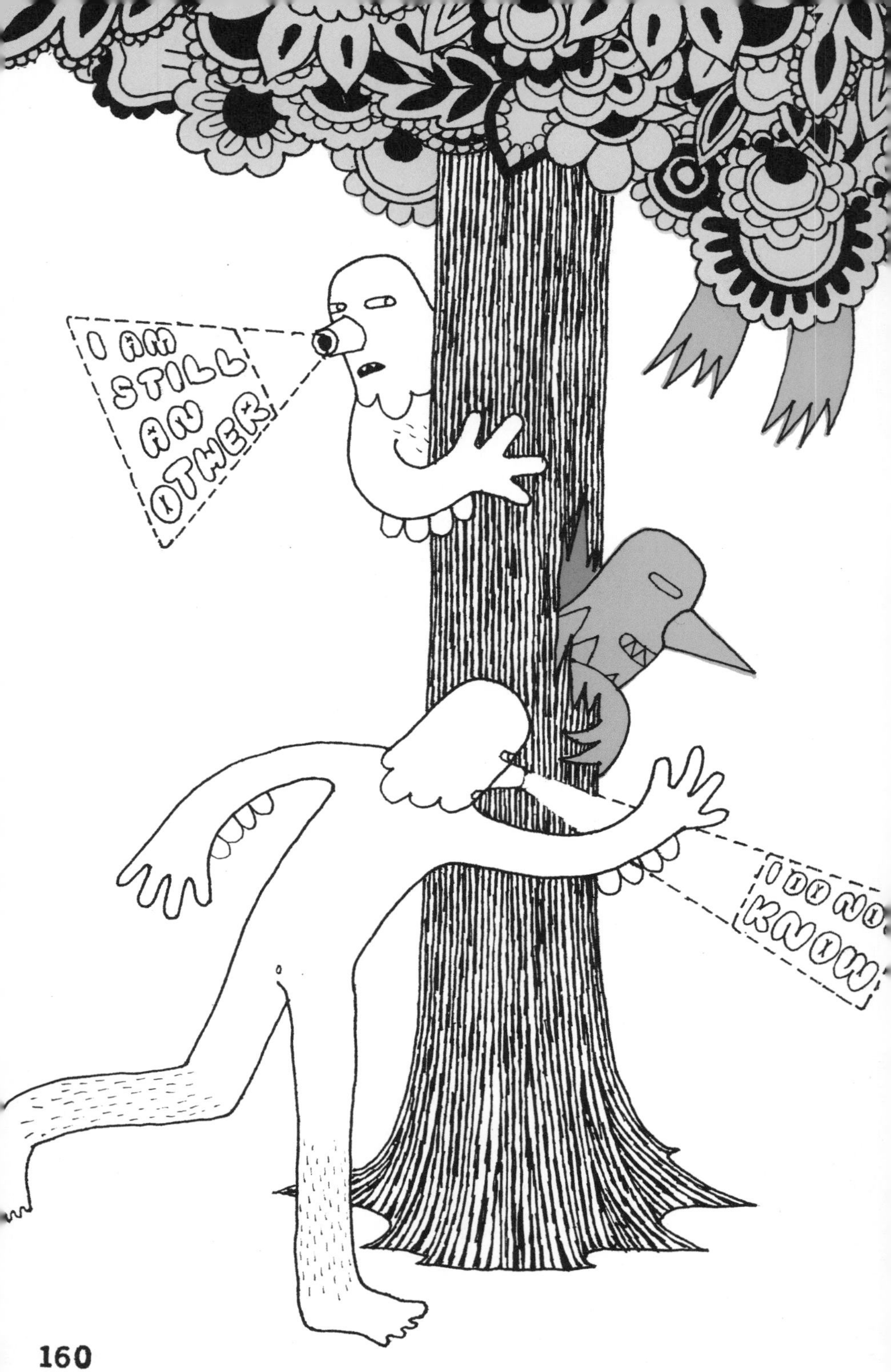
I AM STILL AN OTHER
I DO NO
KNOW

ALL MEMORIE
WILL RETURN

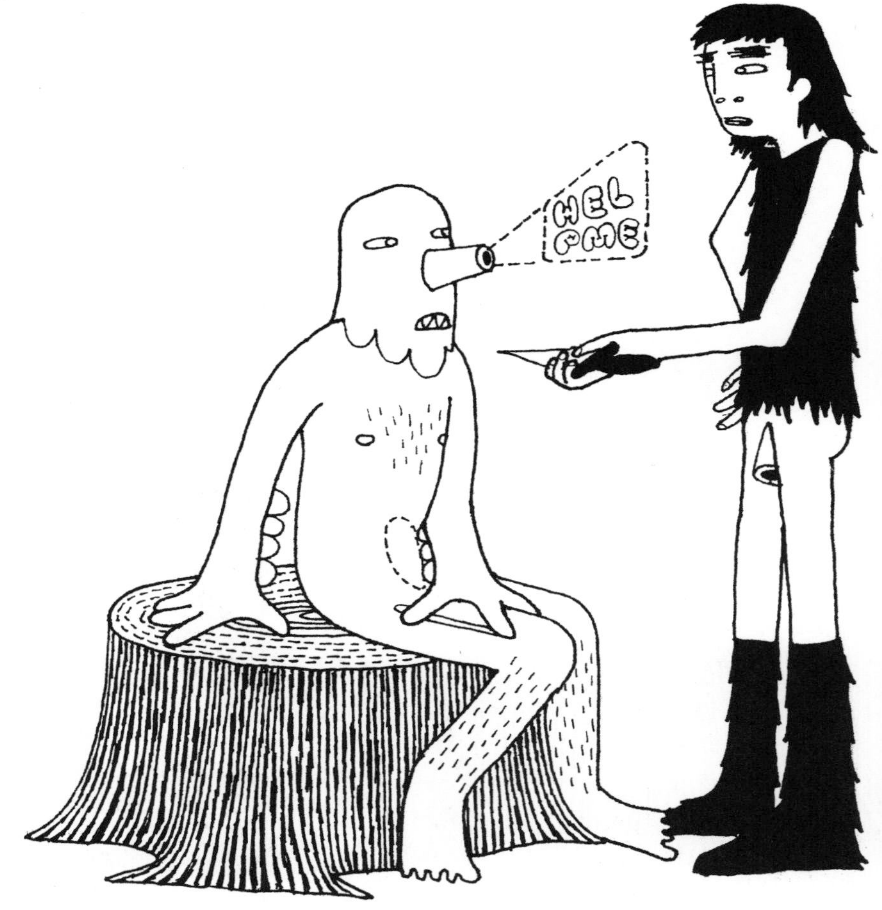
HEL
PME

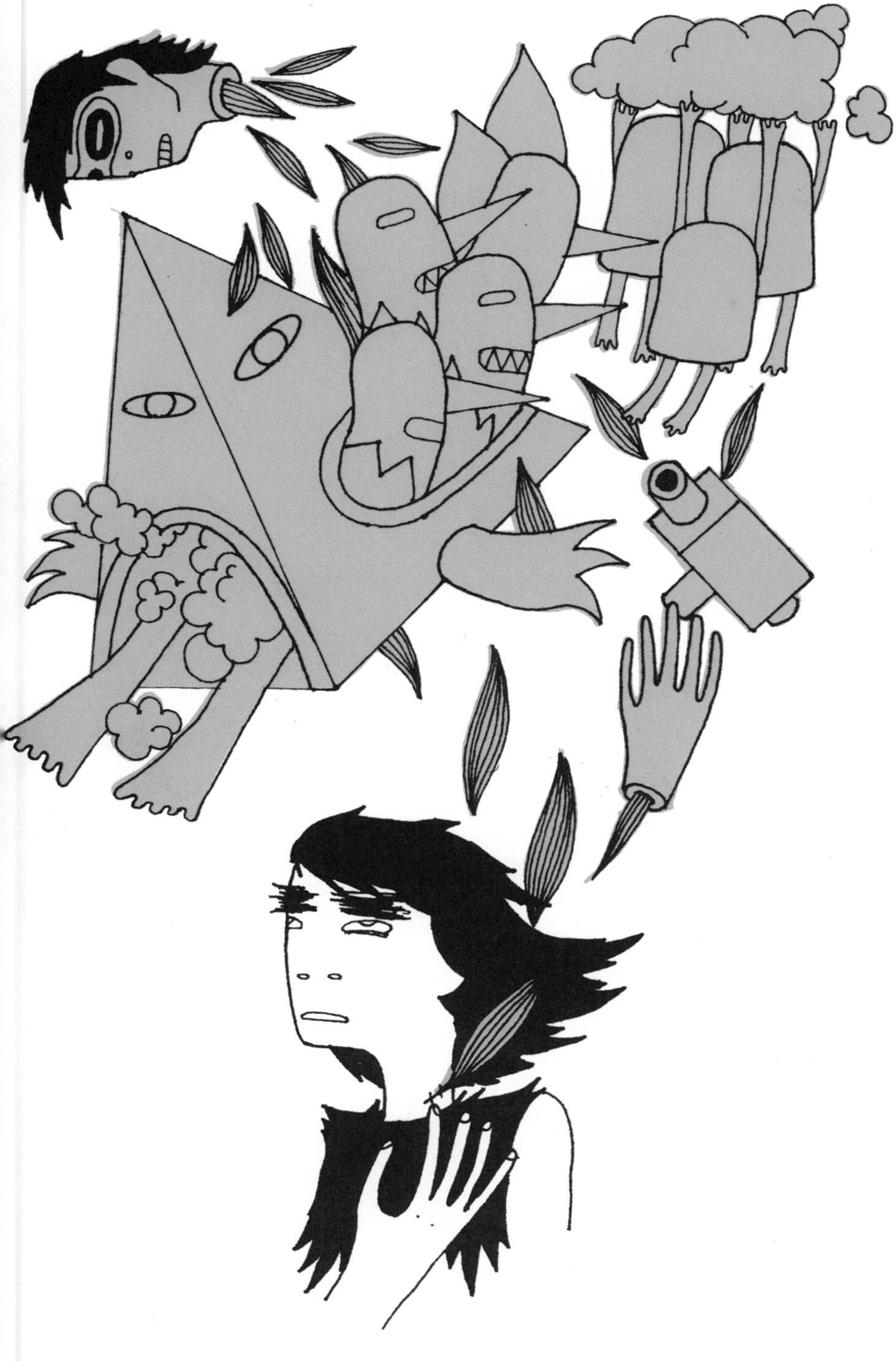

HELP YRSELF

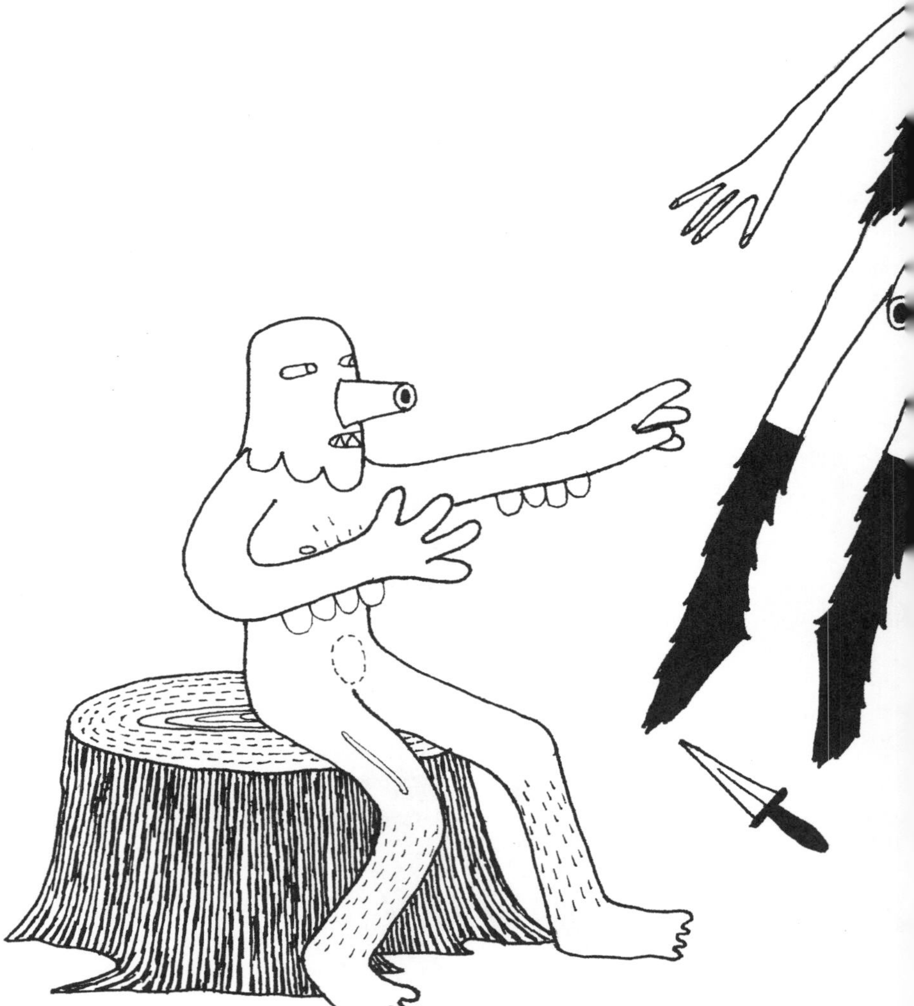

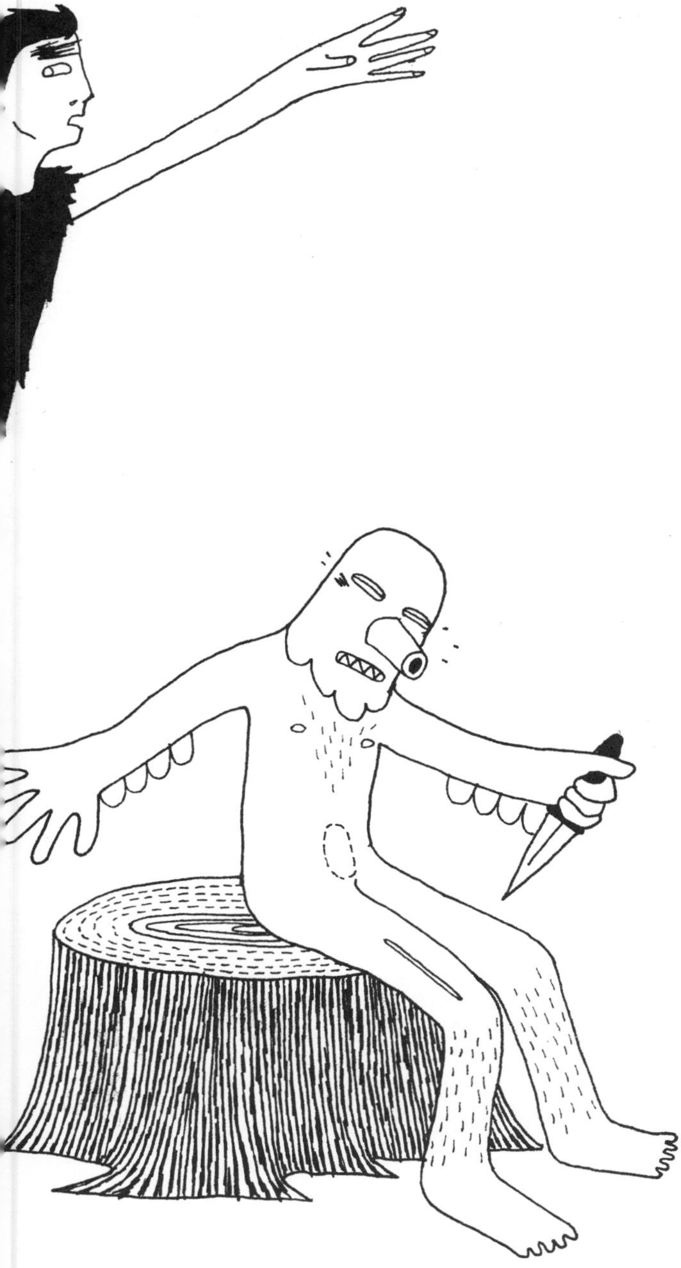

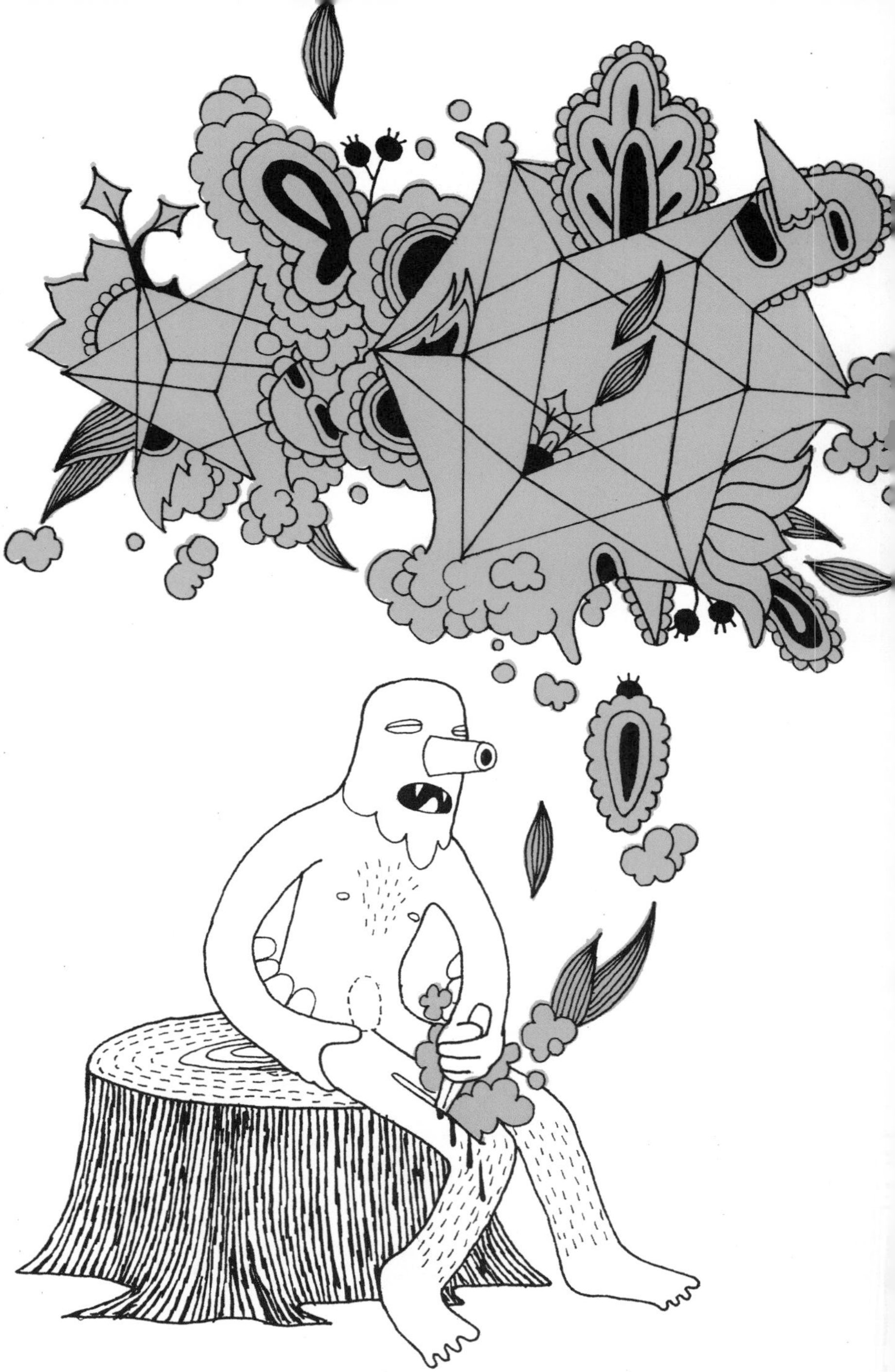

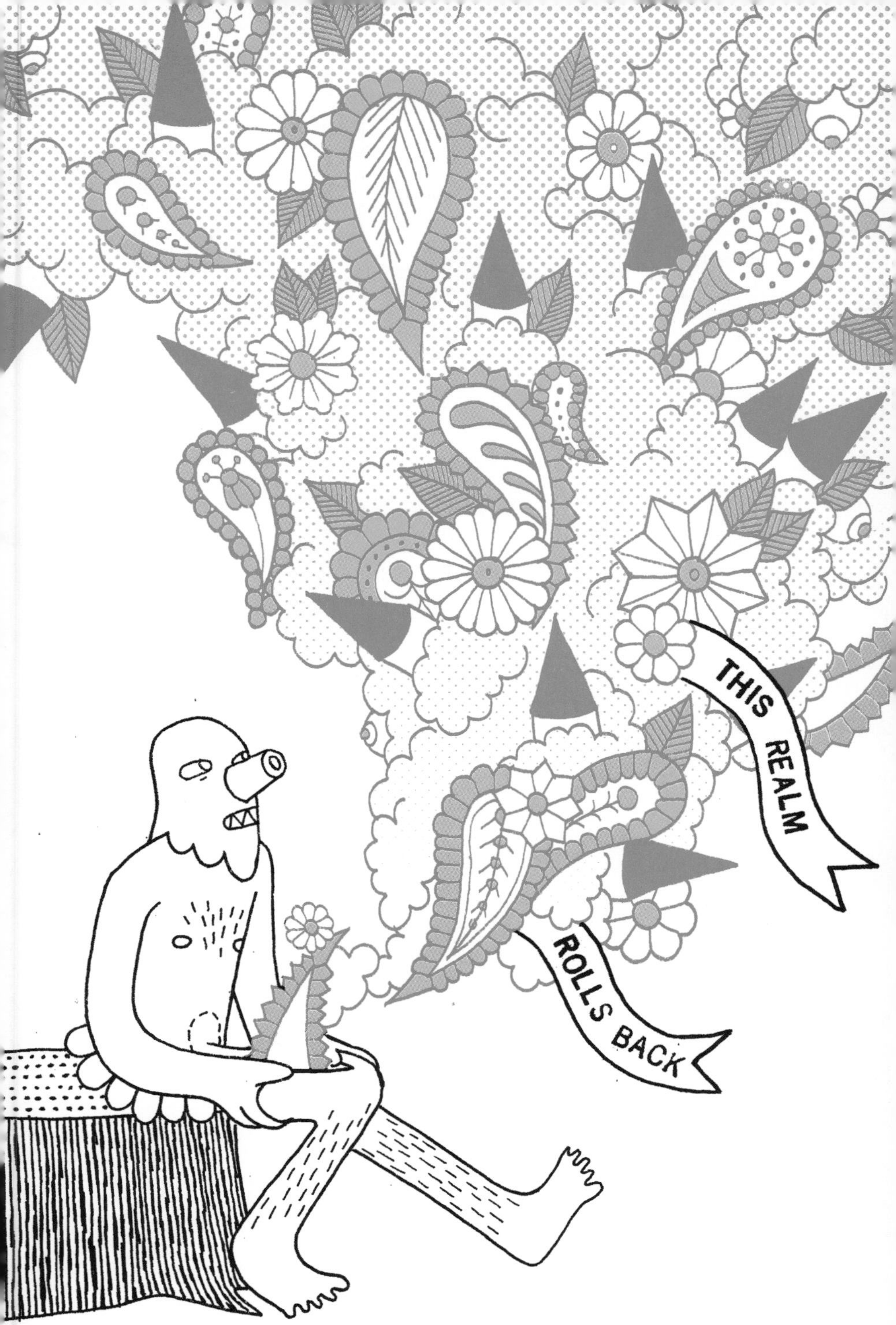
THIS REALM
ROLLS BACK

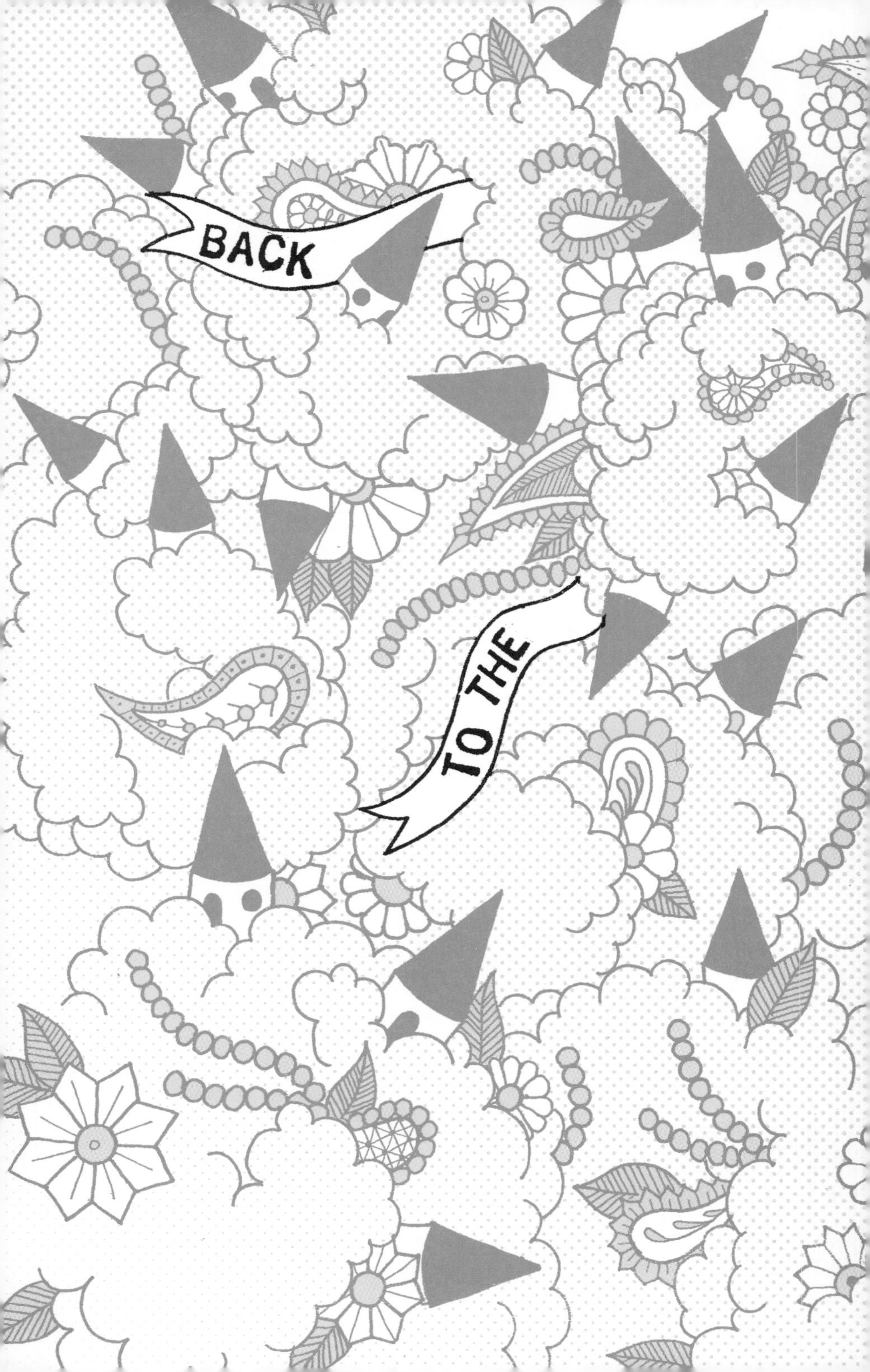
BACK
TO THE

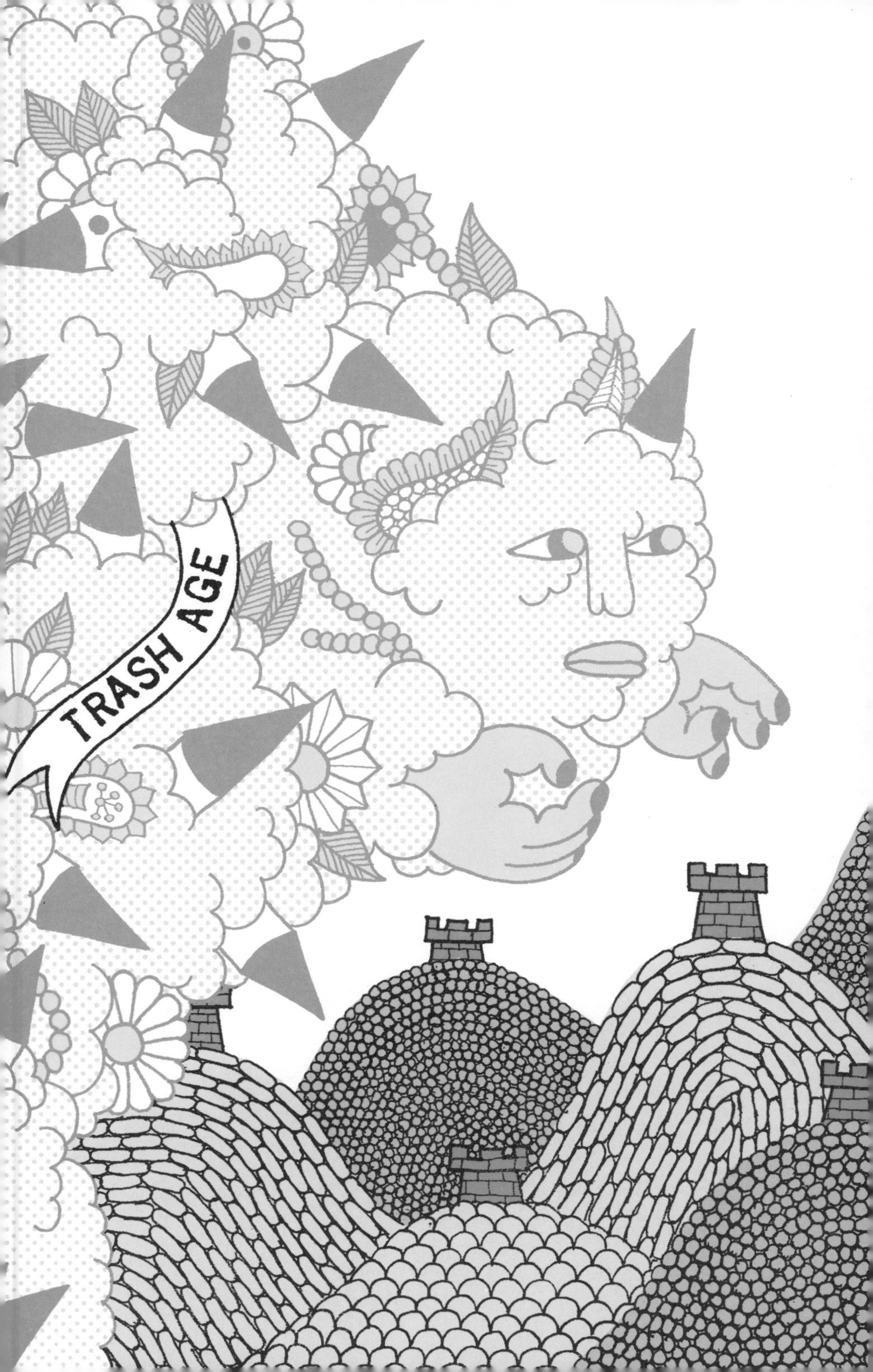
TRASH AGE

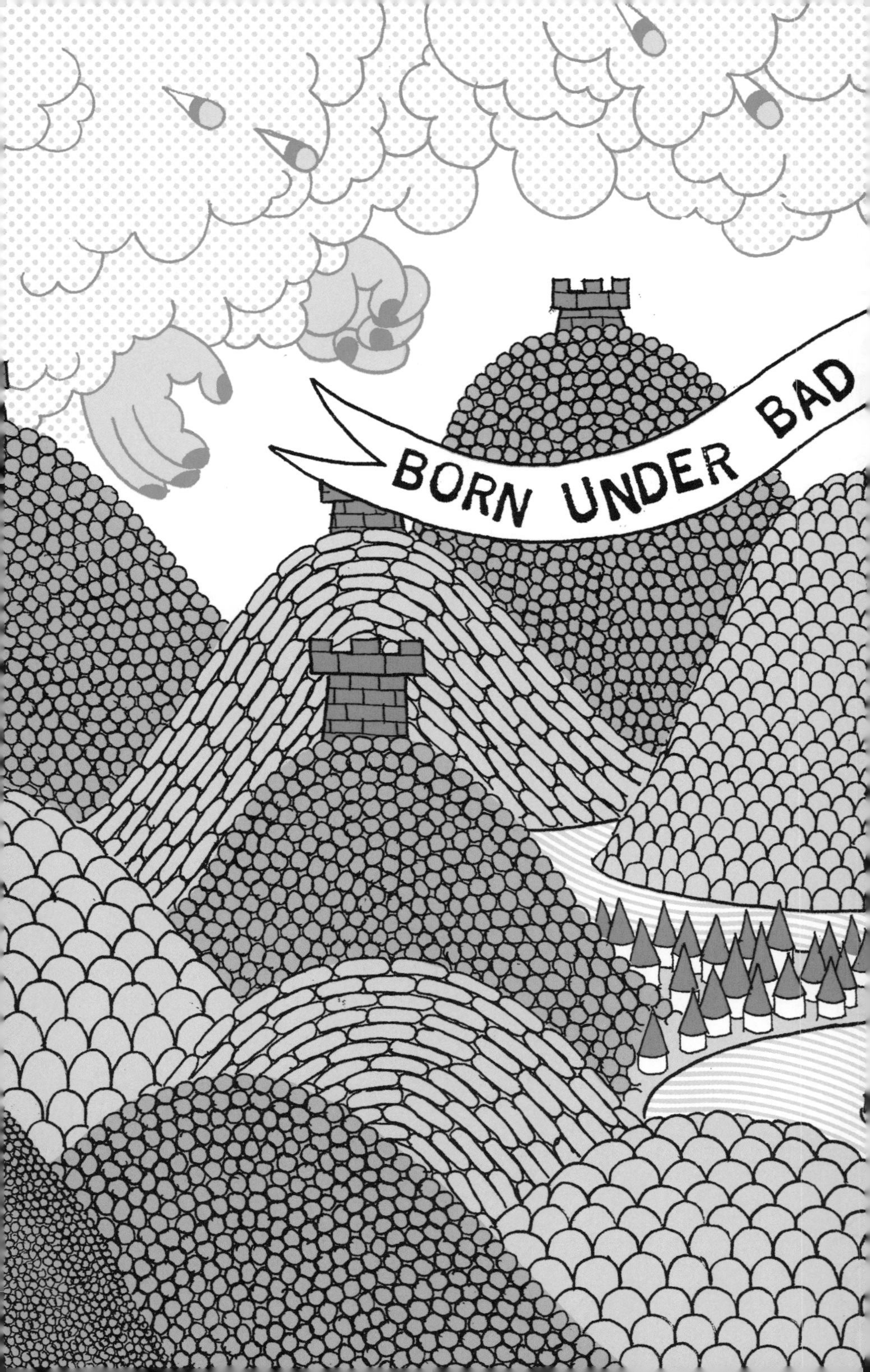
BORN UNDER BAD

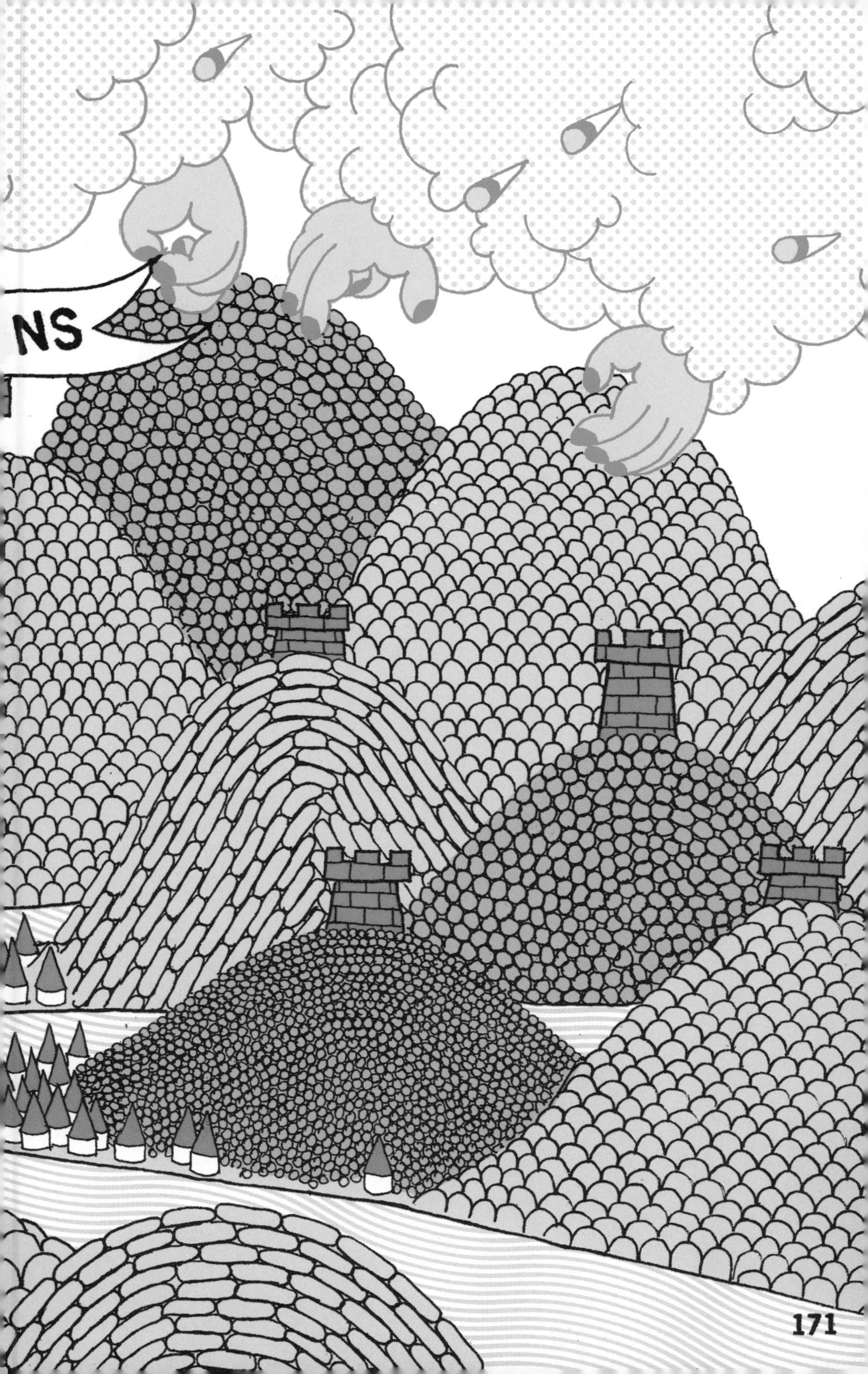
NS

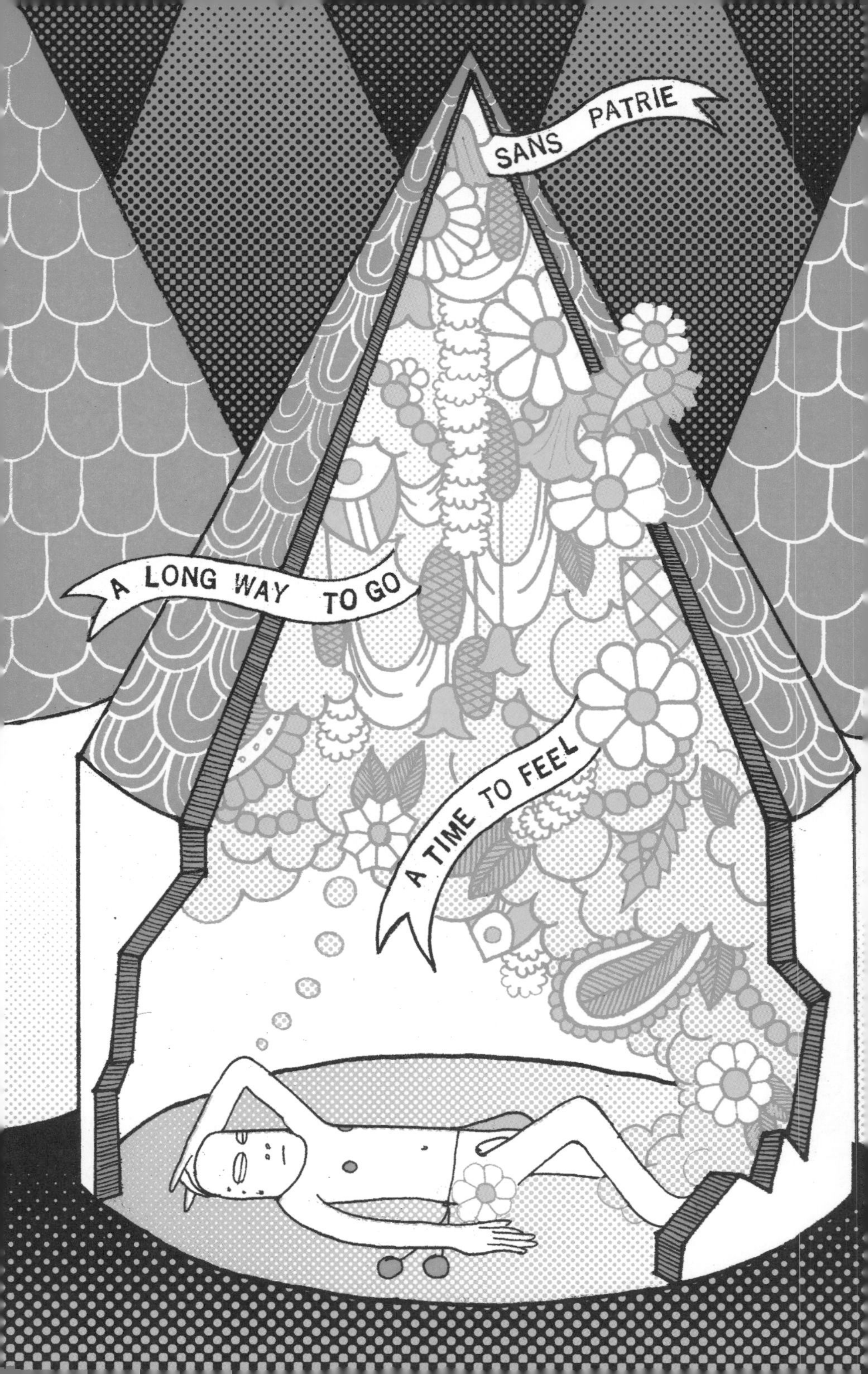
SANS PATRIE
A LONG WAY TO GO
A TIME TO FEEL

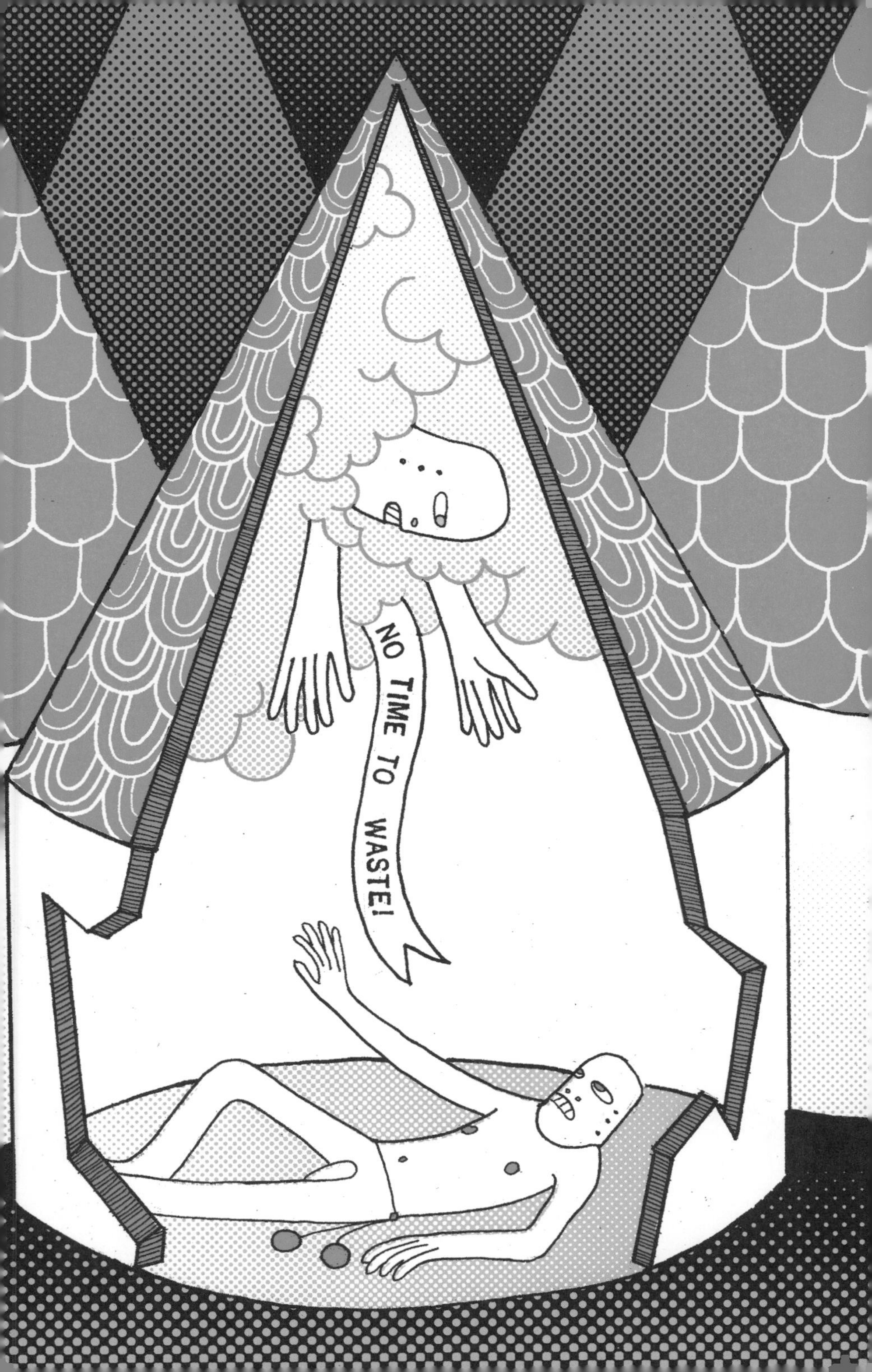
NO TIME TO WASTE!

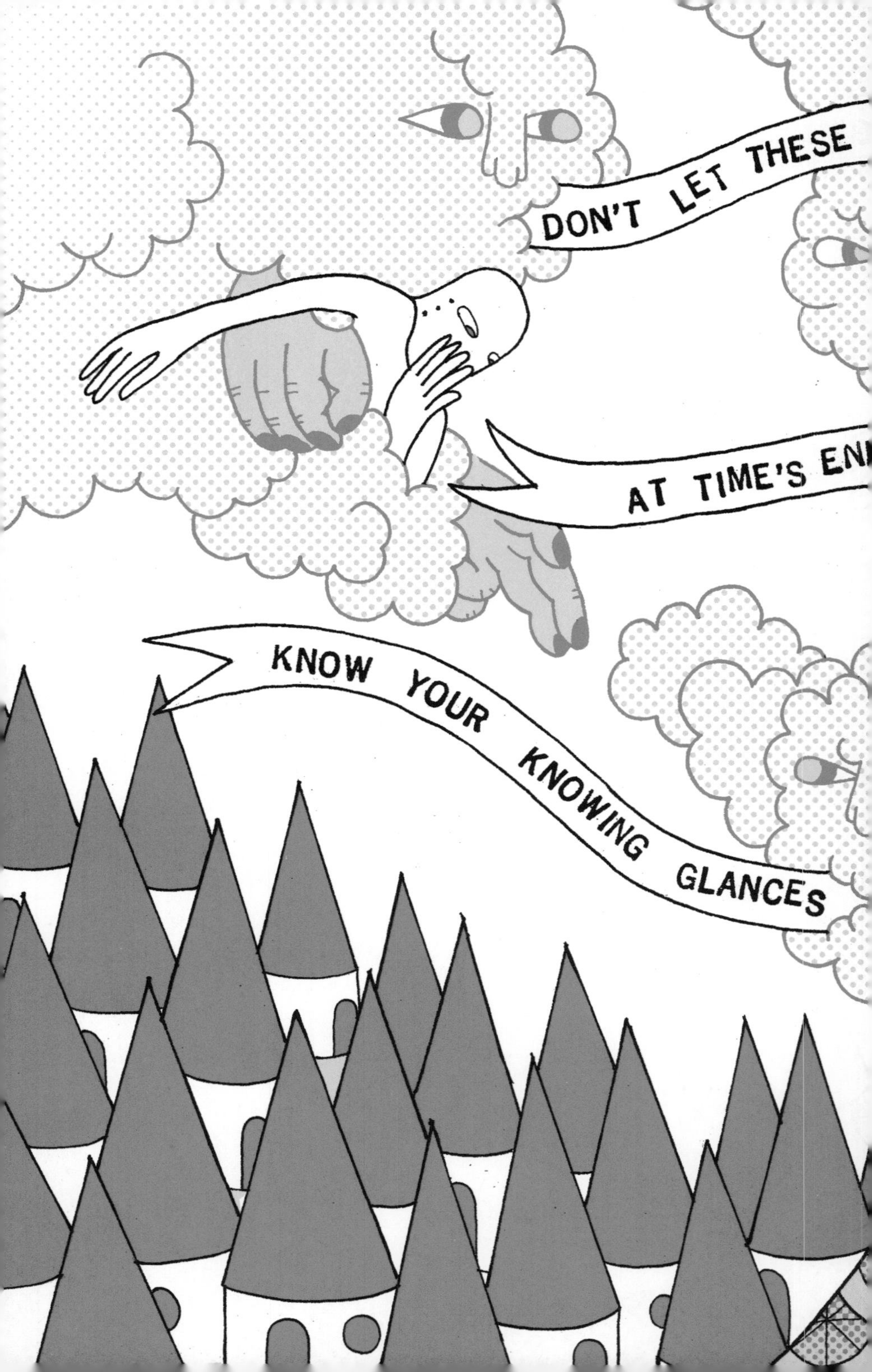
DON'T LET THESE
AT TIME'S EN
KNOW YOUR KNOWING GLANCES

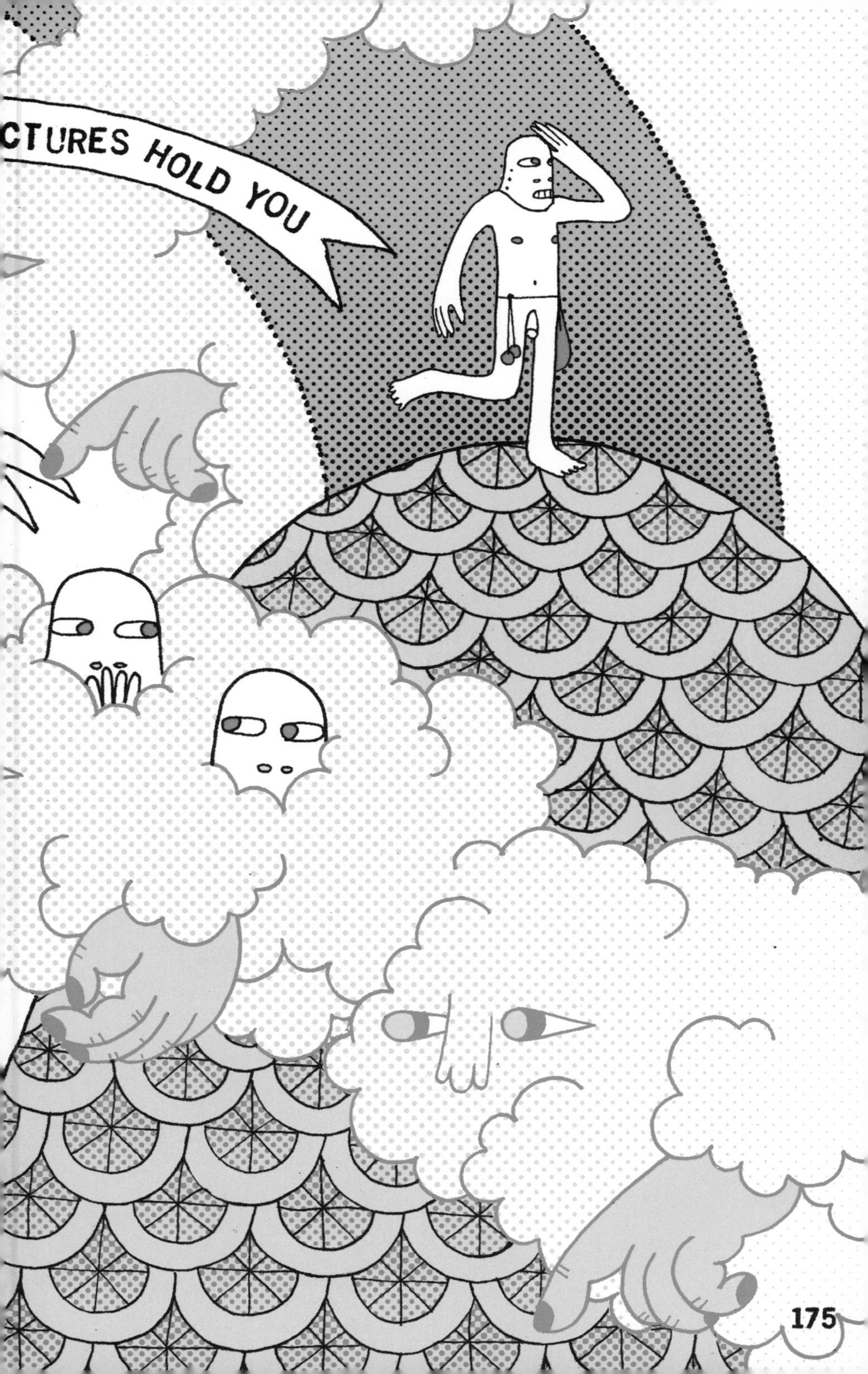
CTURES HOLD YOU

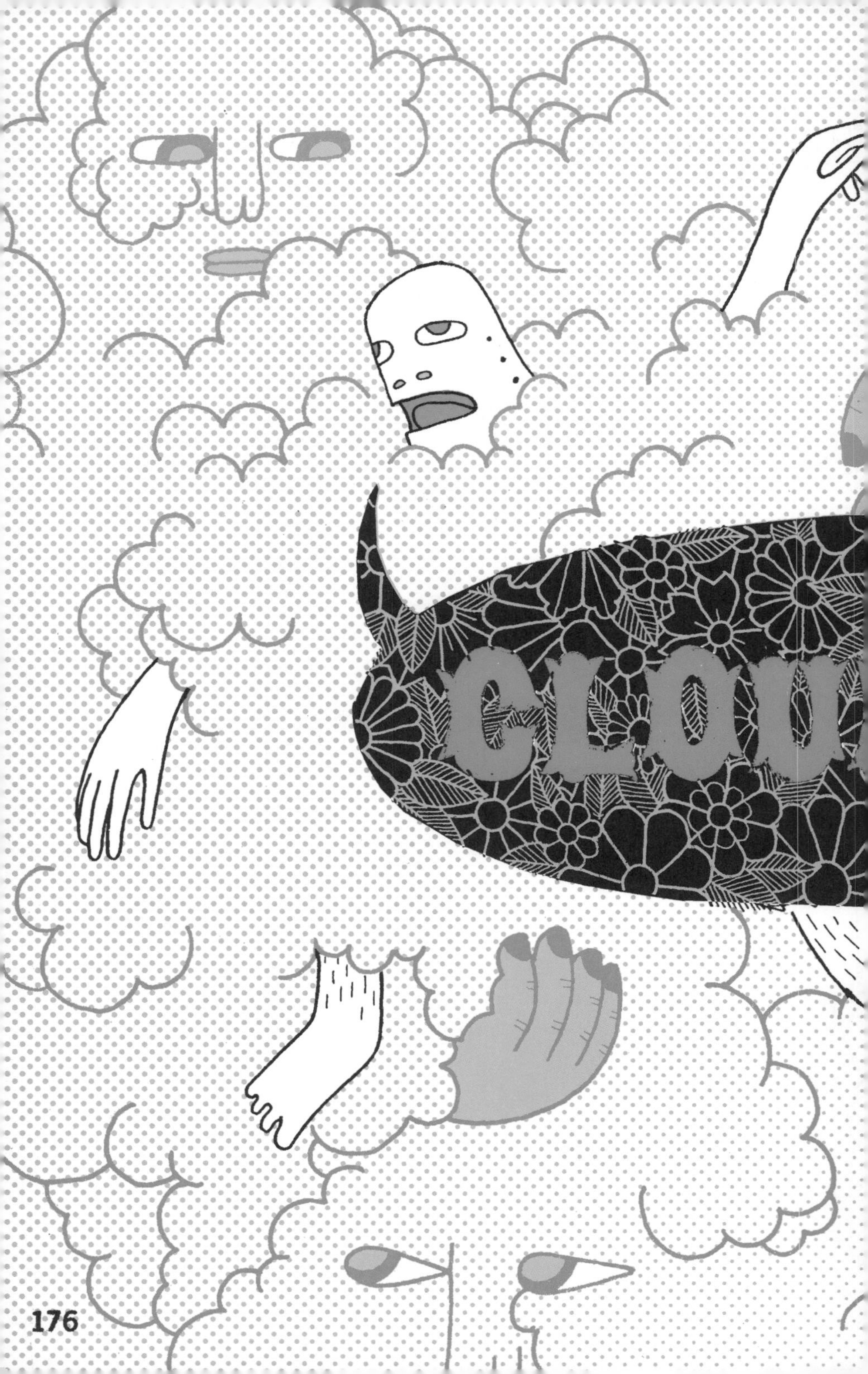
CLOU

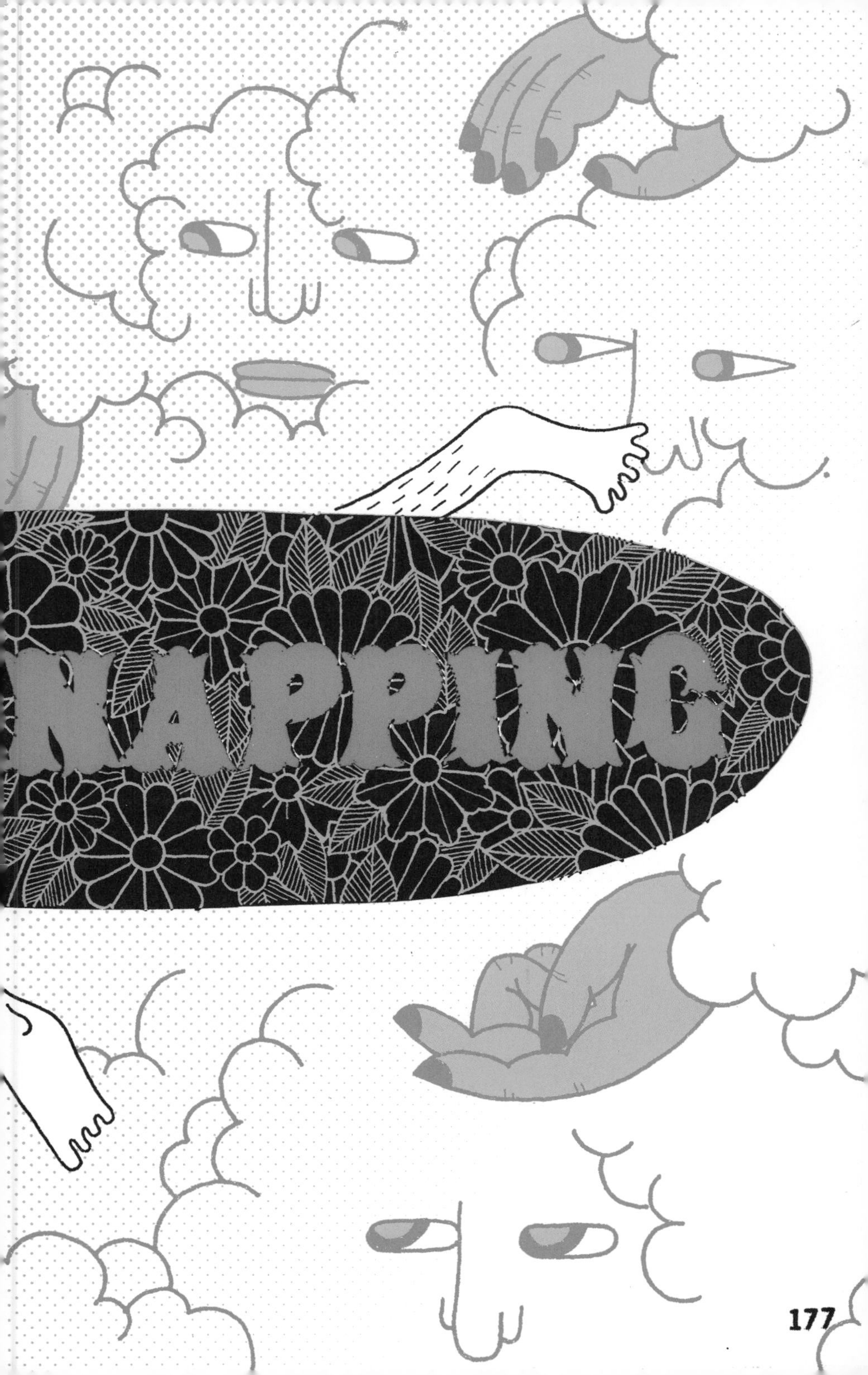
NAPPING

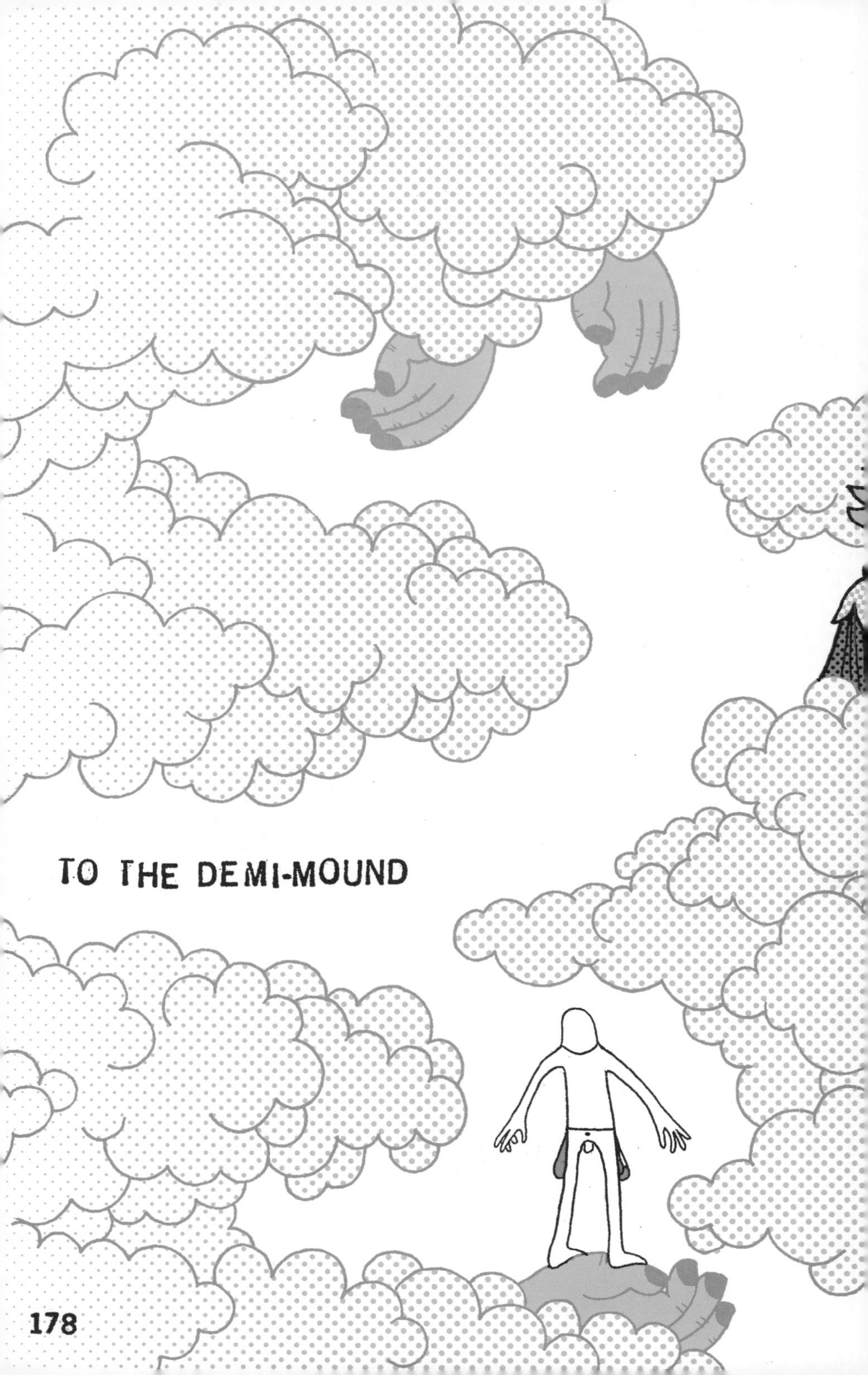
TO THE DEMI-MOUND

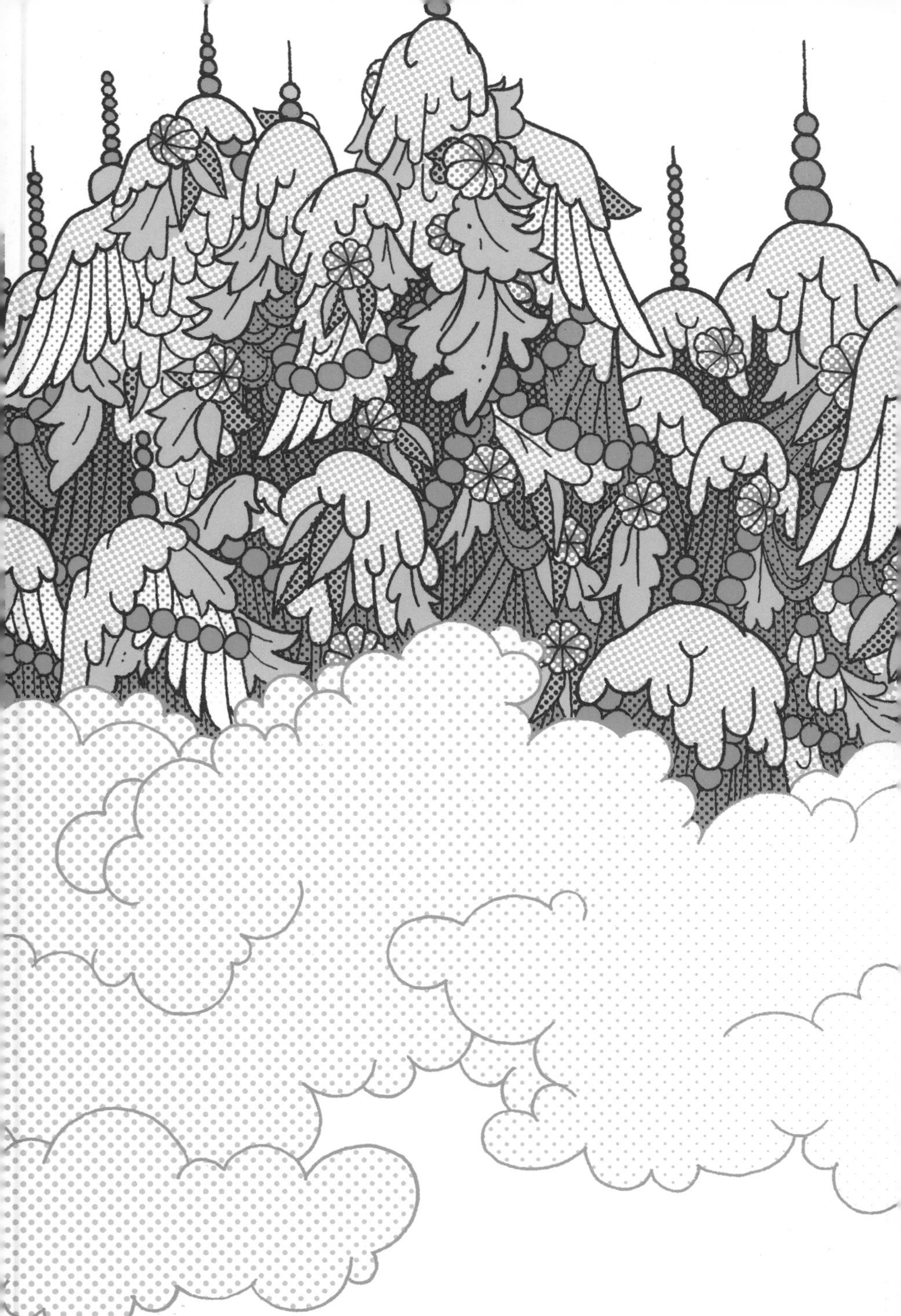

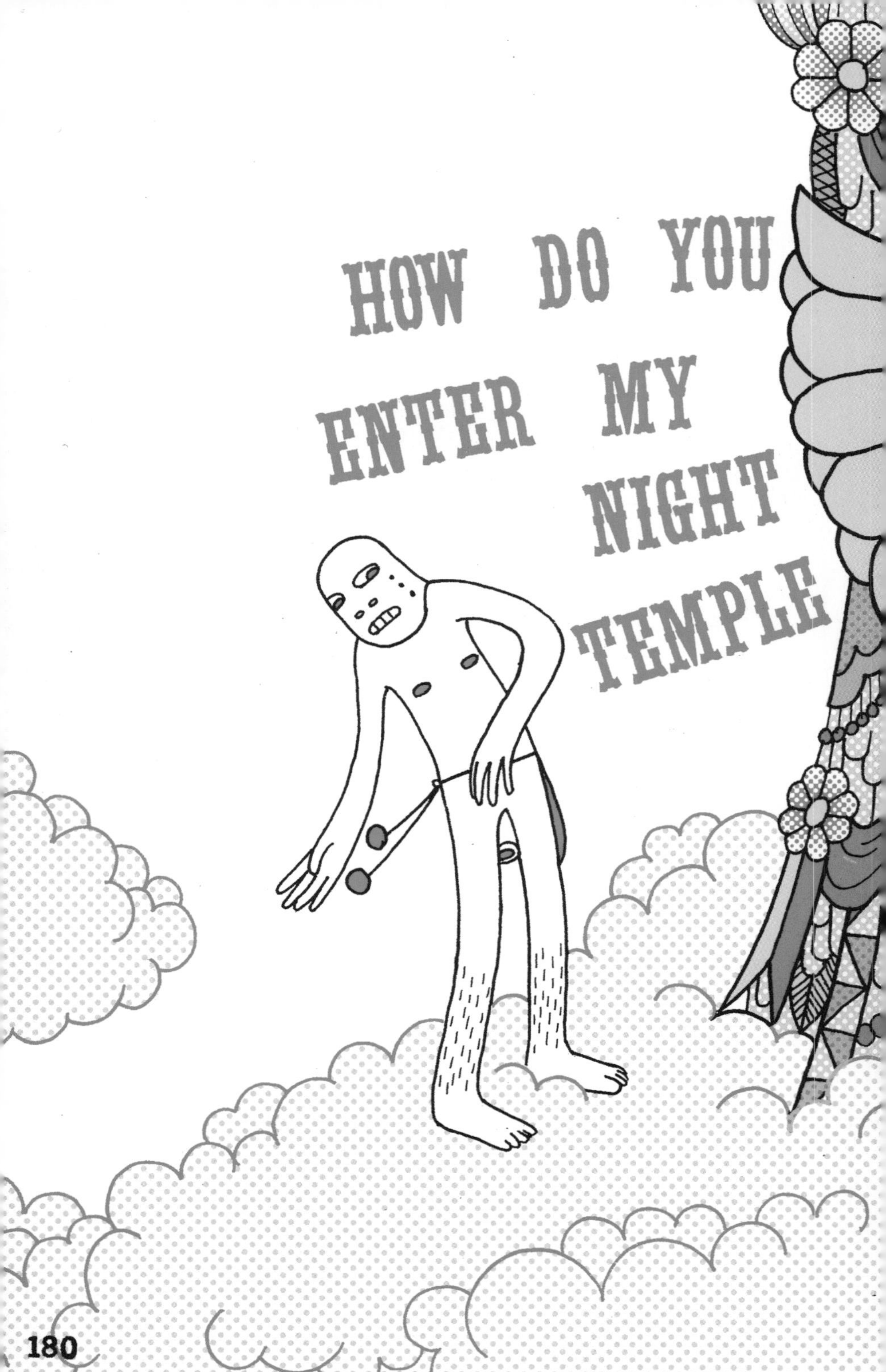
HOW DO YOU
ENTER MY
NIGHT
TEMPLE

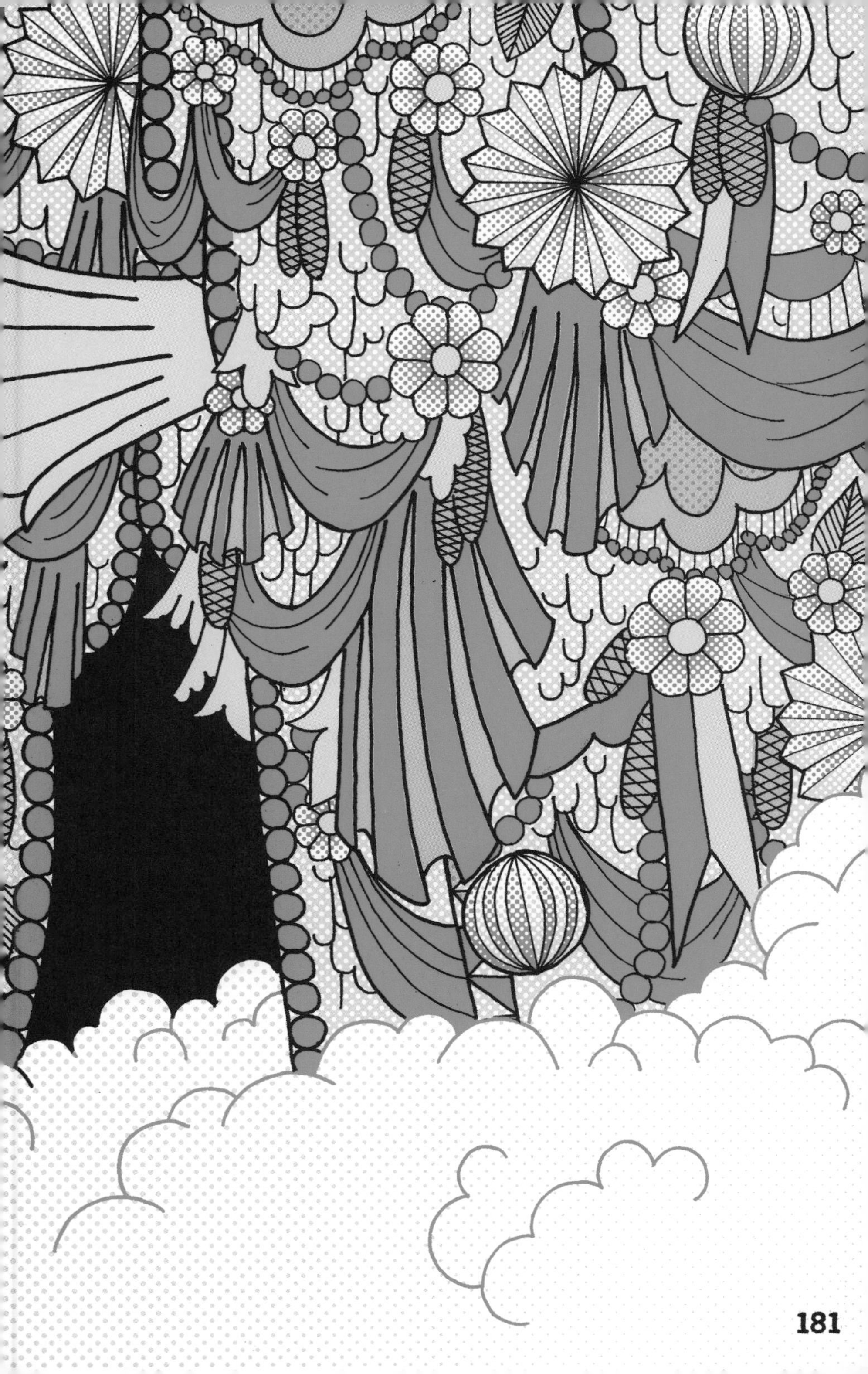

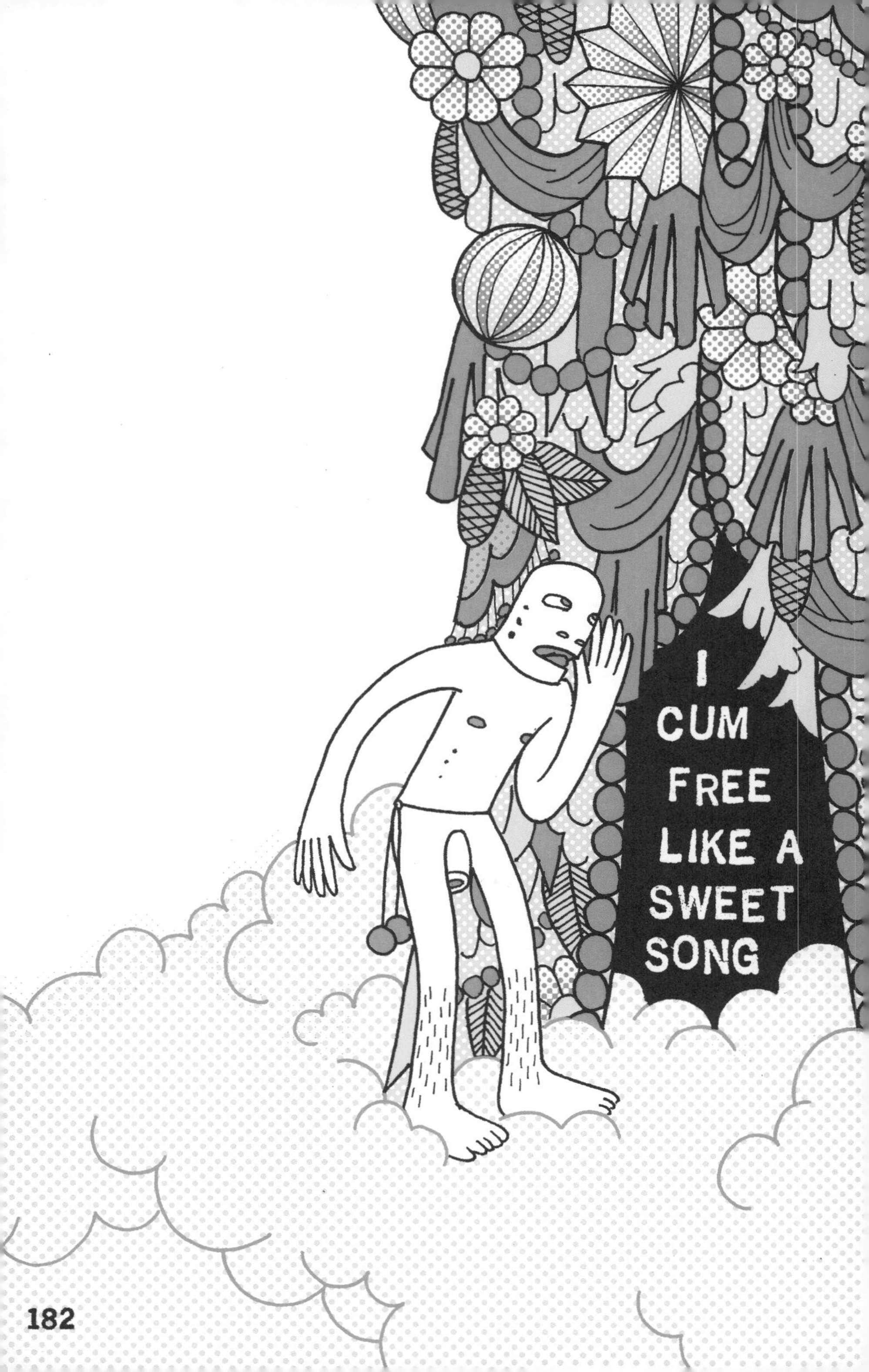
I CUM FREE LIKE A SWEET SONG

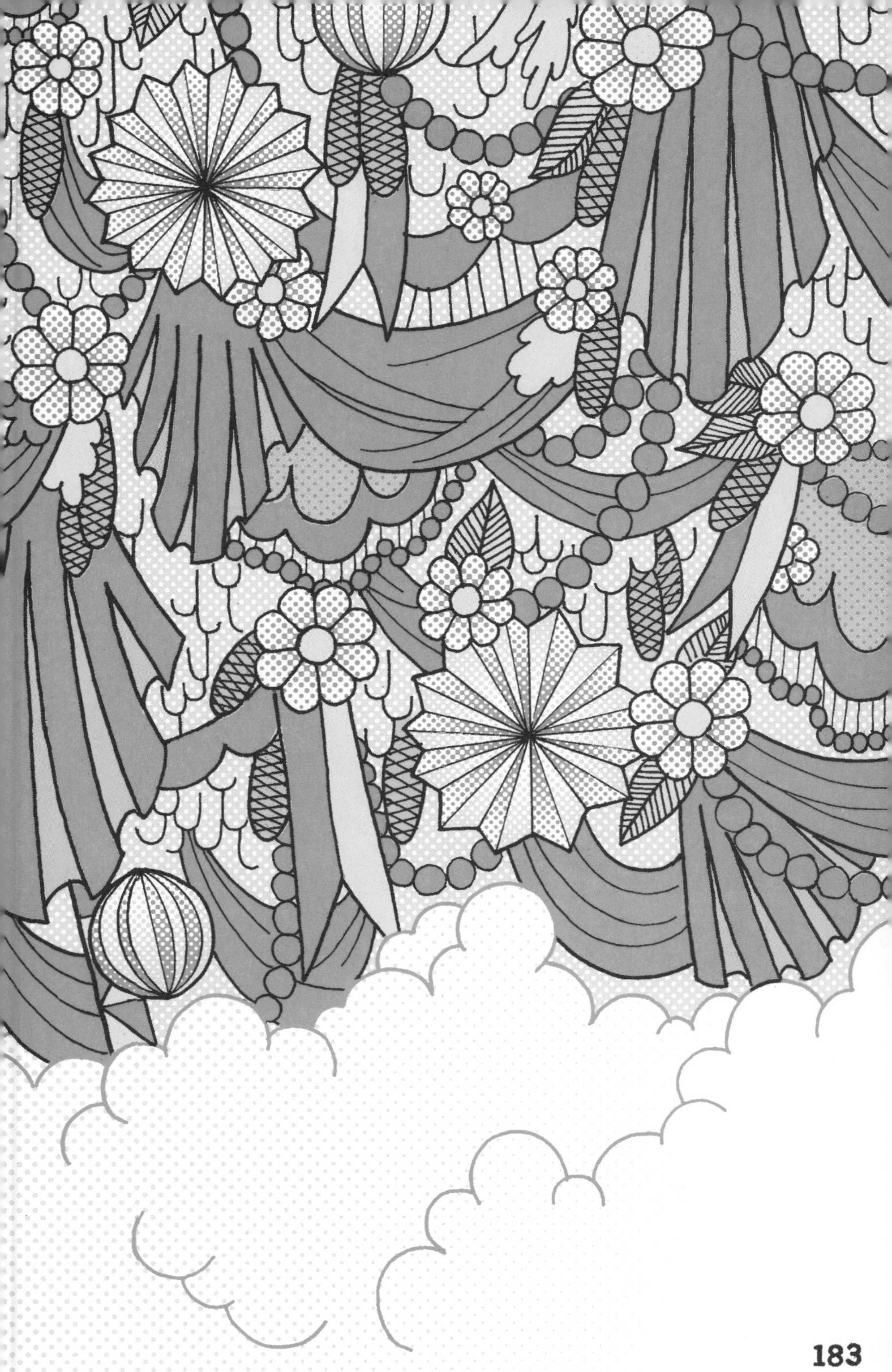

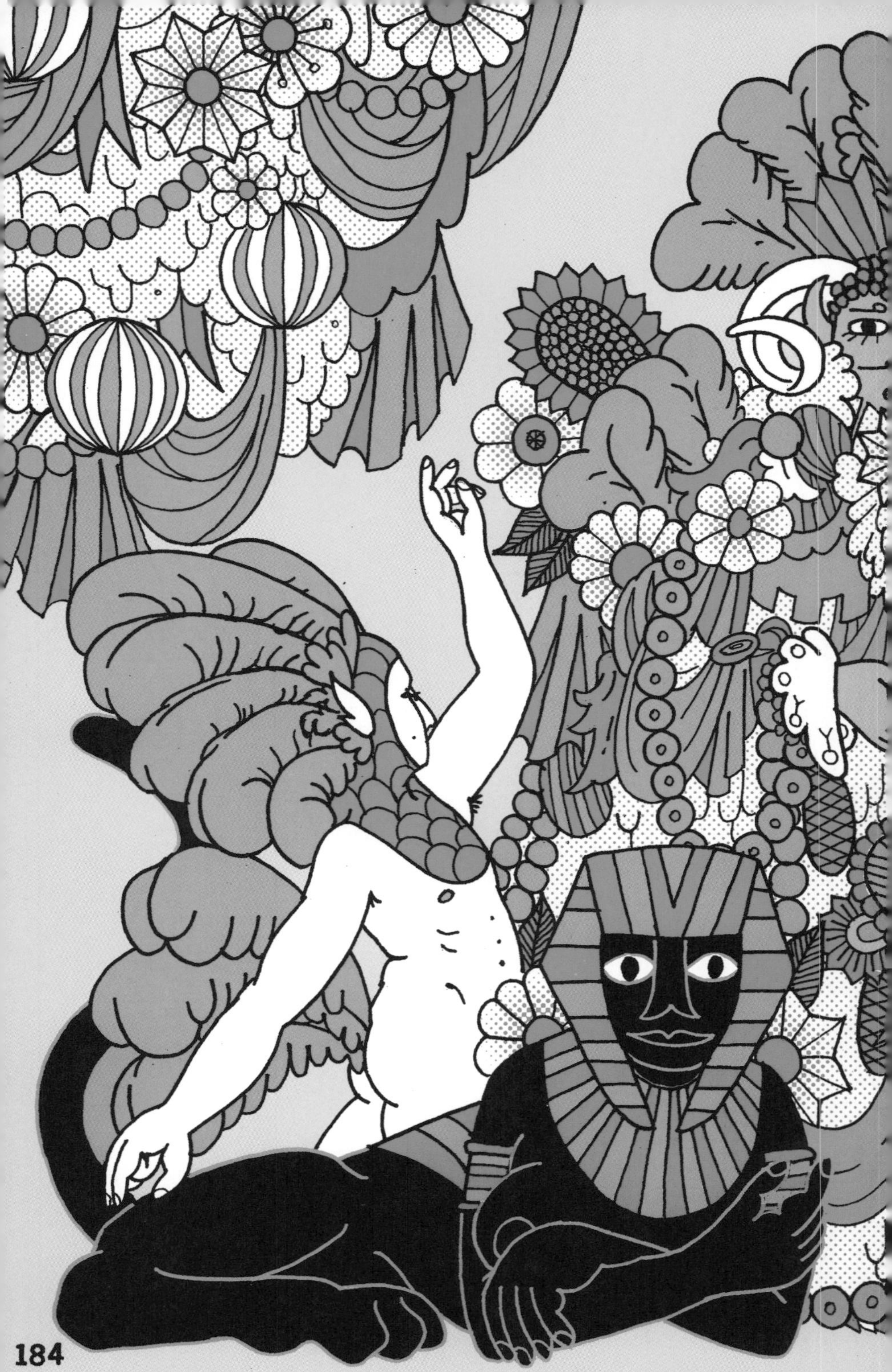

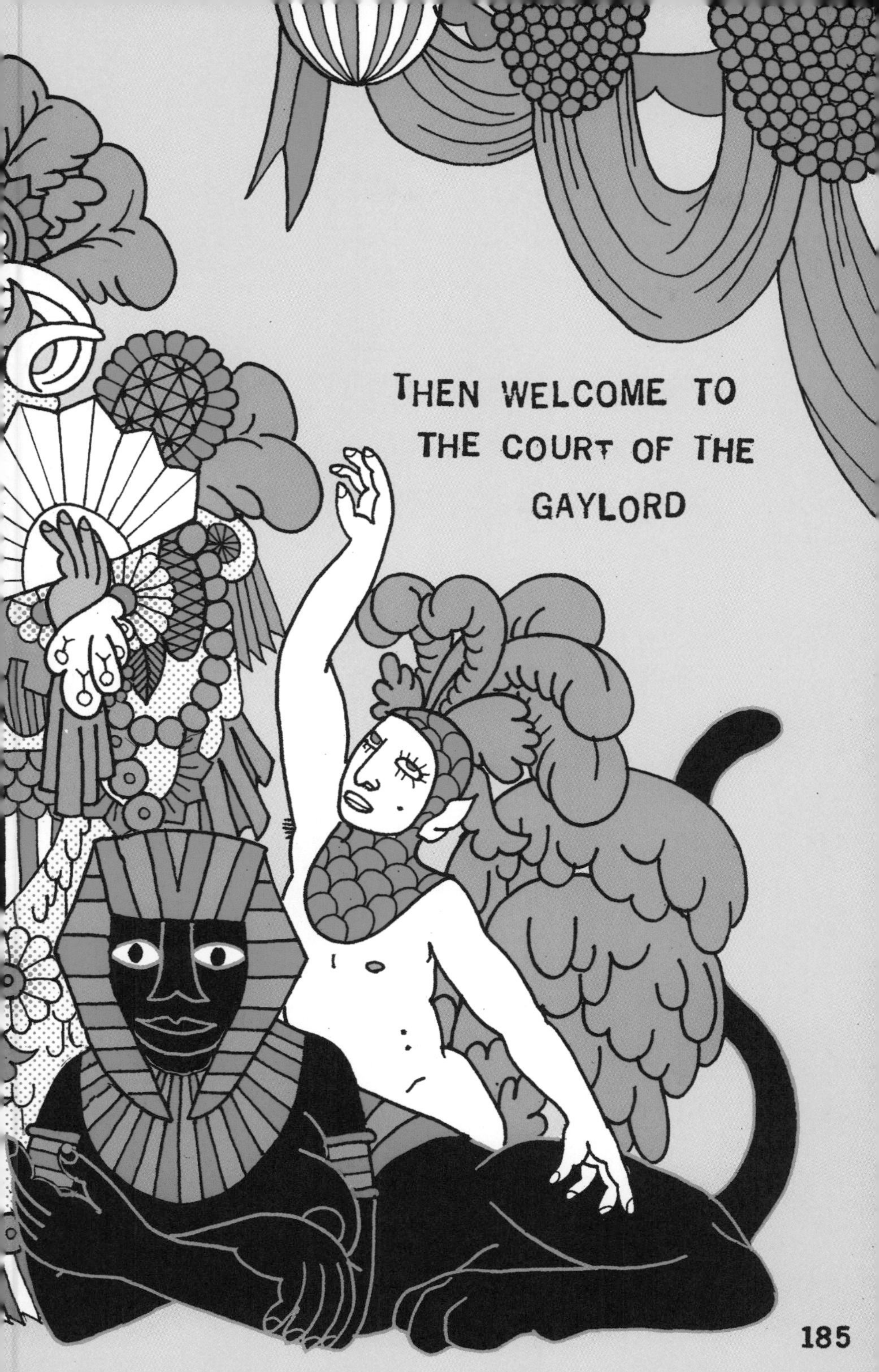
THEN WELCOME TO
THE COURT OF THE
GAYLORD

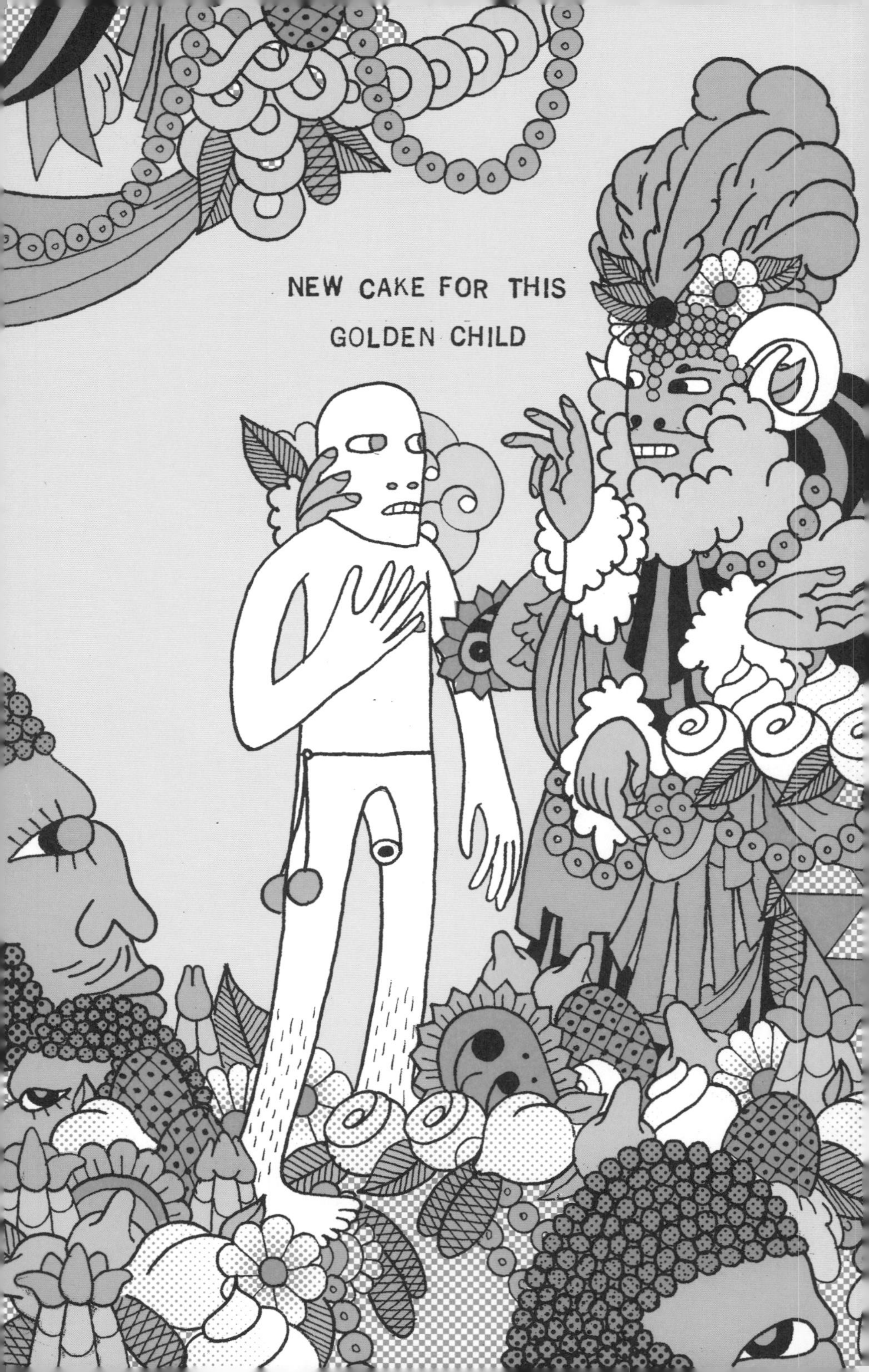
NEW CAKE FOR THIS
GOLDEN CHILD

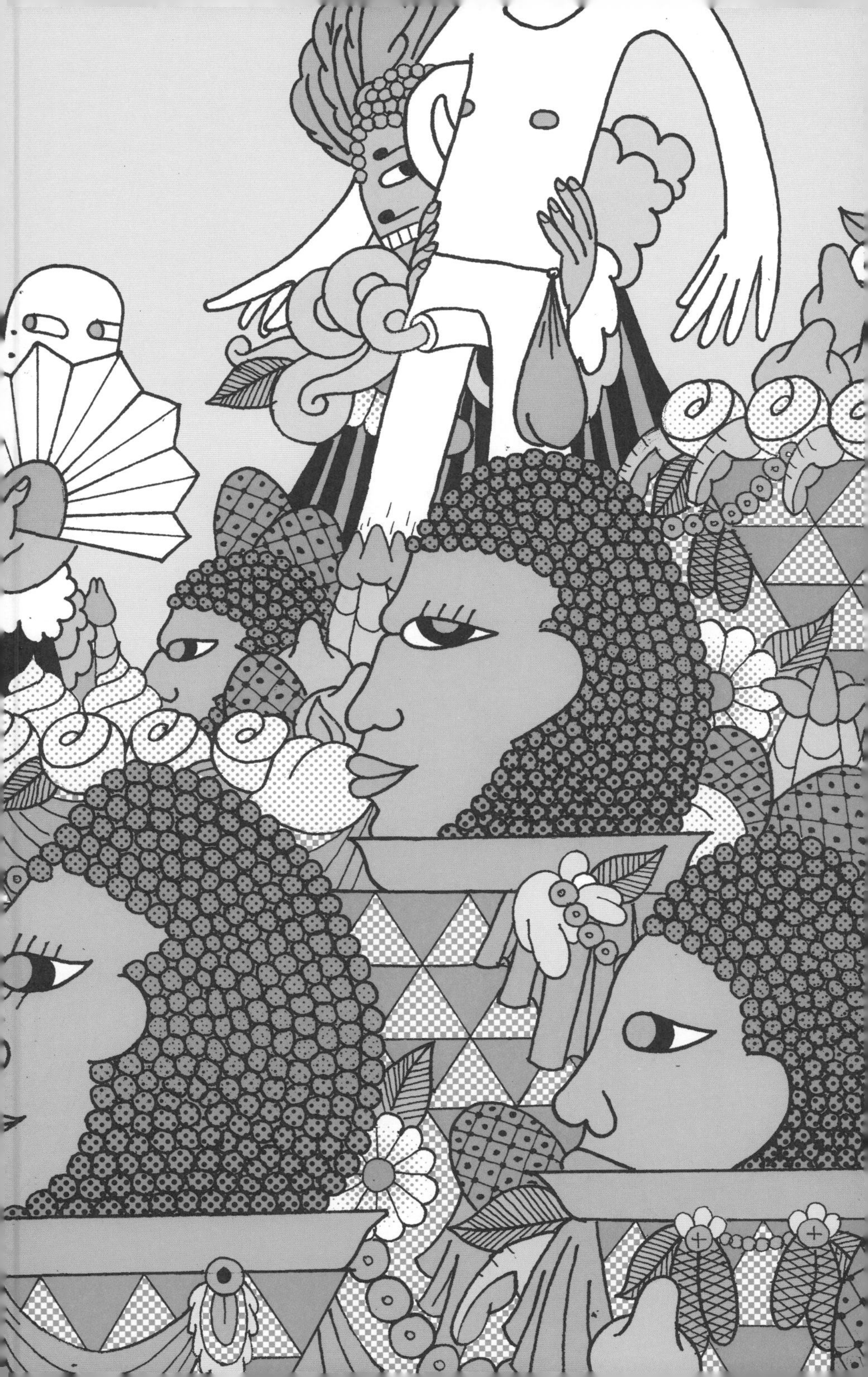

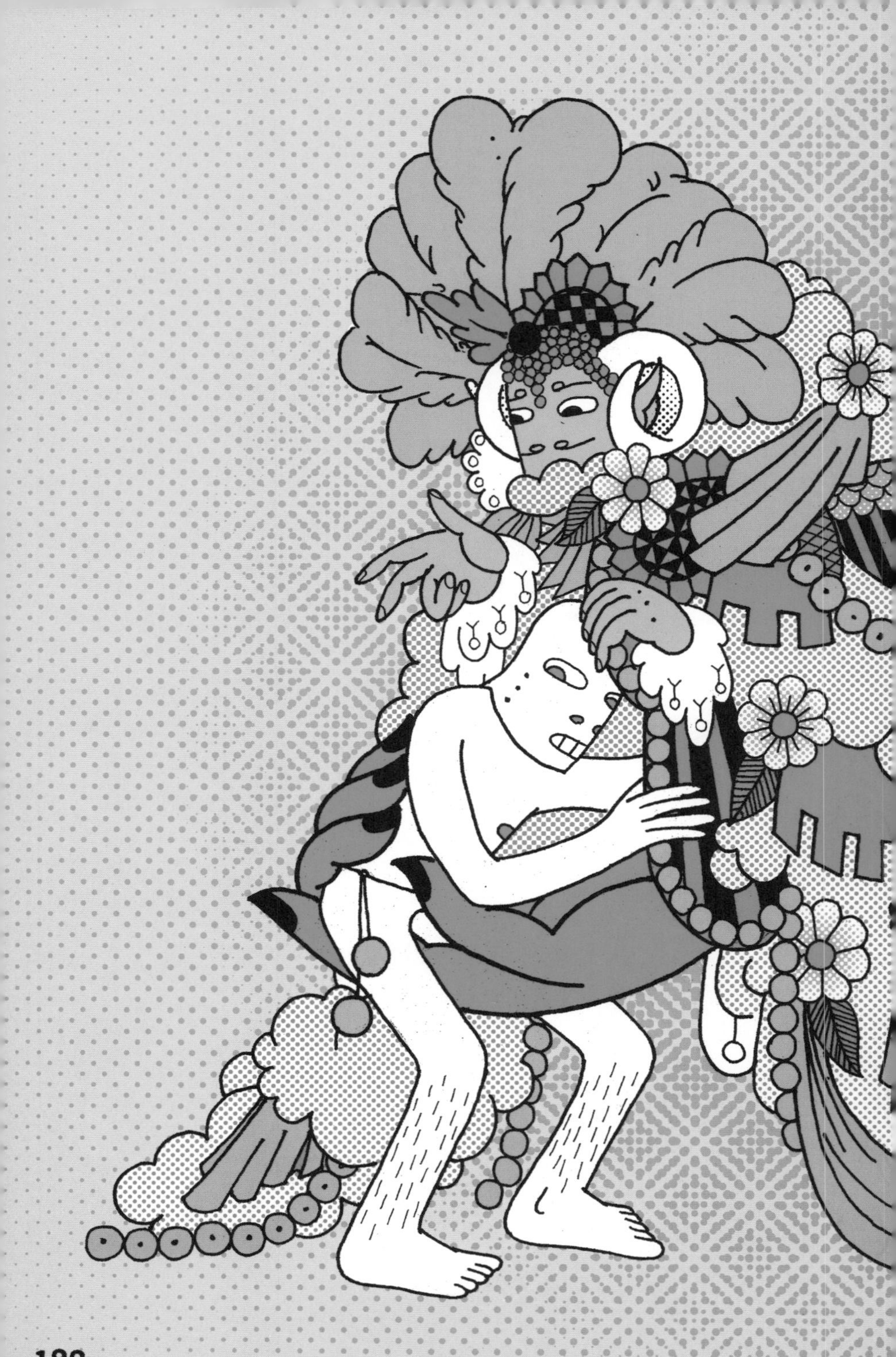

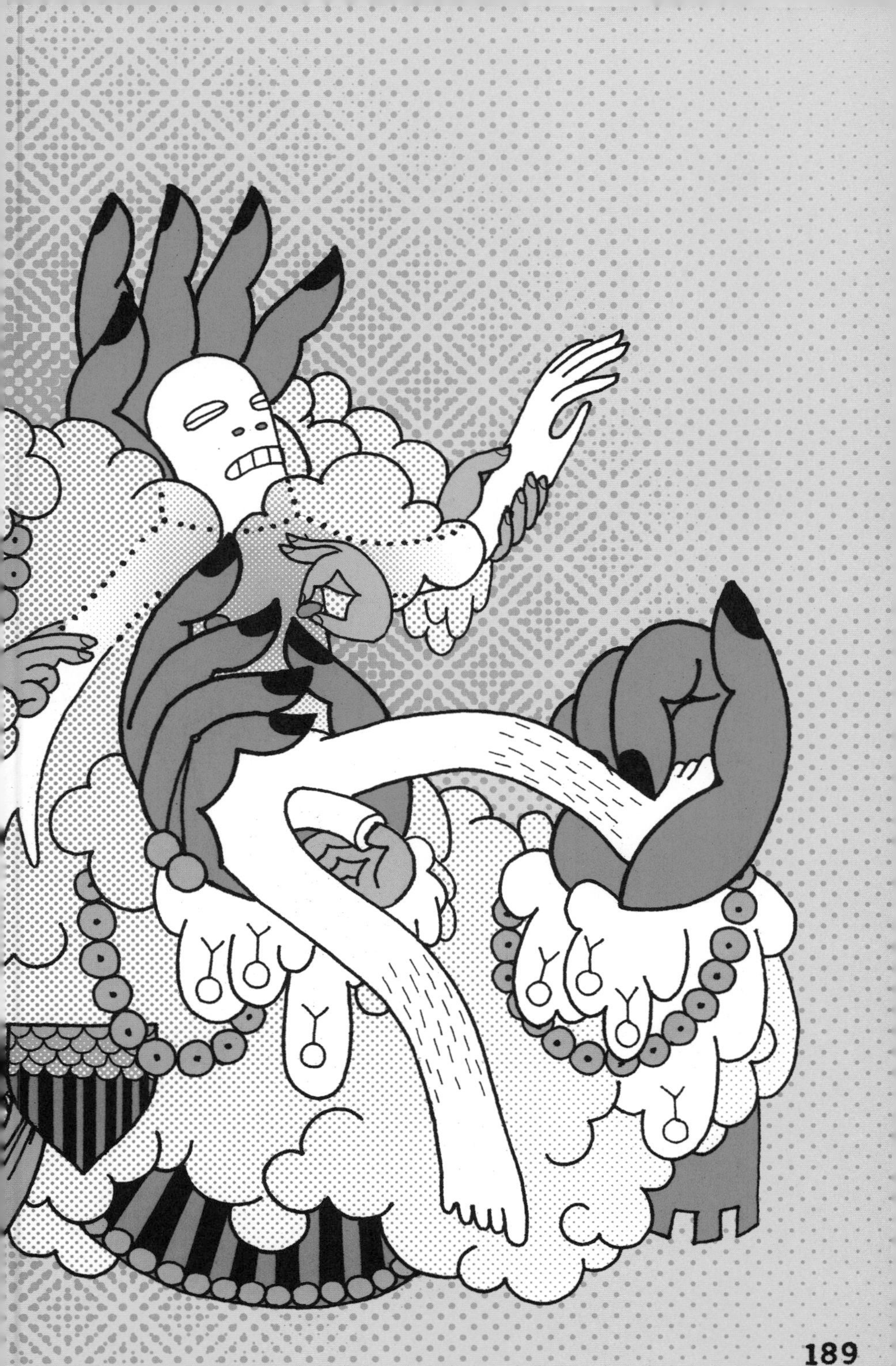

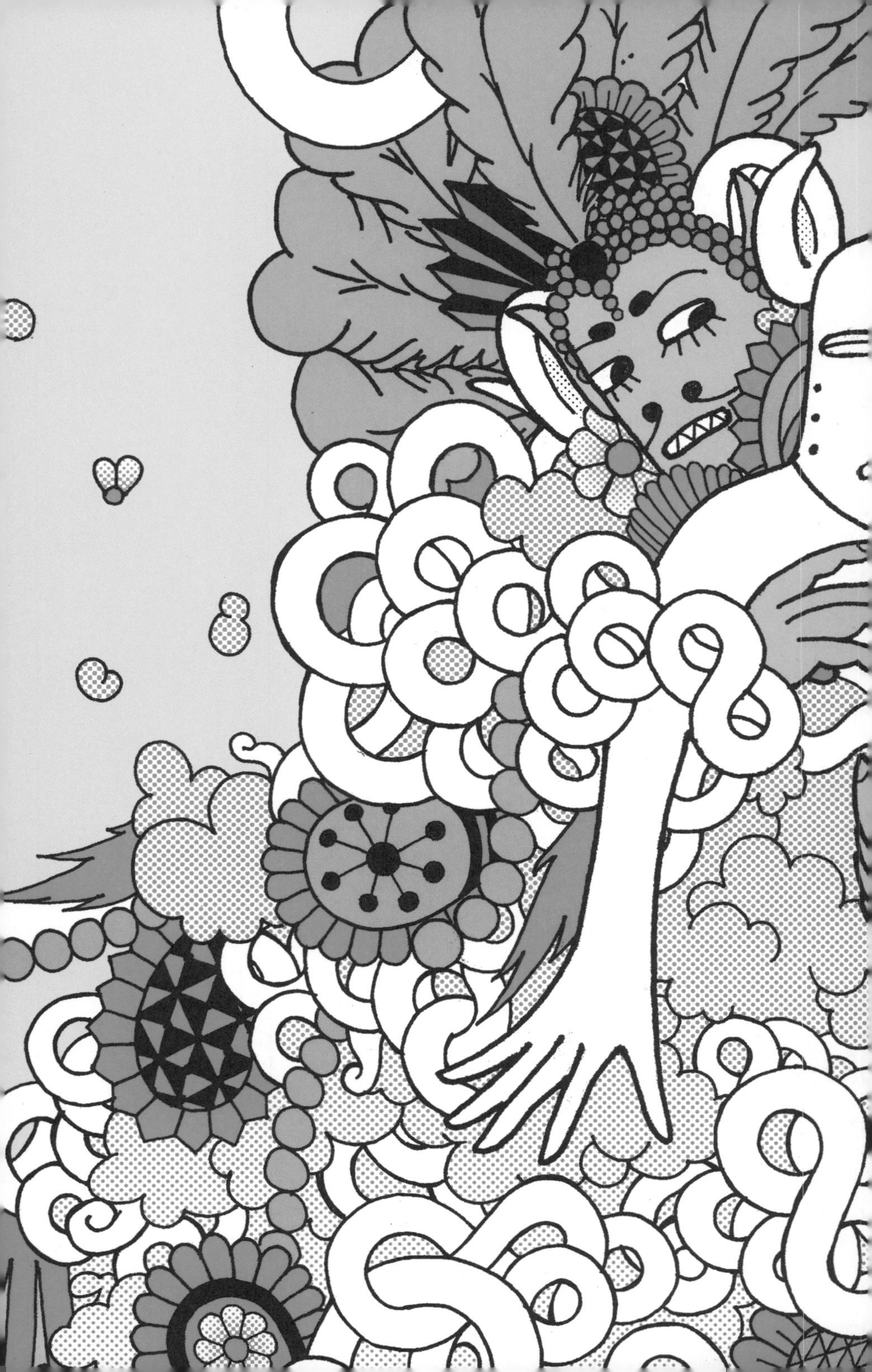

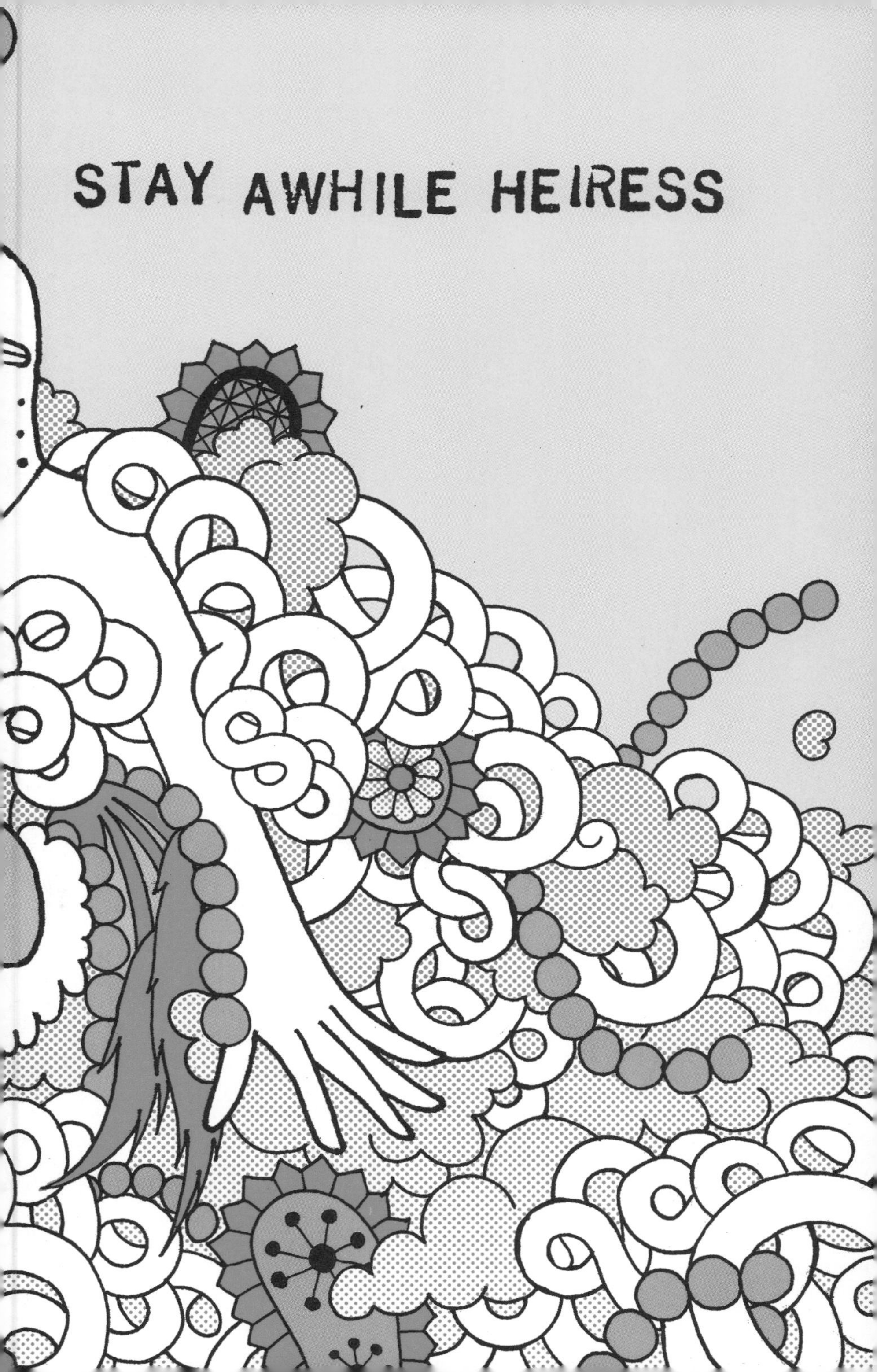
STAY AWHILE HEIRESS

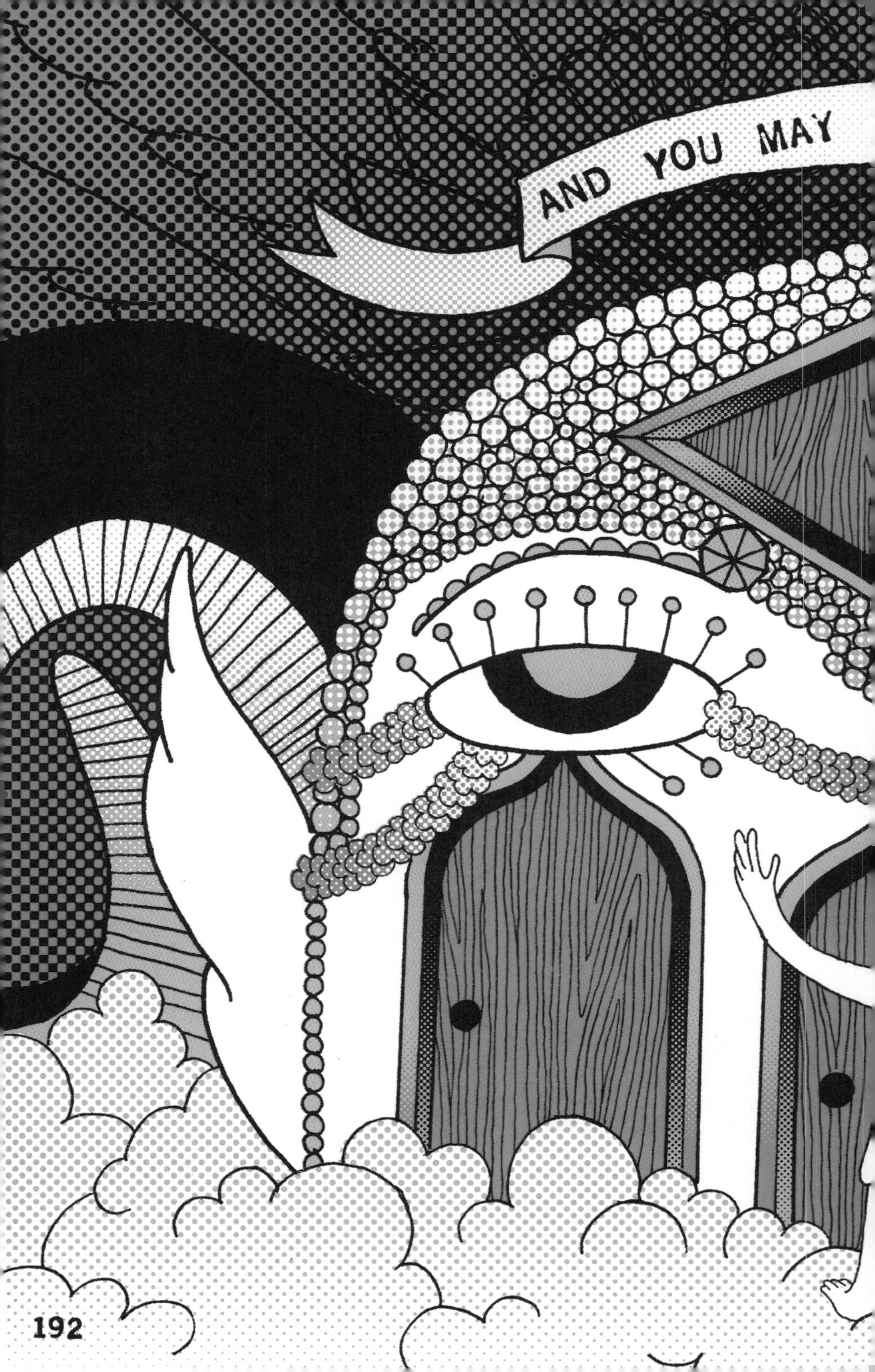
AND YOU MAY

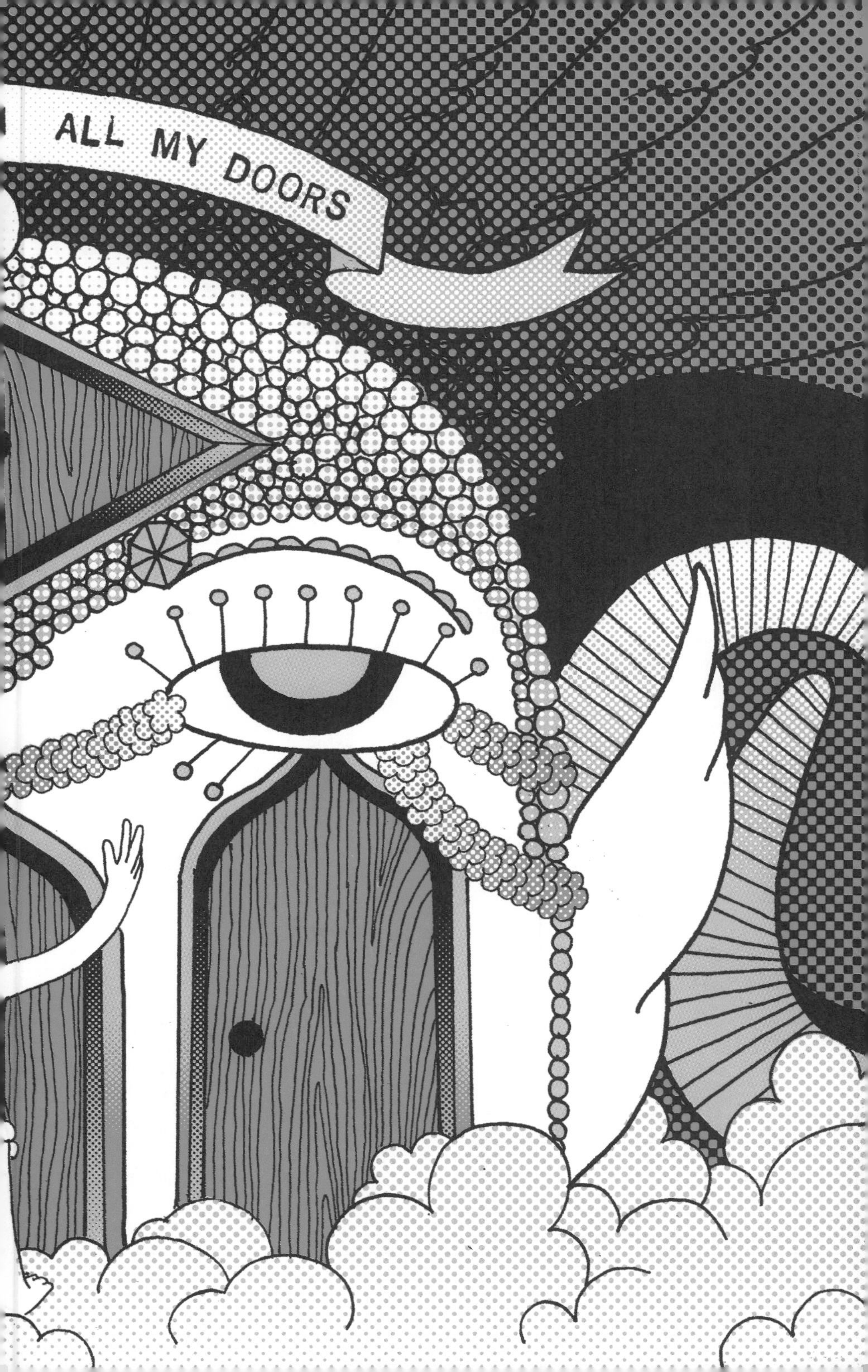
ALL MY DOORS

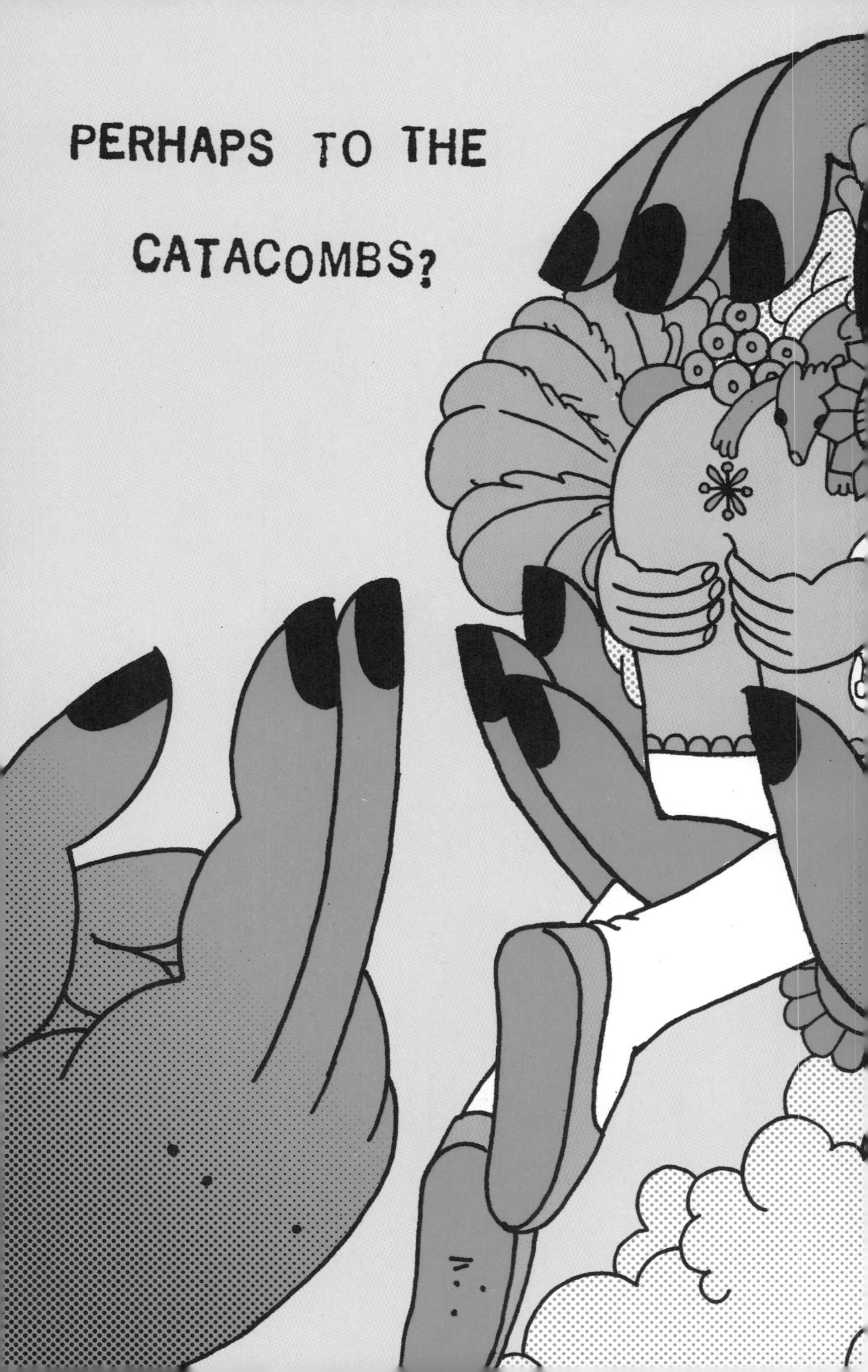
PERHAPS TO THE CATACOMBS?

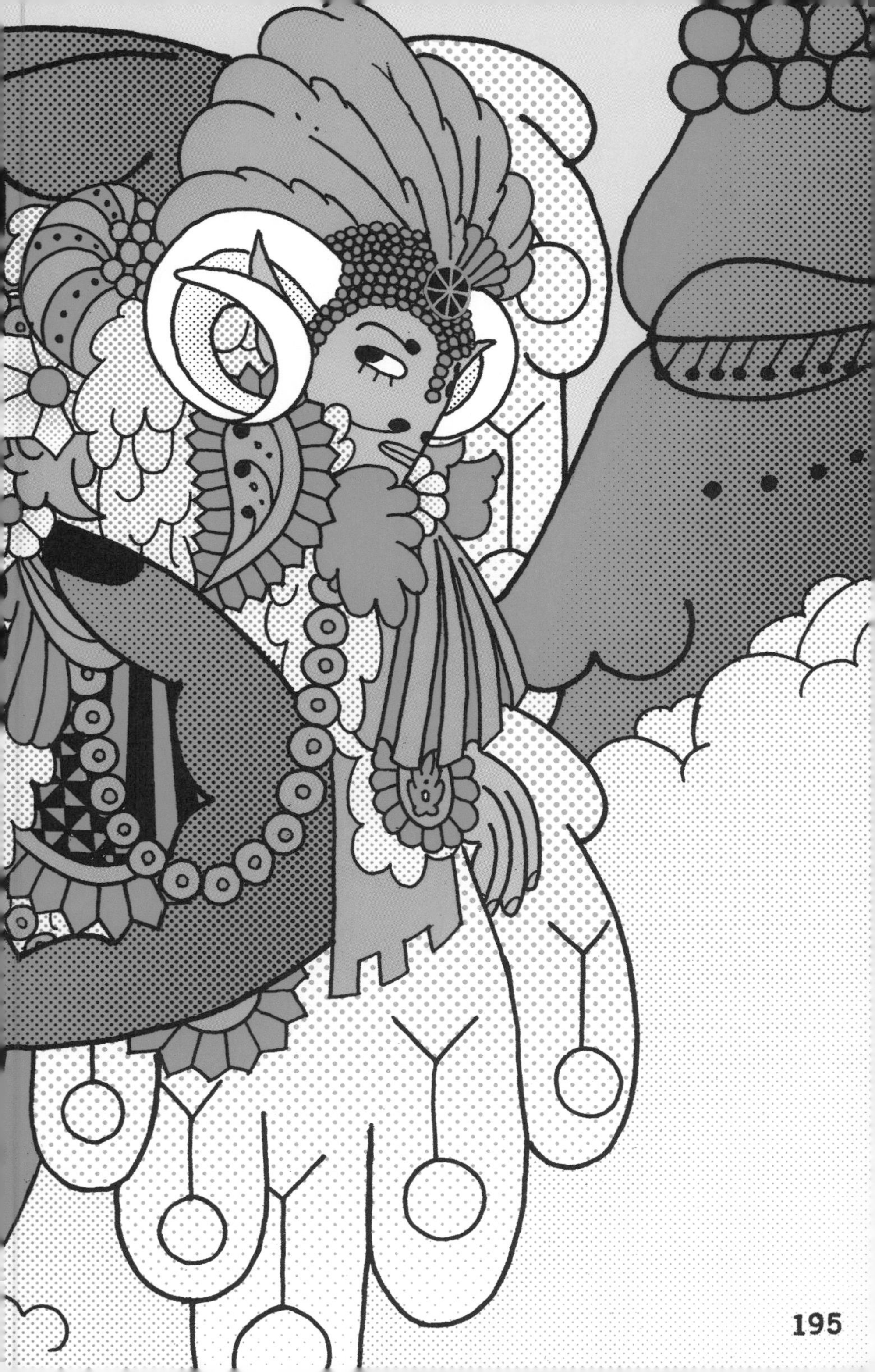

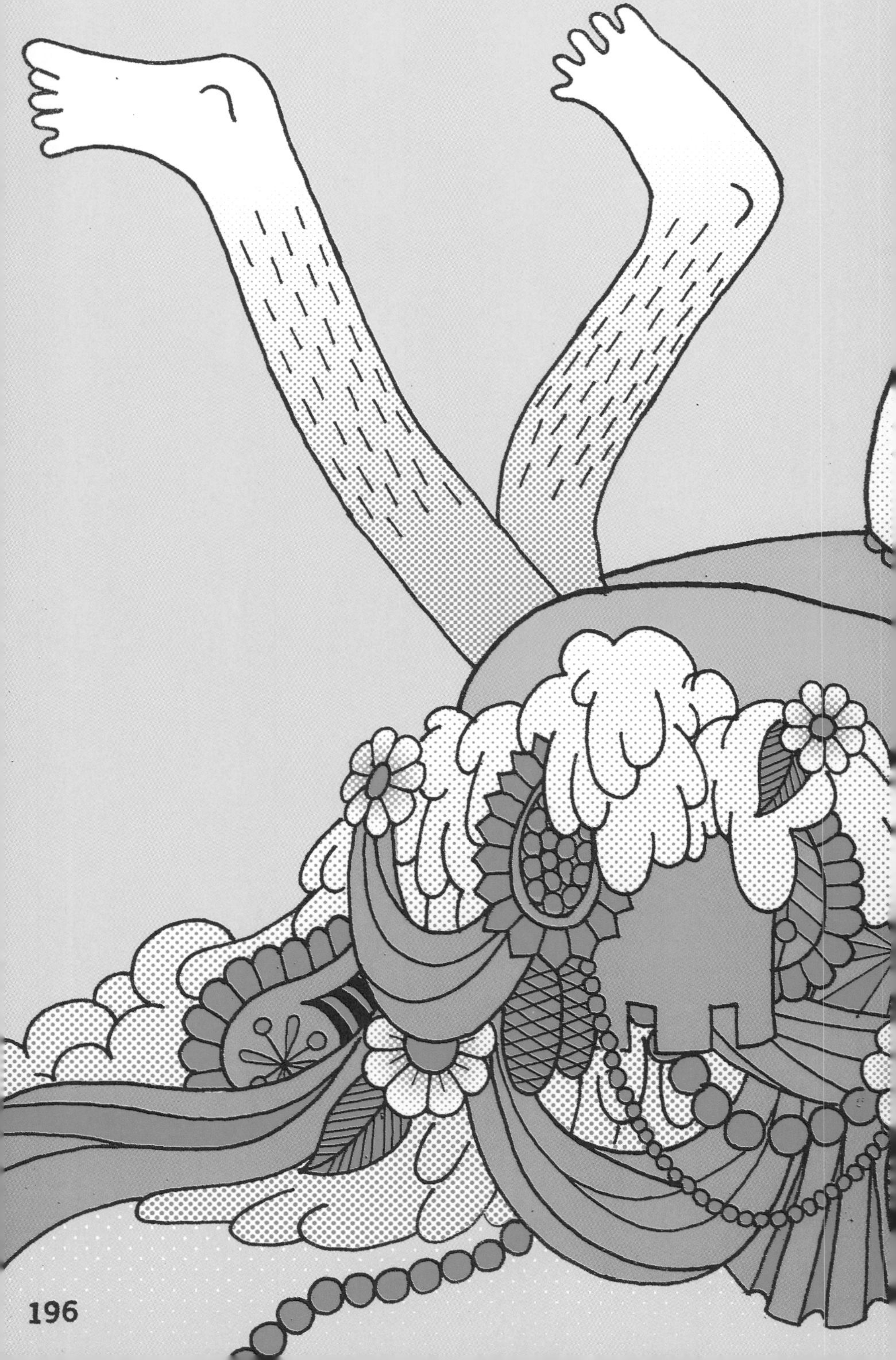

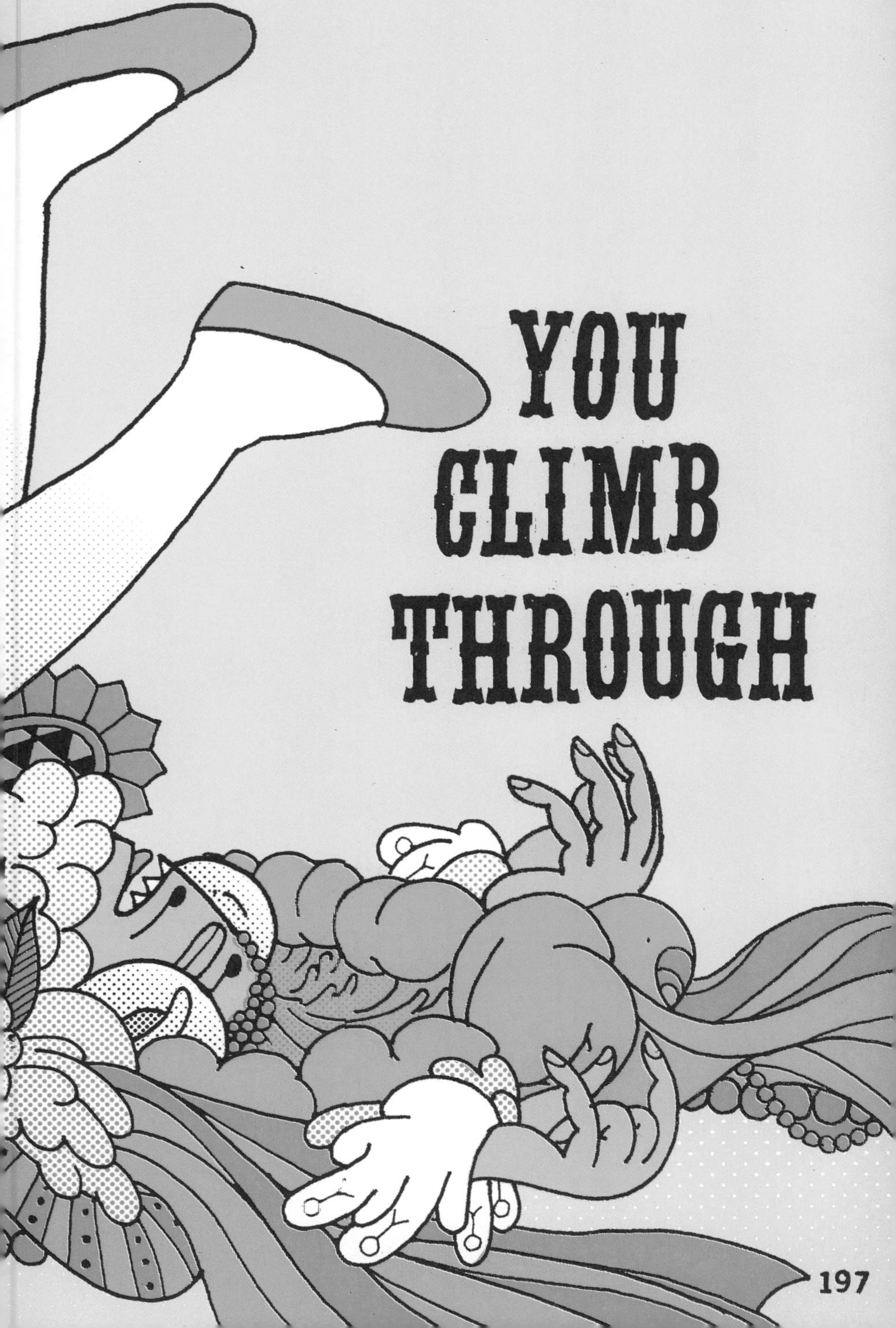
YOU
CLIMB
THROUGH

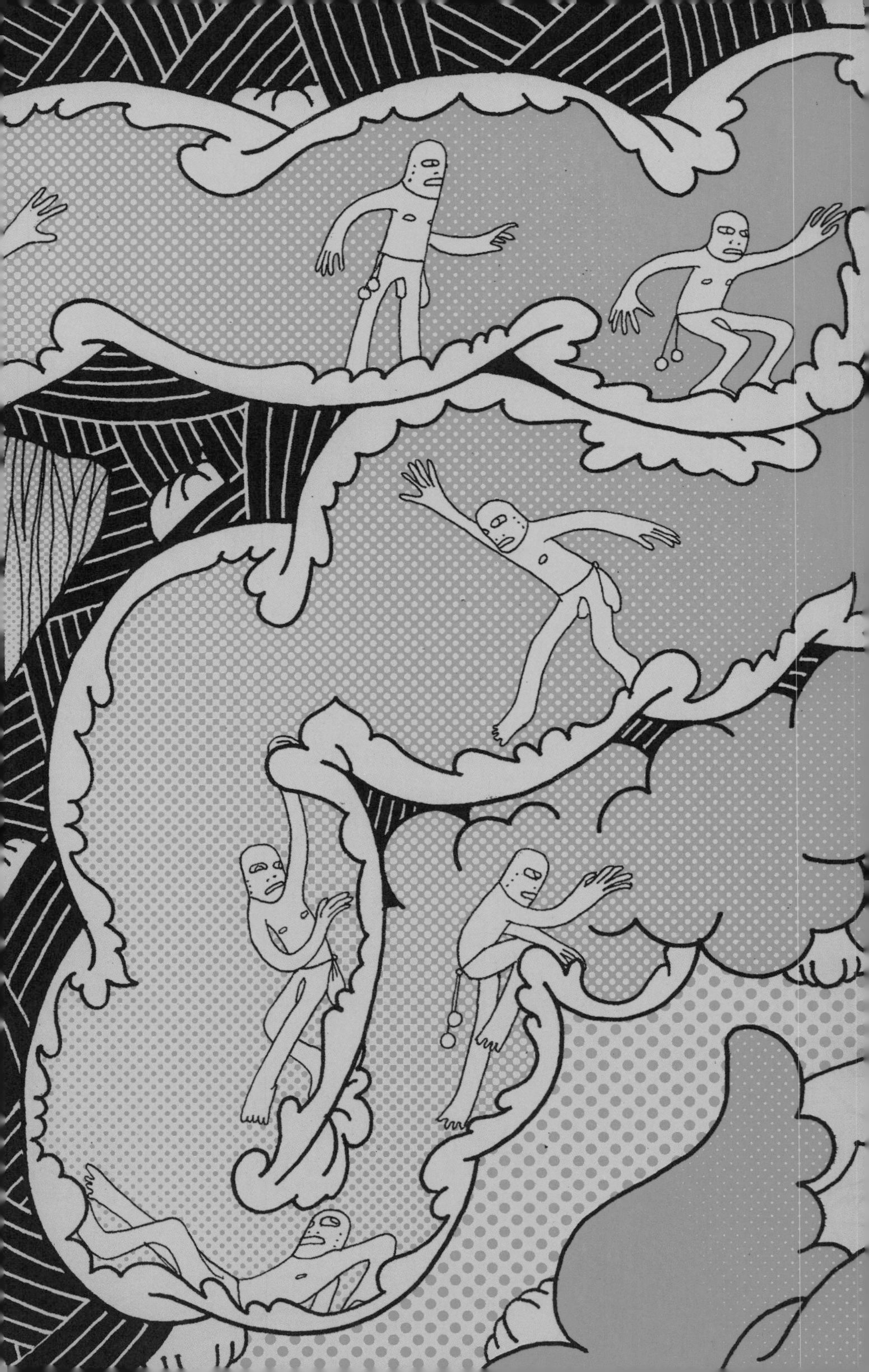

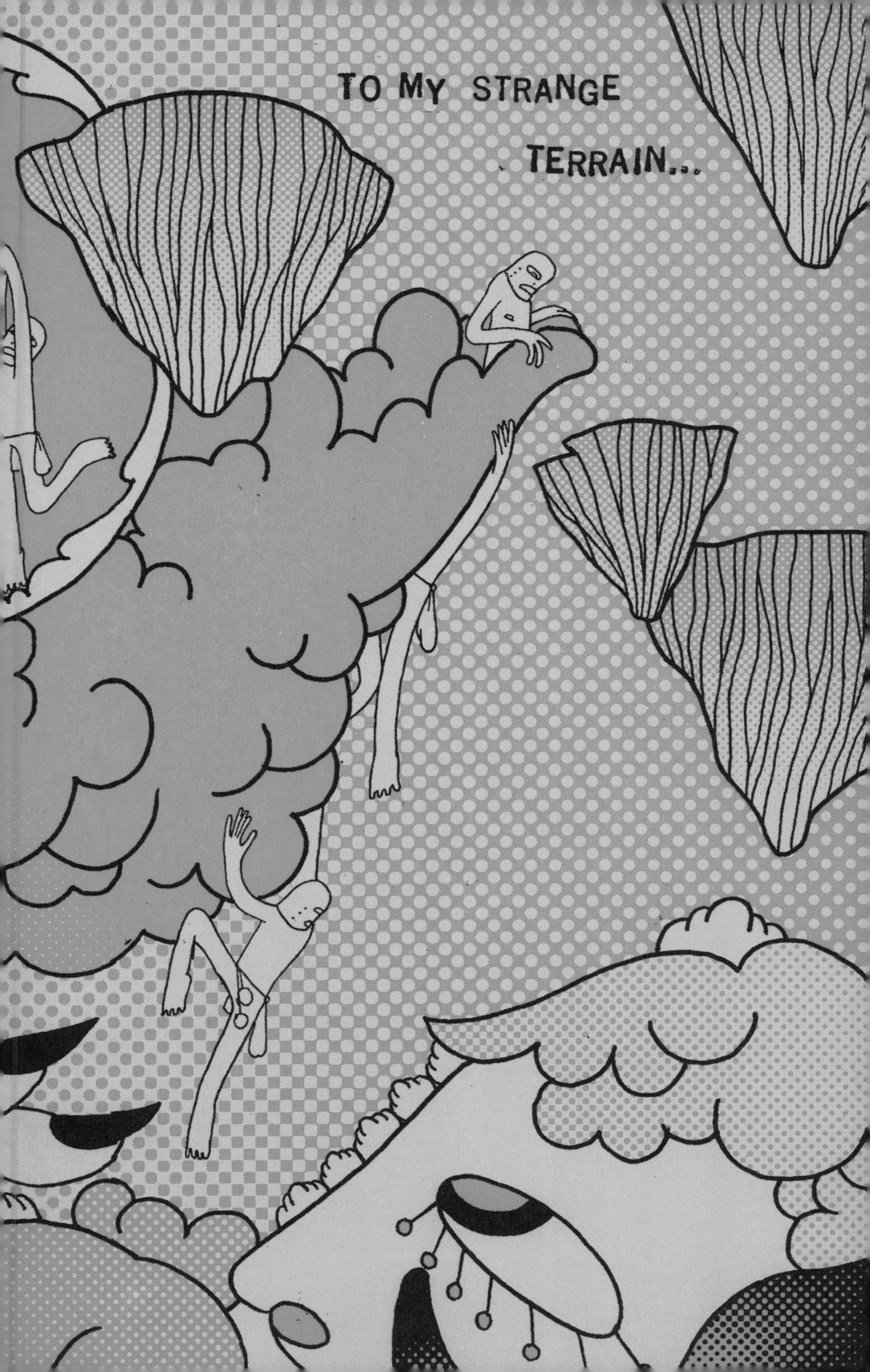
TO MY STRANGE
TERRAIN...

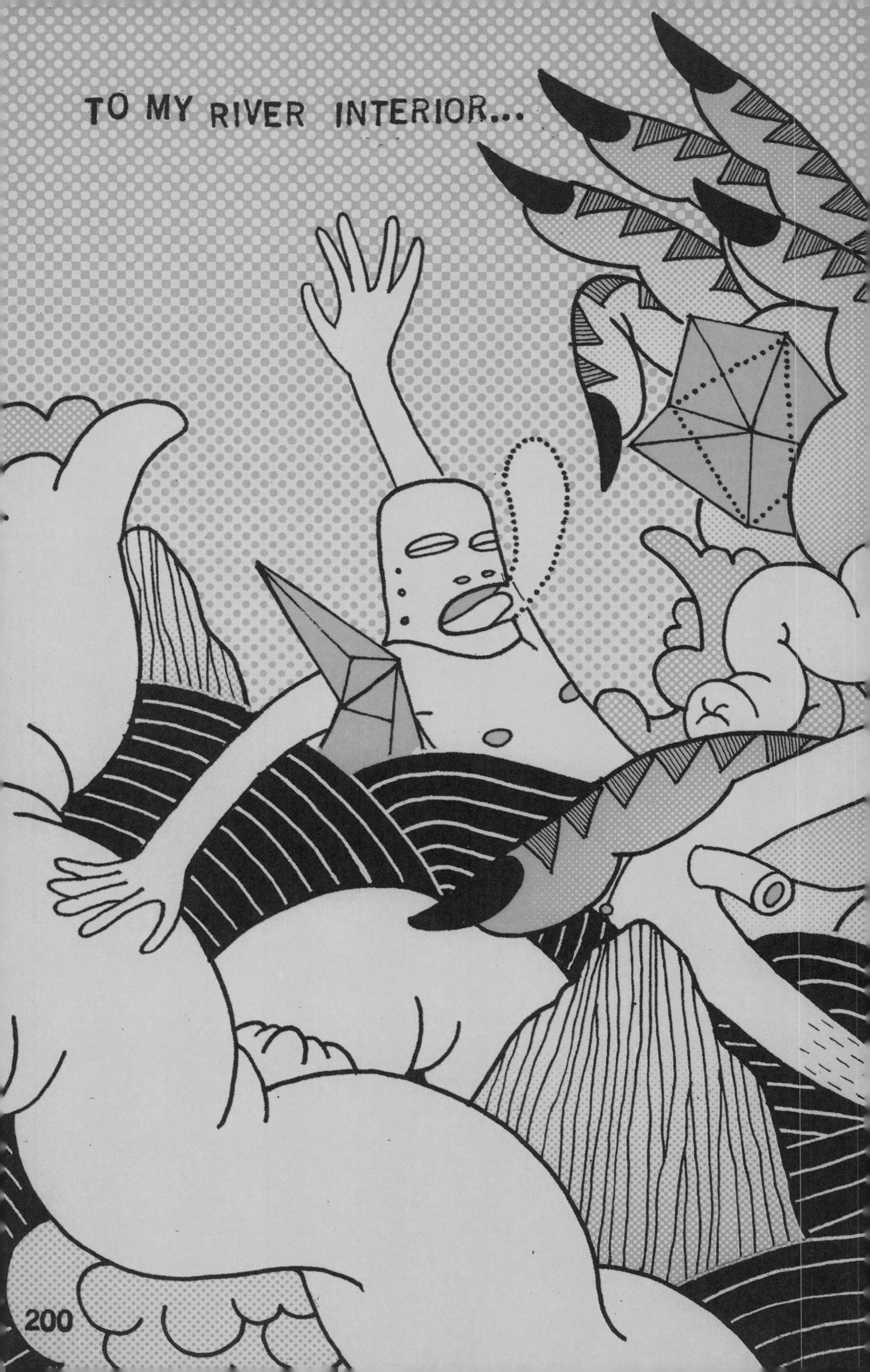
TO MY RIVER INTERIOR...

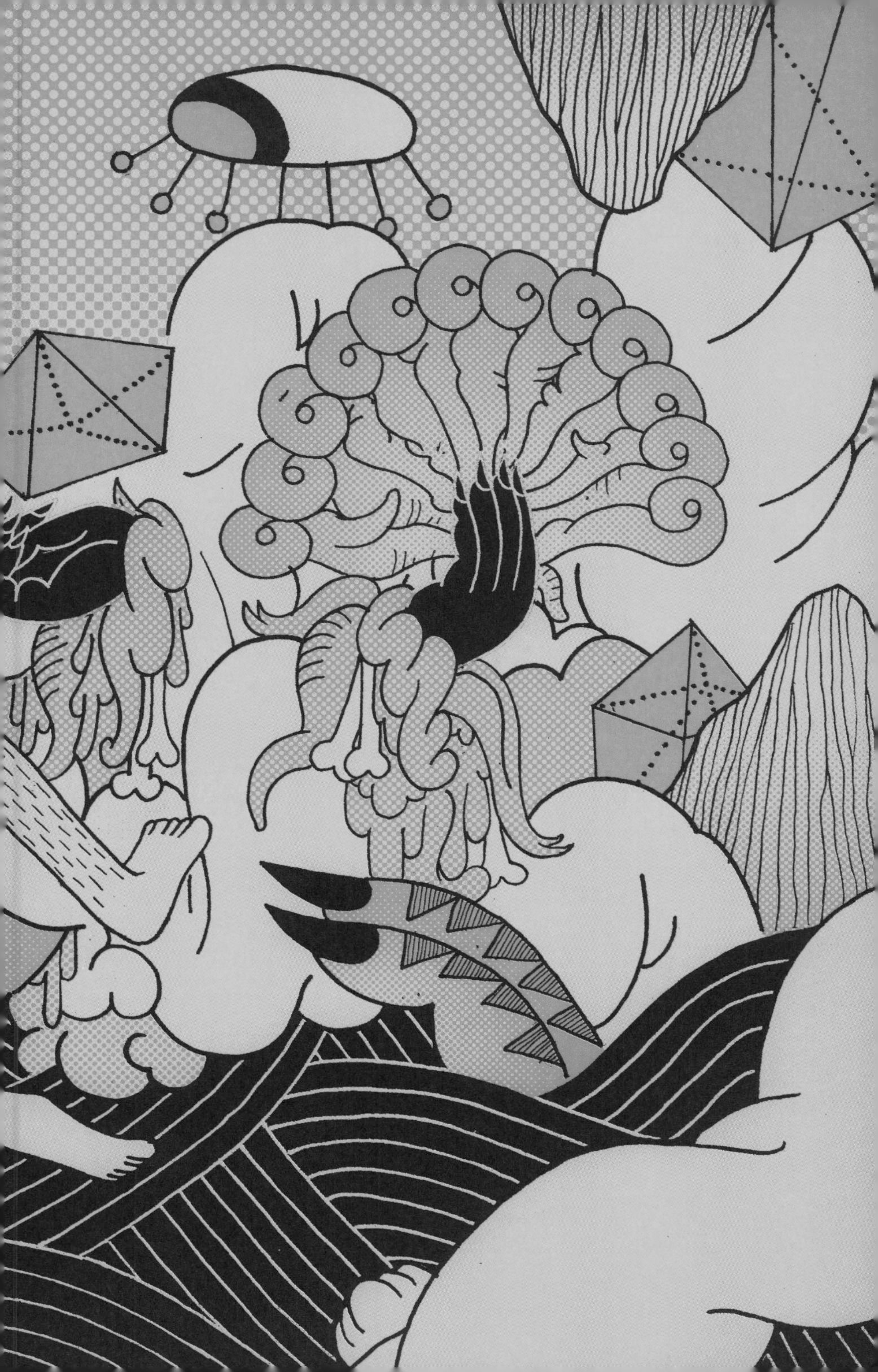

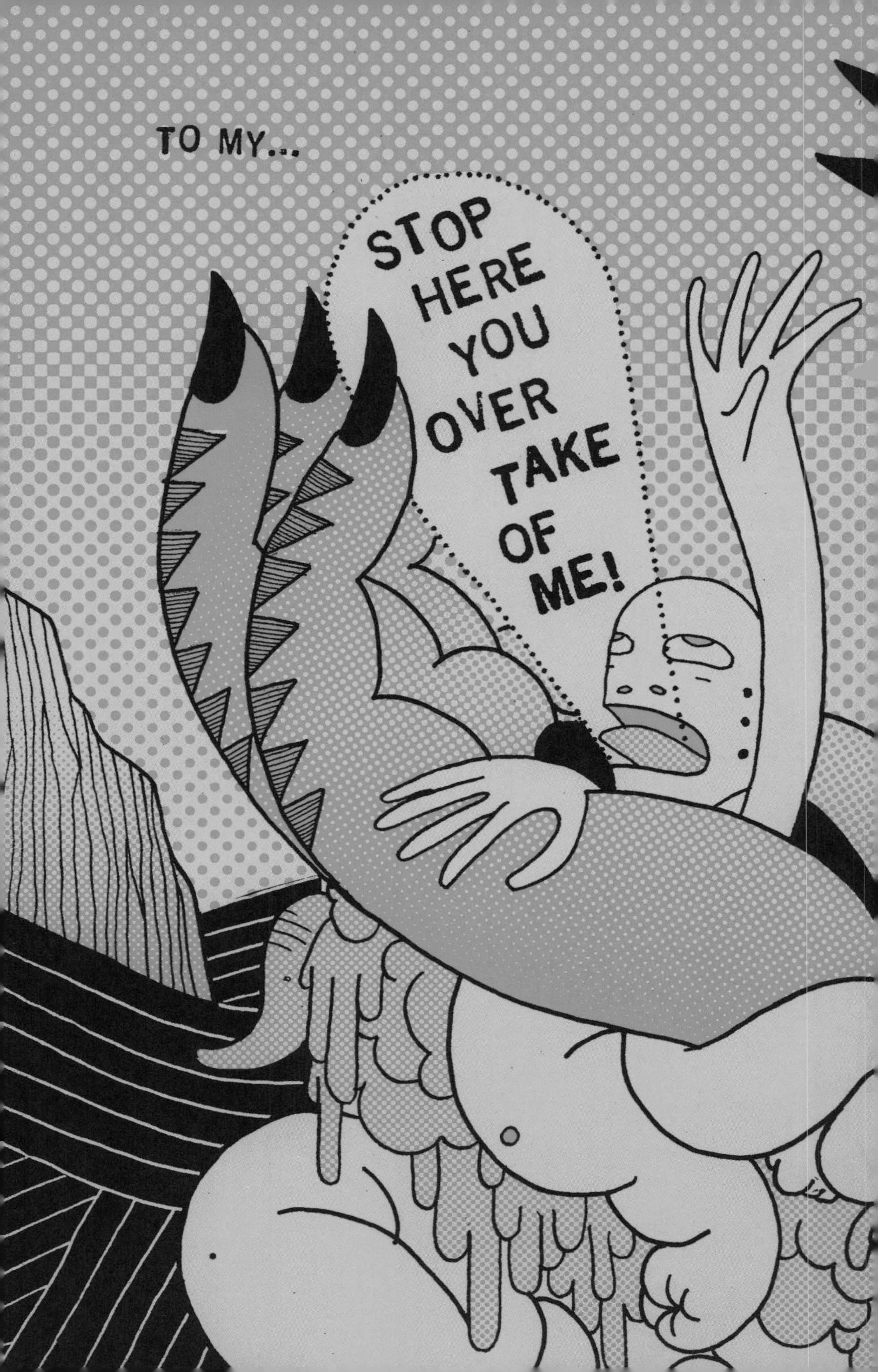
TO MY...
STOP HERE YOU OVER TAKE OF ME!

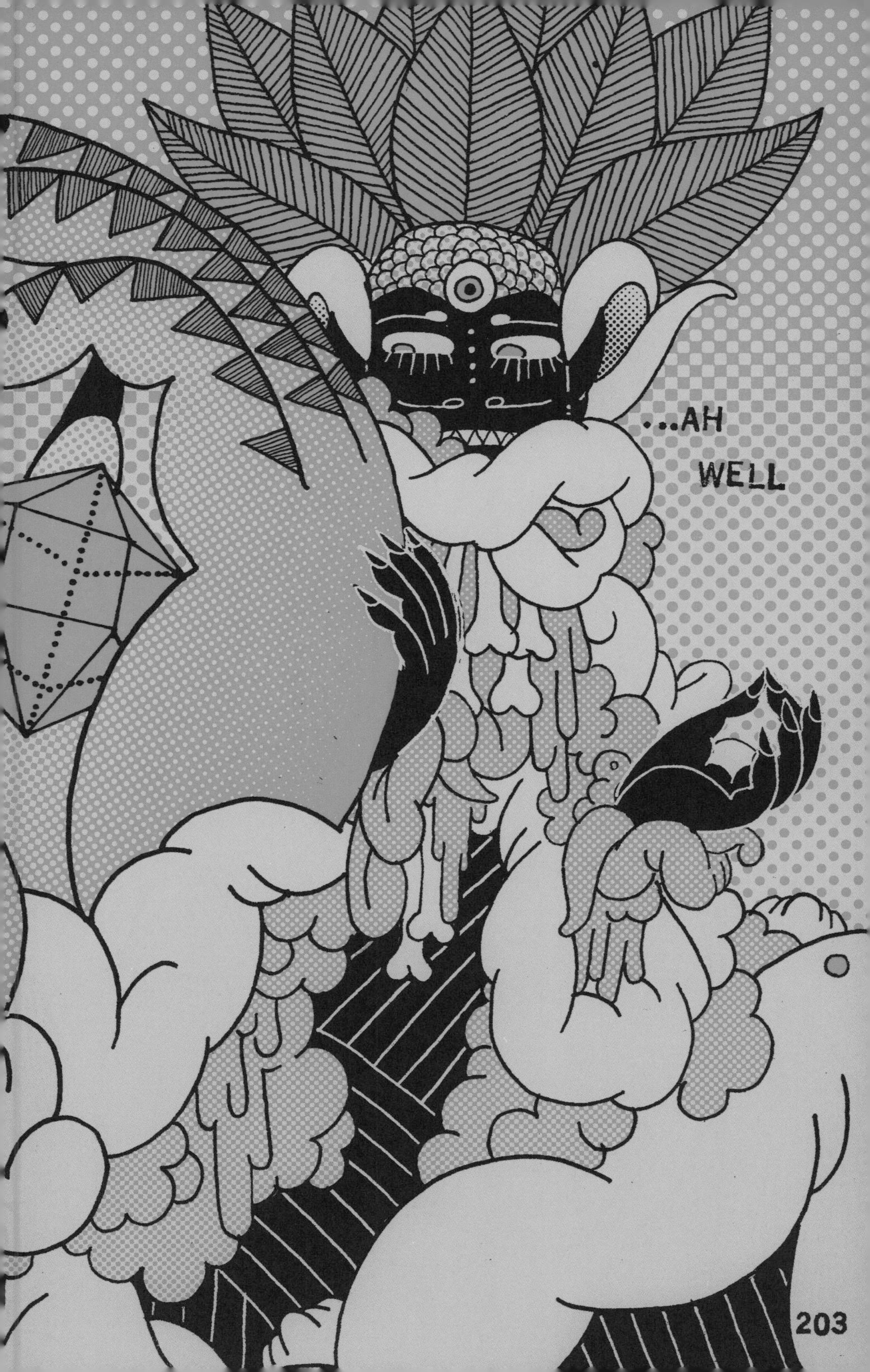
...AH
WELL

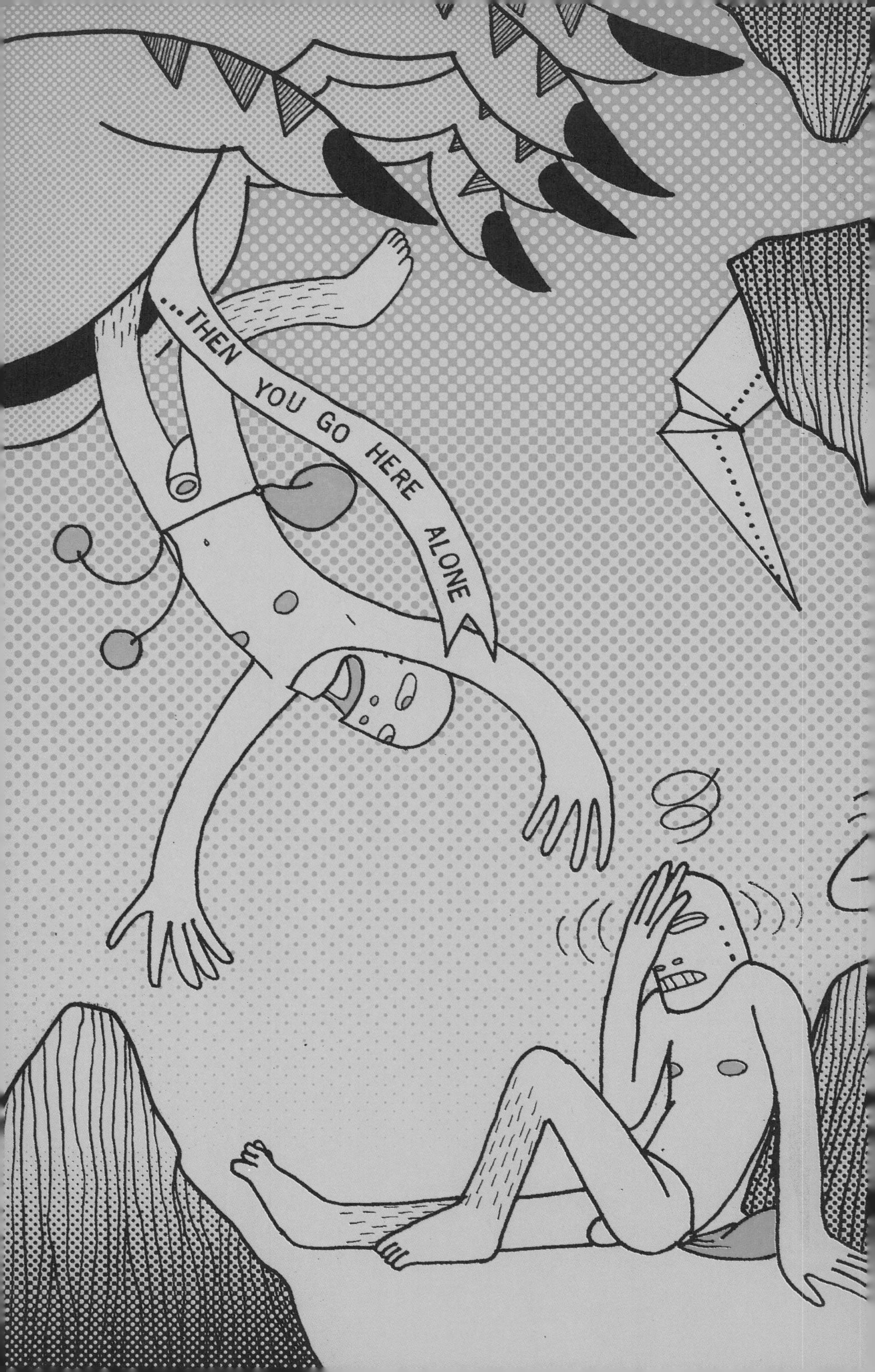
...THEN YOU GO HERE ALONE

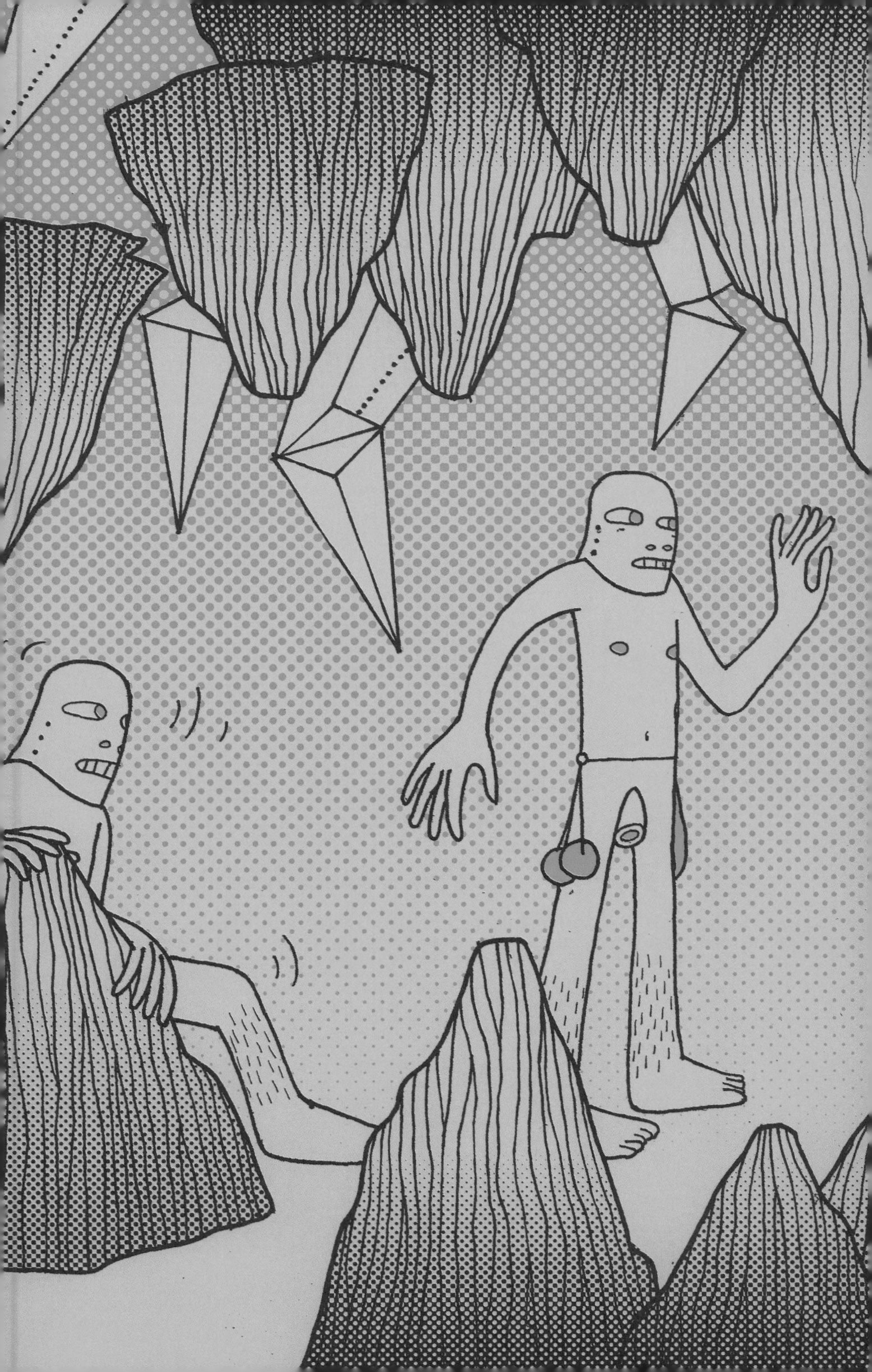

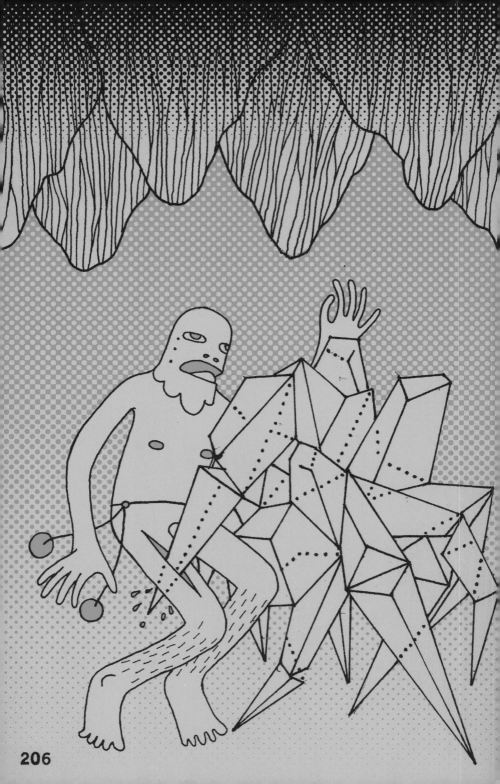

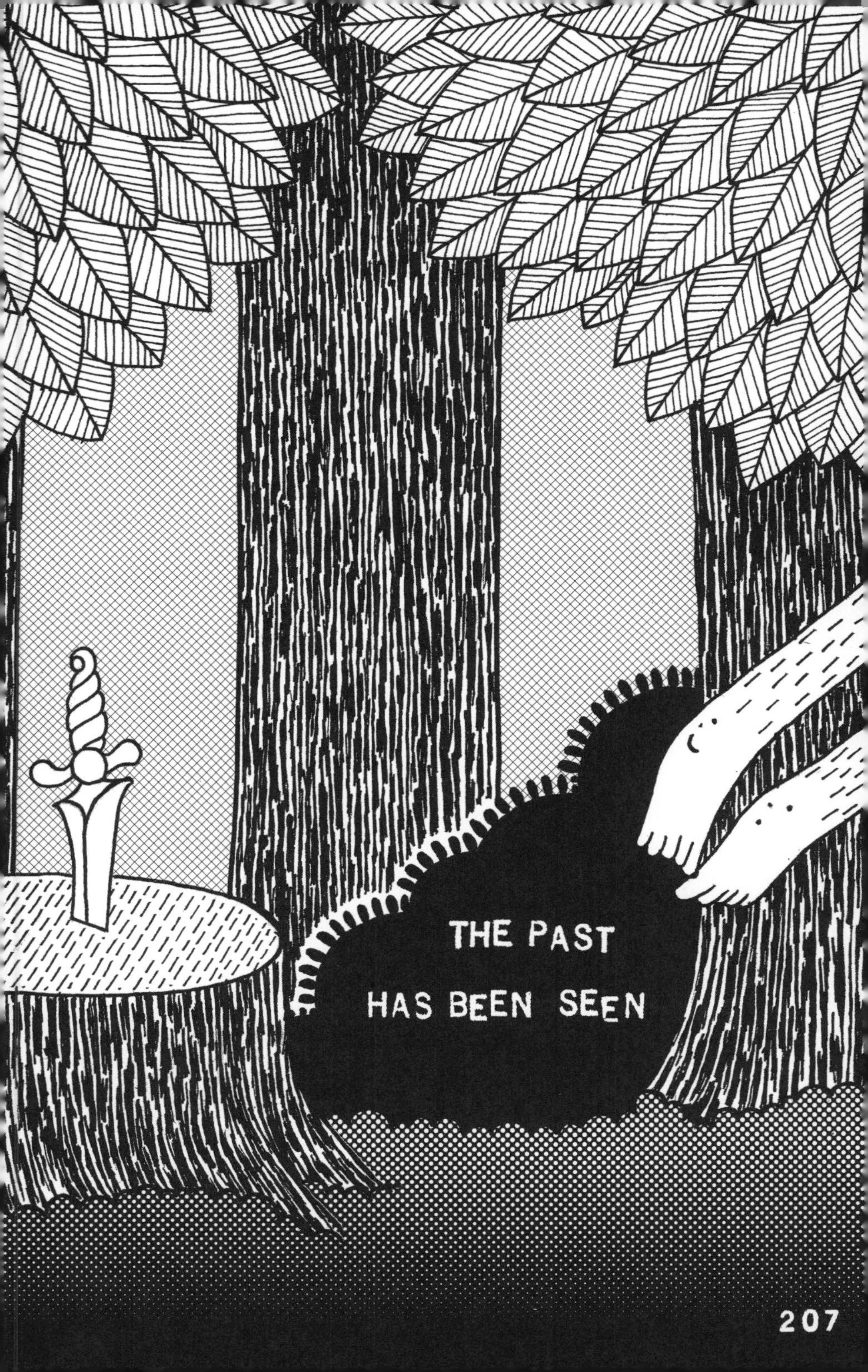
THE PAST
HAS BEEN SEEN

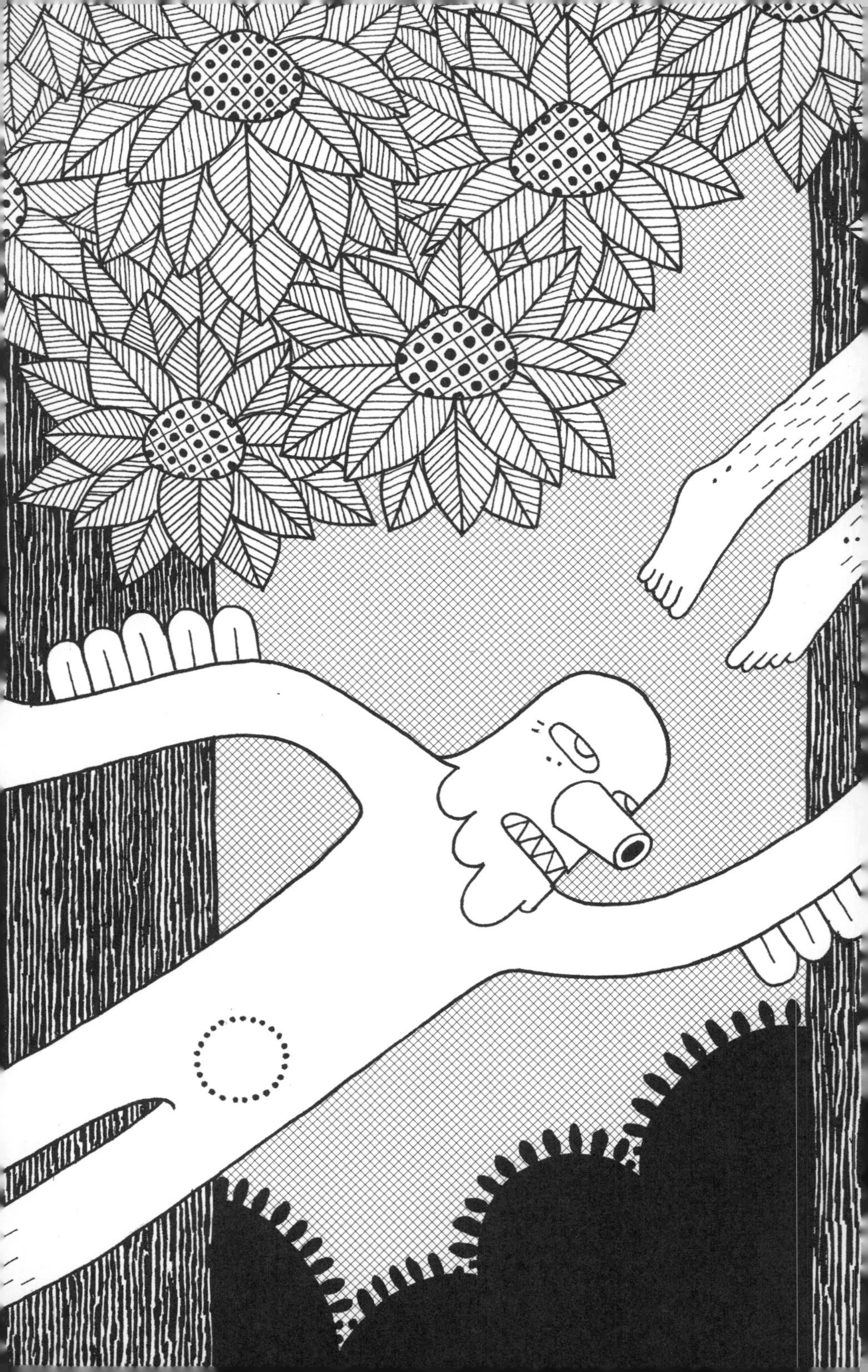

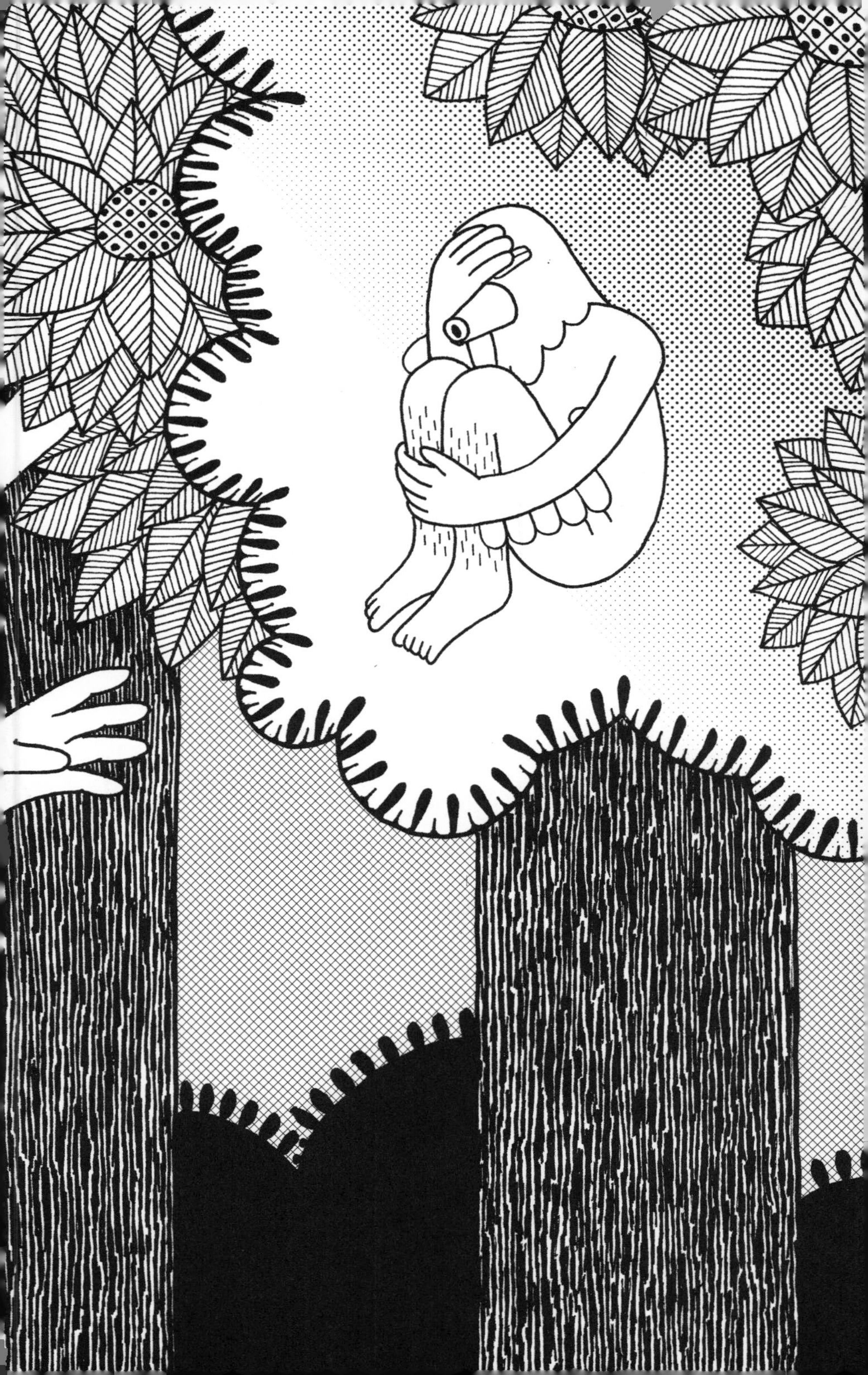

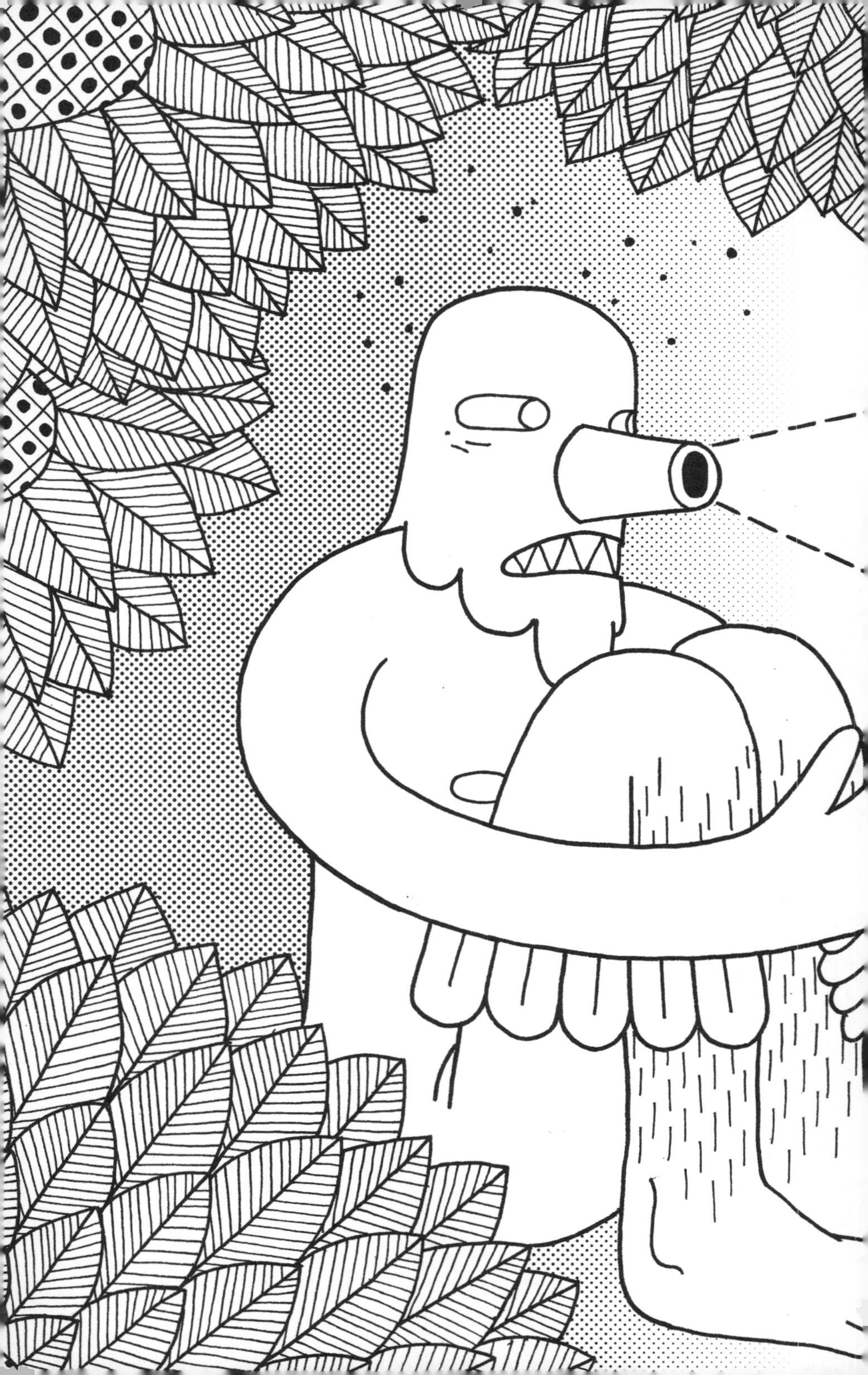

WHAT DO YOU DO ONCE YOU KNOW

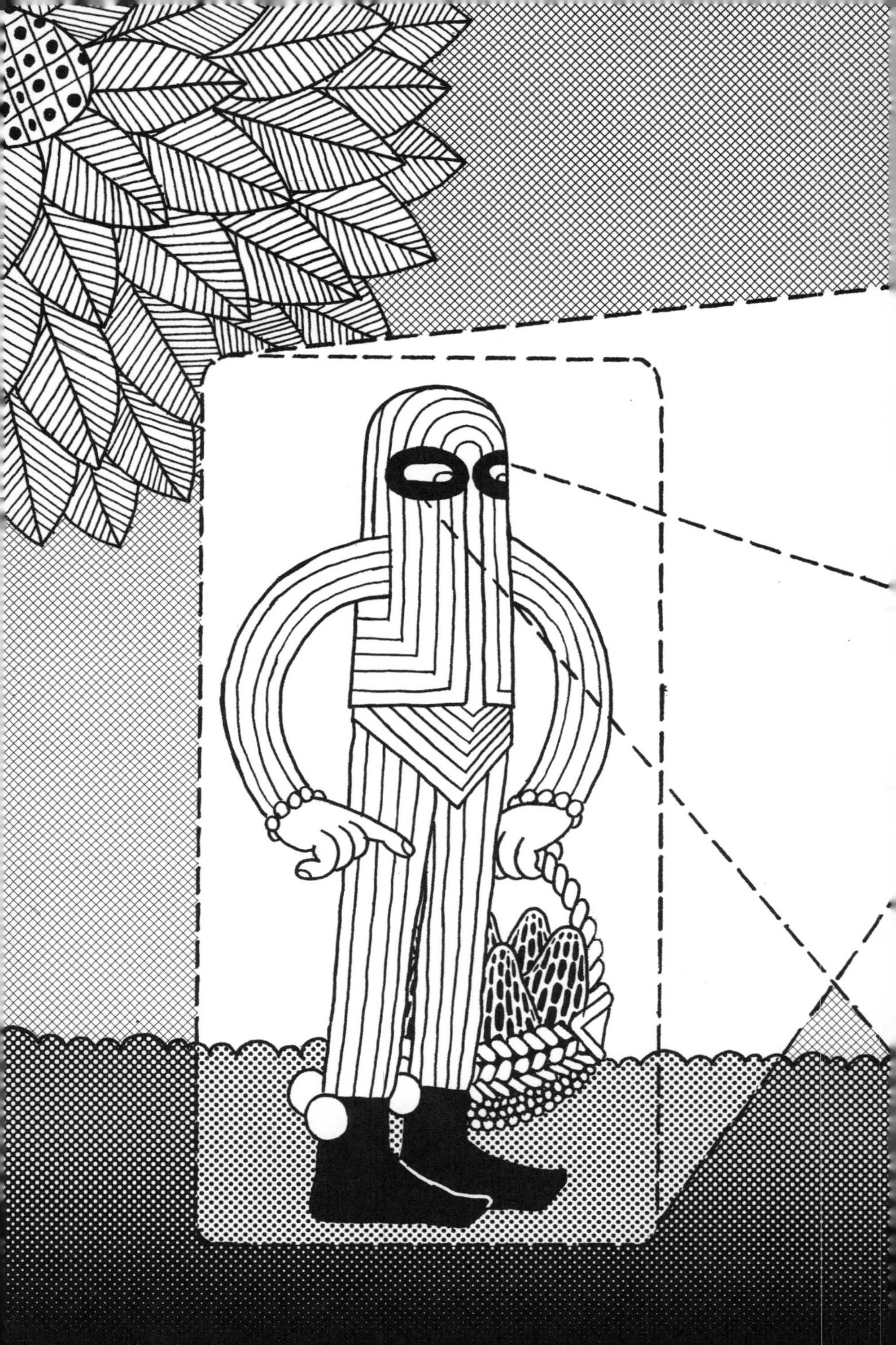

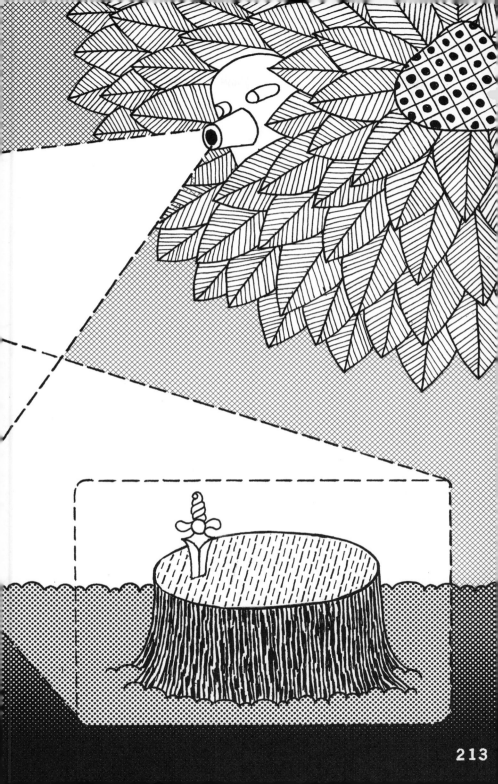

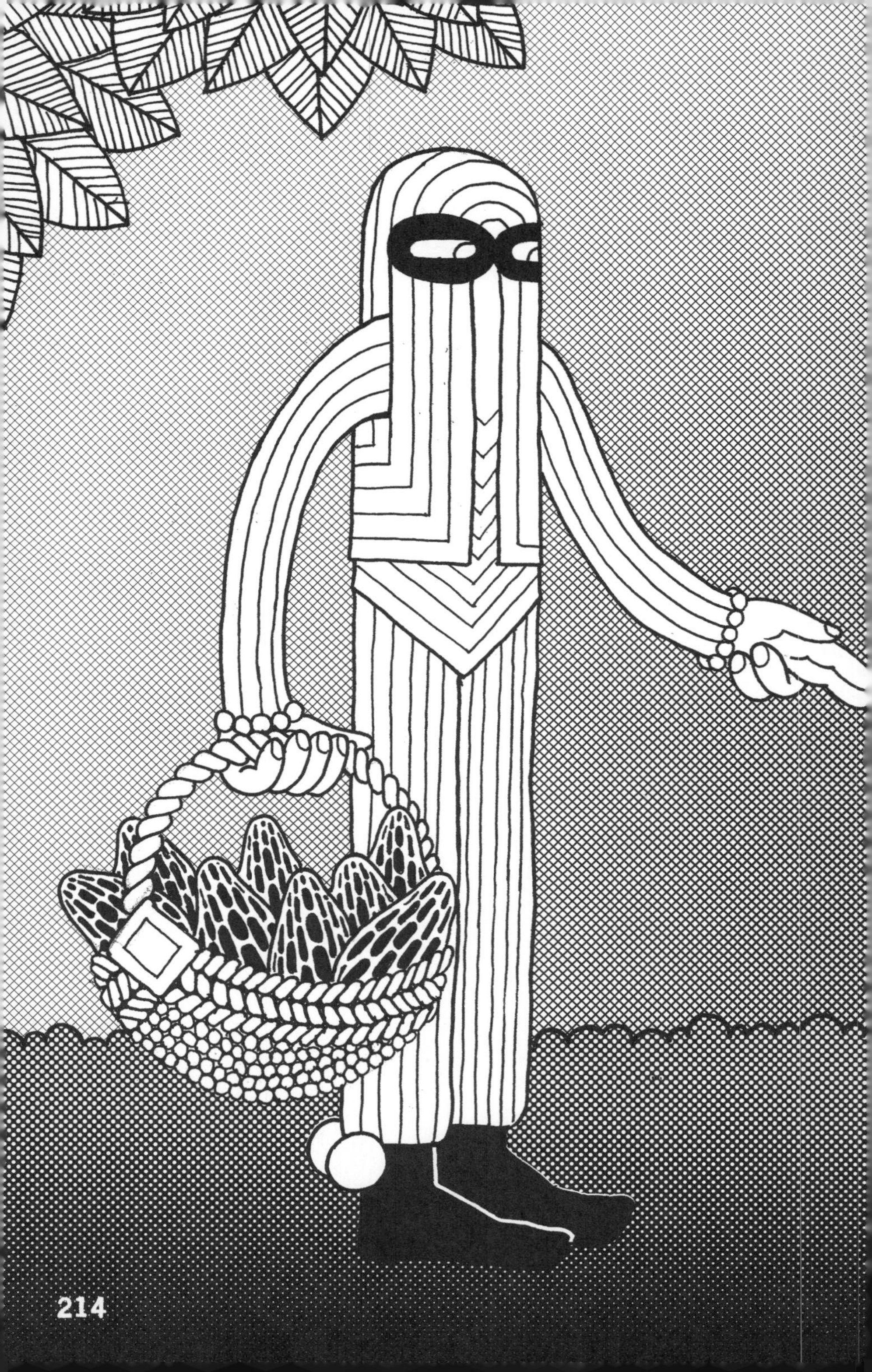

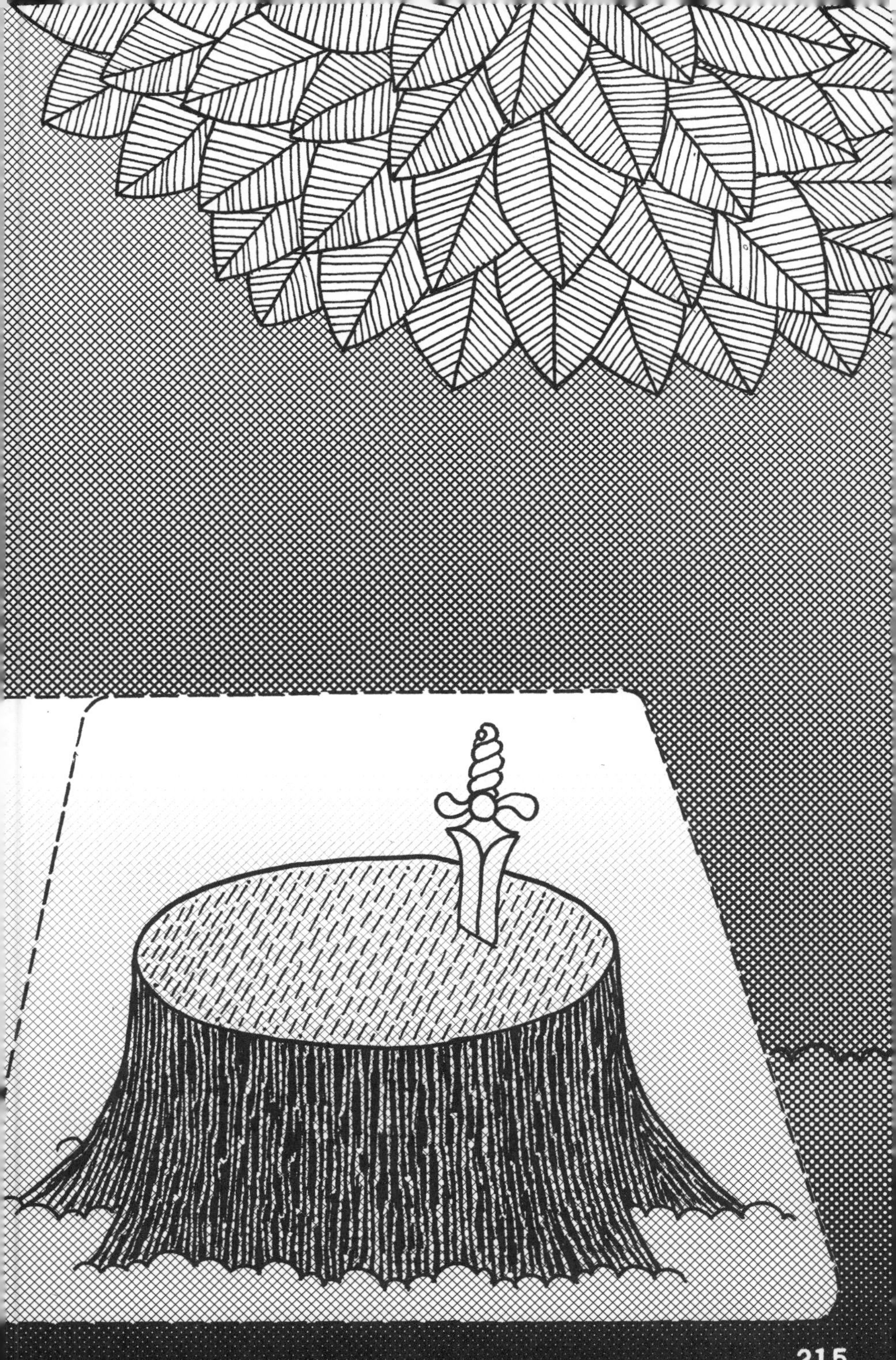

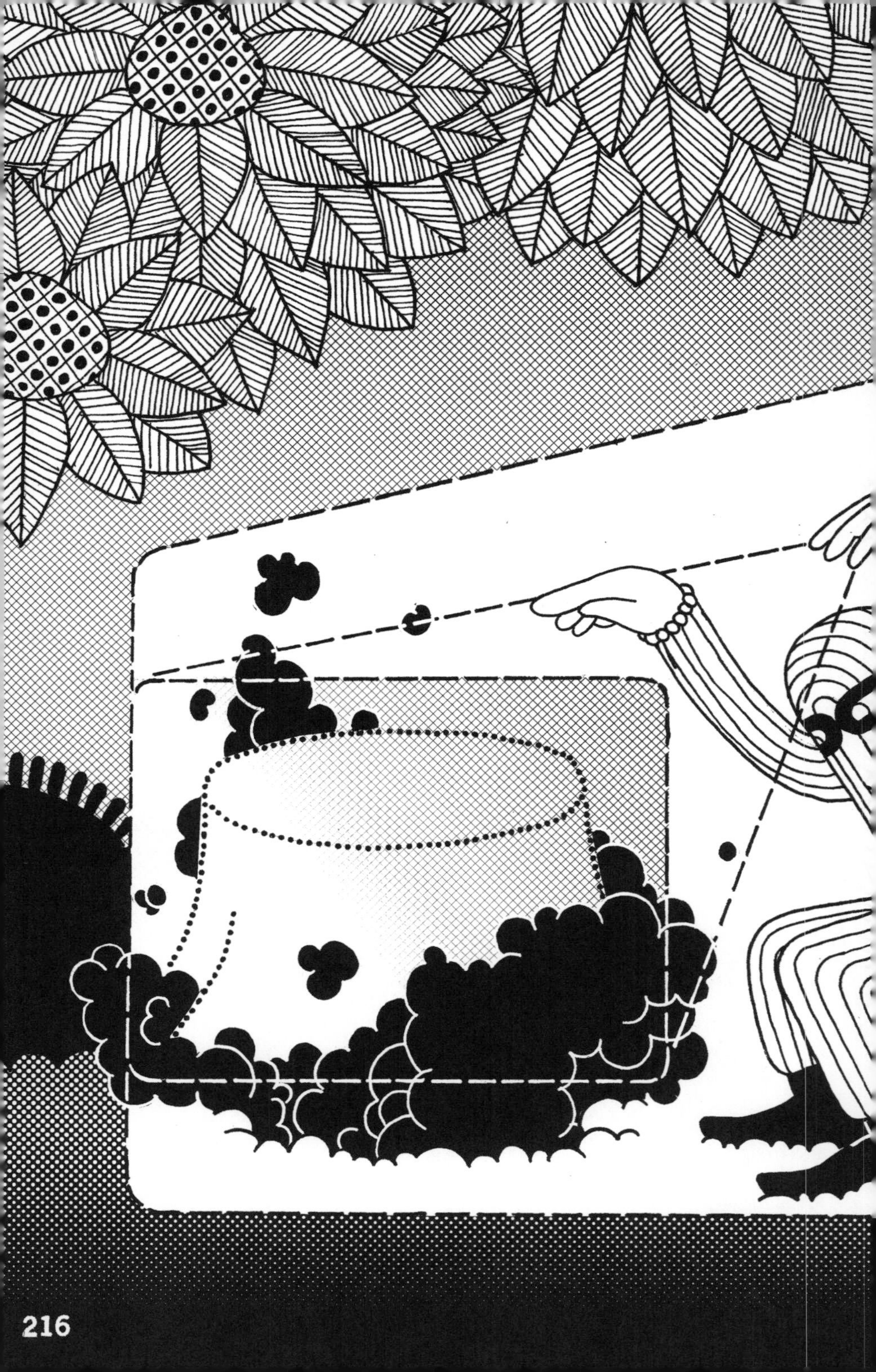

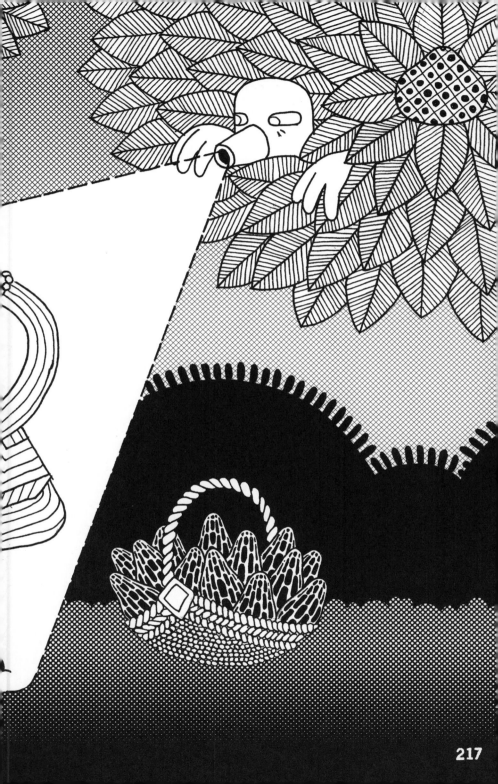

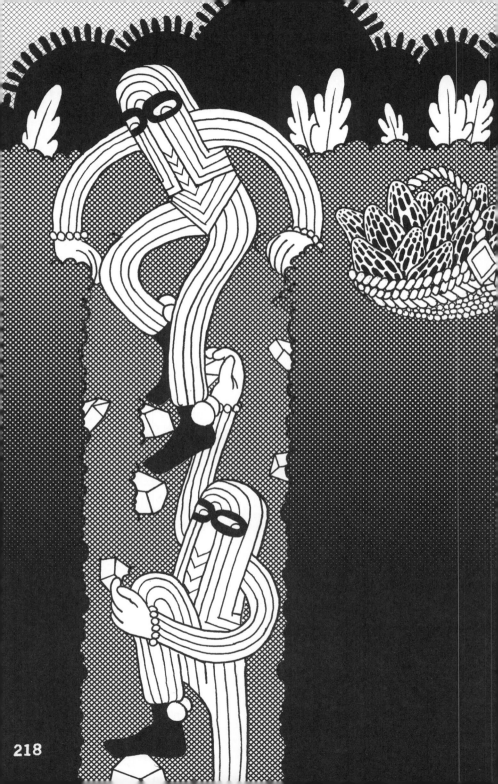

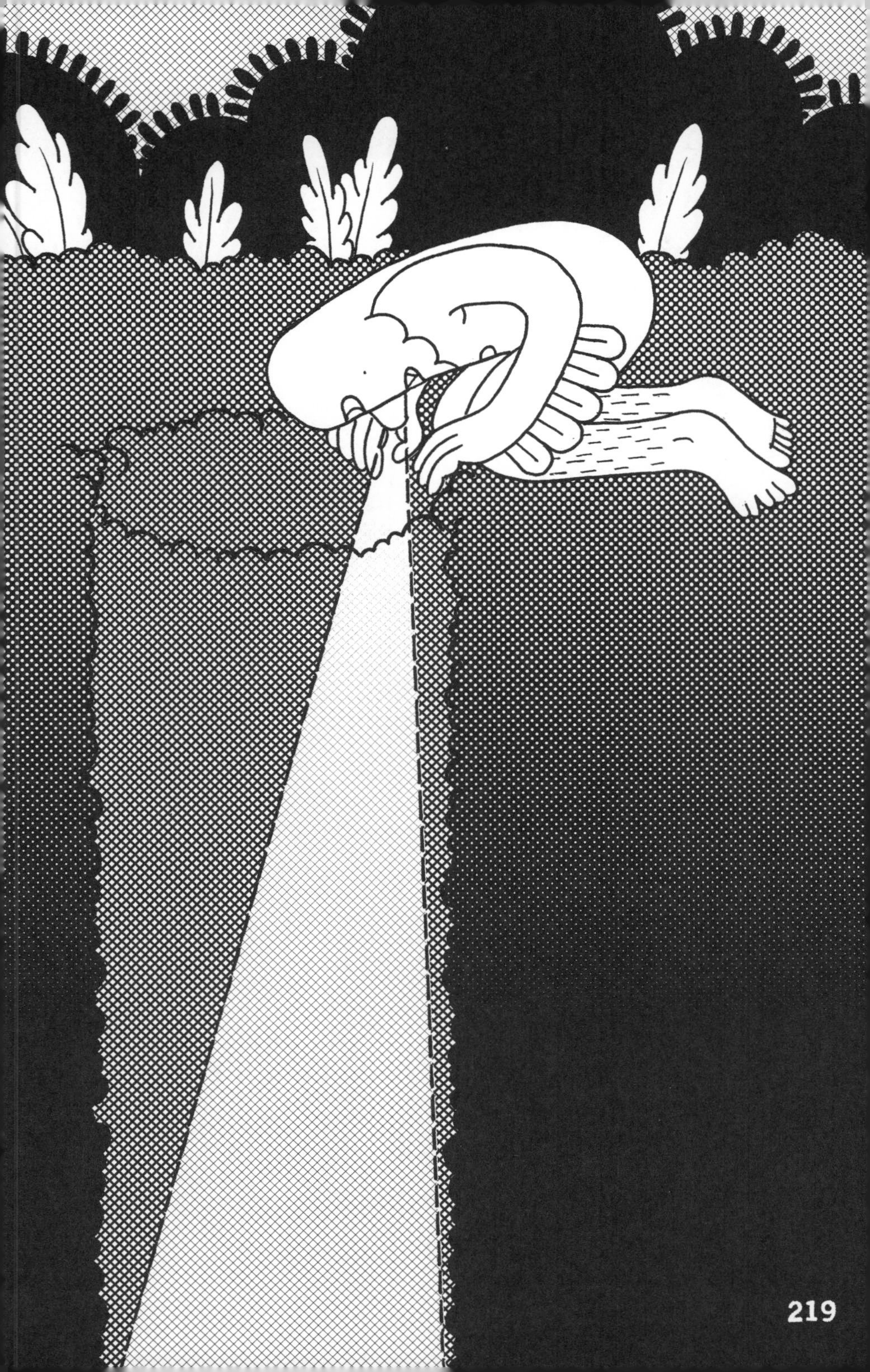

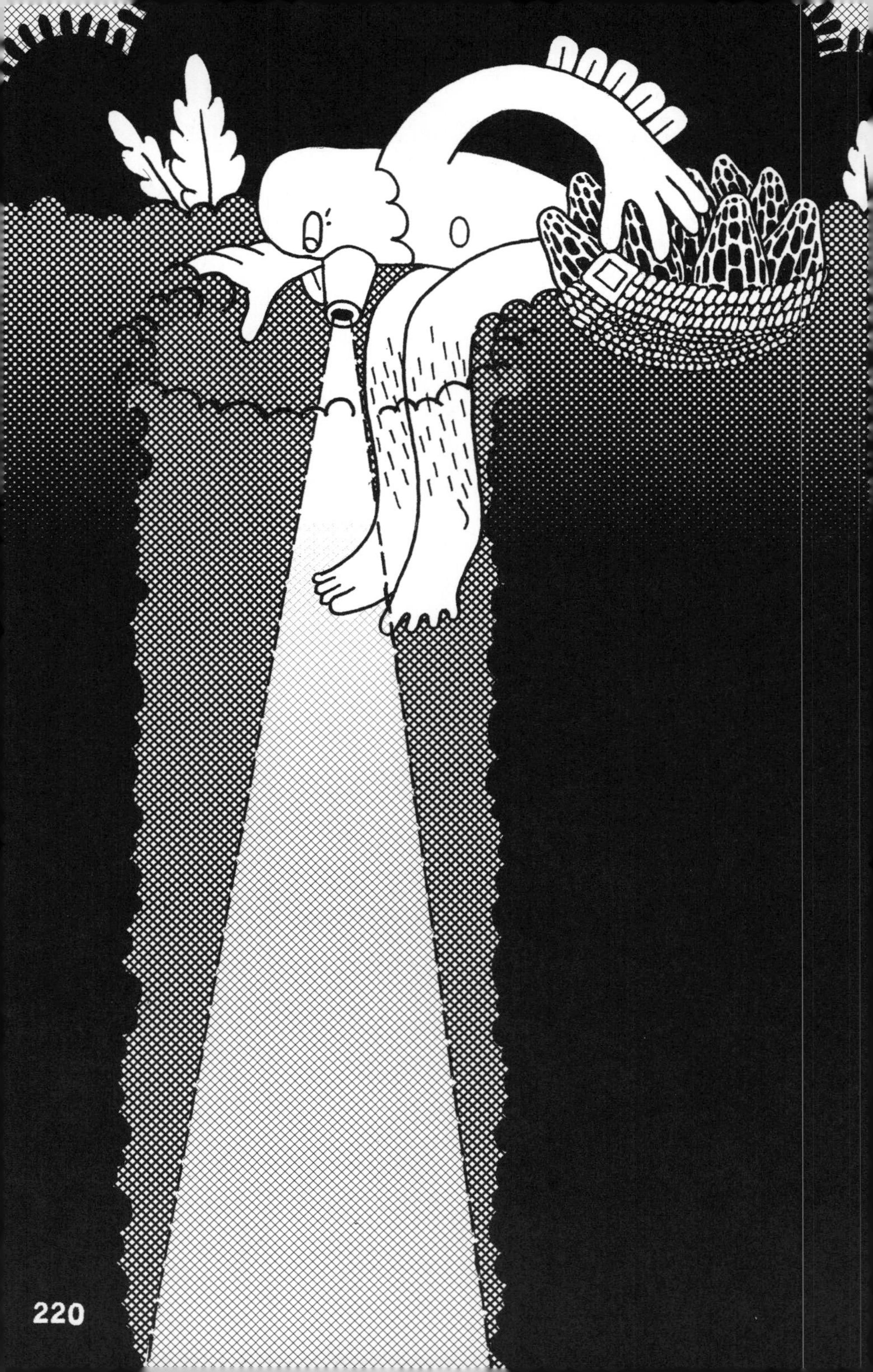

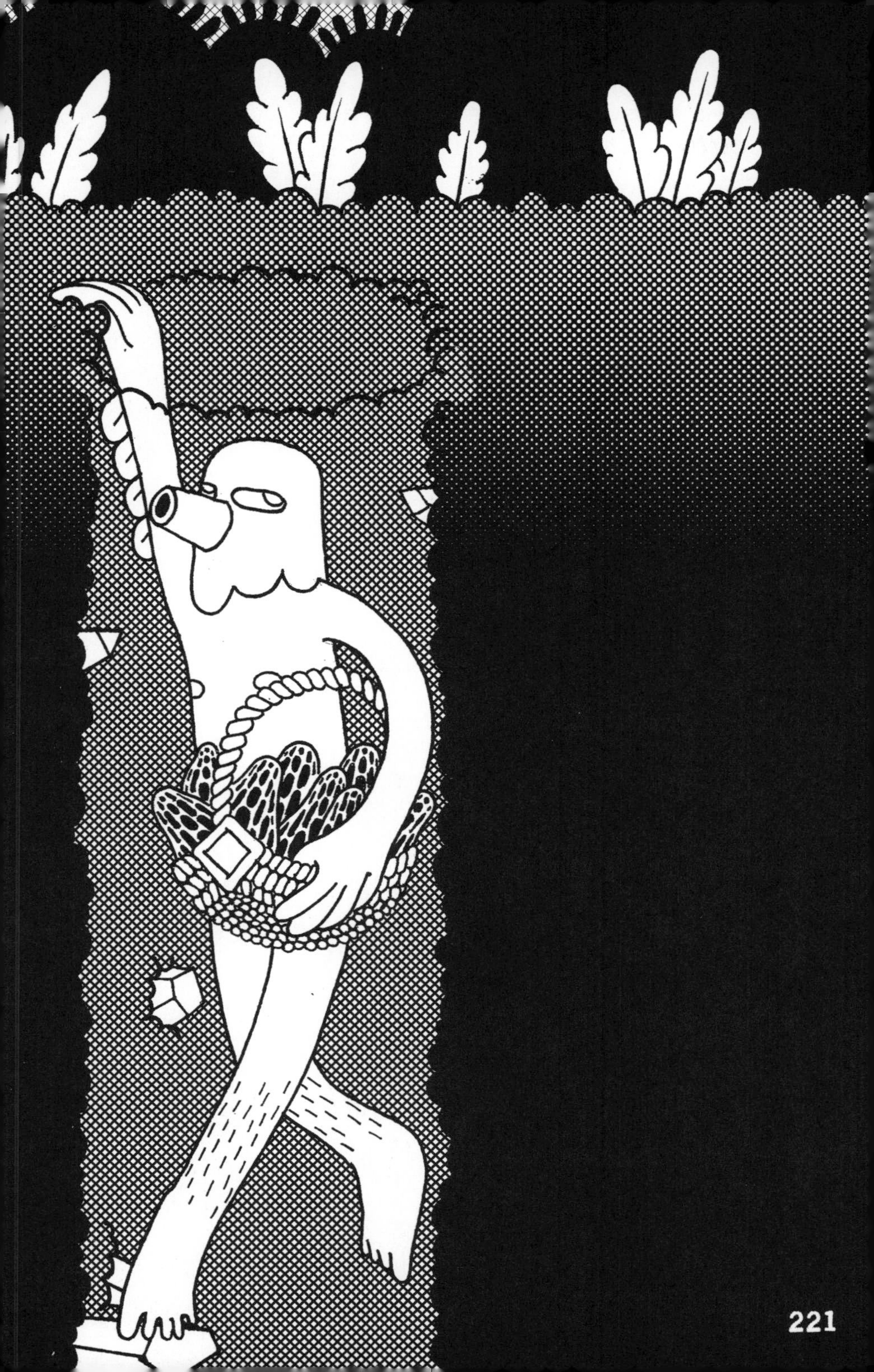

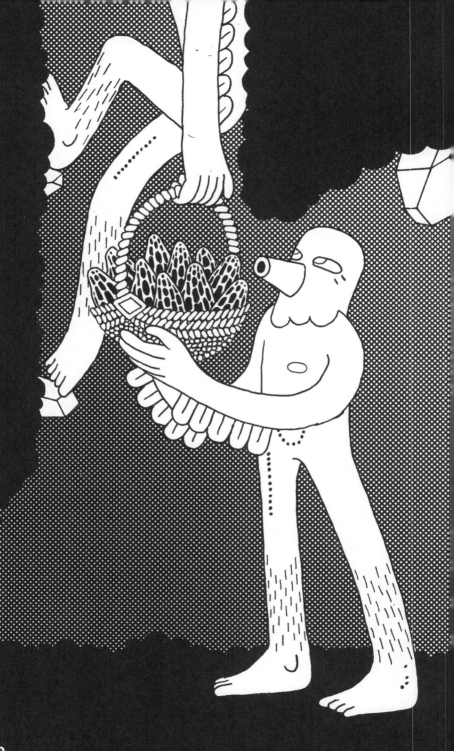

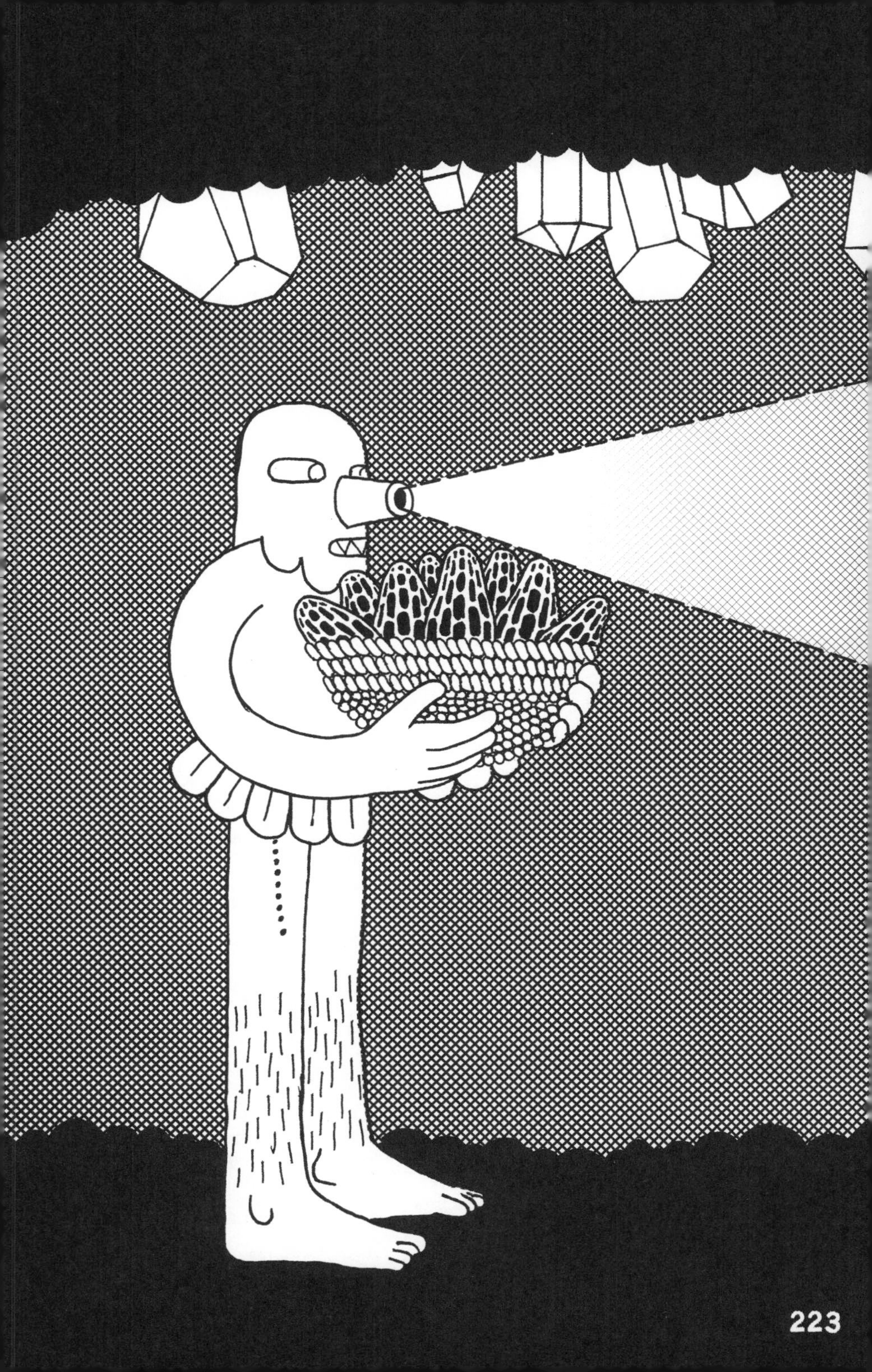

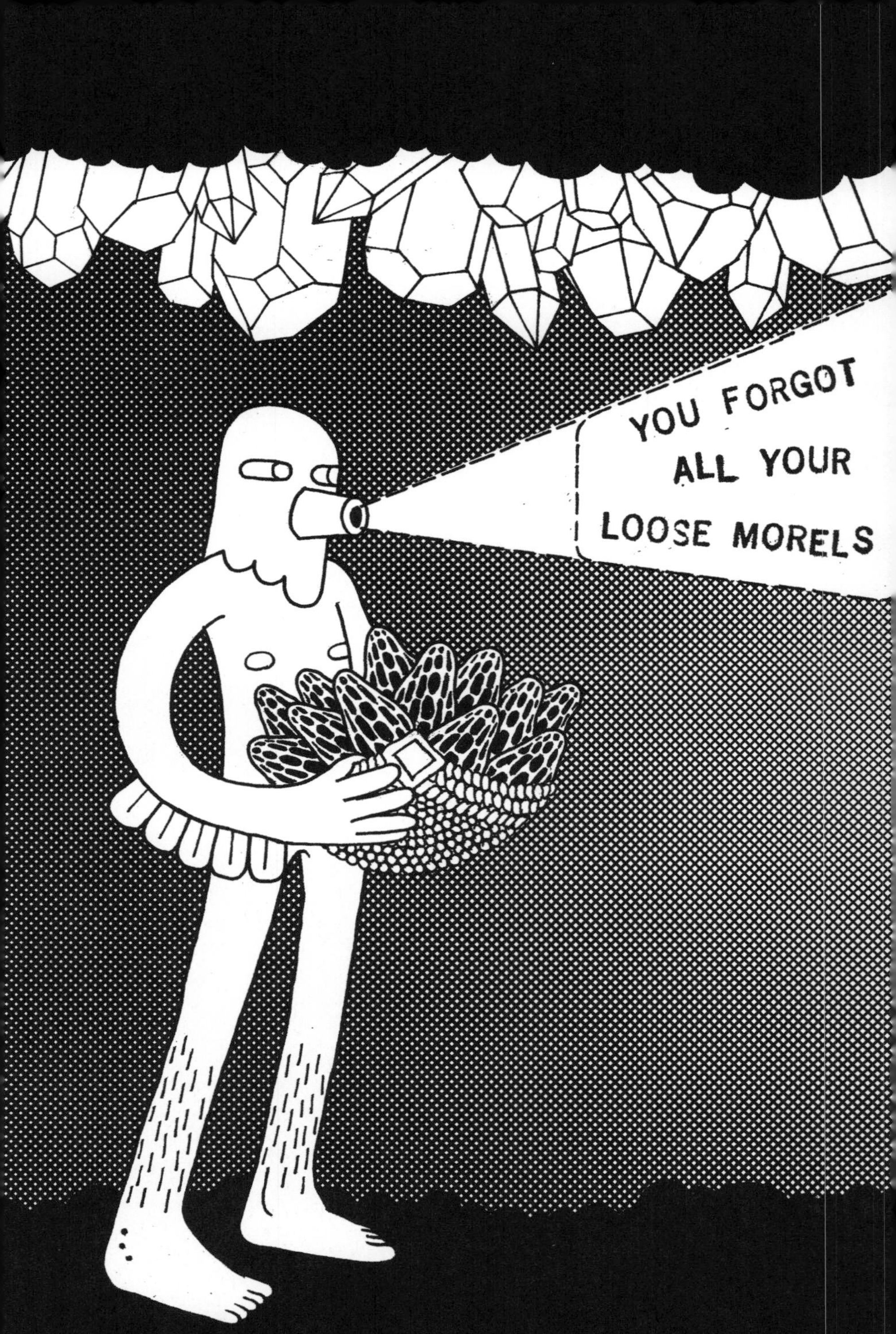
YOU FORGOT ALL YOUR LOOSE MORELS

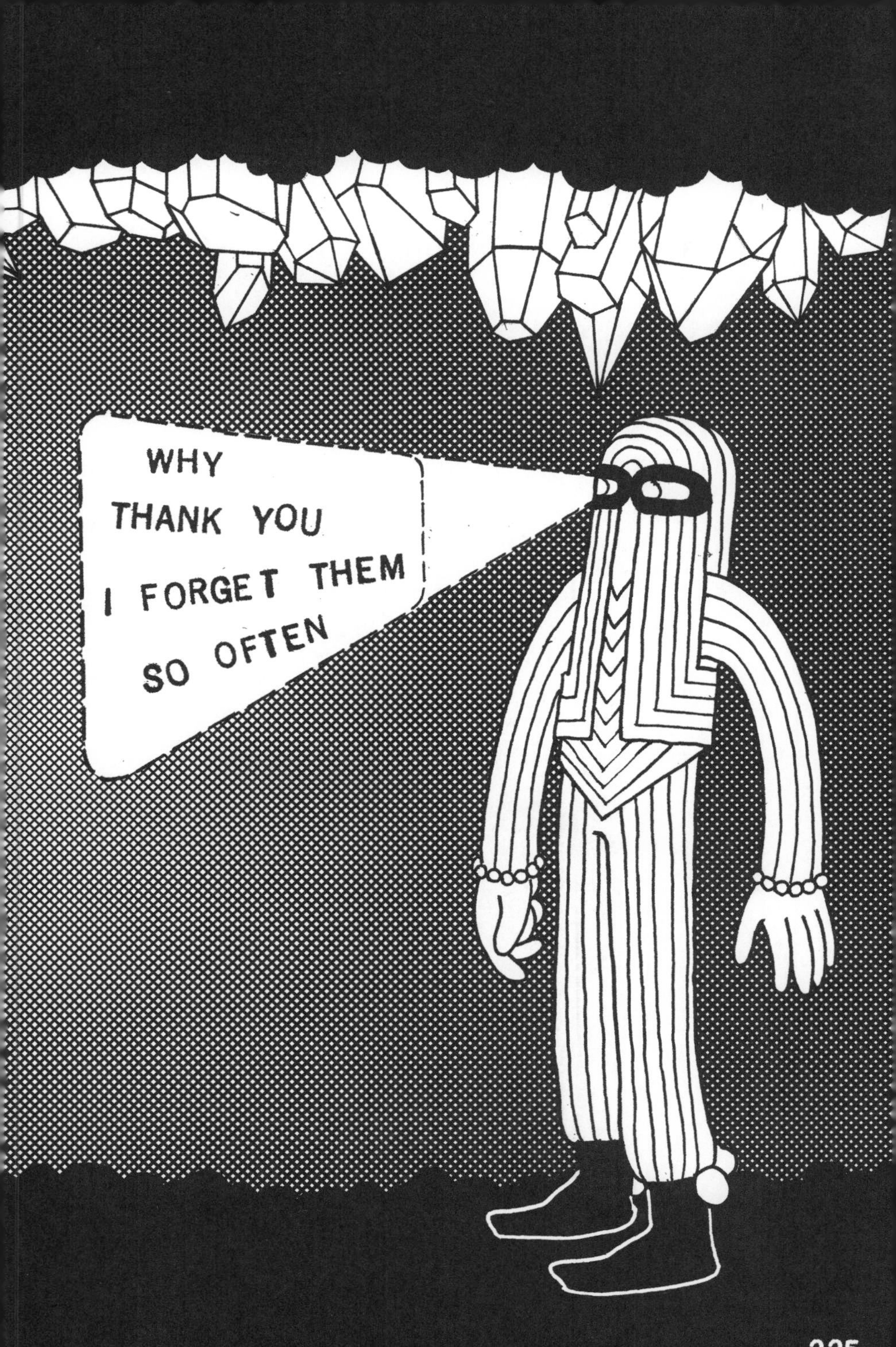
WHY THANK YOU I FORGET THEM SO OFTEN

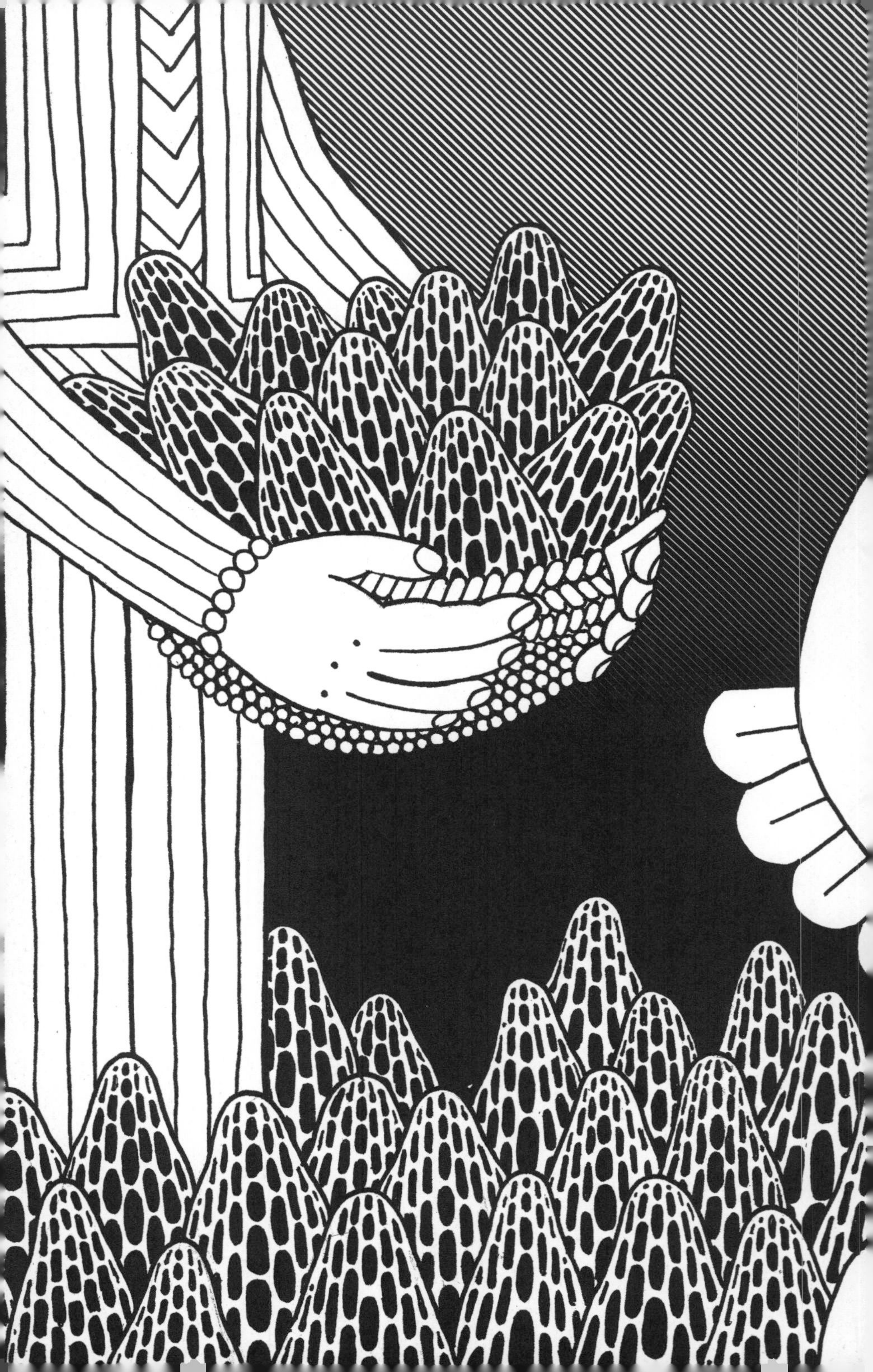

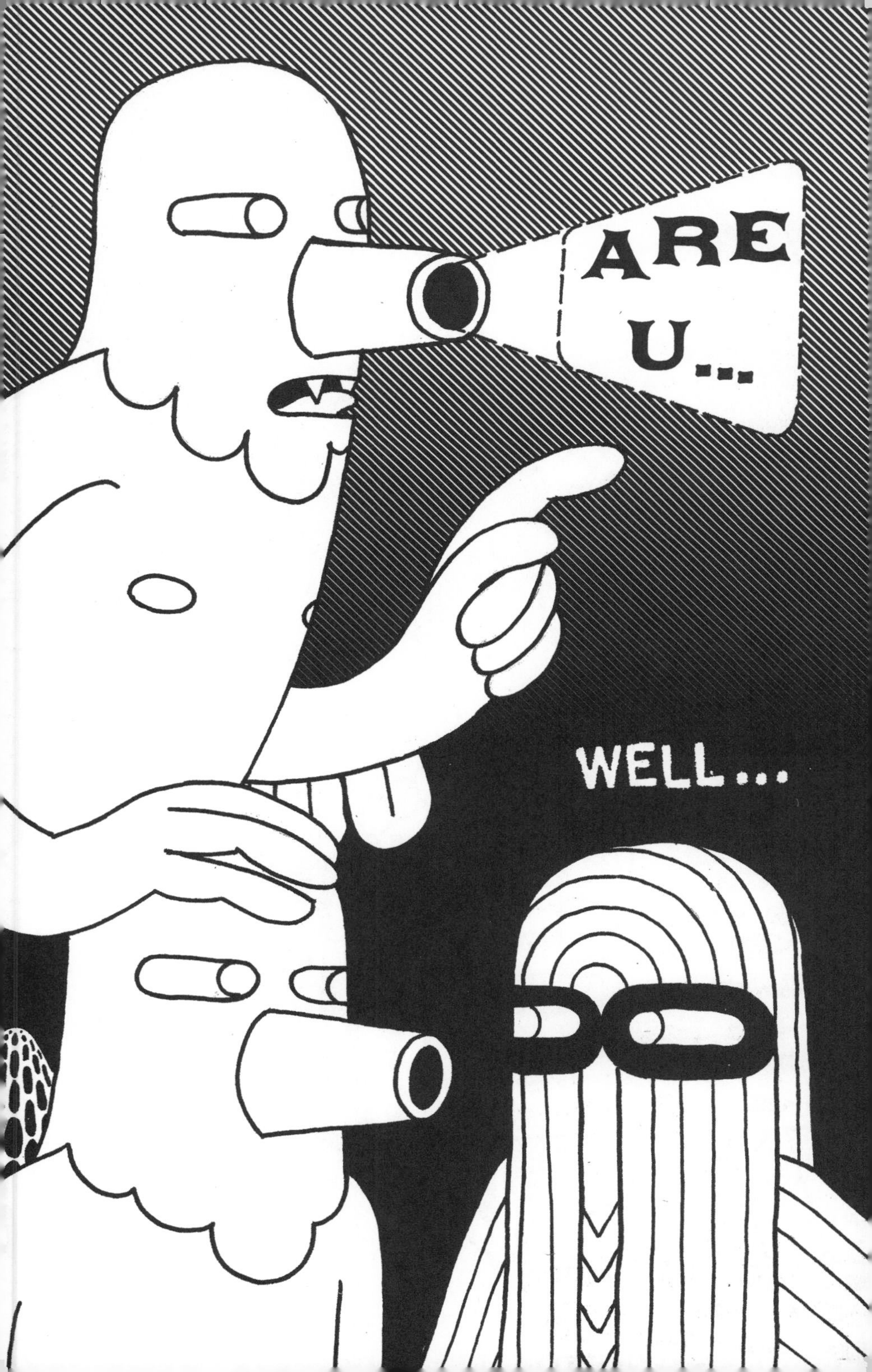
ARE U...
WELL...

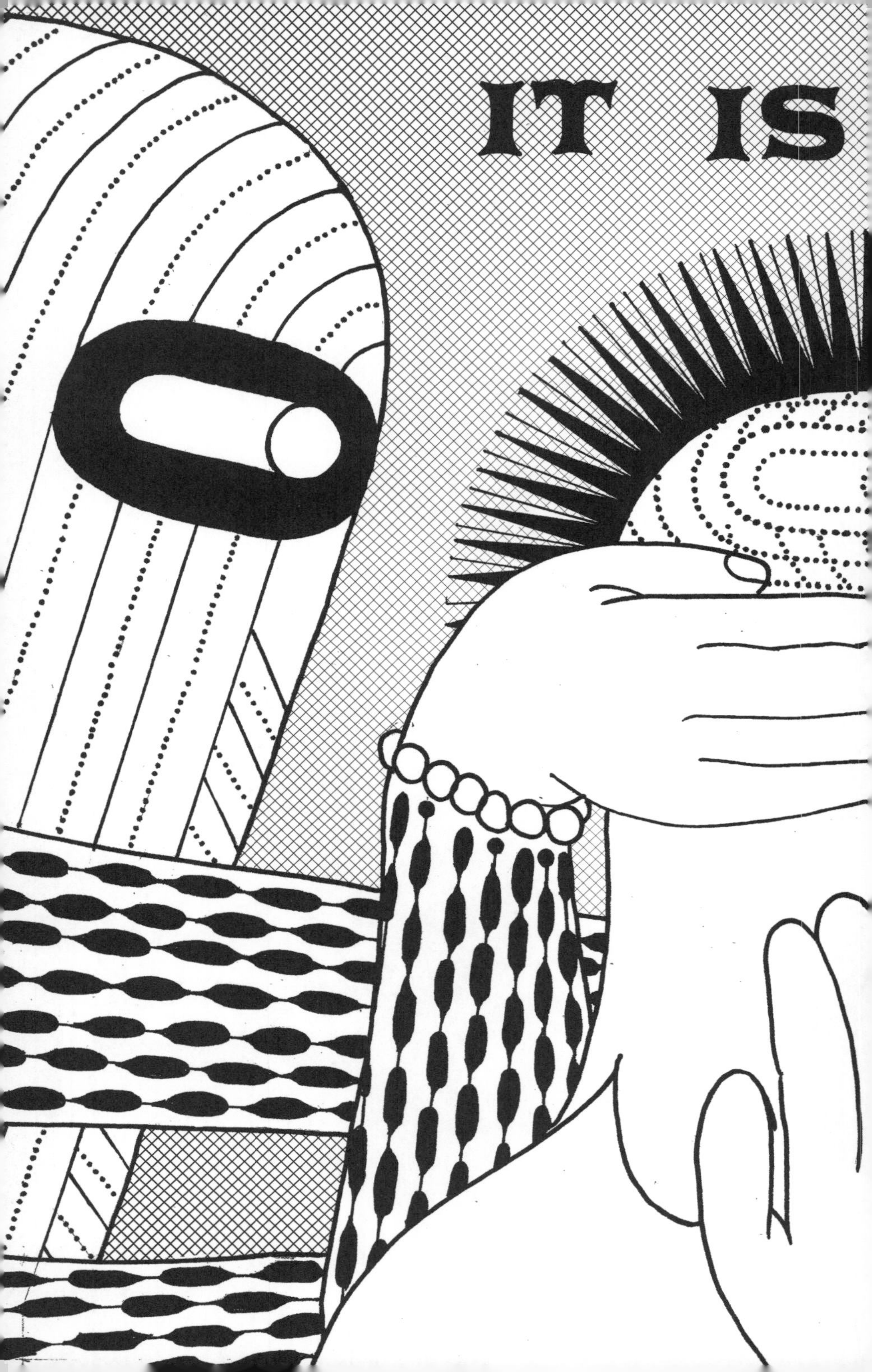
IT IS

LIKE THIS

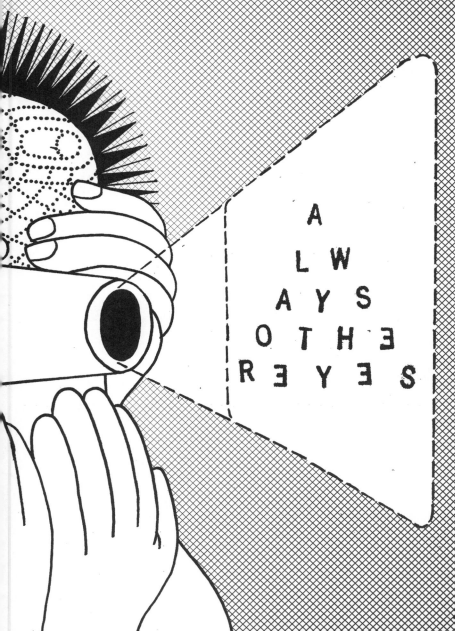

A
LW
AYS
OTHƎ
RƎYƎS

O P E N

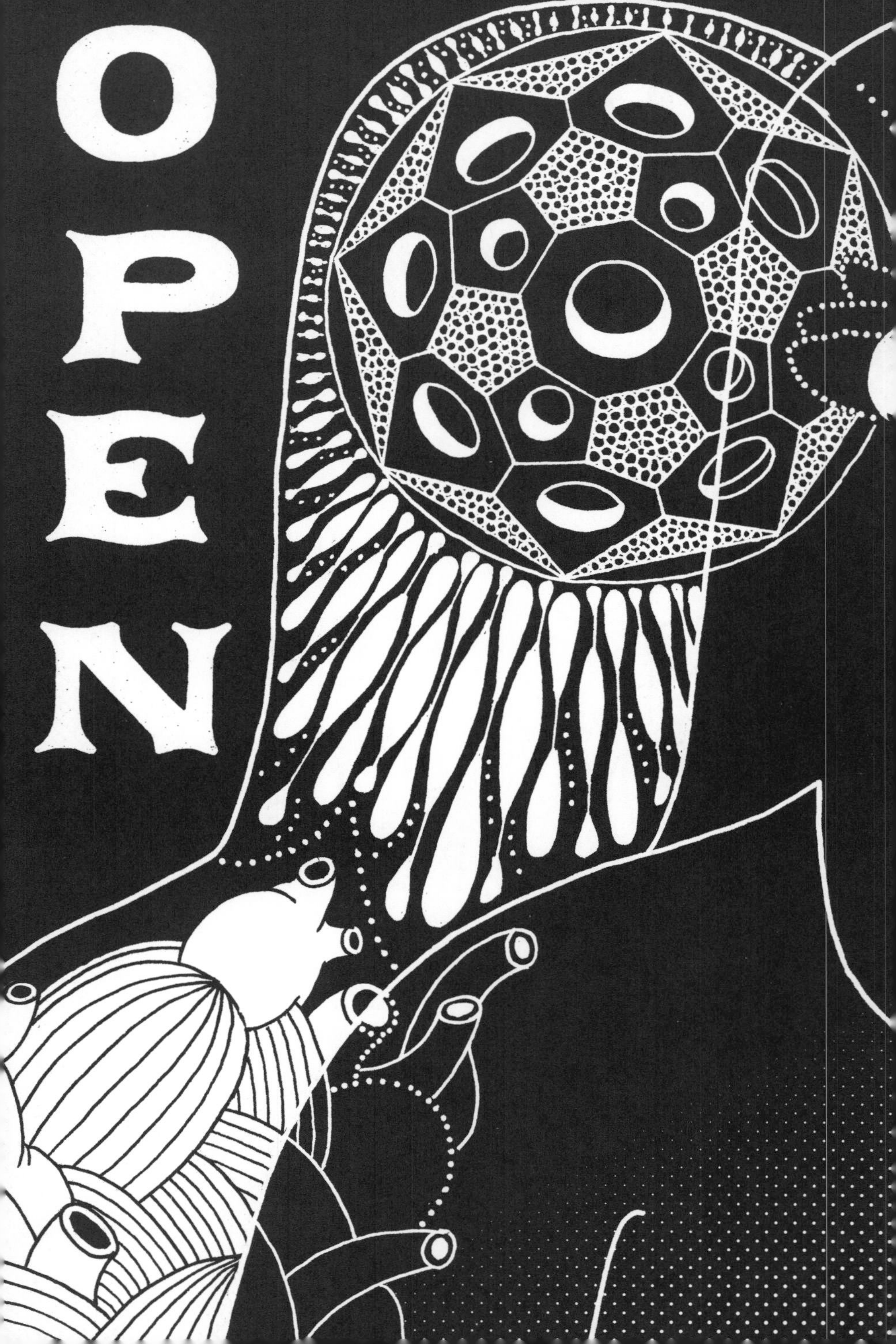

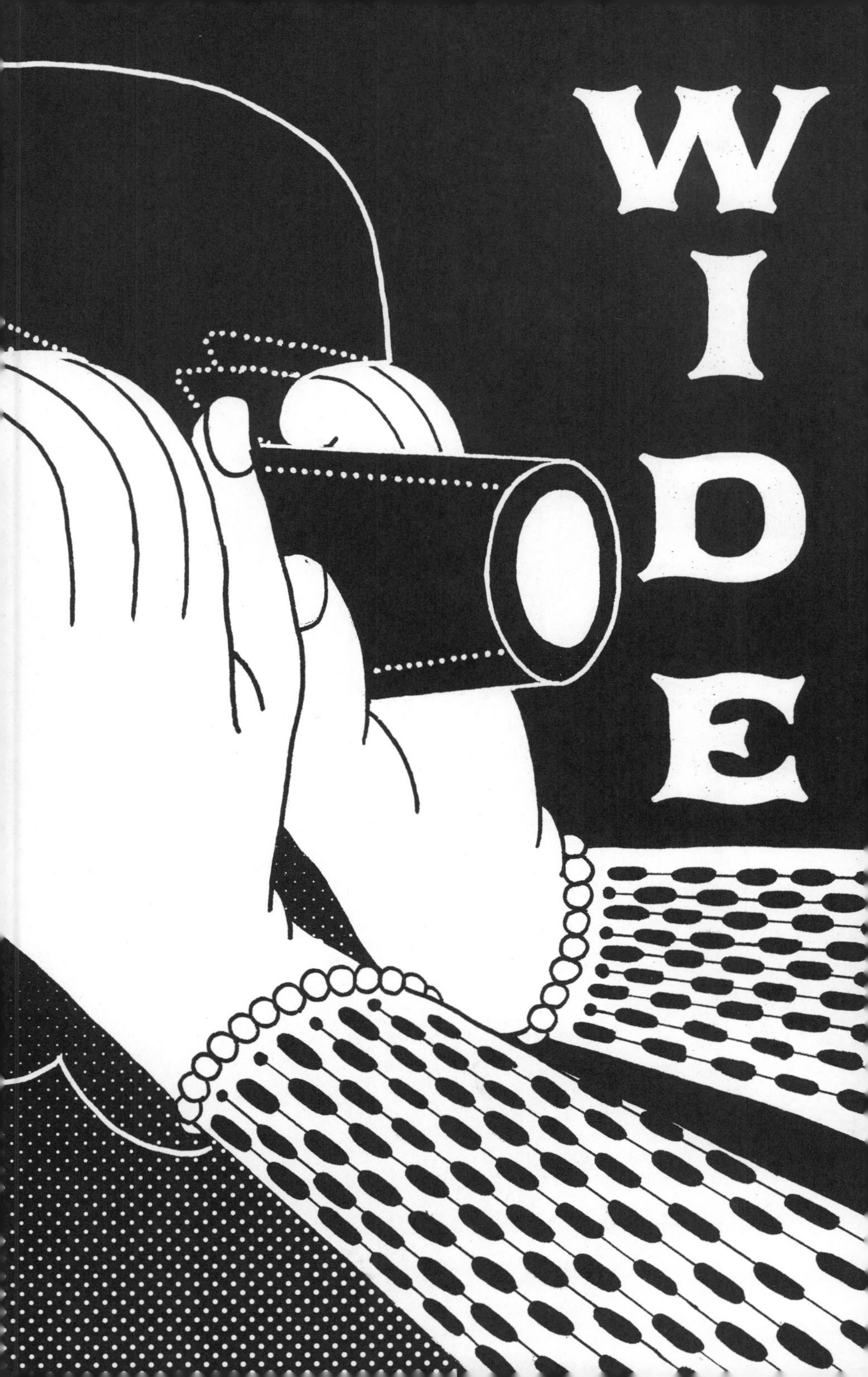
WIDE

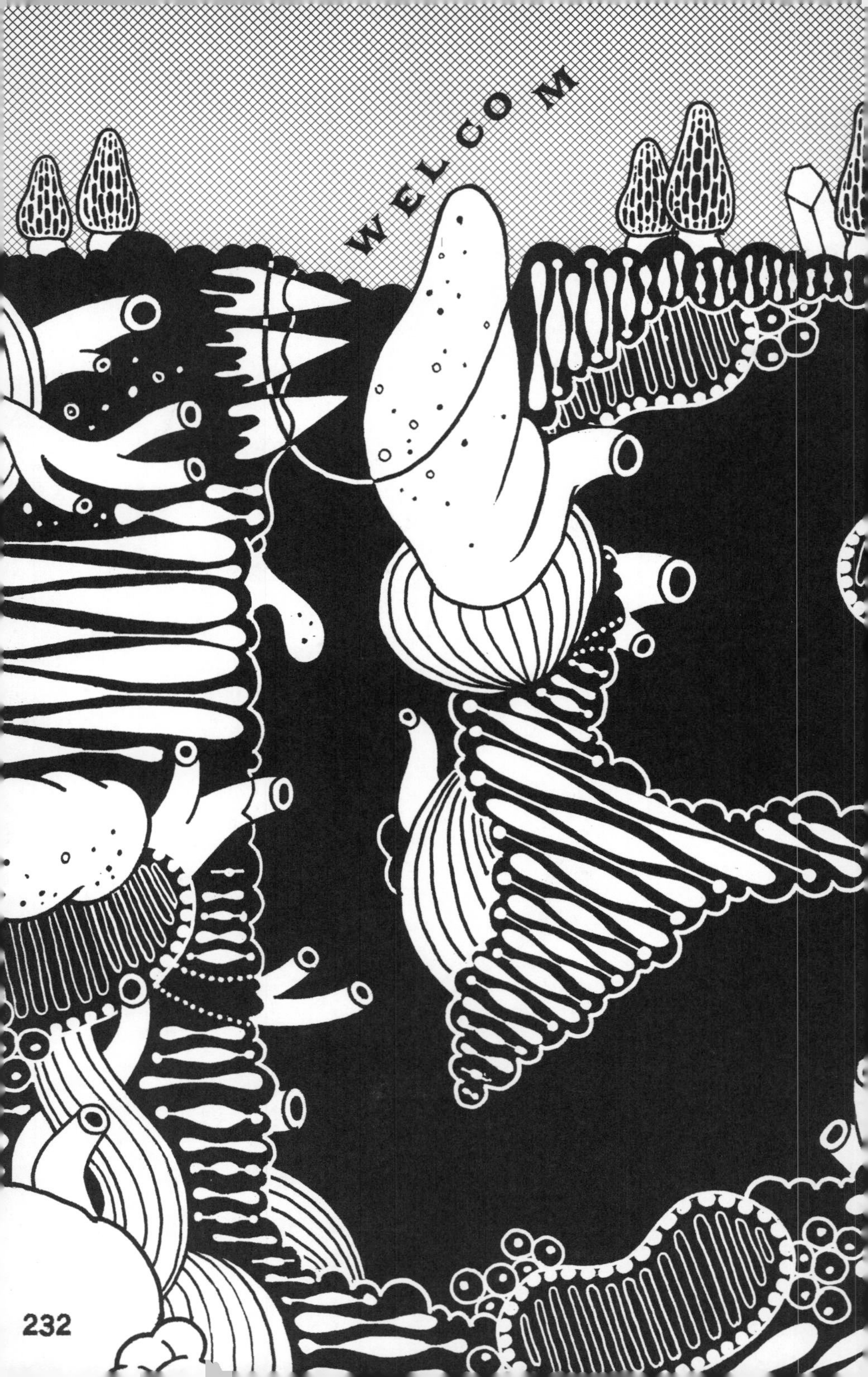
WELCOM

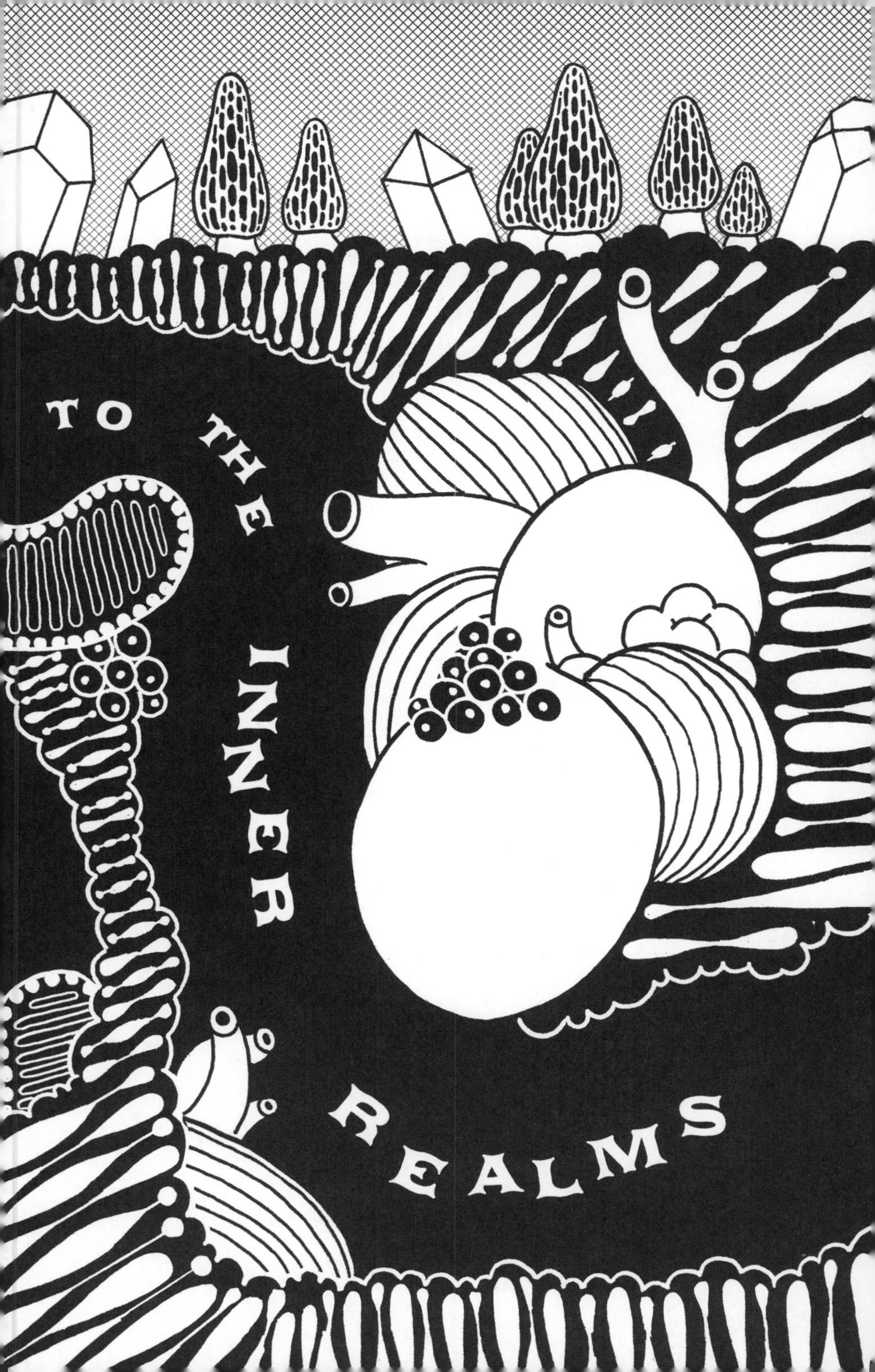
TO THE INNER REALMS

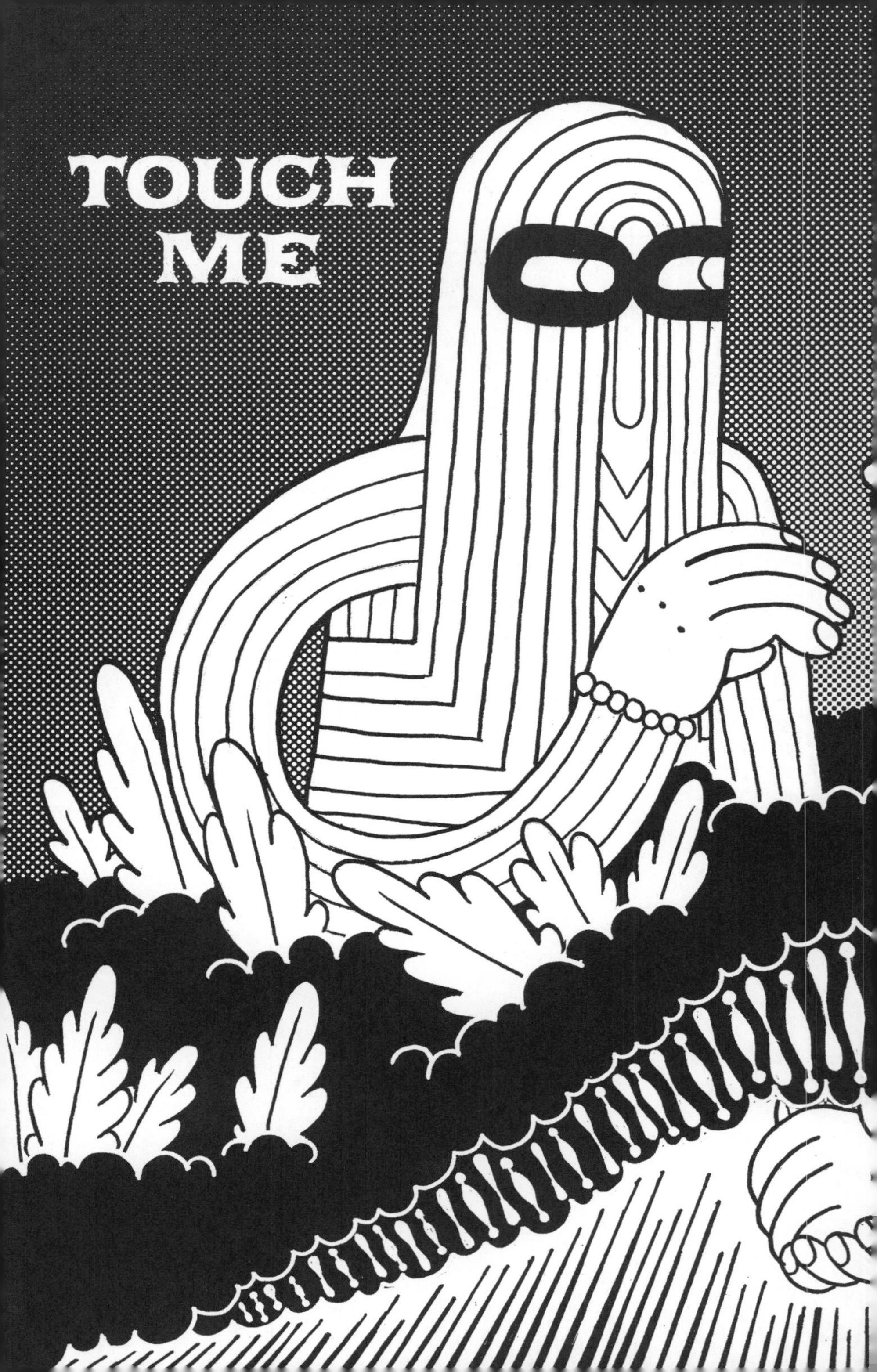
TOUCH
ME

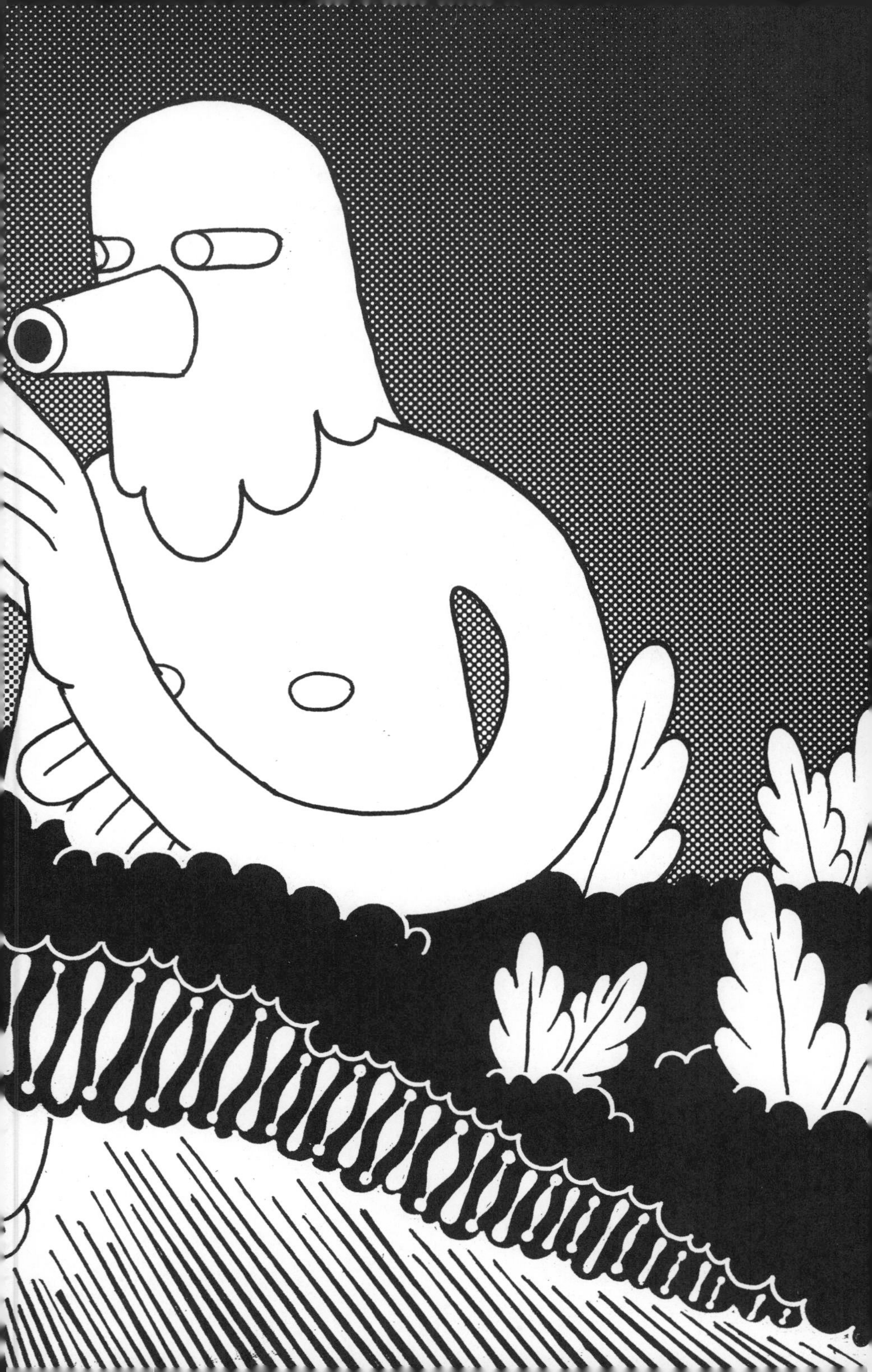

...AND SHOW

YR

SENSE

OF

SELF

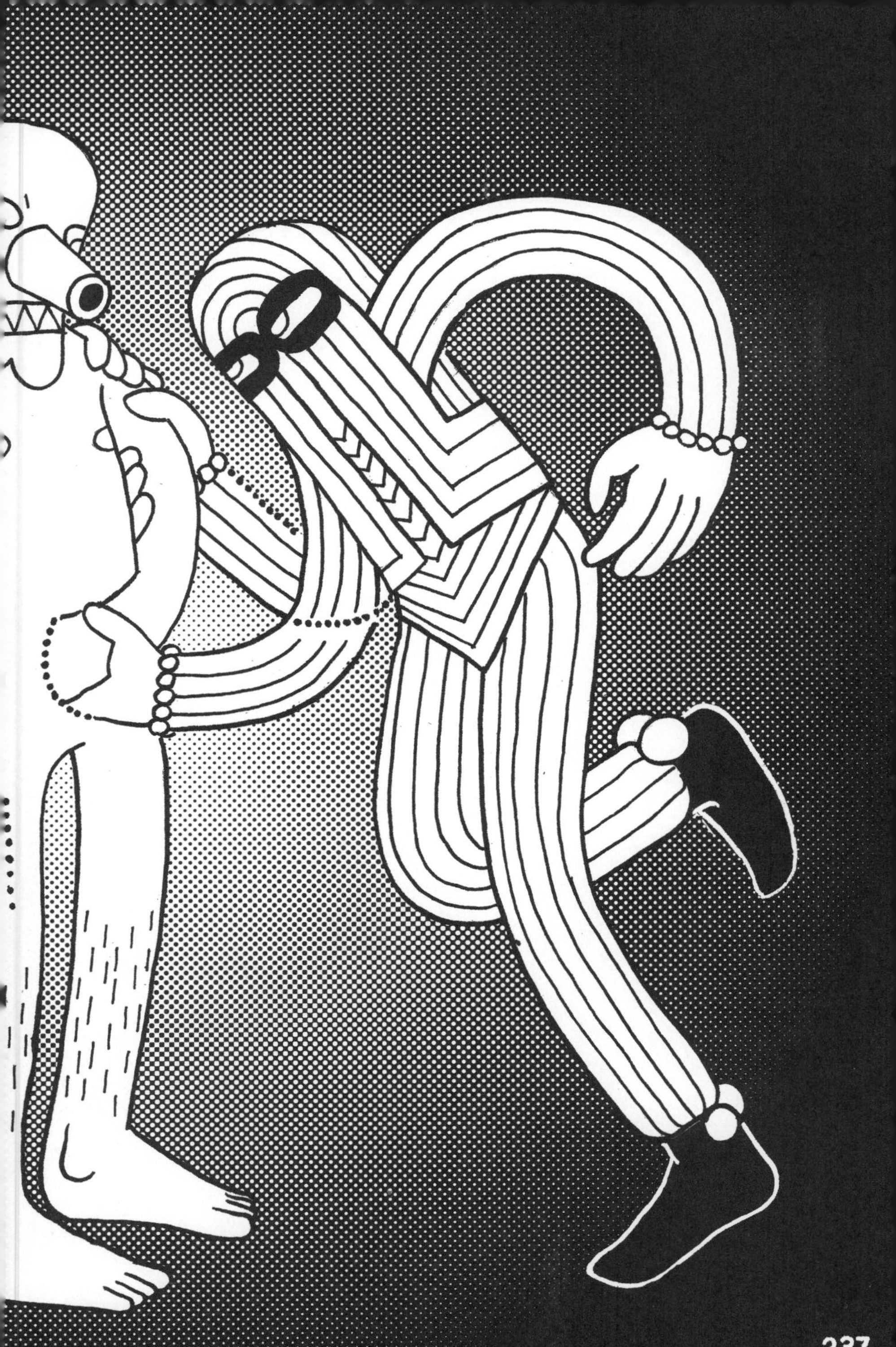

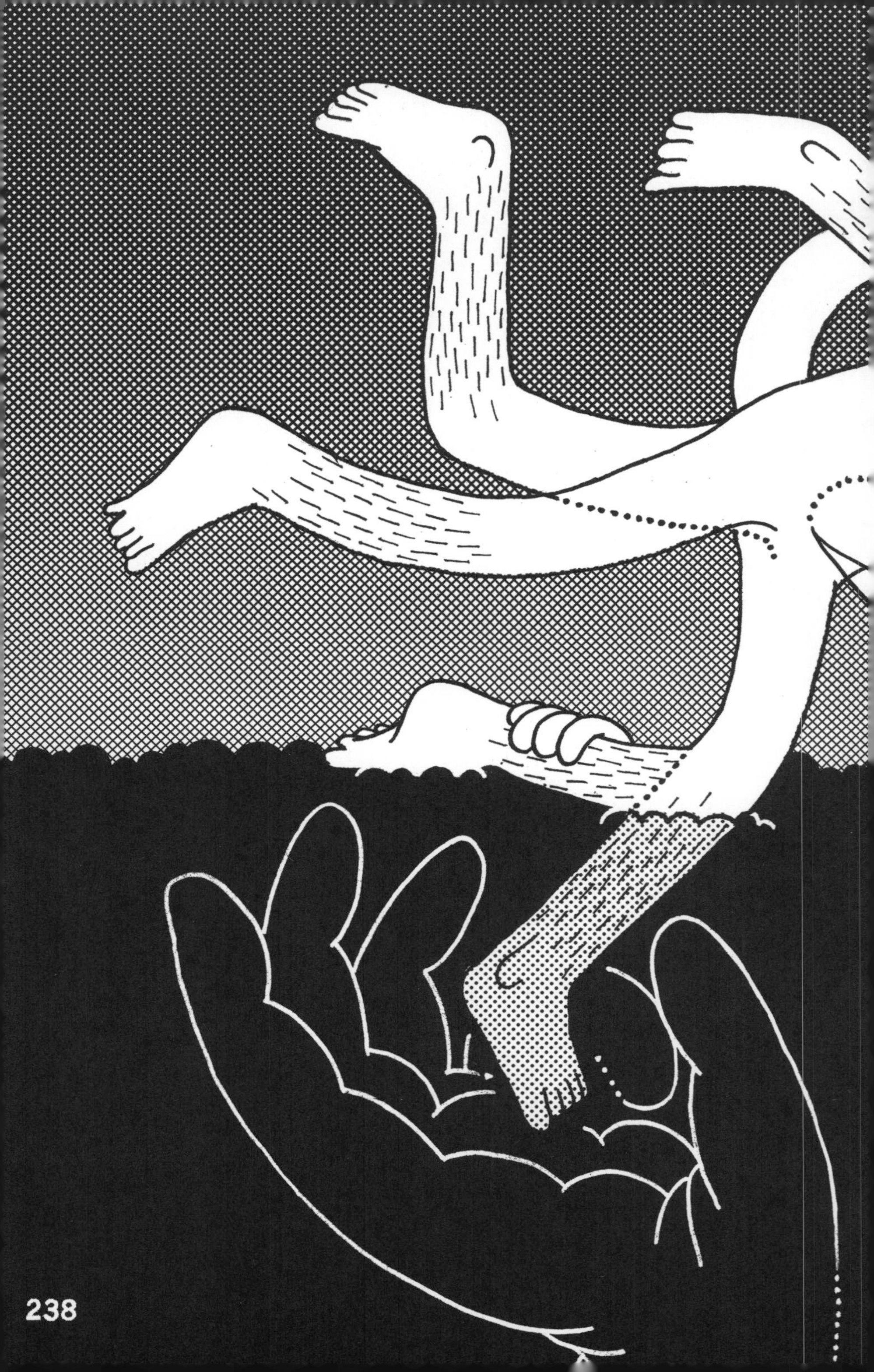

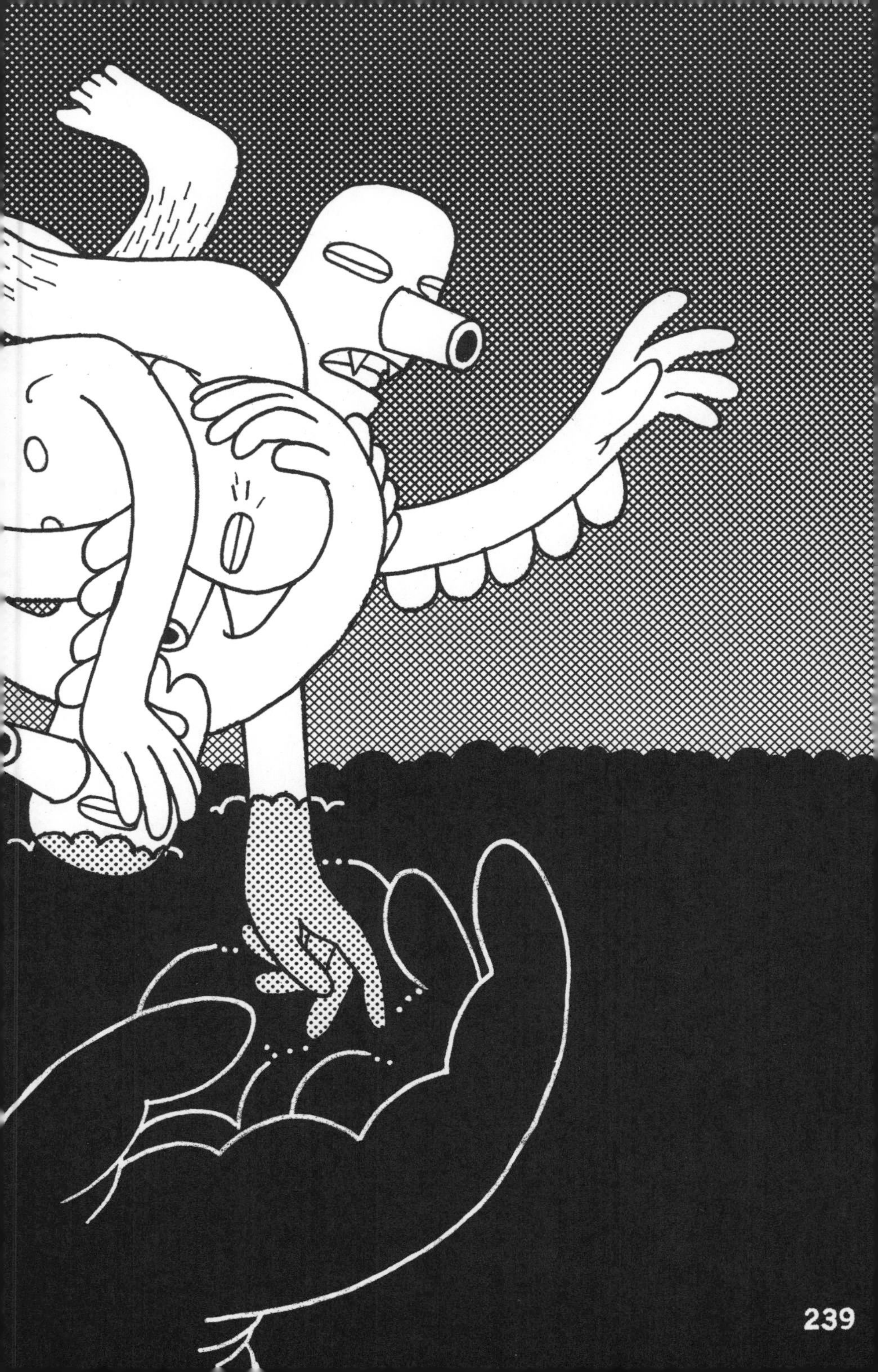

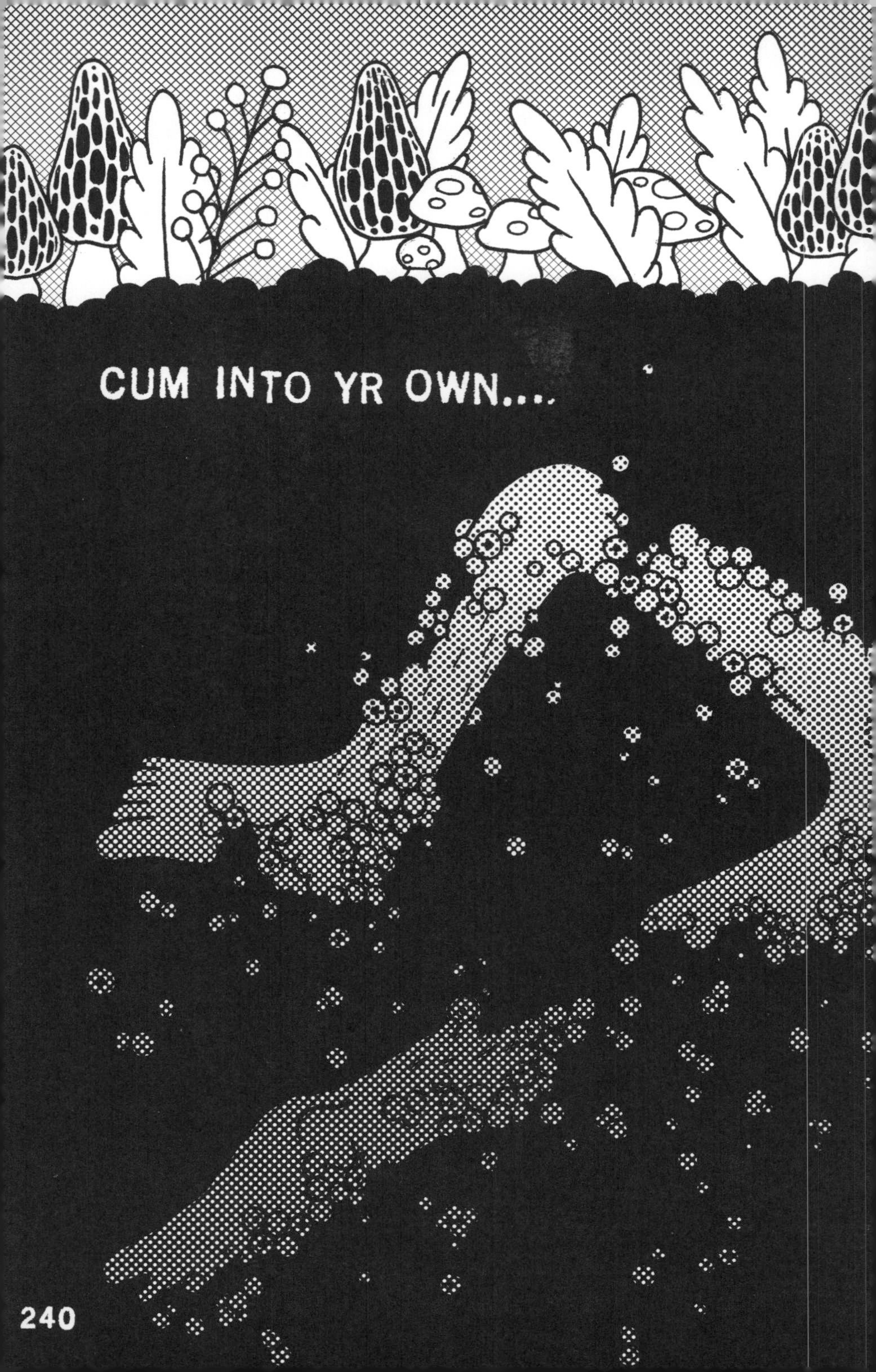
CUM INTO YR OWN....

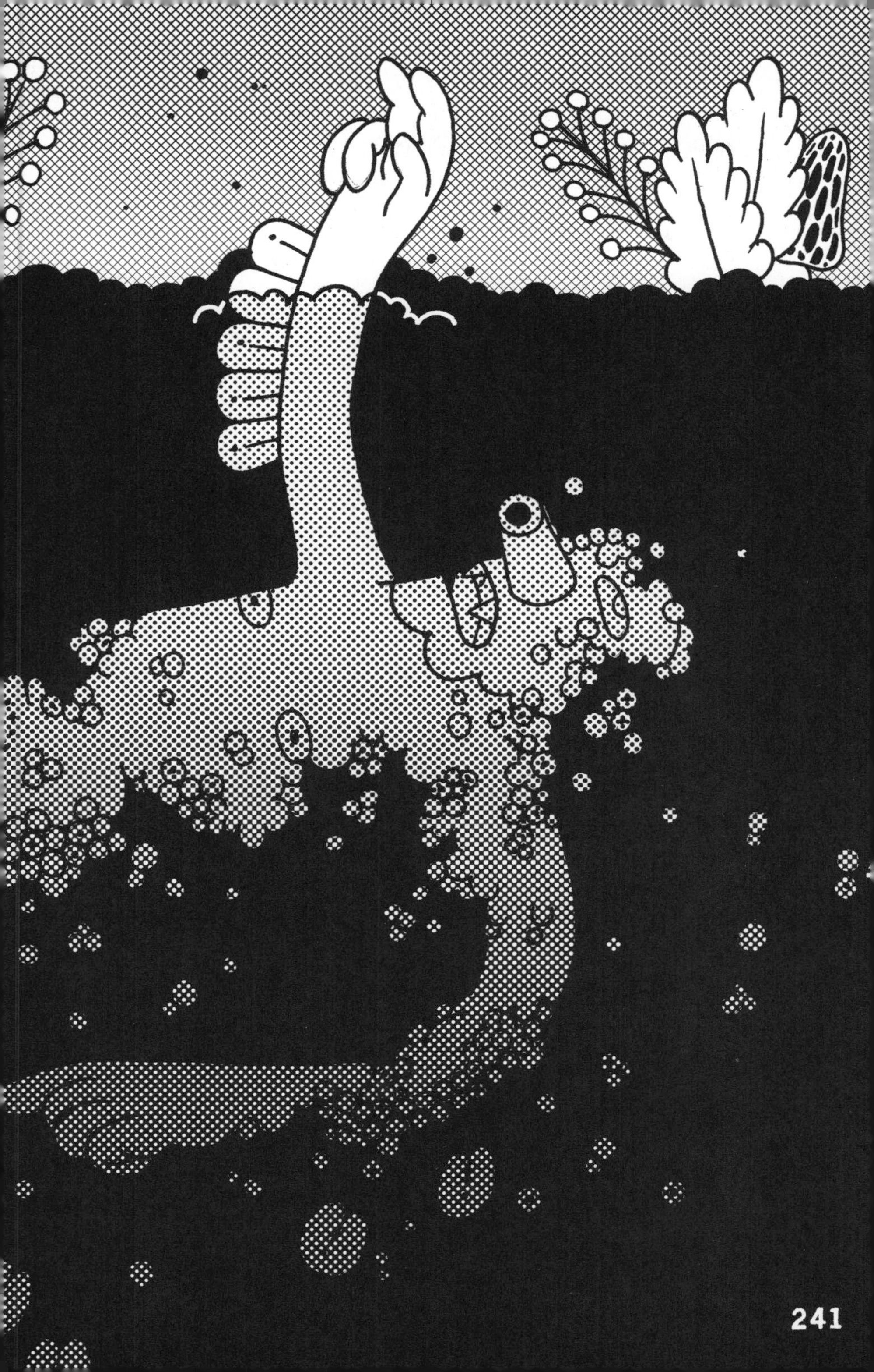

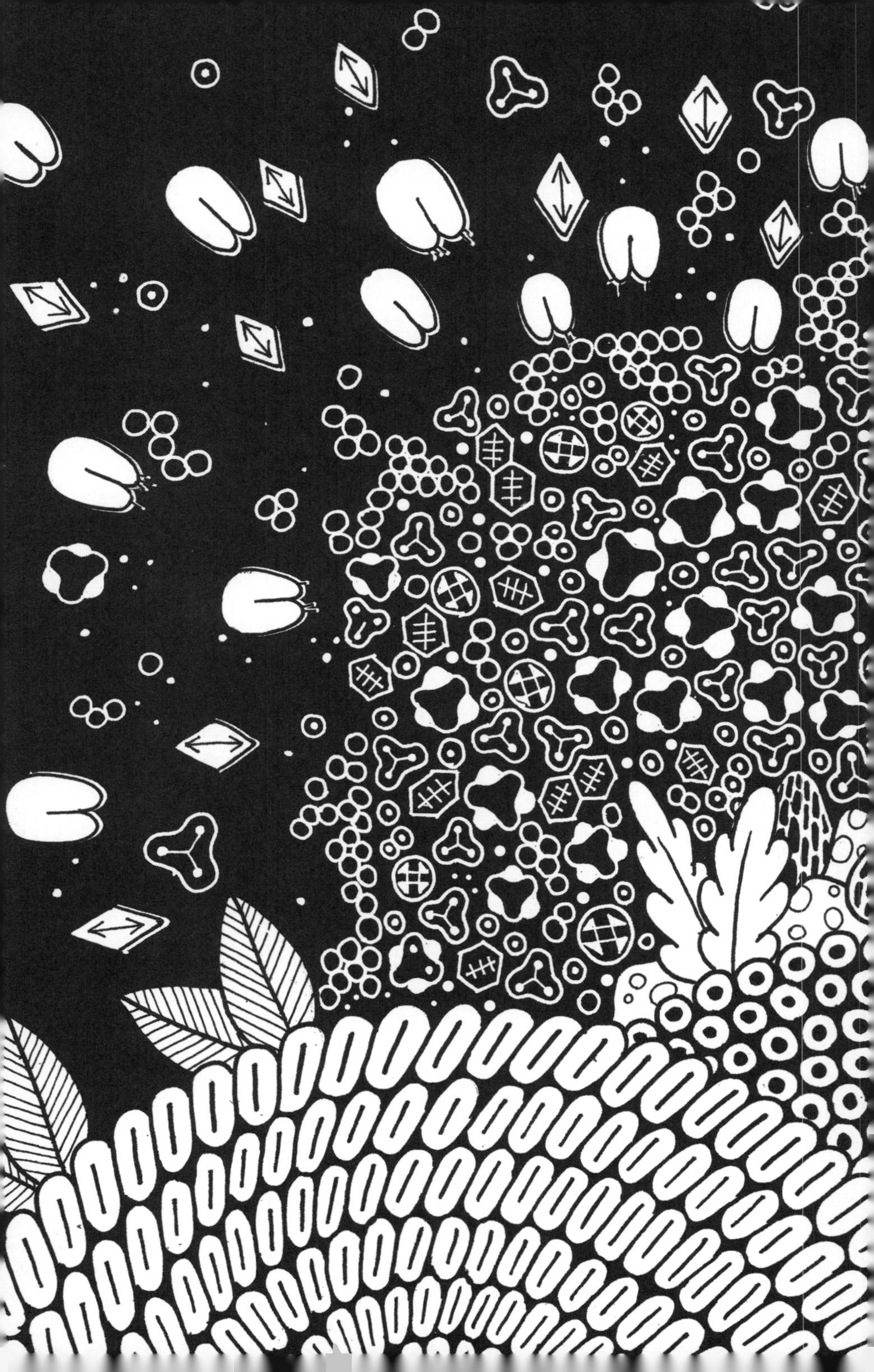

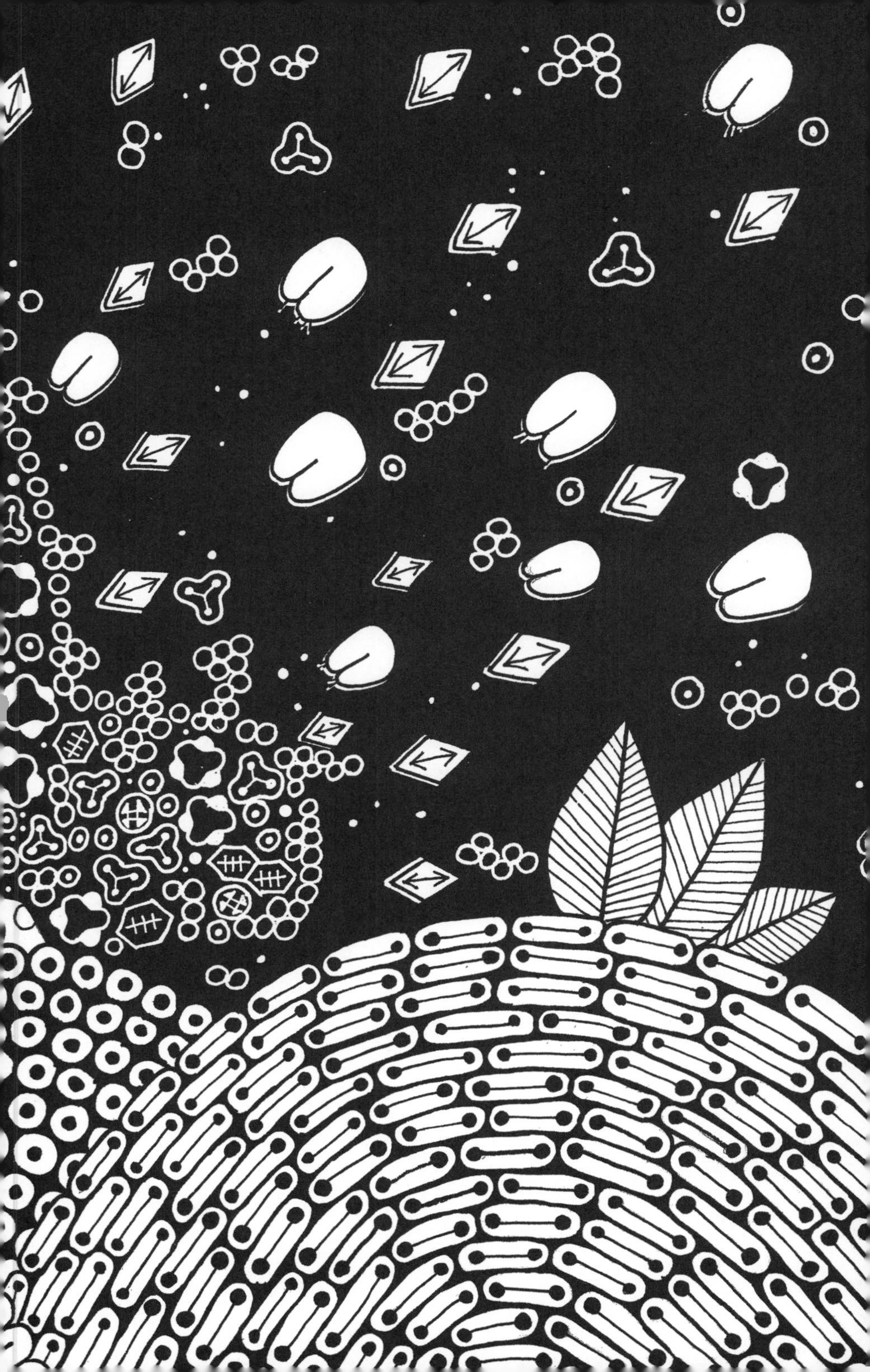

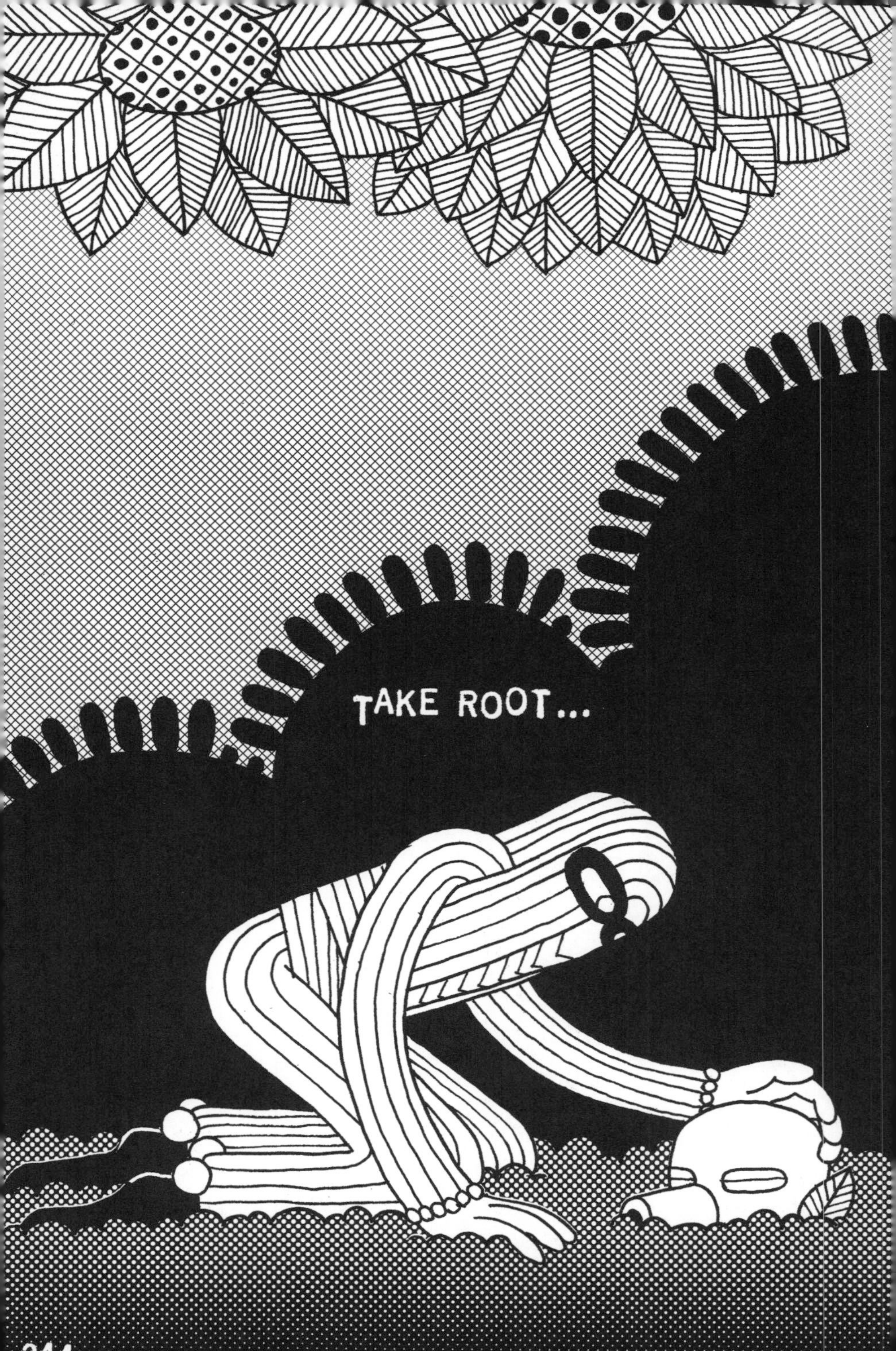
TAKE ROOT...

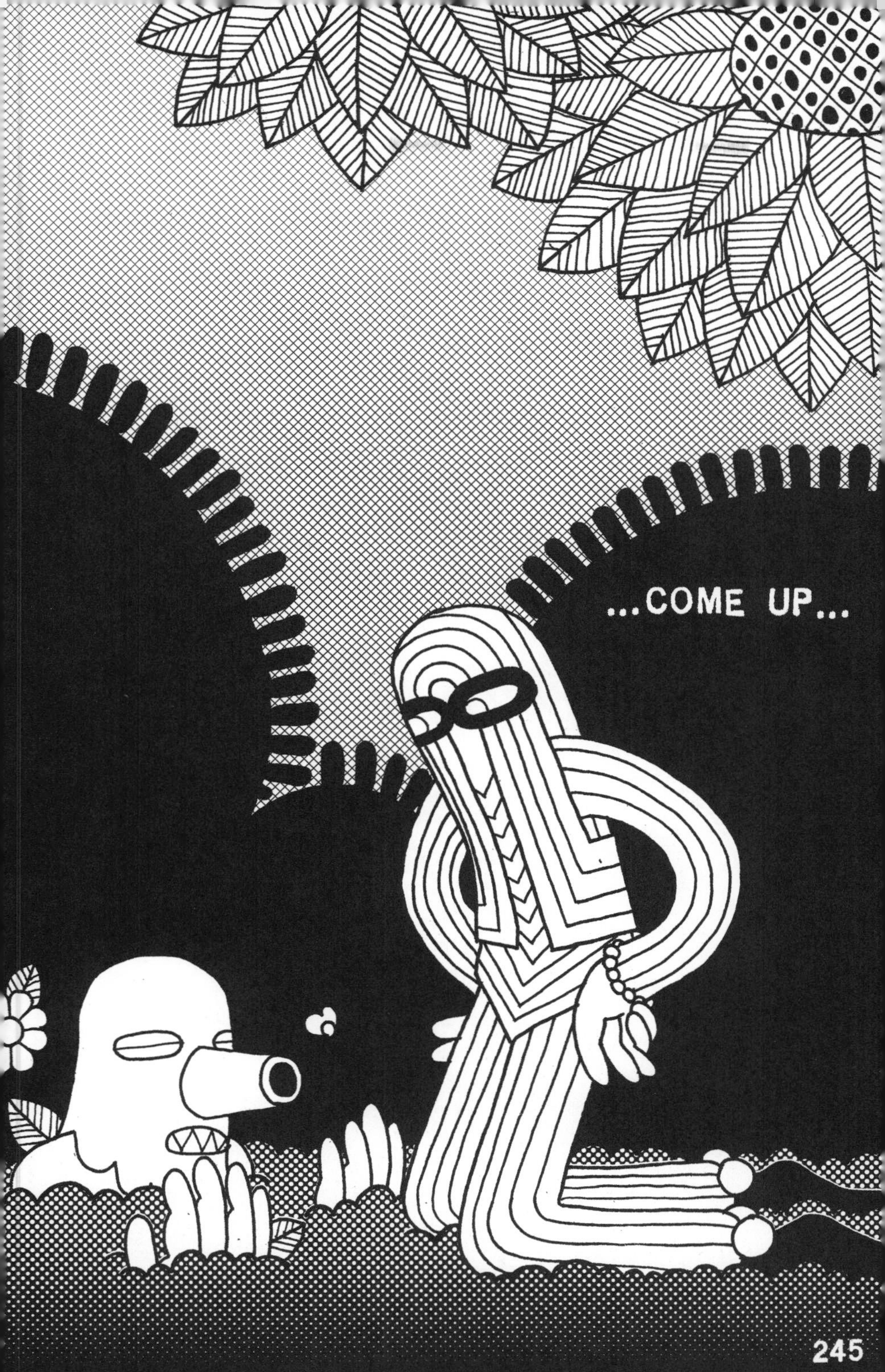
...COME UP...

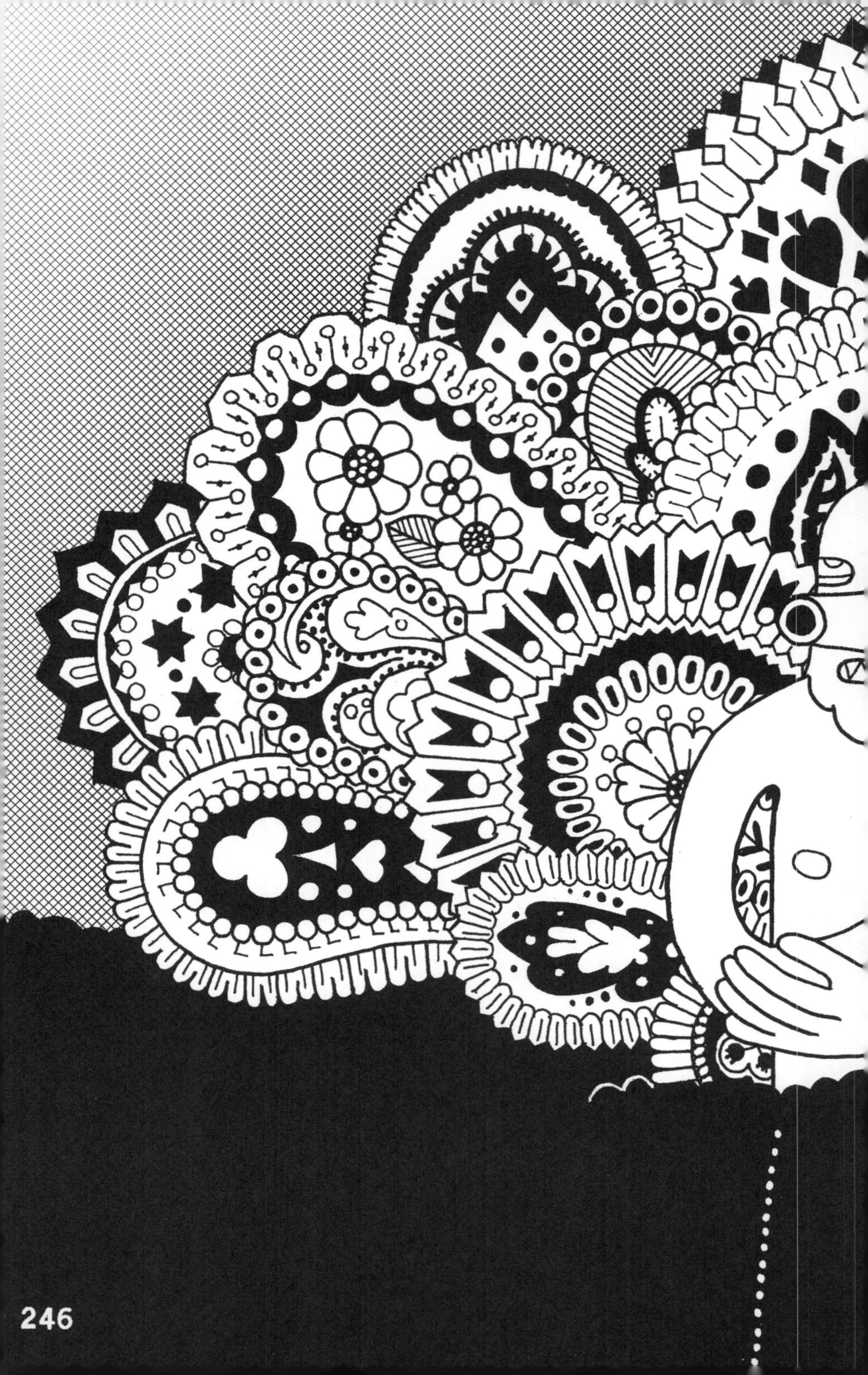

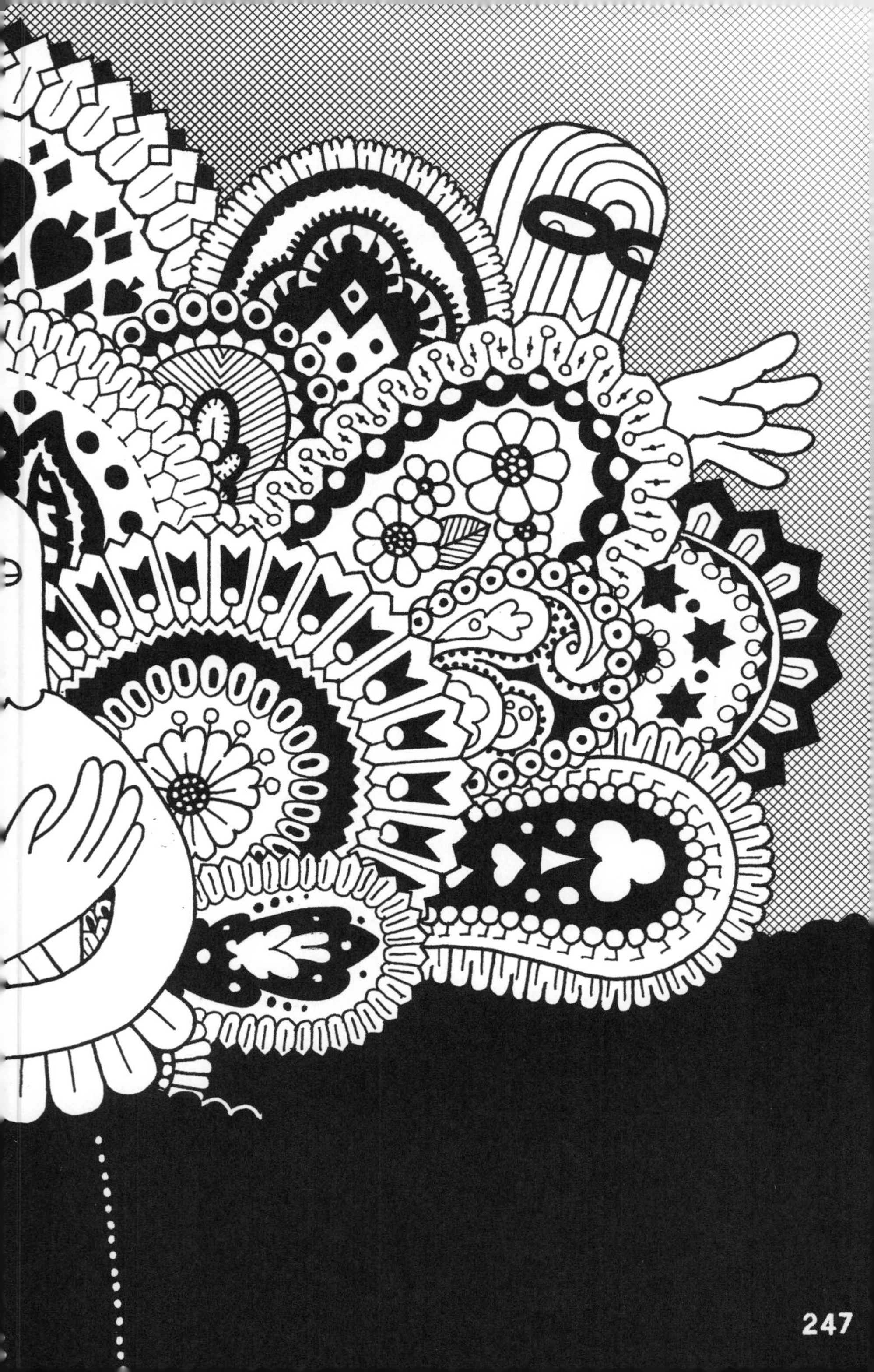

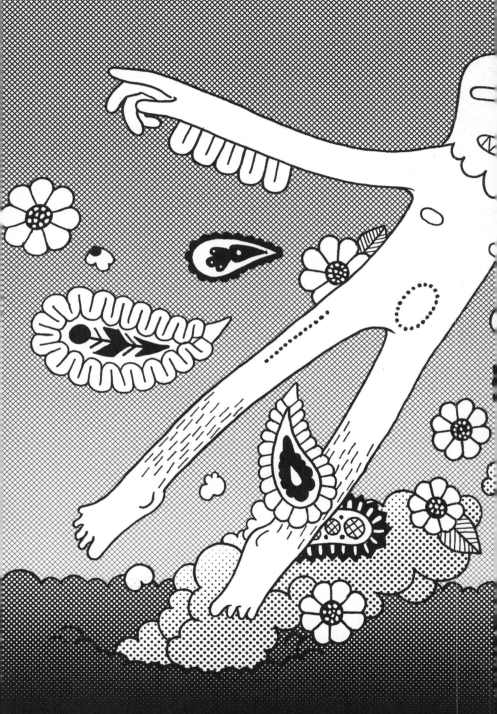

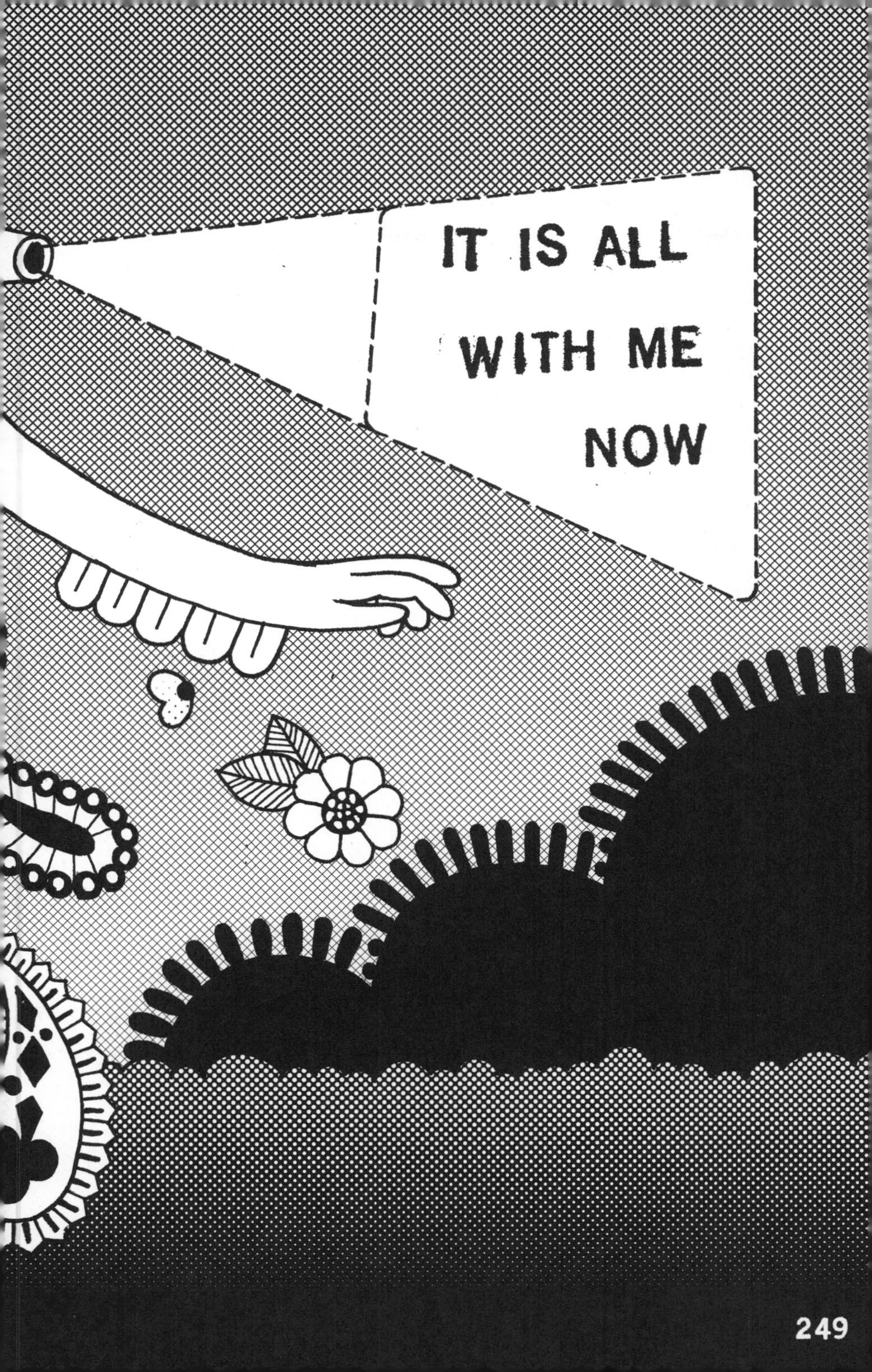
IT IS ALL
WITH ME
NOW

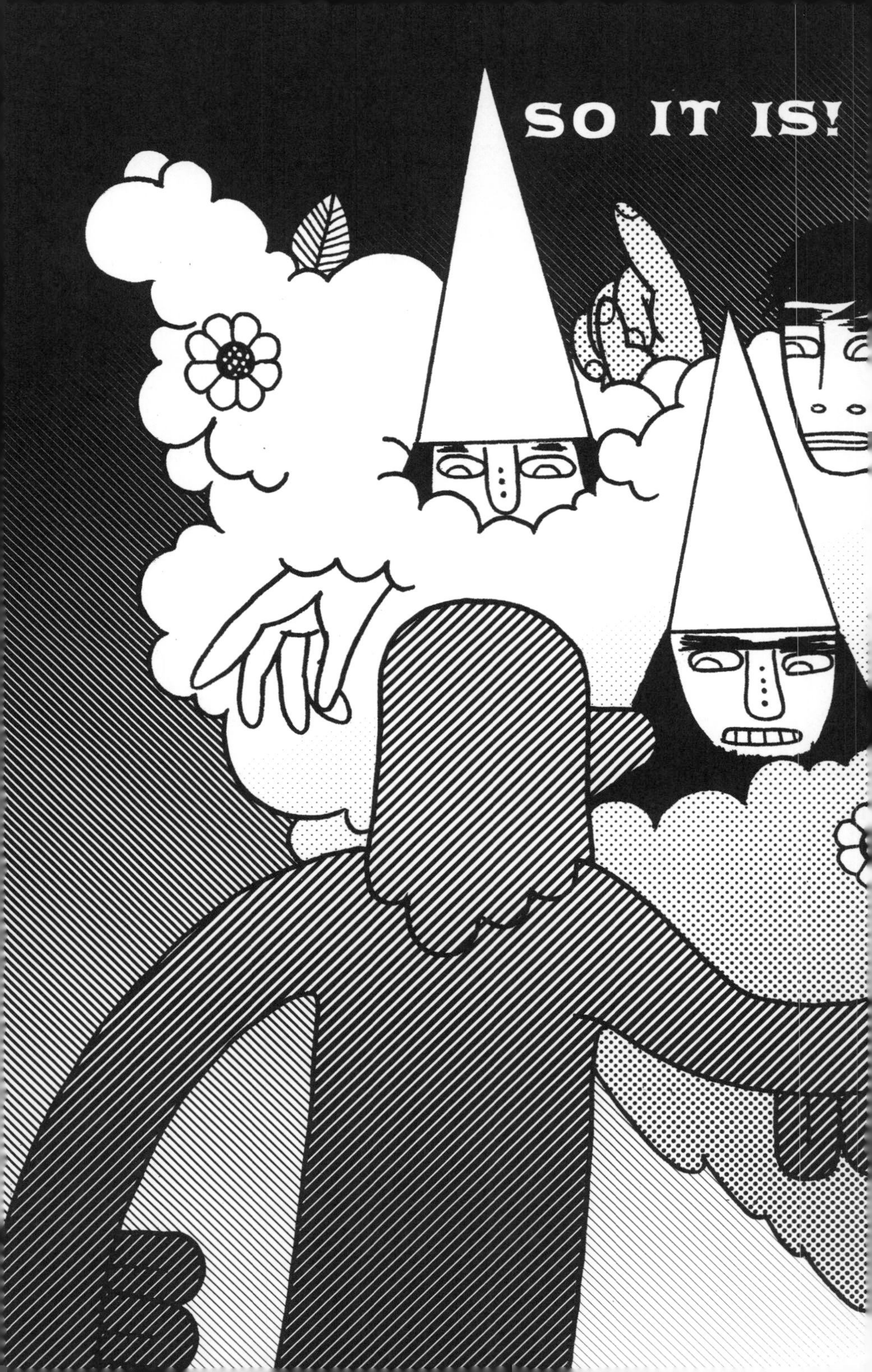
SO IT IS!

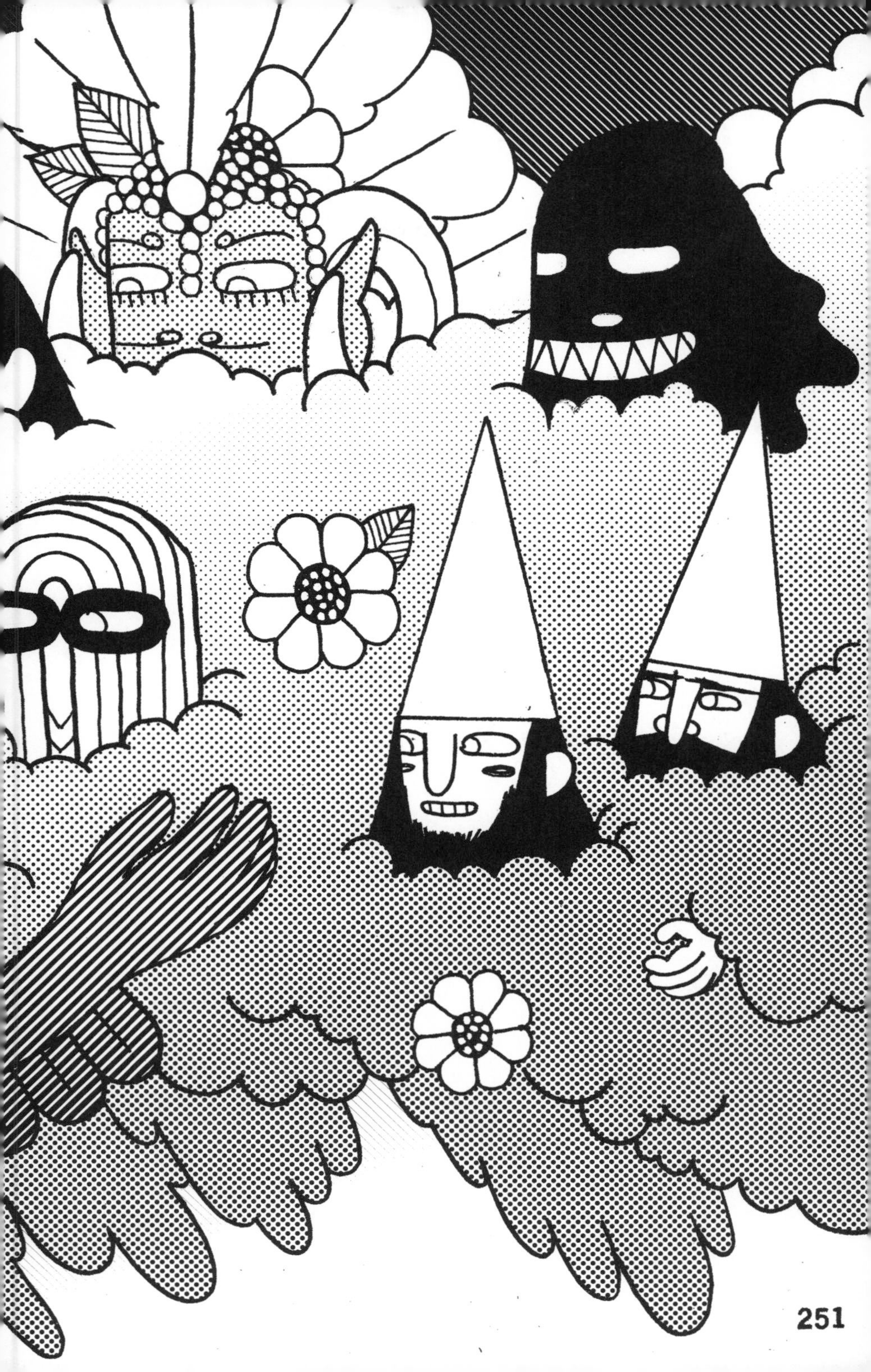

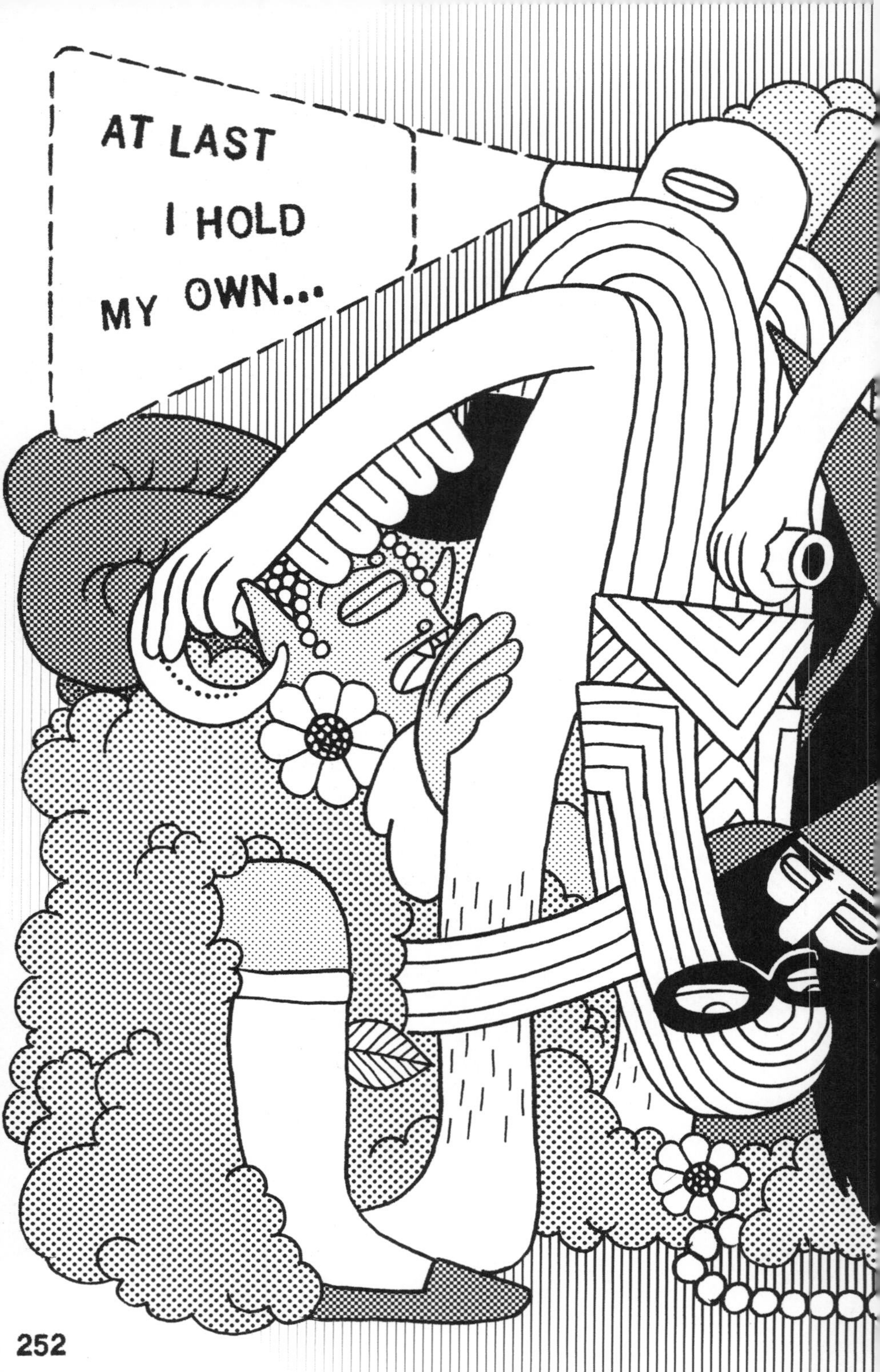
AT LAST I HOLD MY OWN...

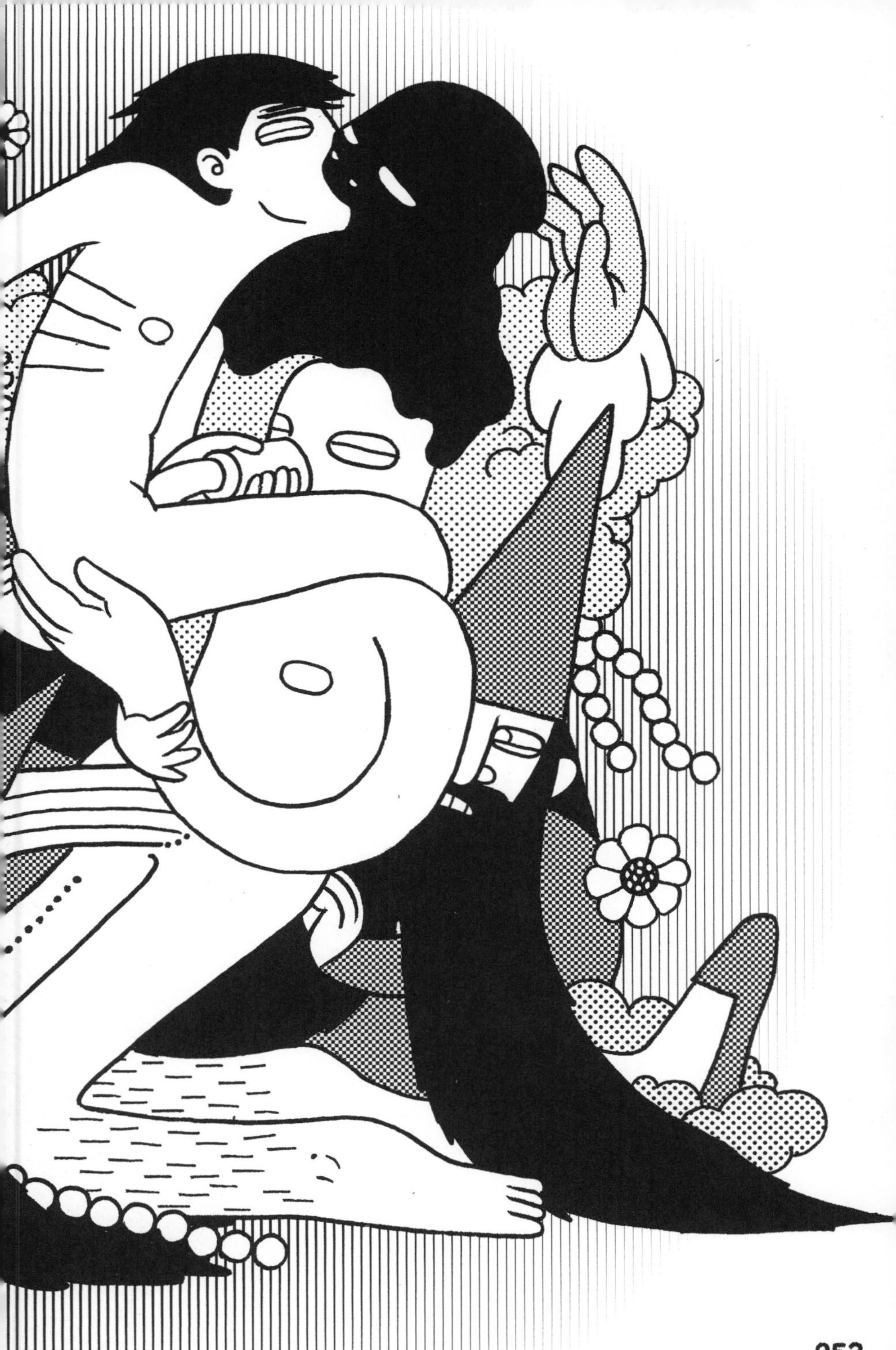

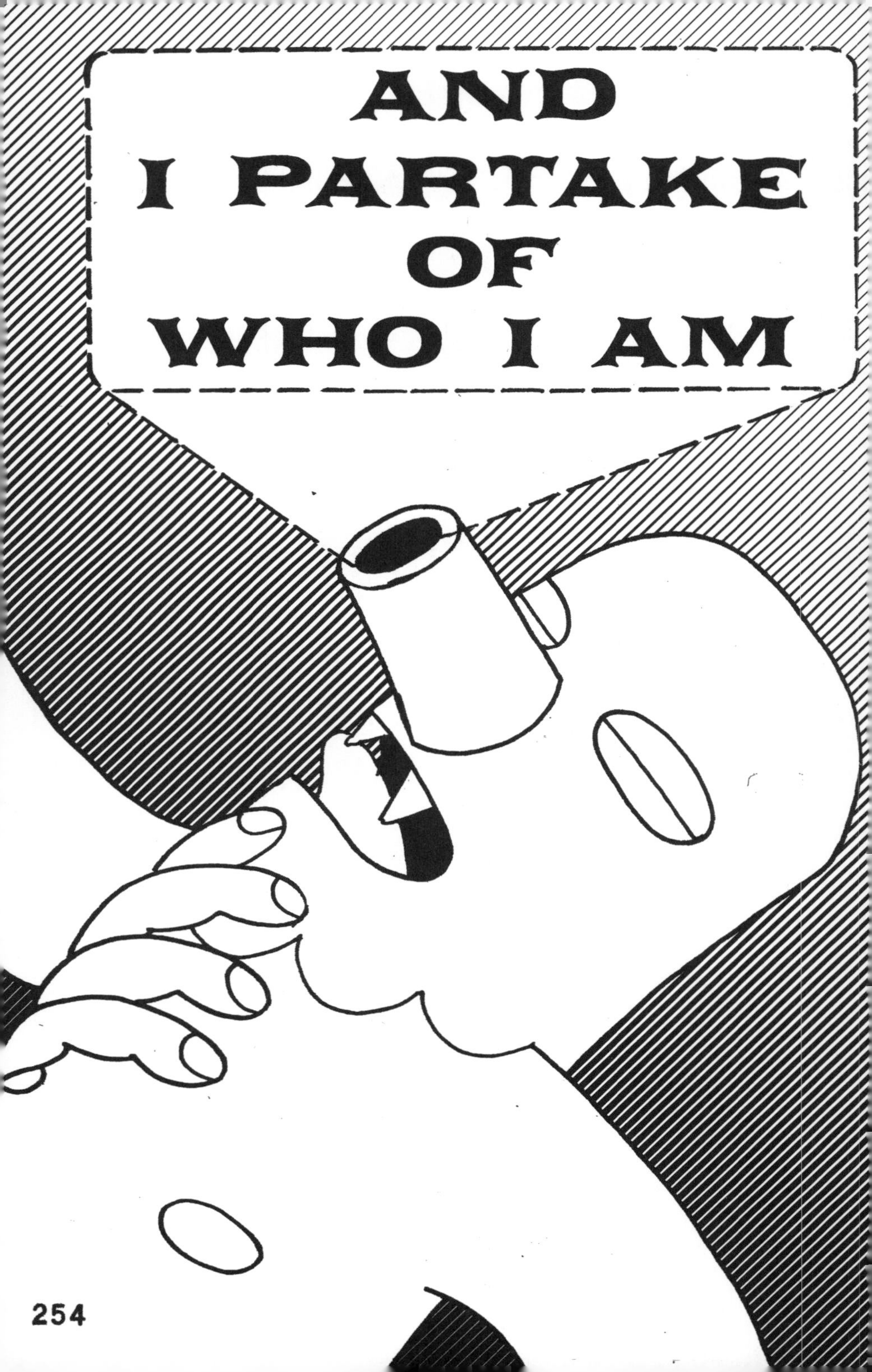
AND I PARTAKE OF WHO I AM